THE COMPLETE ADVENTURES OF
JOHNNY MUTTON

www.hmhco.com

The text of this book is set in Tykewriter.
The illustrations are pen and ink and digitally created.

ISBN: 978-0-544-32404-6

Manufactured in China
SCP 10 9 8 7 6 5 4 3 2 1

4500479277

THE COMPLETE ADVENTURES OF

JOHNNY MUTTON

STORIES AND PICTURES BY

JAMES PROIMOS

HOUGHTON MIFFLIN HARCOURT
BOSTON   NEW YORK

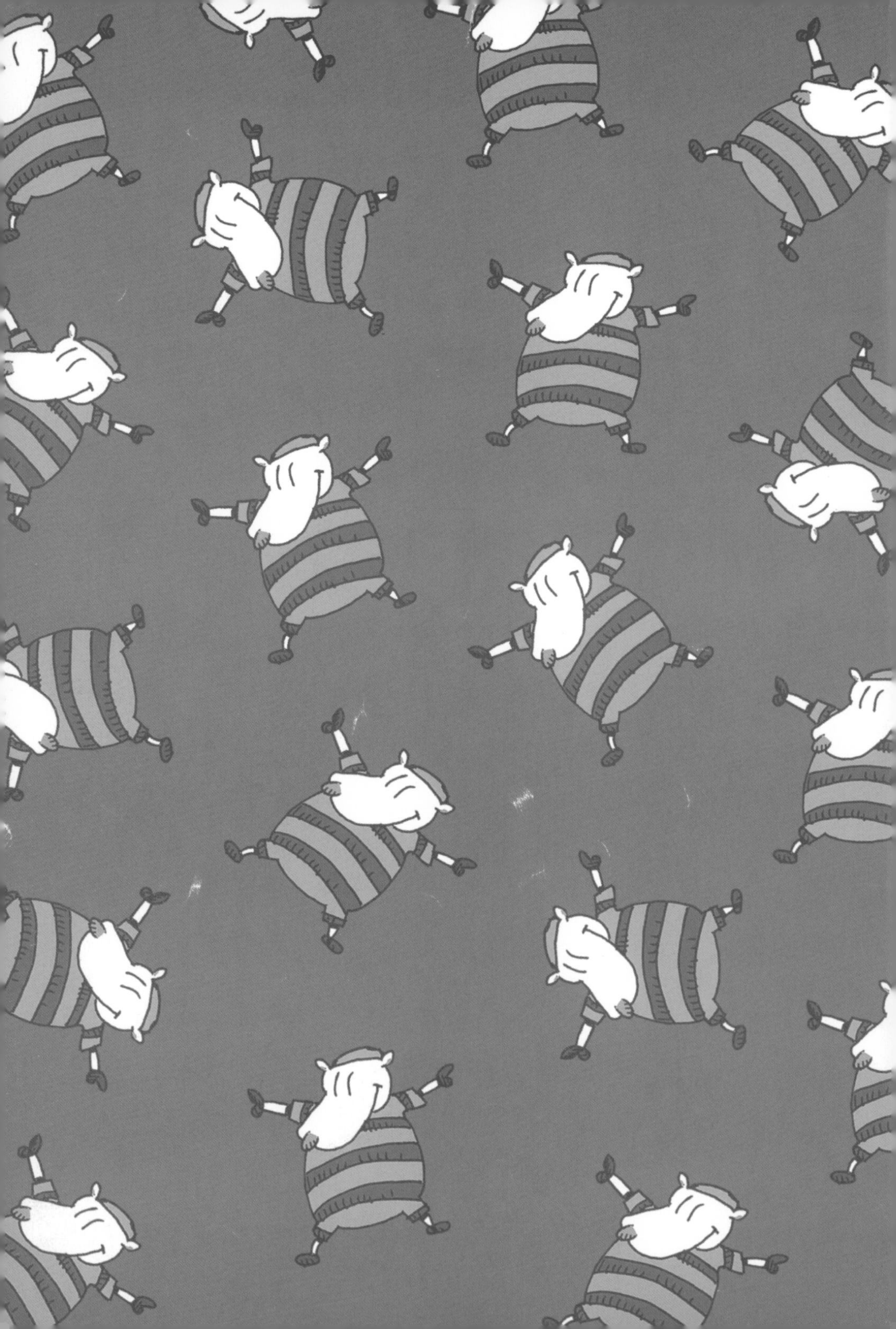

THE MANY ADVENTURES OF
JOHNNY MUTTON

JOHNNY MUTTON, HE'S SO HIM!

MUTTON SOUP

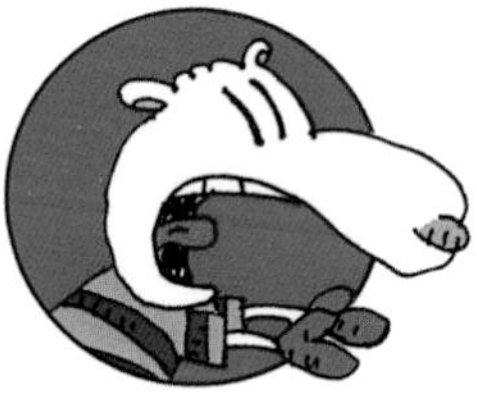

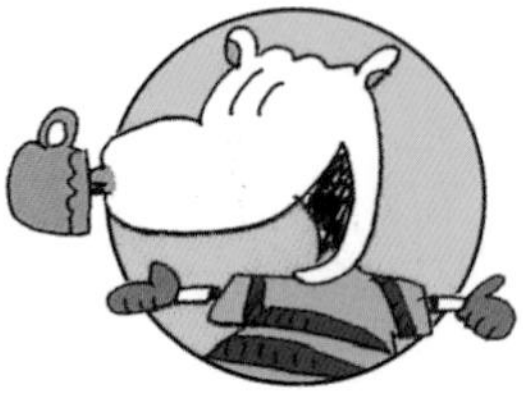

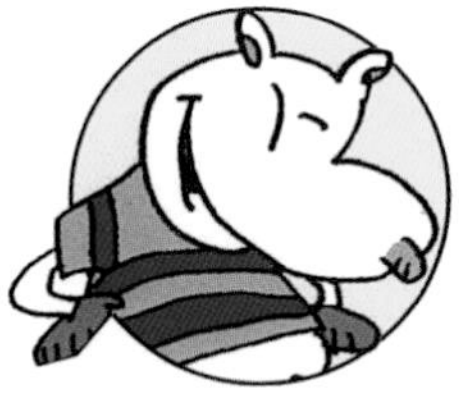

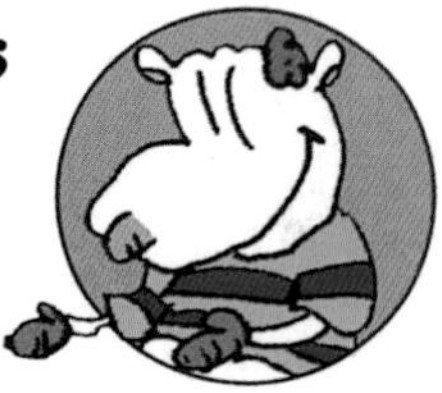

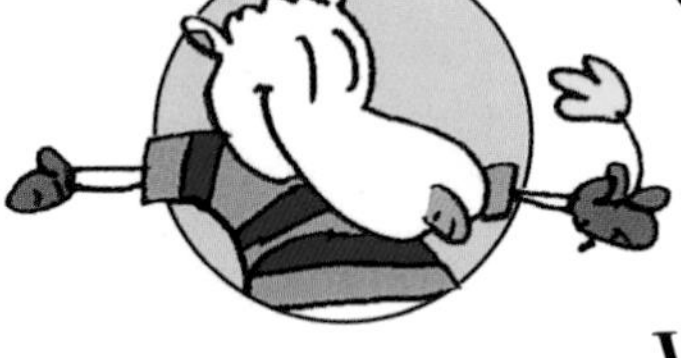

EXTRAS, EXTRAS, READ ALL ABOUT IT!

THE MANY ADVENTURES OF
JOHNNY MUTTON

For Annie and Jimmy

Baby Steps

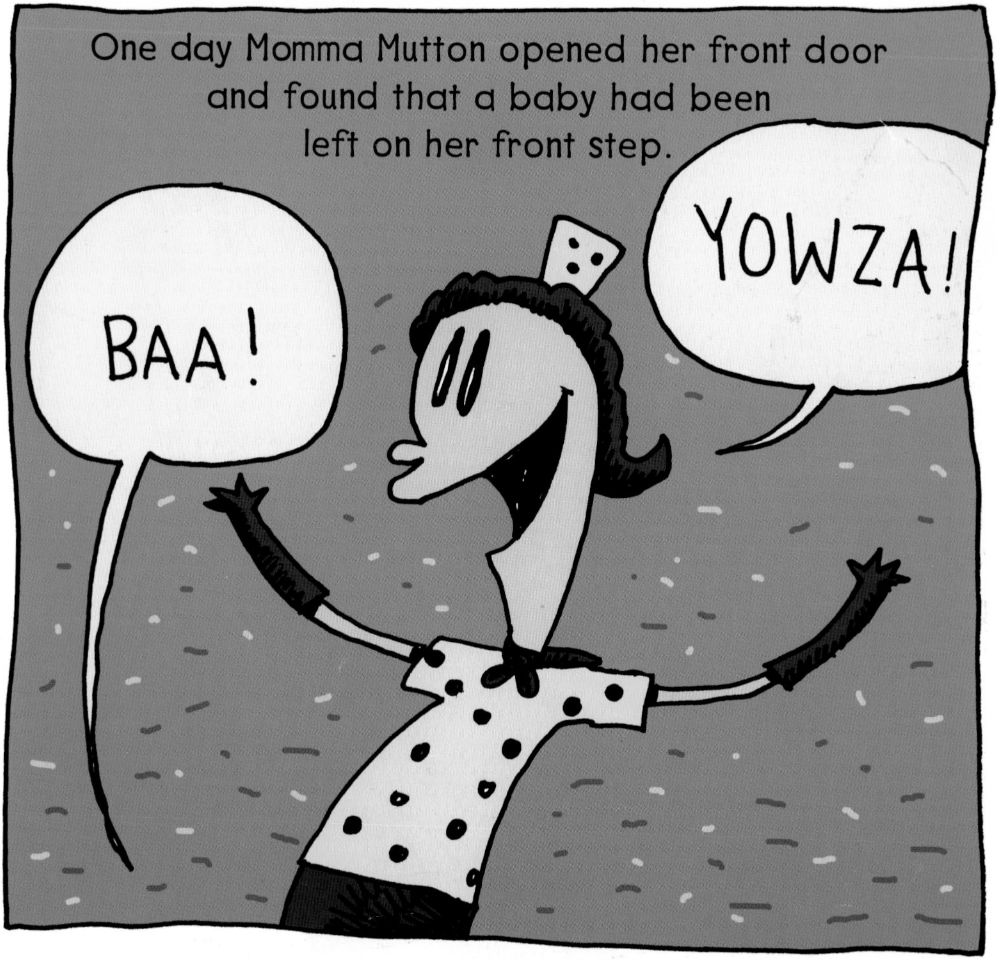
One day Momma Mutton opened her front door and found that a baby had been left on her front step.
BAA!
YOWZA!

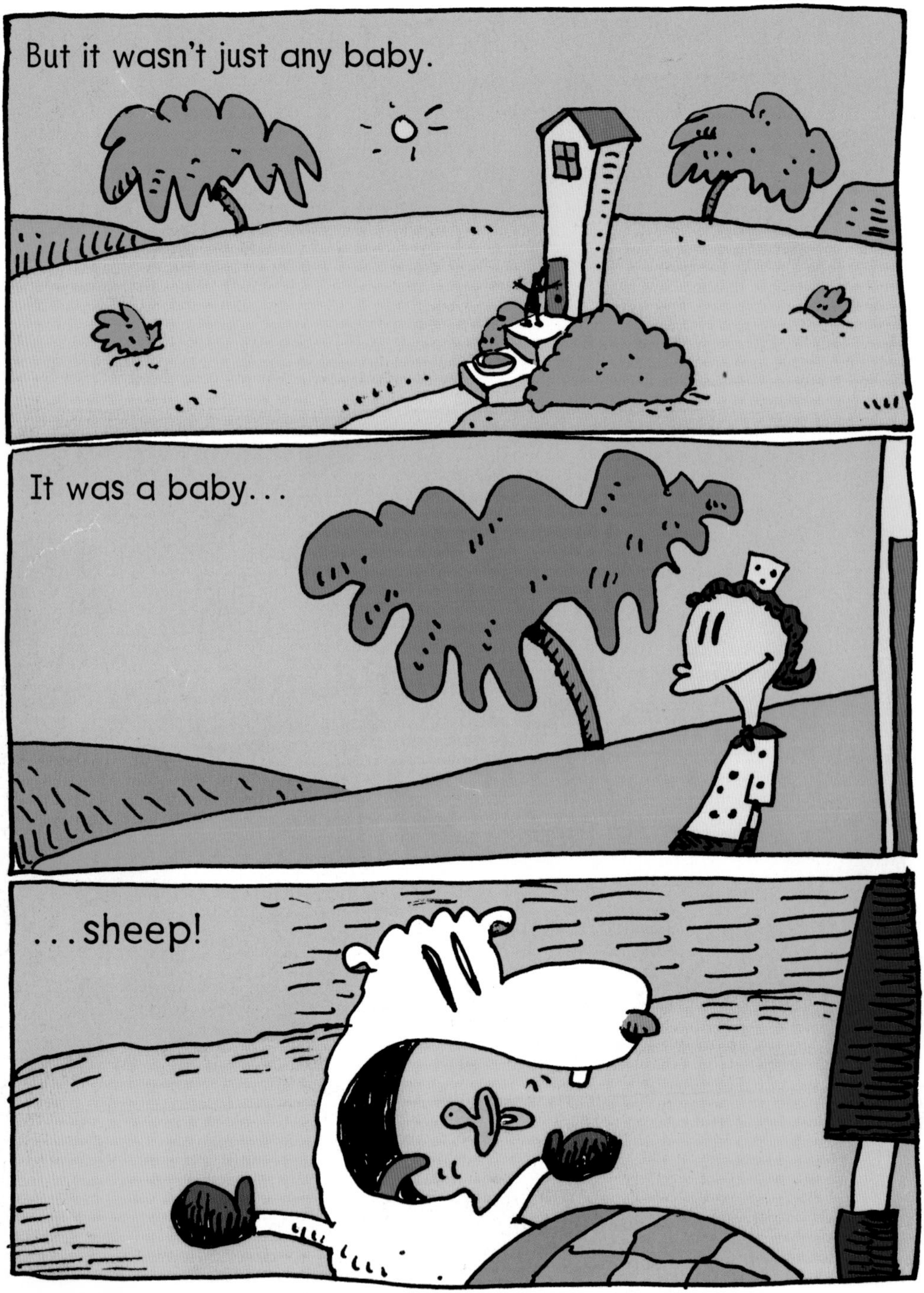
But it wasn't just any baby.
It was a baby...
...sheep!

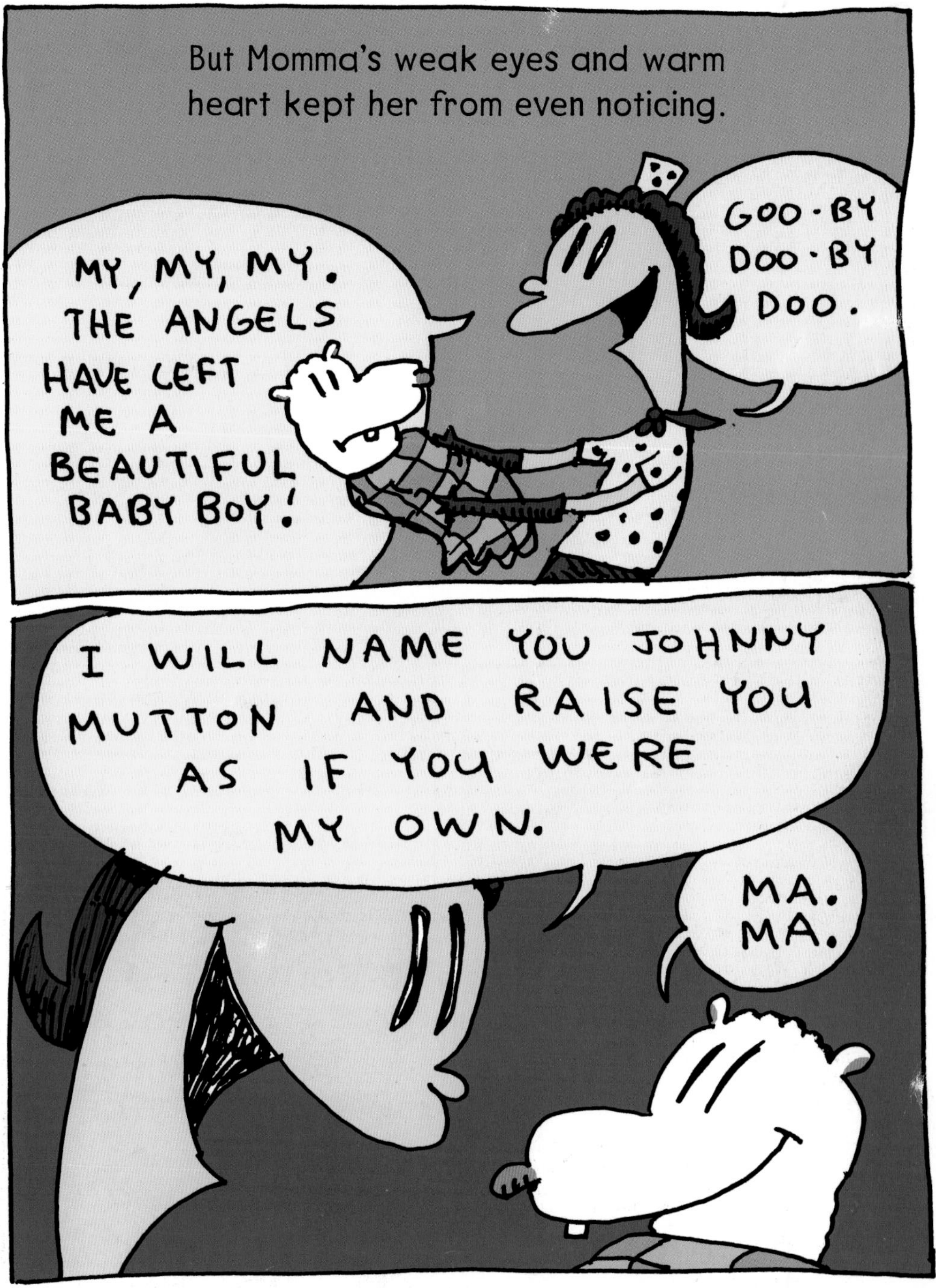
But Momma's weak eyes and warm heart kept her from even noticing.
MY, MY, MY. THE ANGELS HAVE LEFT ME A BEAUTIFUL BABY BOY!
GOO-BY DOO-BY DOO.
I WILL NAME YOU JOHNNY MUTTON AND RAISE YOU AS IF YOU WERE MY OWN.
MA. MA.

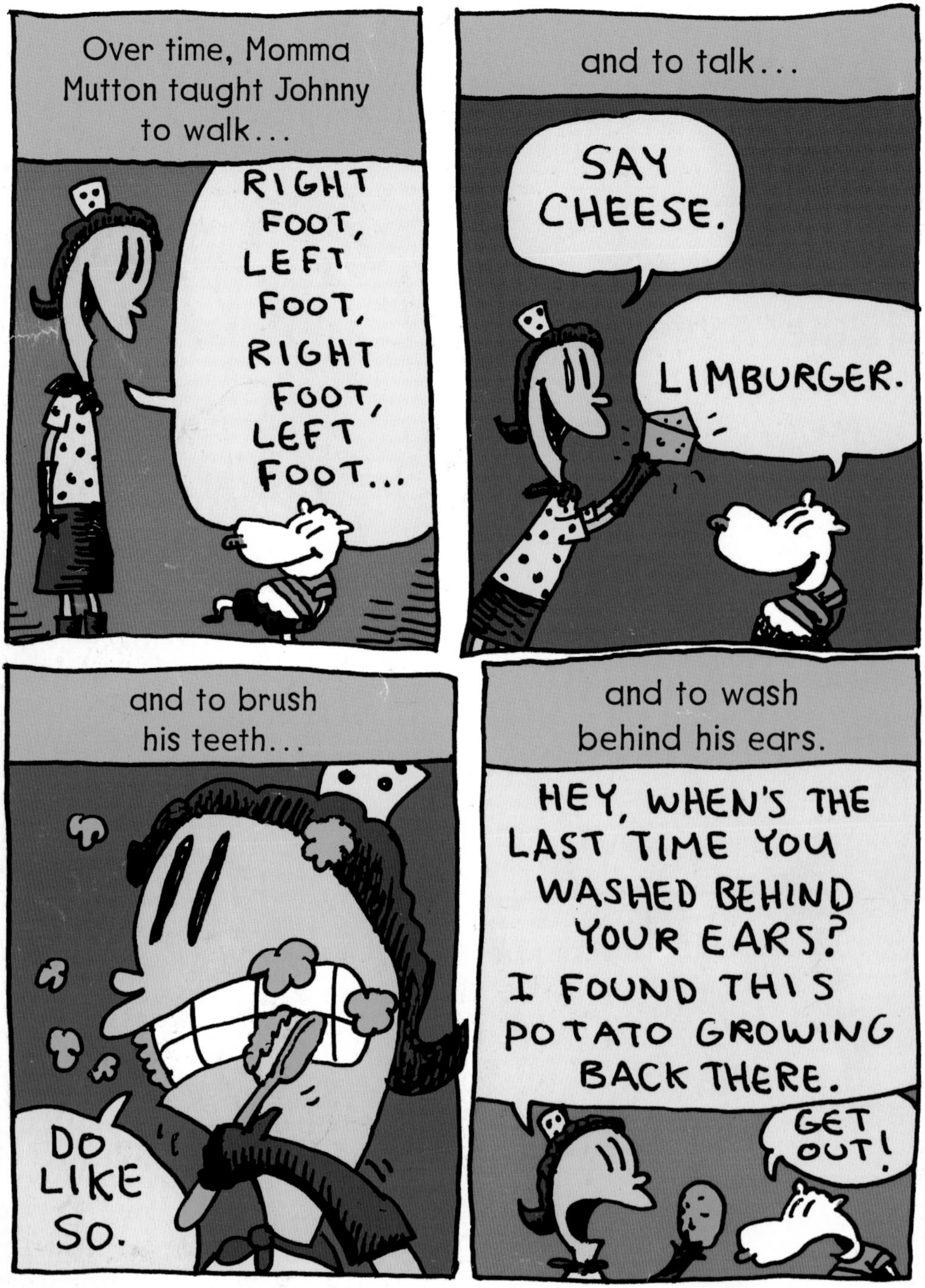
Over time, Momma Mutton taught Johnny to walk...
RIGHT FOOT, LEFT FOOT, RIGHT FOOT, LEFT FOOT...
and to talk...
SAY CHEESE.
LIMBURGER.
and to brush his teeth...
DO LIKE SO.
and to wash behind his ears.
HEY, WHEN'S THE LAST TIME YOU WASHED BEHIND YOUR EARS? I FOUND THIS POTATO GROWING BACK THERE.
GET OUT!

Although Johnny often got those last two confused.

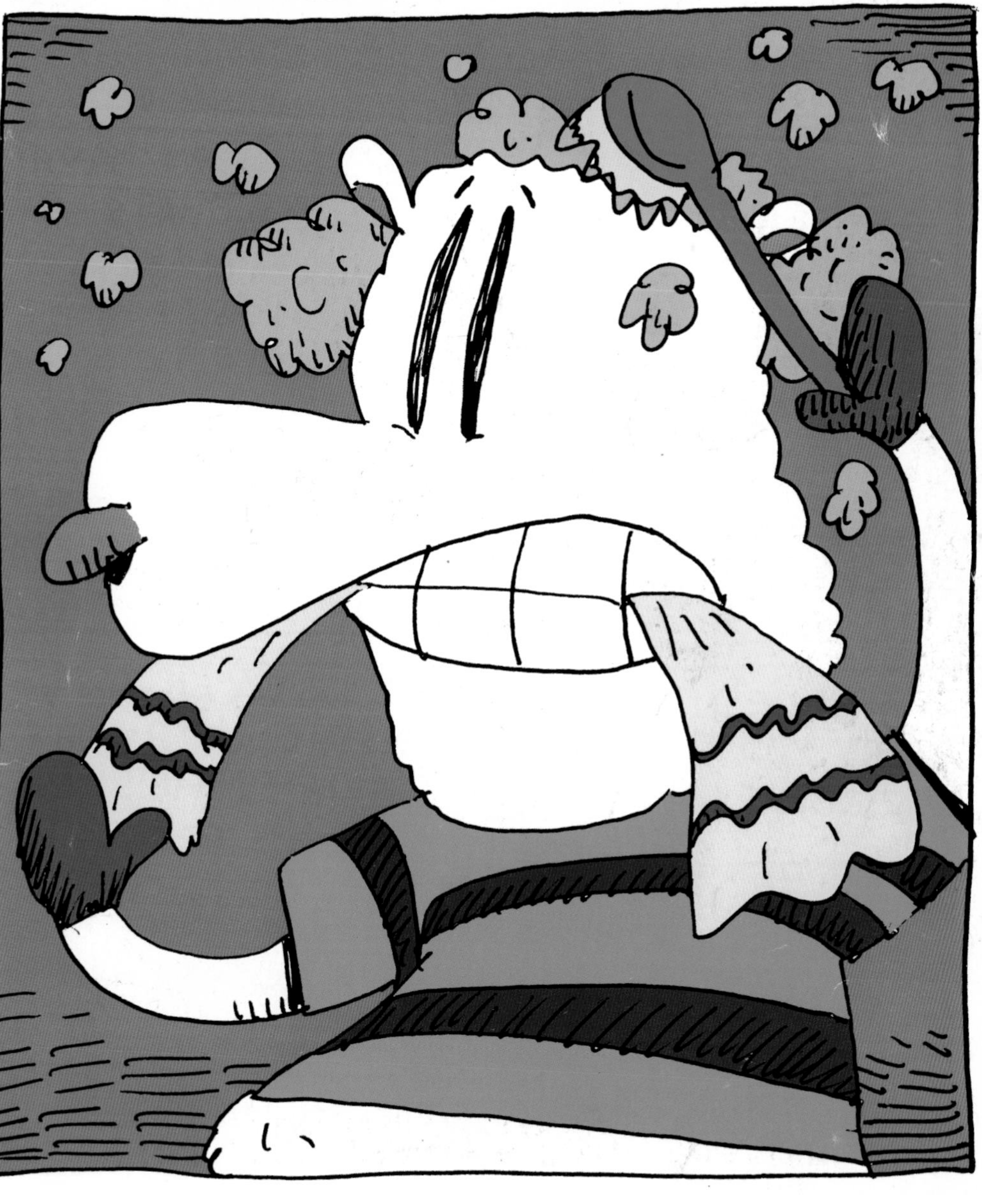

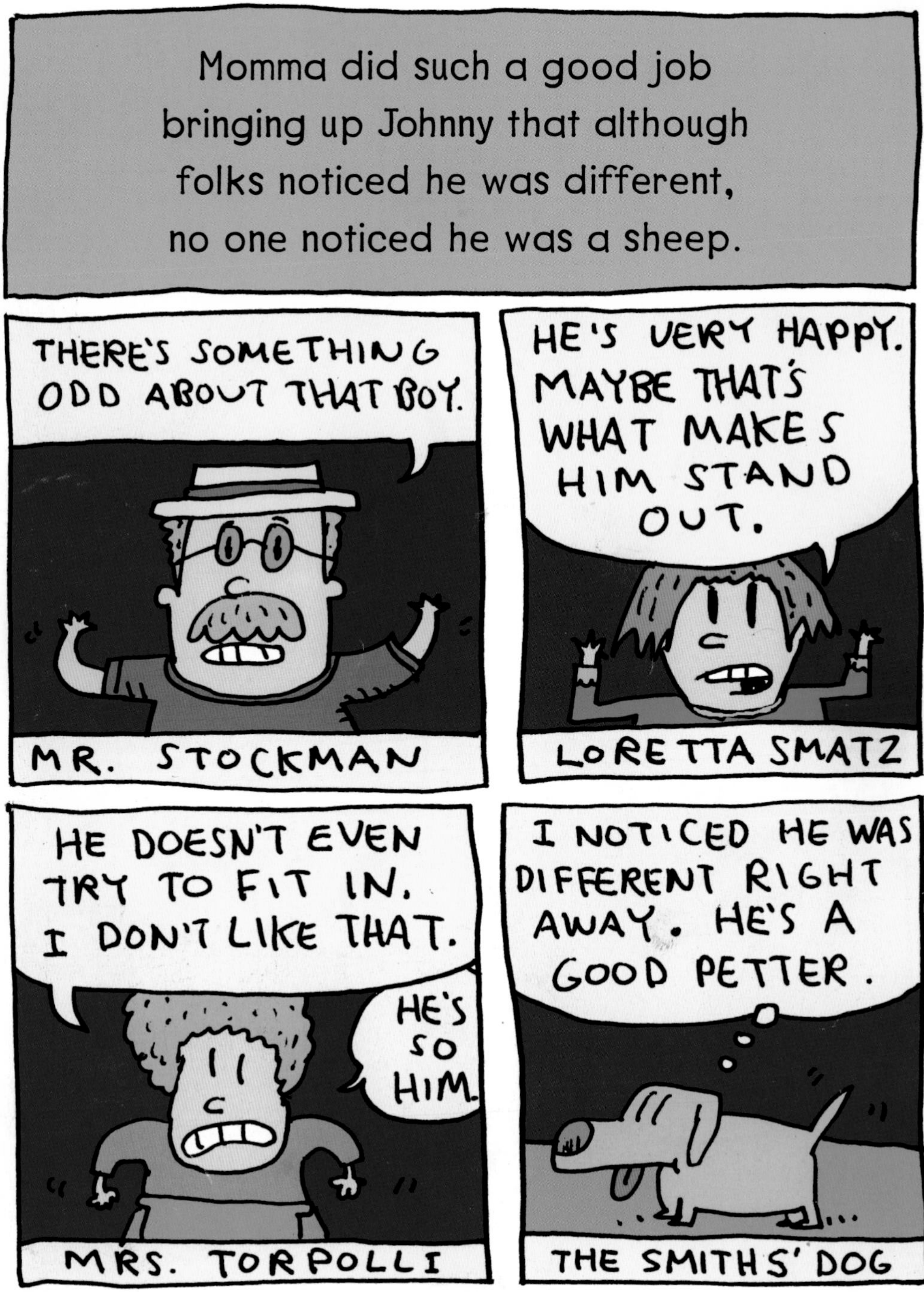
Momma did such a good job bringing up Johnny that although folks noticed he was different, no one noticed he was a sheep.
THERE'S SOMETHING ODD ABOUT THAT BOY.
MR. STOCKMAN
HE'S VERY HAPPY. MAYBE THAT'S WHAT MAKES HIM STAND OUT.
LORETTA SMATZ
HE DOESN'T EVEN TRY TO FIT IN. I DON'T LIKE THAT.
HE'S SO HIM.
MRS. TORPOLLI
I NOTICED HE WAS DIFFERENT RIGHT AWAY. HE'S A GOOD PETTER.
THE SMITHS' DOG

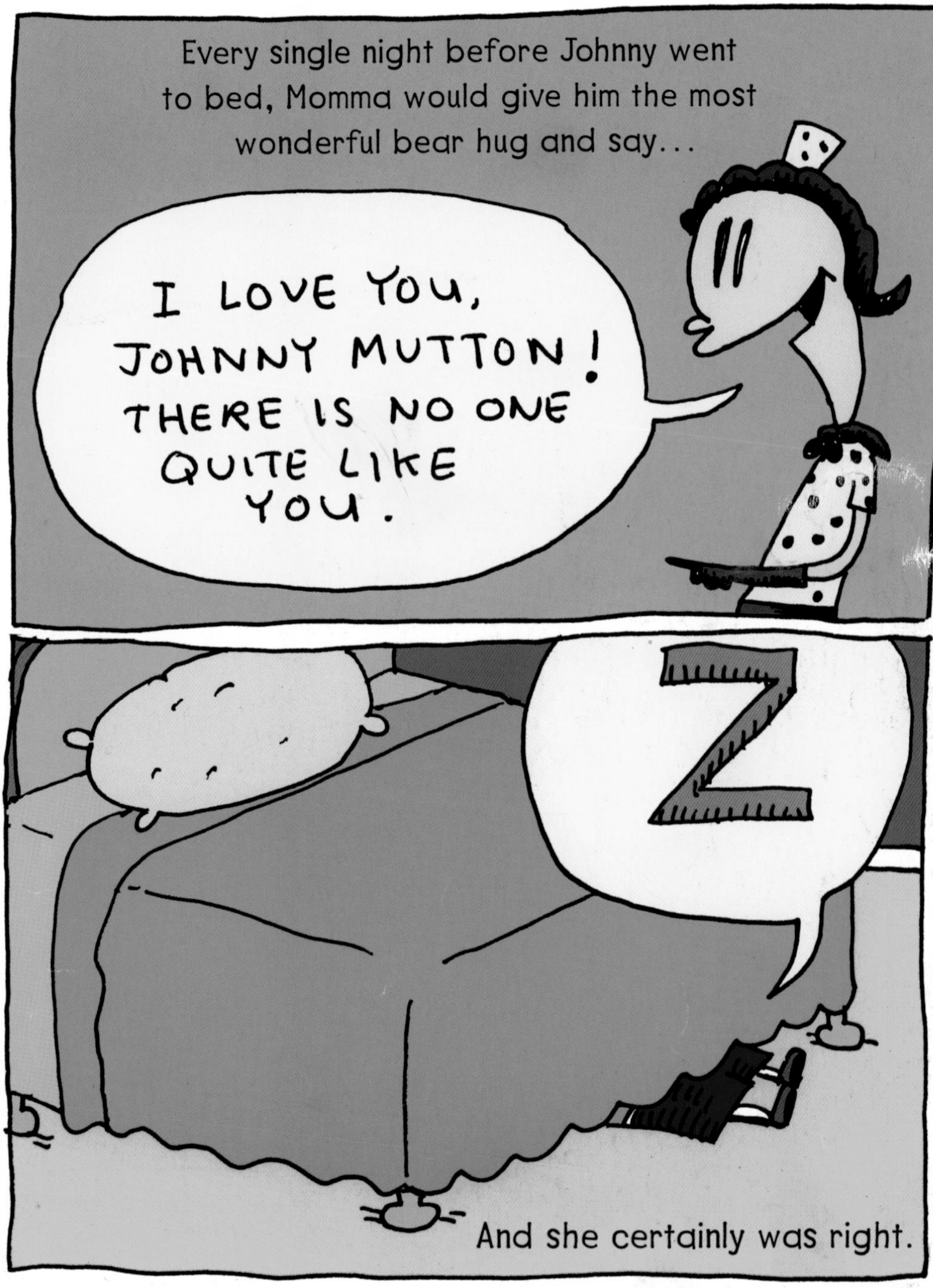
Every single night before Johnny went to bed, Momma would give him the most wonderful bear hug and say...
I LOVE YOU, JOHNNY MUTTON! THERE IS NO ONE QUITE LIKE YOU.
Z
And she certainly was right.

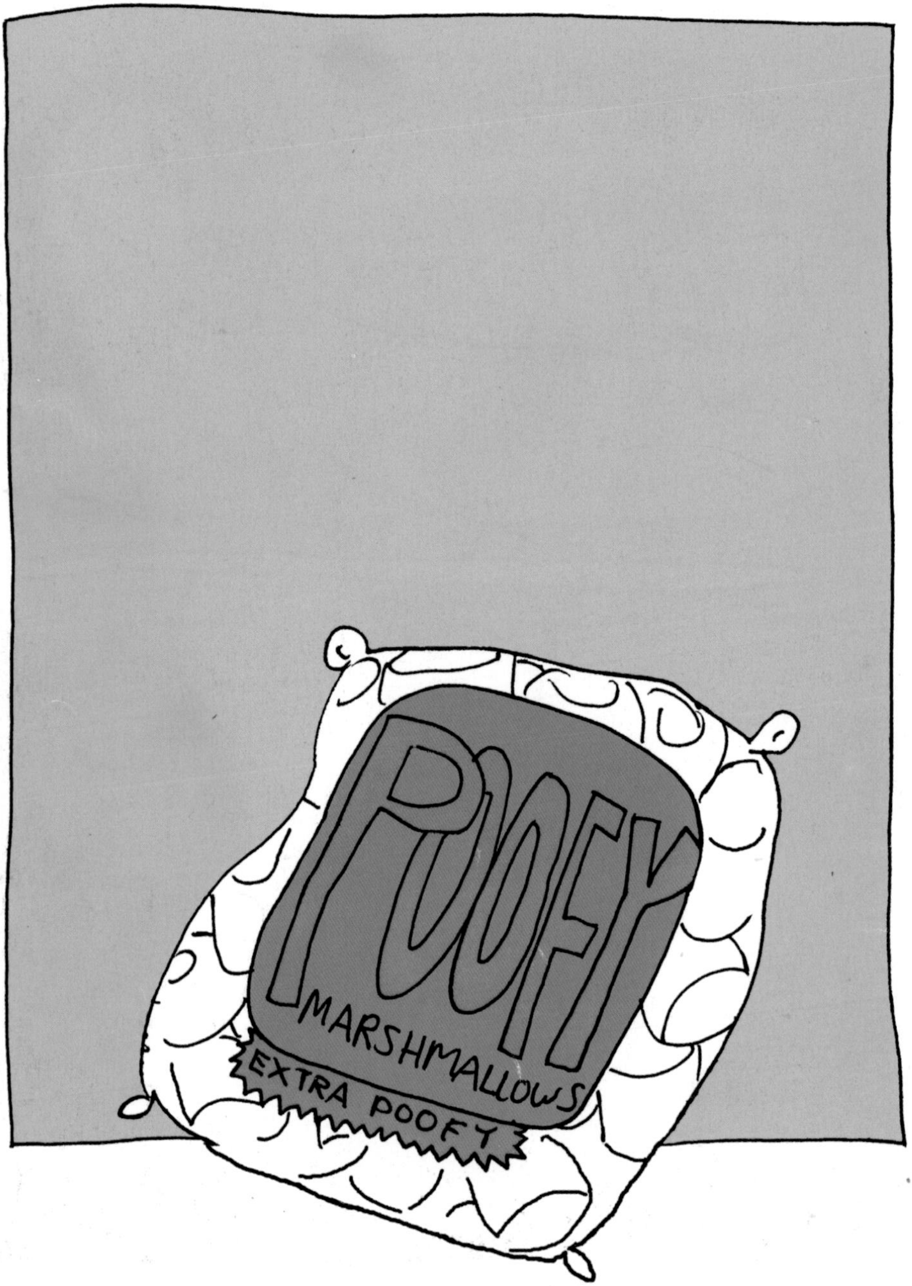
POOFY
MARSHMALLOWS
EXTRA POOFY

More Fun Than a Bag of Marshmallows

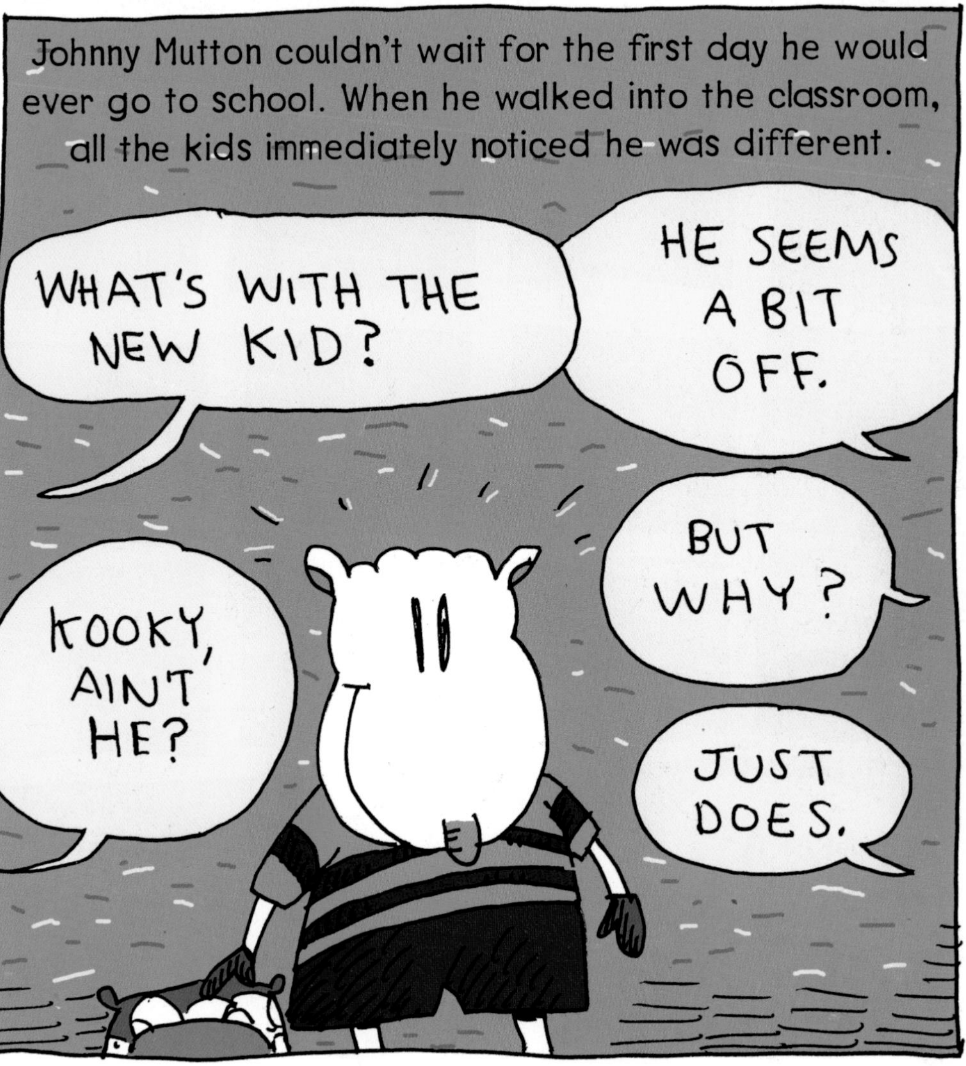
Johnny Mutton couldn't wait for the first day he would ever go to school. When he walked into the classroom, all the kids immediately noticed he was different.
WHAT'S WITH THE NEW KID?
HE SEEMS A BIT OFF.
KOOKY, AIN'T HE?
BUT WHY?
JUST DOES.

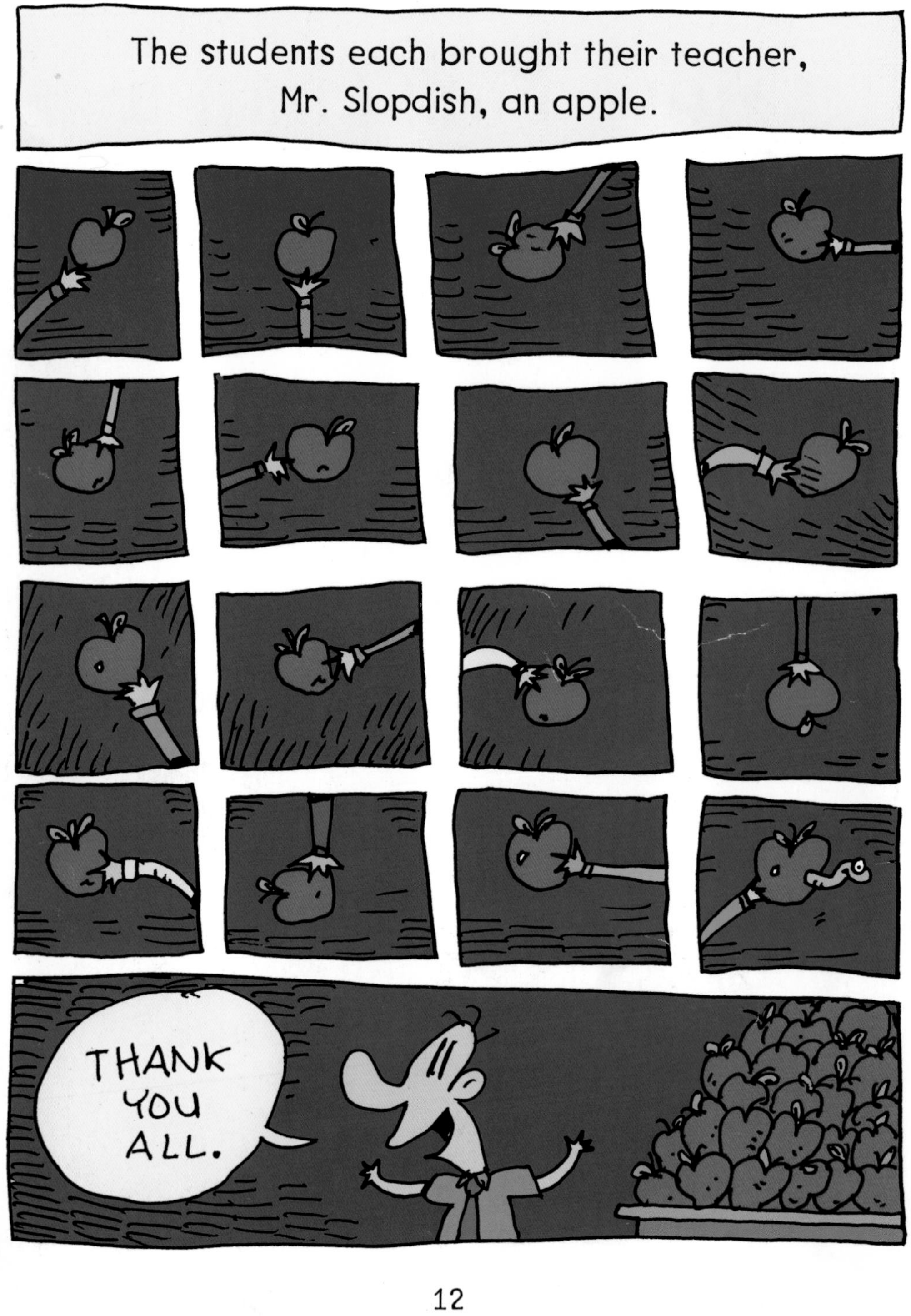
The students each brought their teacher, Mr. Slopdish, an apple.
THANK YOU ALL.

Johnny brought him a
bag of marshmallows.

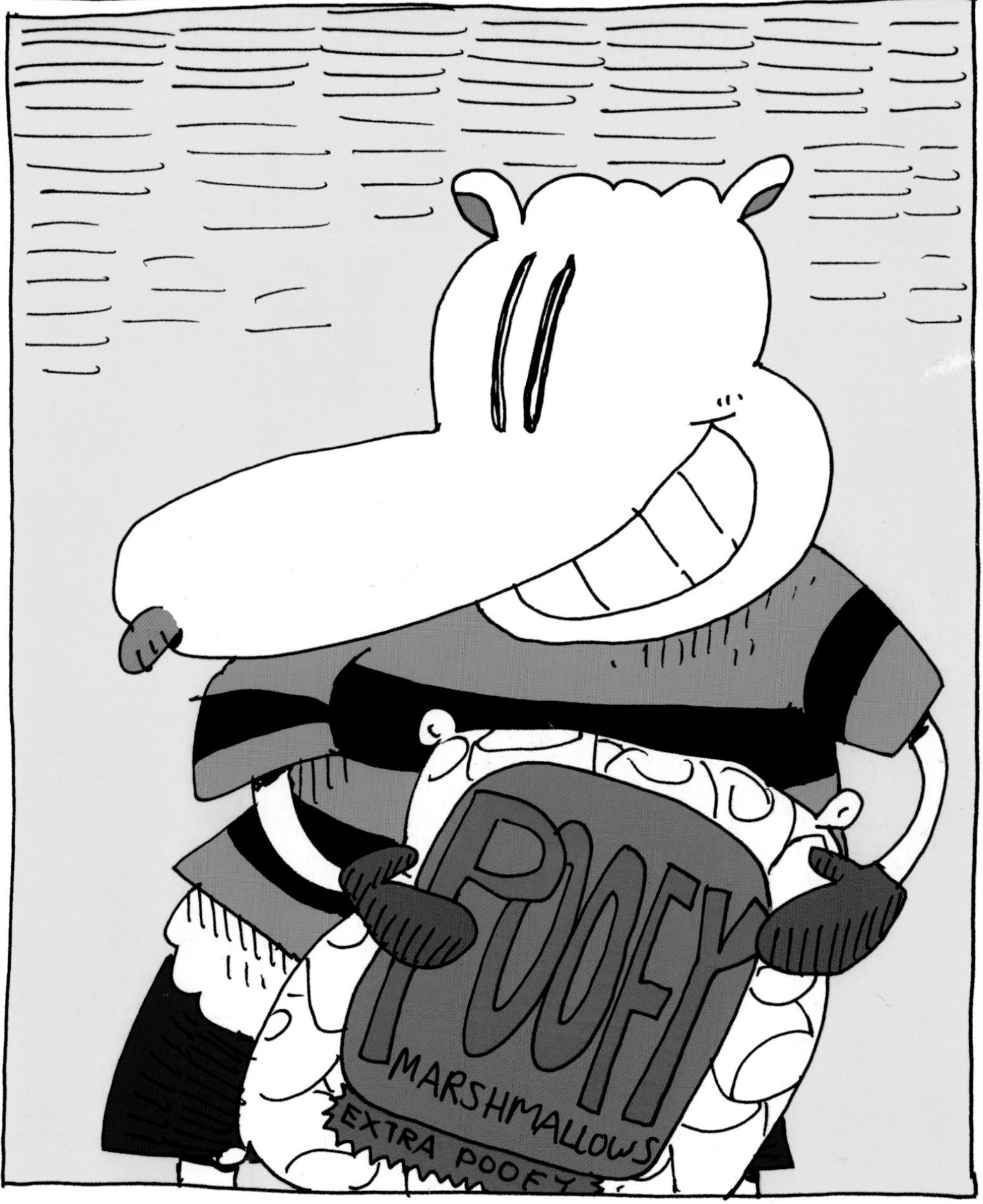
POOFY
MARSHMALLOWS
EXTRA POOFY

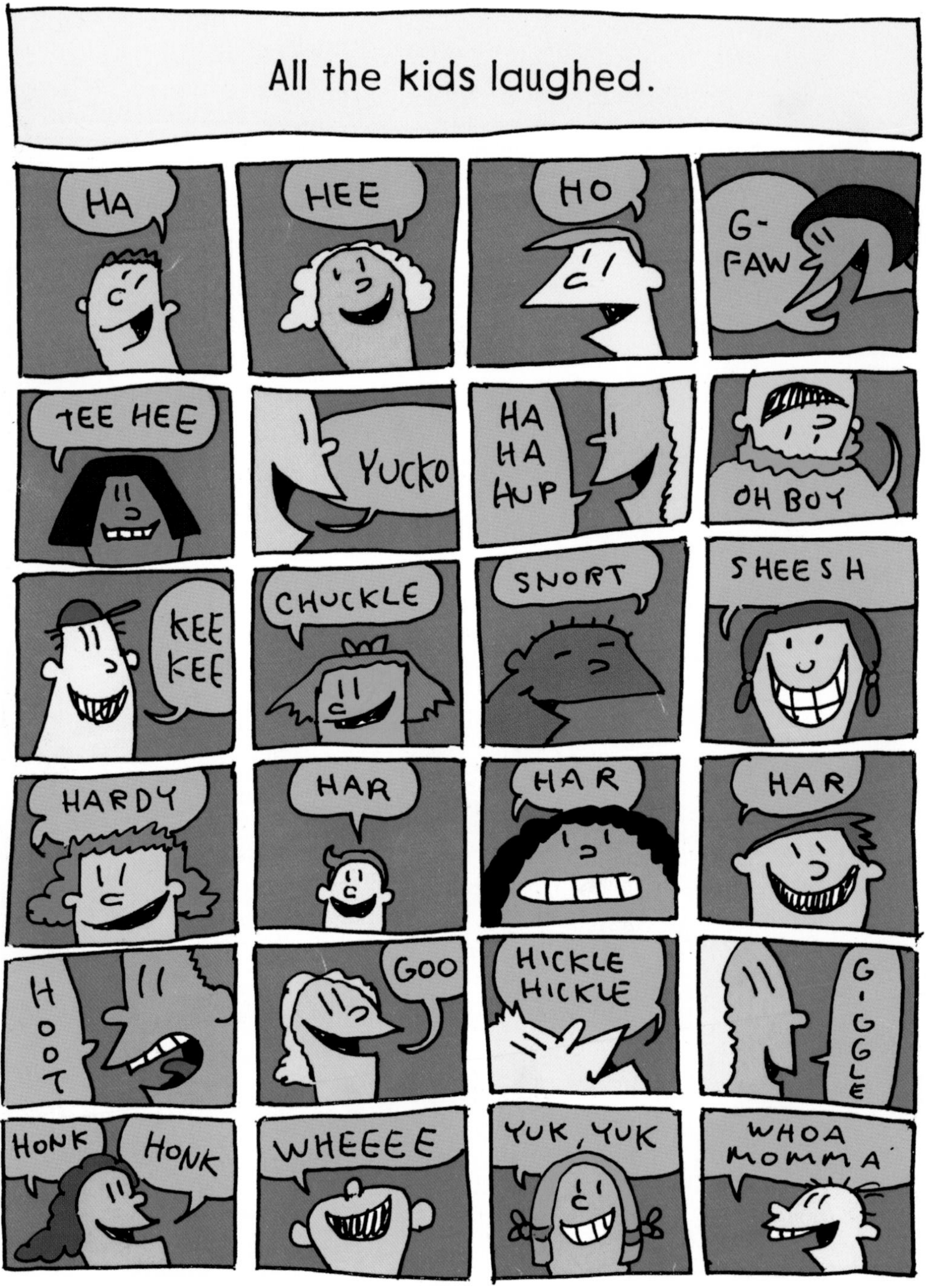
All the kids laughed.
HA
HEE
HO
G-FAW
TEE HEE
YUCKO
HA HA HUP
OH BOY
KEE KEE
CHUCKLE
SNORT
SHEESH
HARDY
HAR
HAR
HAR
HOOT
GOO
HICKLE HICKLE
GIGGLE
HONK
HONK
WHEEEEE
YUK, YUK
WHOA MOMMA

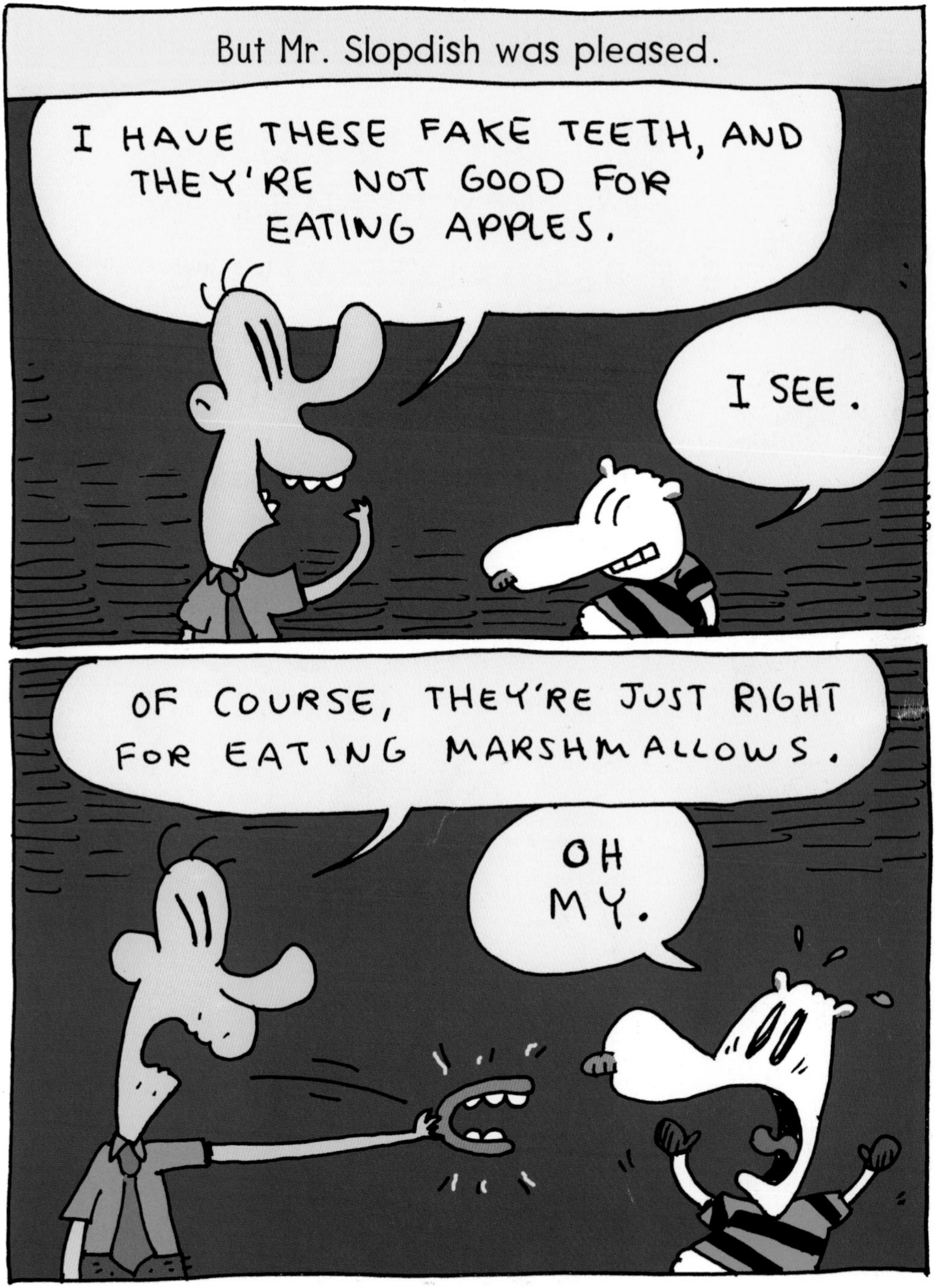
But Mr. Slopdish was pleased.
I HAVE THESE FAKE TEETH, AND THEY'RE NOT GOOD FOR EATING APPLES.
I SEE.
OF COURSE, THEY'RE JUST RIGHT FOR EATING MARSHMALLOWS.
OH MY.

And then Mr. Slopdish said...

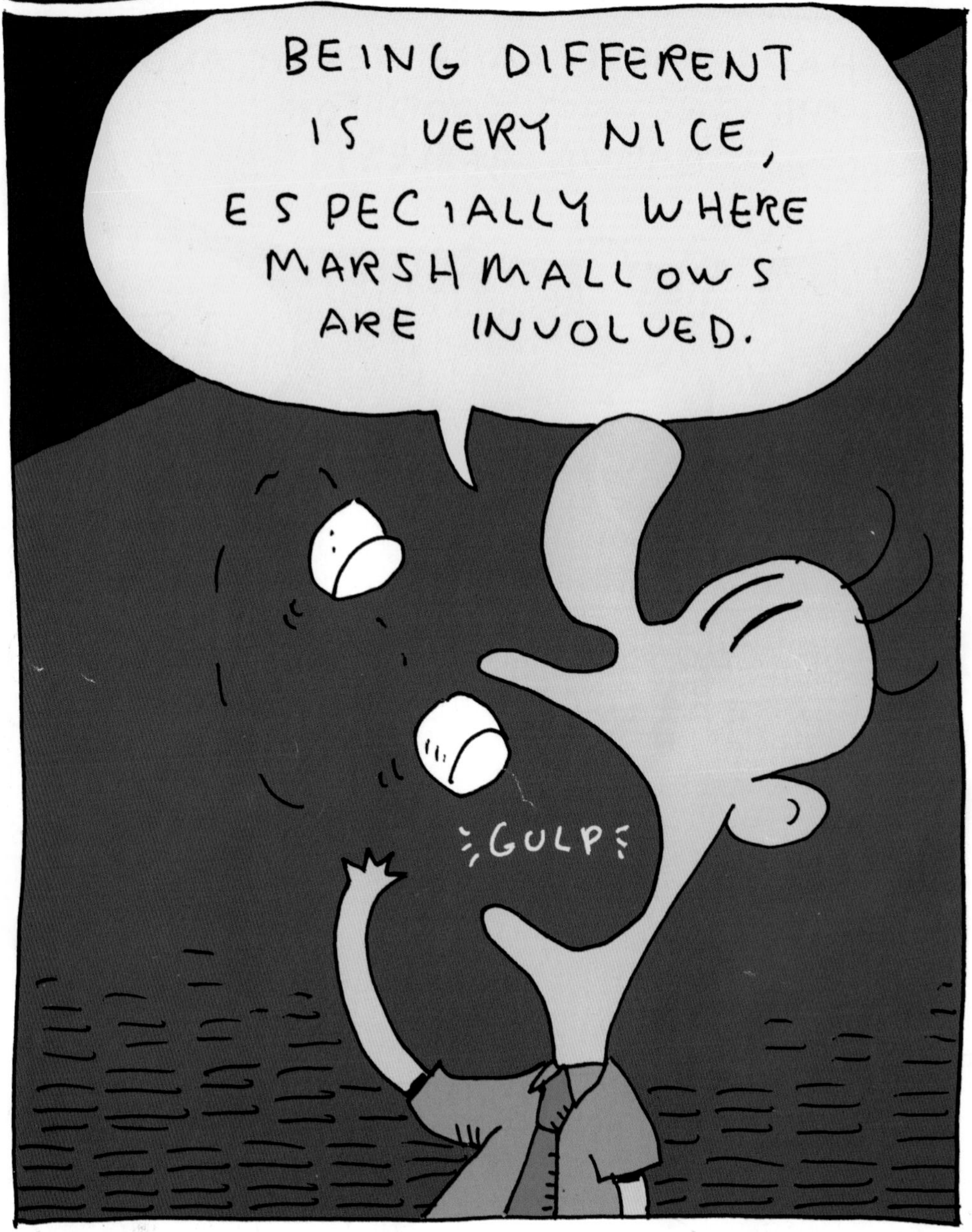

But Johnny didn't hear that because he was in the closet, hiding from those creepy fake teeth.

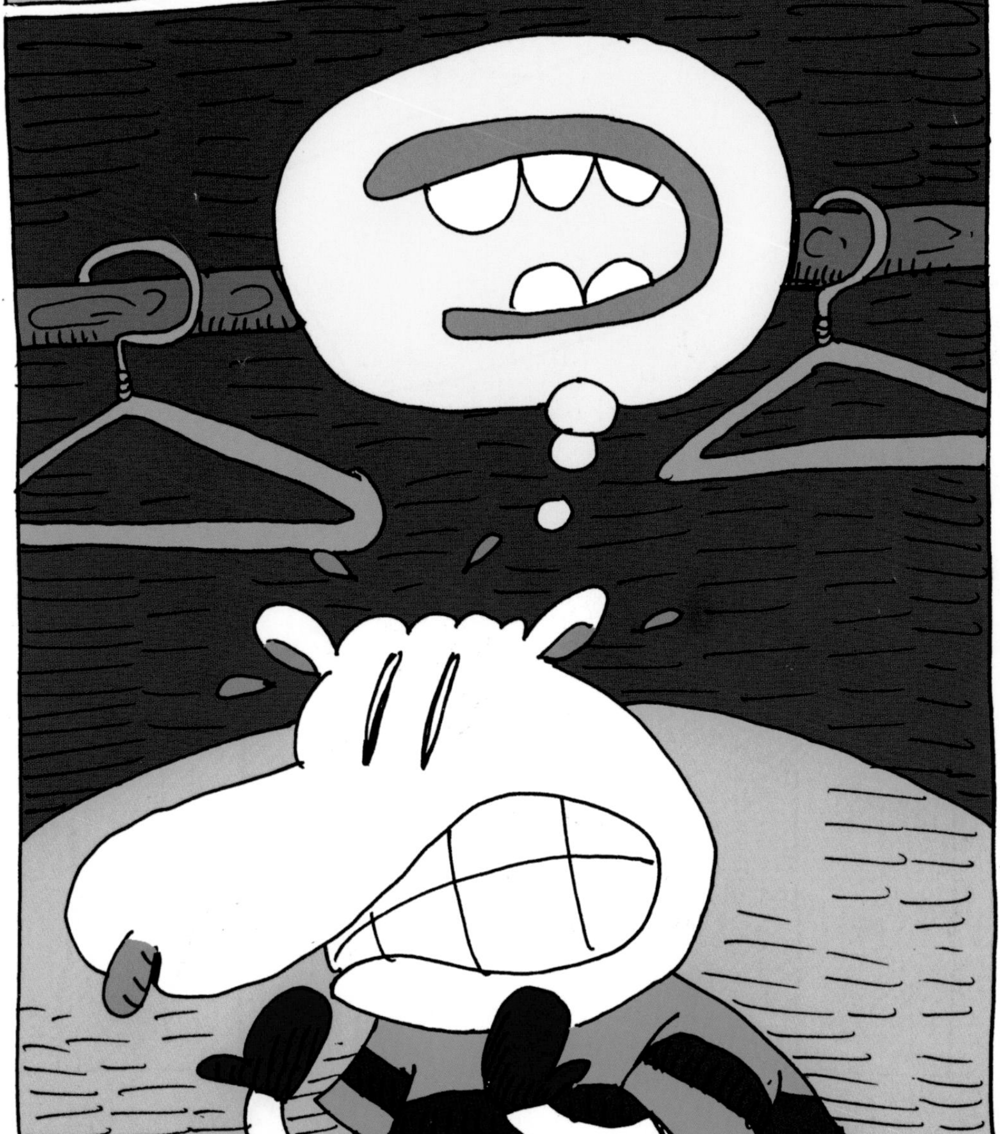

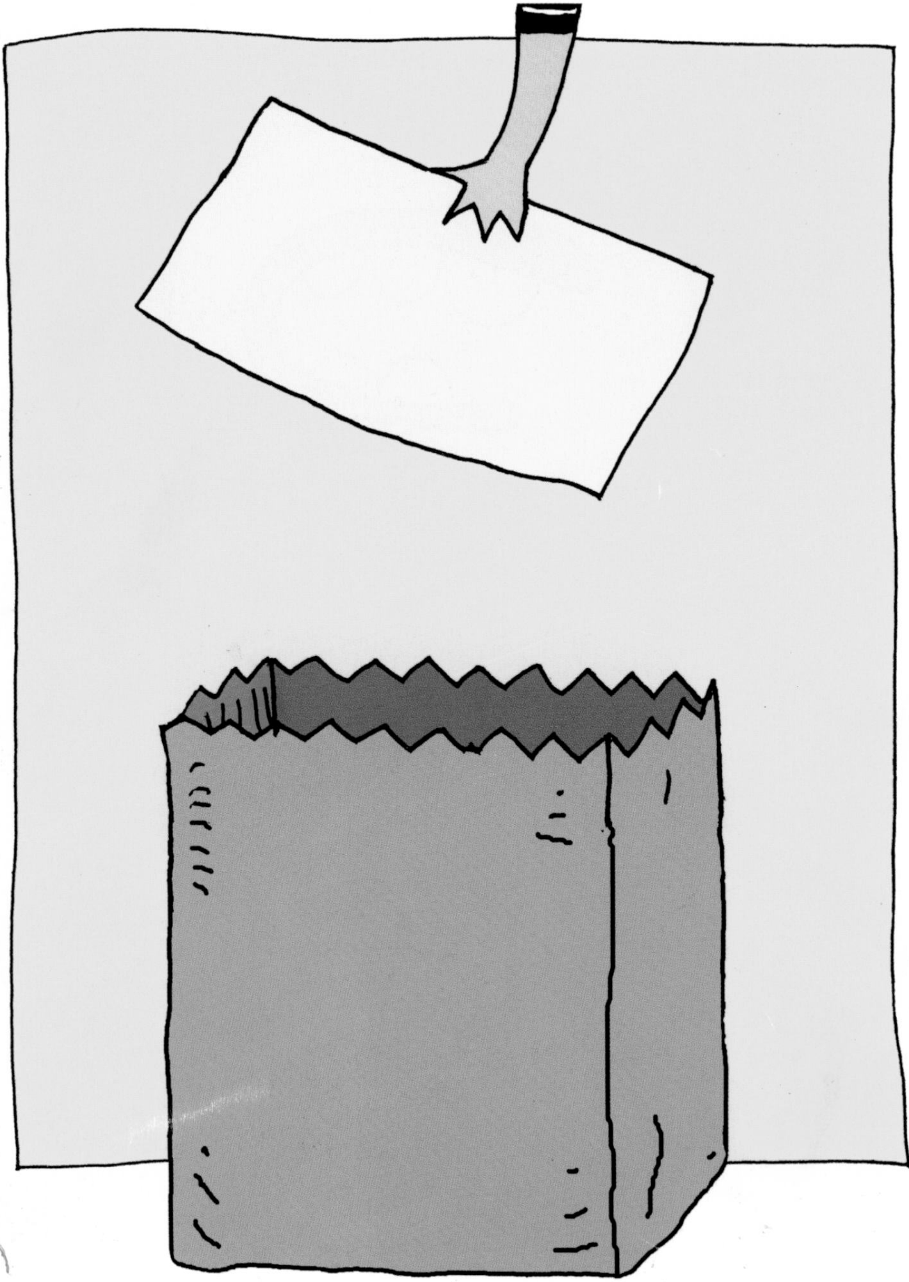

Spell Binding

There was a big spelling bee at Johnny Mutton's school. The parents of all the children came to watch.
CAT
K-
WRONG!
DOG
P-
WRONG!
SOCK
C-
WRONG!
WRONG
R-
WRONG!
Kids were dropping like flies.

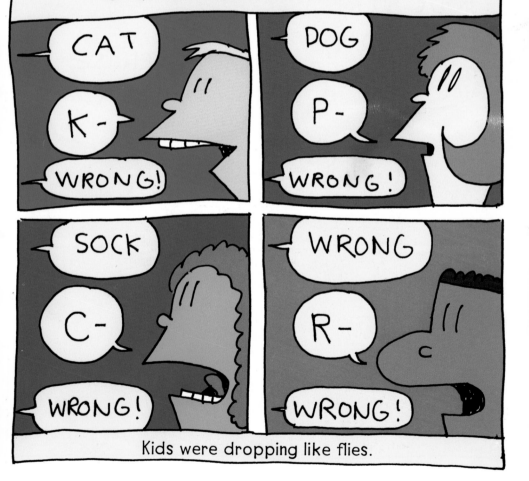

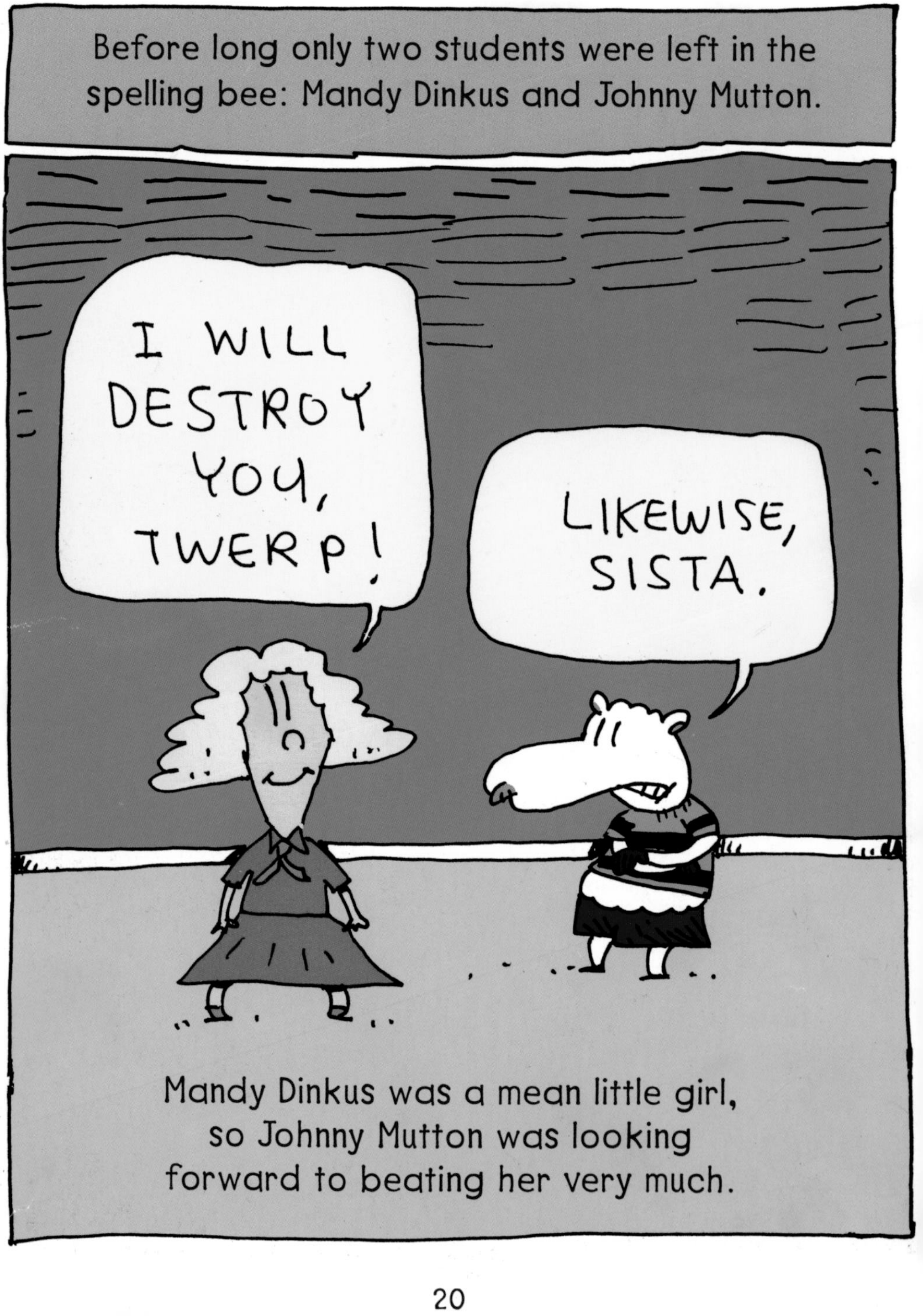
Before long only two students were left in the spelling bee: Mandy Dinkus and Johnny Mutton.
I WILL DESTROY YOU, TWERP!
LIKEWISE, SISTA.
Mandy Dinkus was a mean little girl, so Johnny Mutton was looking forward to beating her very much.

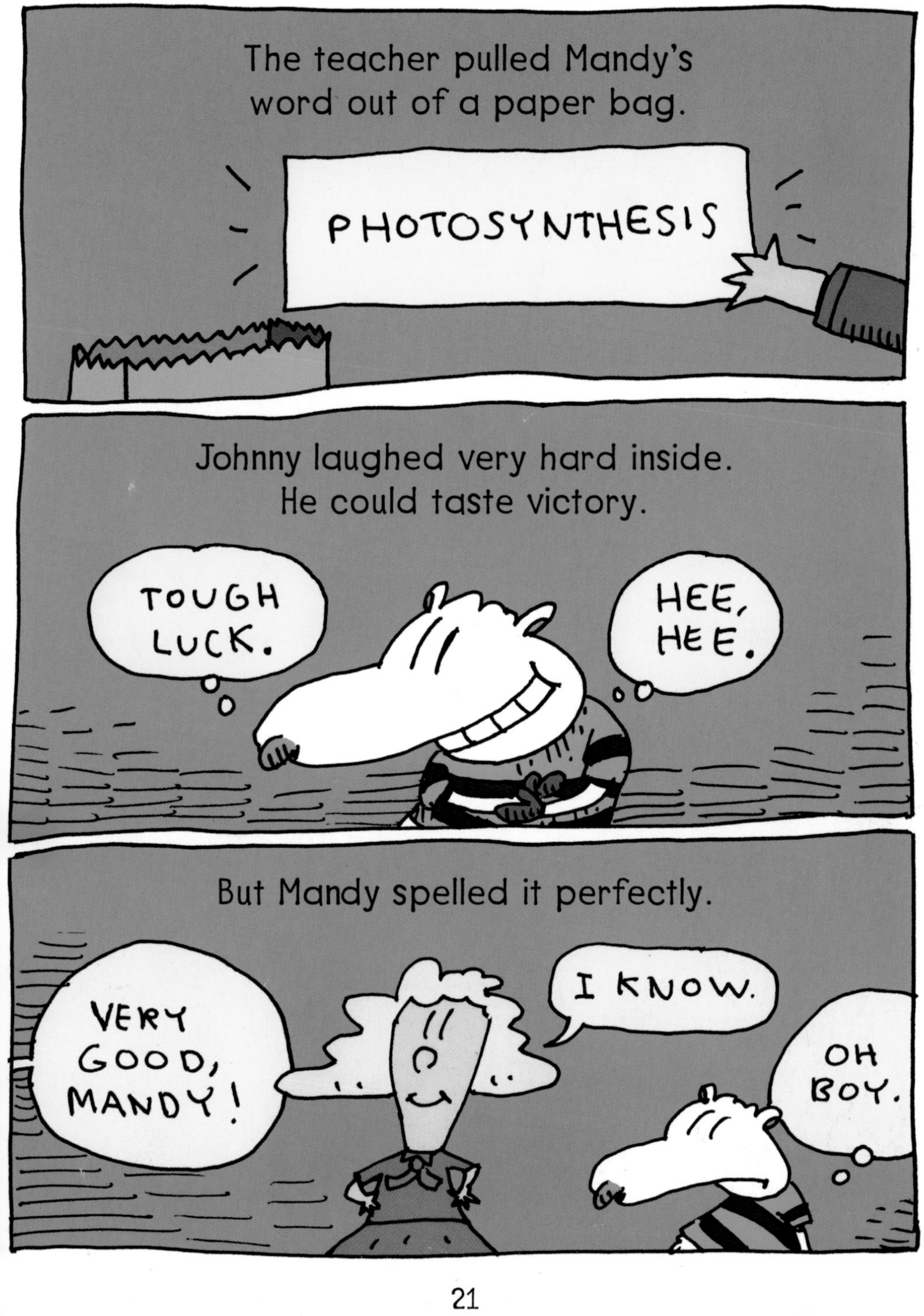
The teacher pulled Mandy's word out of a paper bag.
PHOTOSYNTHESIS
Johnny laughed very hard inside. He could taste victory.
TOUGH LUCK.
HEE, HEE.
But Mandy spelled it perfectly.
VERY GOOD, MANDY!
I KNOW.
OH BOY.

Next it was Johnny's turn. But just as his teacher was reaching in the bag to pull out his word, the bell rang. The spelling bee would have to be continued the next day.

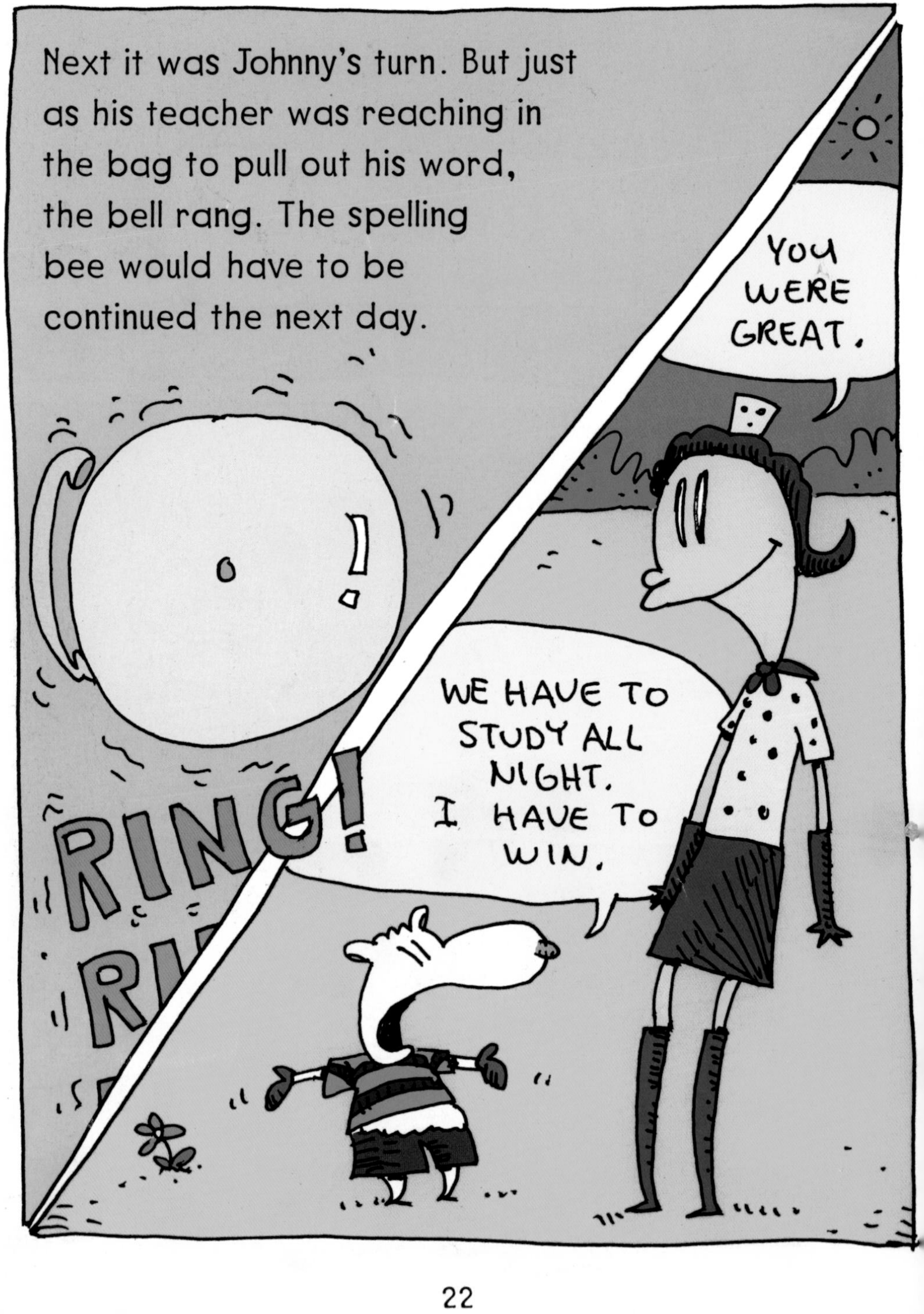
RING!
YOU WERE GREAT.
WE HAVE TO STUDY ALL NIGHT. I HAVE TO WIN.

But Monday night was Momma's tuba practice night, which she never missed. "Some things are more important than winning," said Momma.

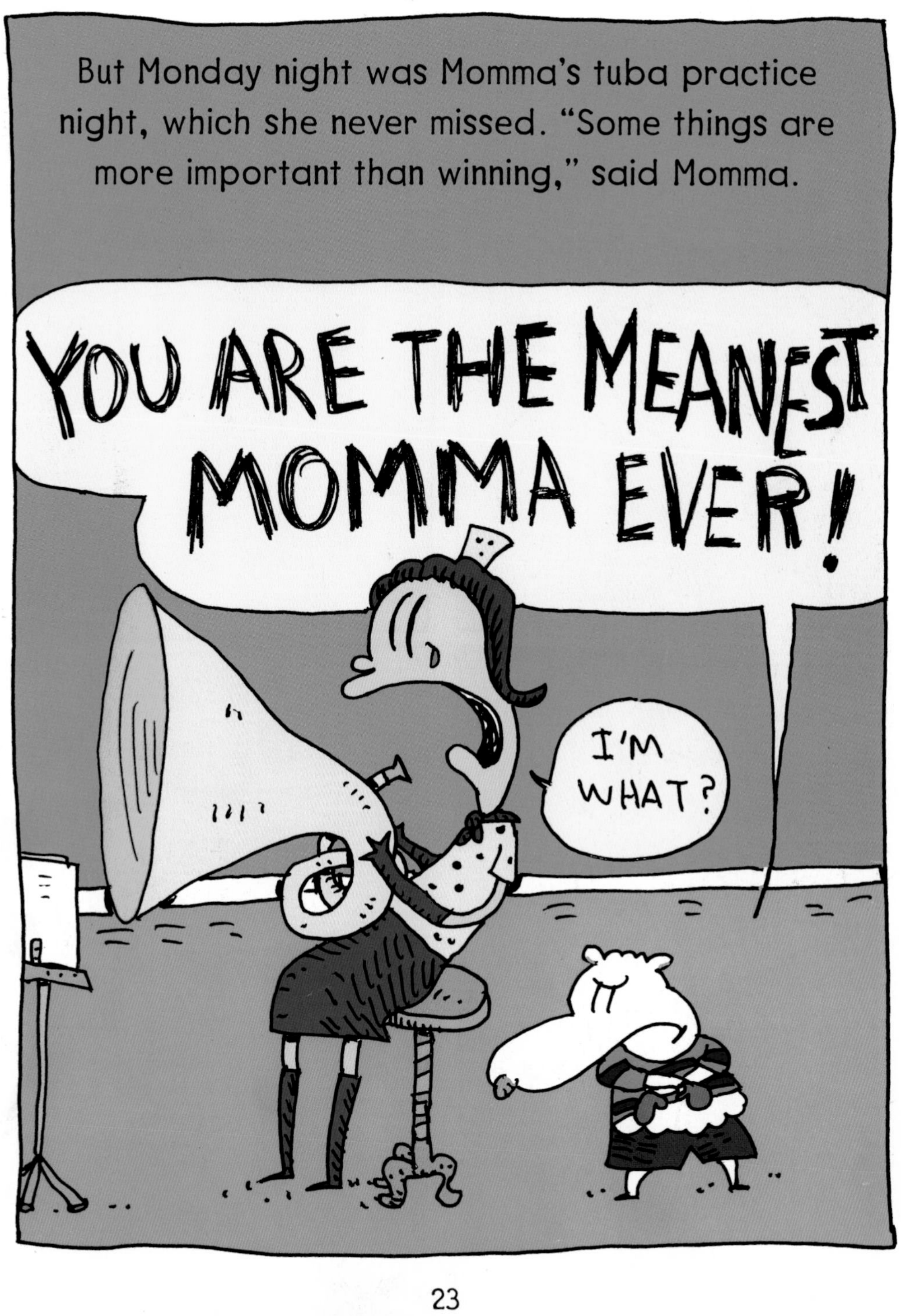
YOU ARE THE MEANEST MOMMA EVER!
I'M WHAT?

The next day the spelling bee resumed.
READY?
READY.
Everyone anxiously waited to see what word would be picked for Johnny to spell.
LOVE
Mandy Dinkus nearly croaked.
NO FAIR. TOO EASY!

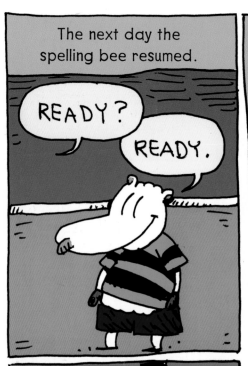

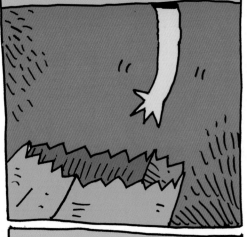

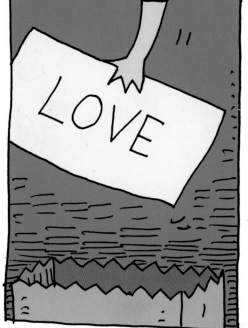

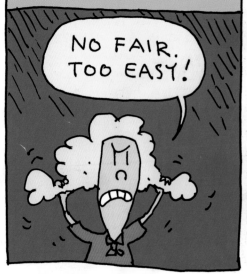

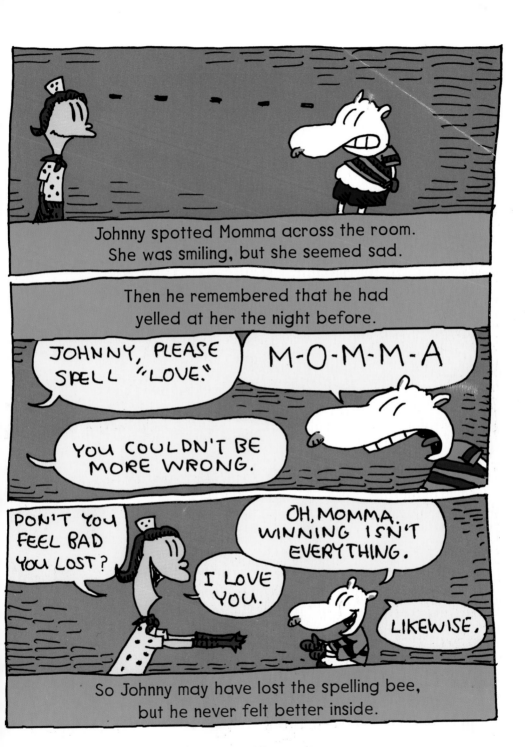

Johnny spotted Momma across the room.
She was smiling, but she seemed sad.

Then he remembered that he had
yelled at her the night before.

JOHNNY, PLEASE SPELL "LOVE."

M-O-M-M-A

YOU COULDN'T BE MORE WRONG.

DON'T YOU FEEL BAD YOU LOST?

OH, MOMMA. WINNING ISN'T EVERYTHING.

I LOVE YOU.

LIKEWISE.

So Johnny may have lost the spelling bee,
but he never felt better inside.

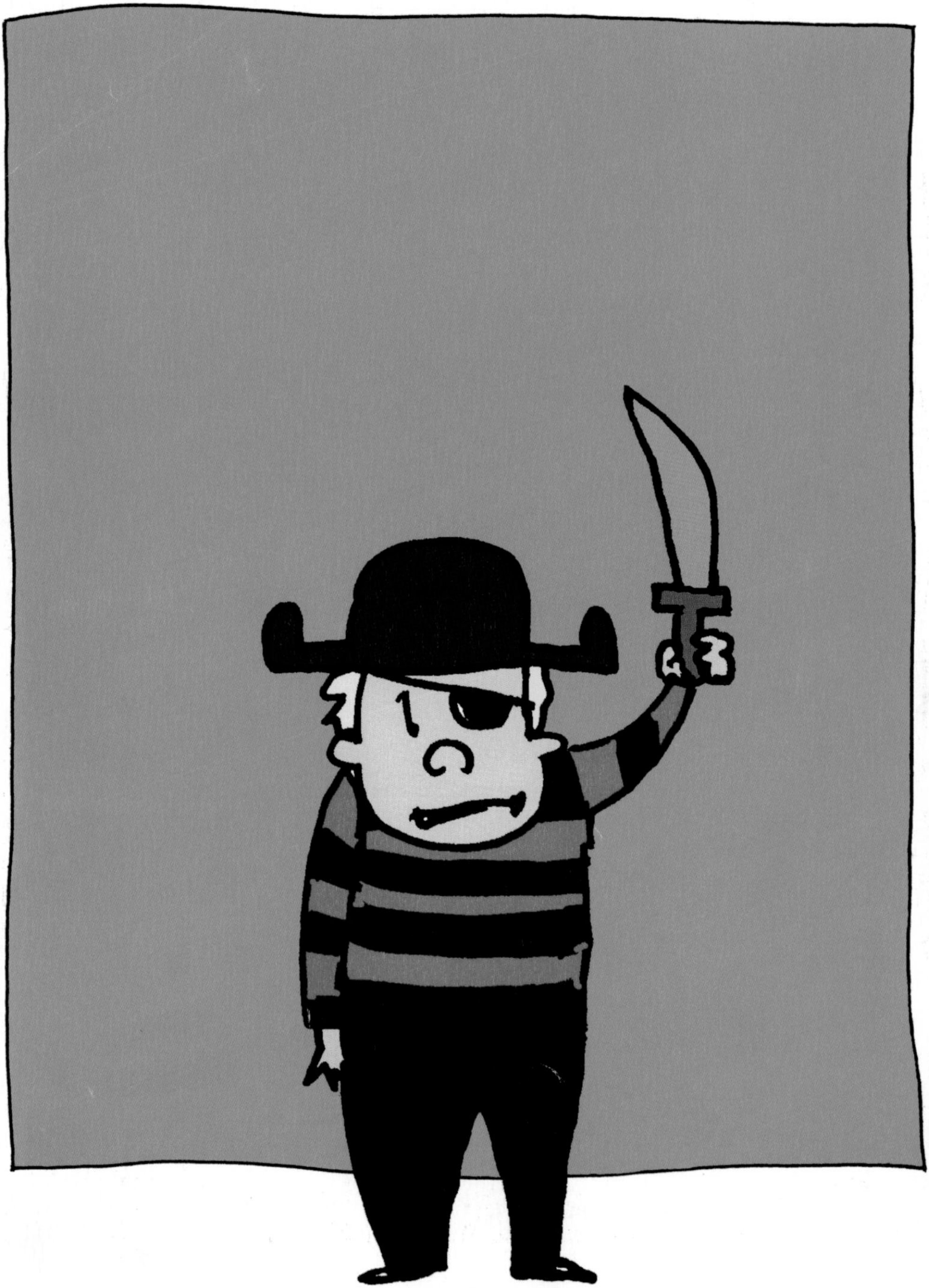

The Pirates Meet the Runny Nose

It was the week before Halloween, and Johnny Mutton was even happier than usual.

MOMMA, THESE SOCKS ARE THE GREENEST AND THE LONGEST.

THE KIDS ARE GONNA LOVE MY COSTUME!

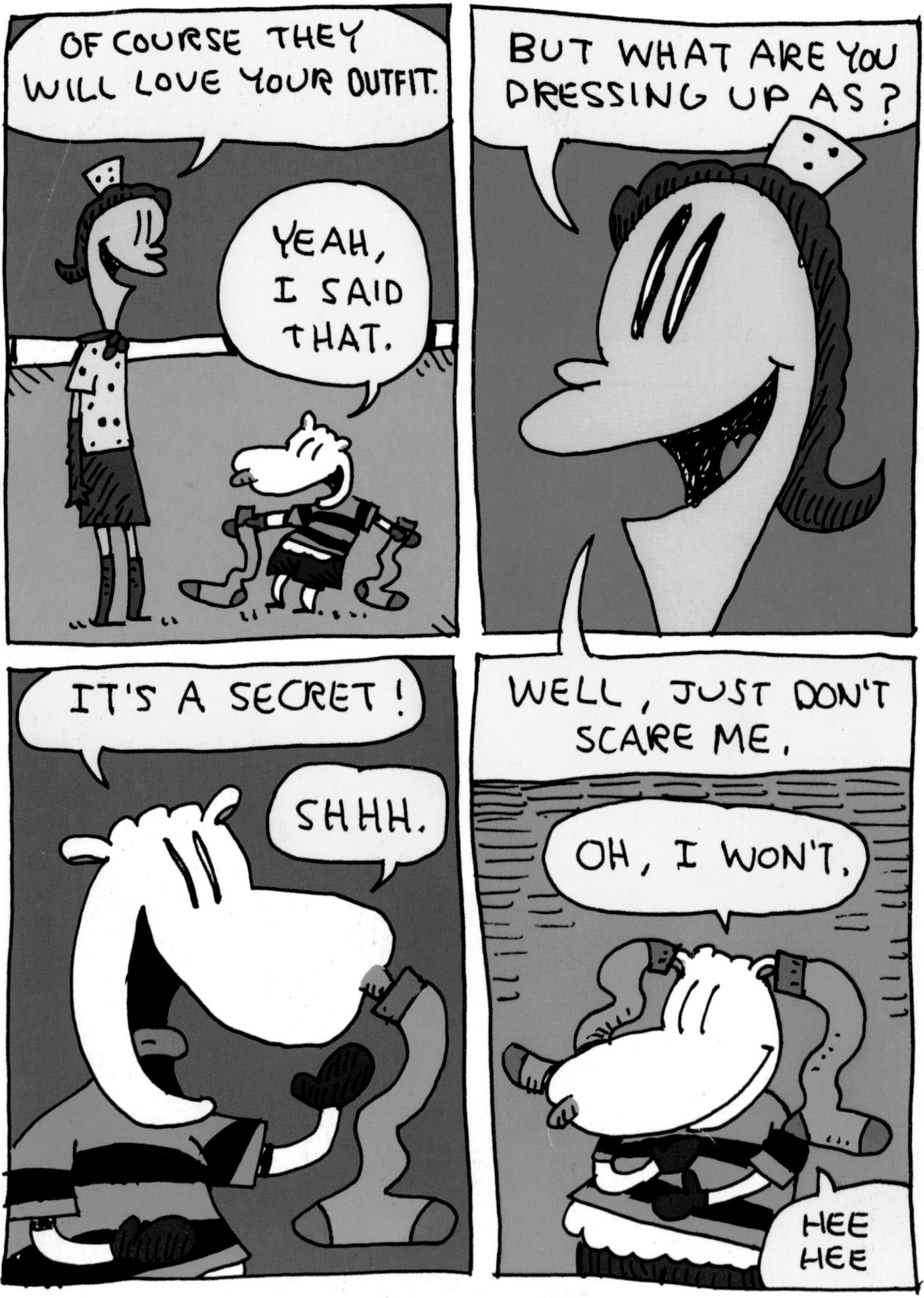
OF COURSE THEY WILL LOVE YOUR OUTFIT.
YEAH, I SAID THAT.
BUT WHAT ARE YOU DRESSING UP AS?
IT'S A SECRET!
SHHH.
WELL, JUST DON'T SCARE ME.
OH, I WON'T.
HEE HEE

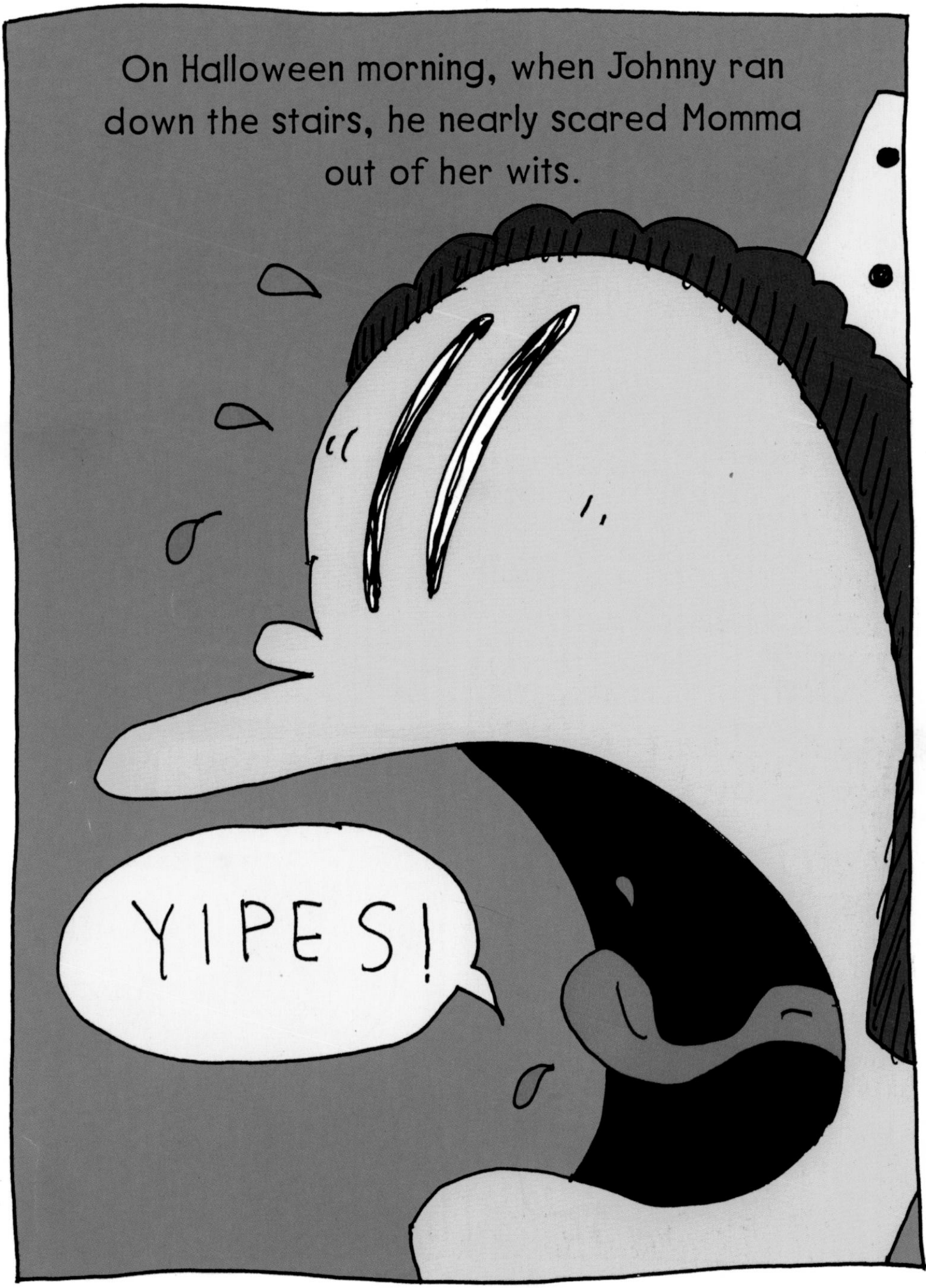
On Halloween morning, when Johnny ran down the stairs, he nearly scared Momma out of her wits.
YIPES!

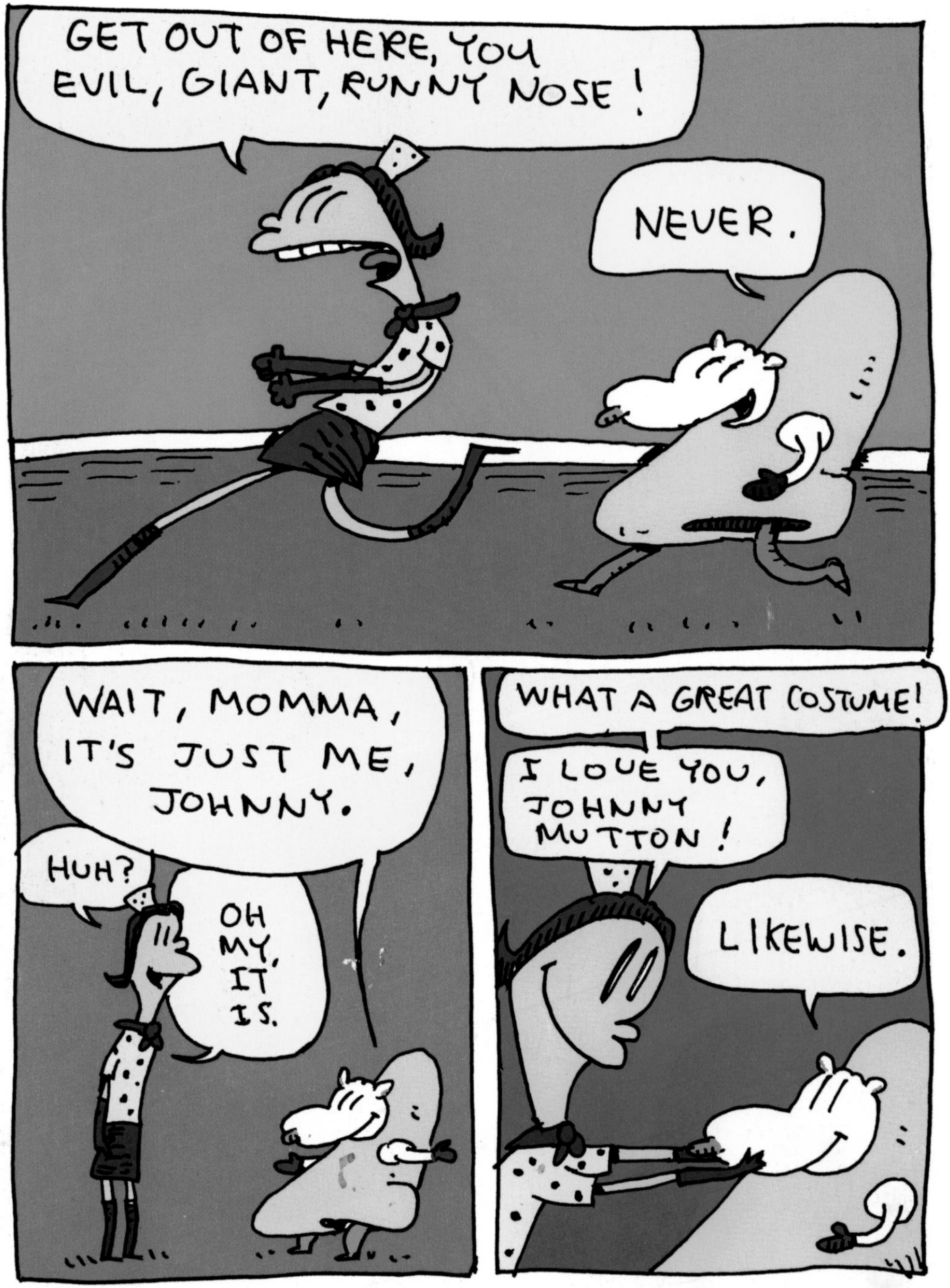
GET OUT OF HERE, YOU EVIL, GIANT, RUNNY NOSE!
NEVER.
WAIT, MOMMA, IT'S JUST ME, JOHNNY.
HUH?
OH MY, IT IS.
WHAT A GREAT COSTUME!
I LOVE YOU, JOHNNY MUTTON!
LIKEWISE.

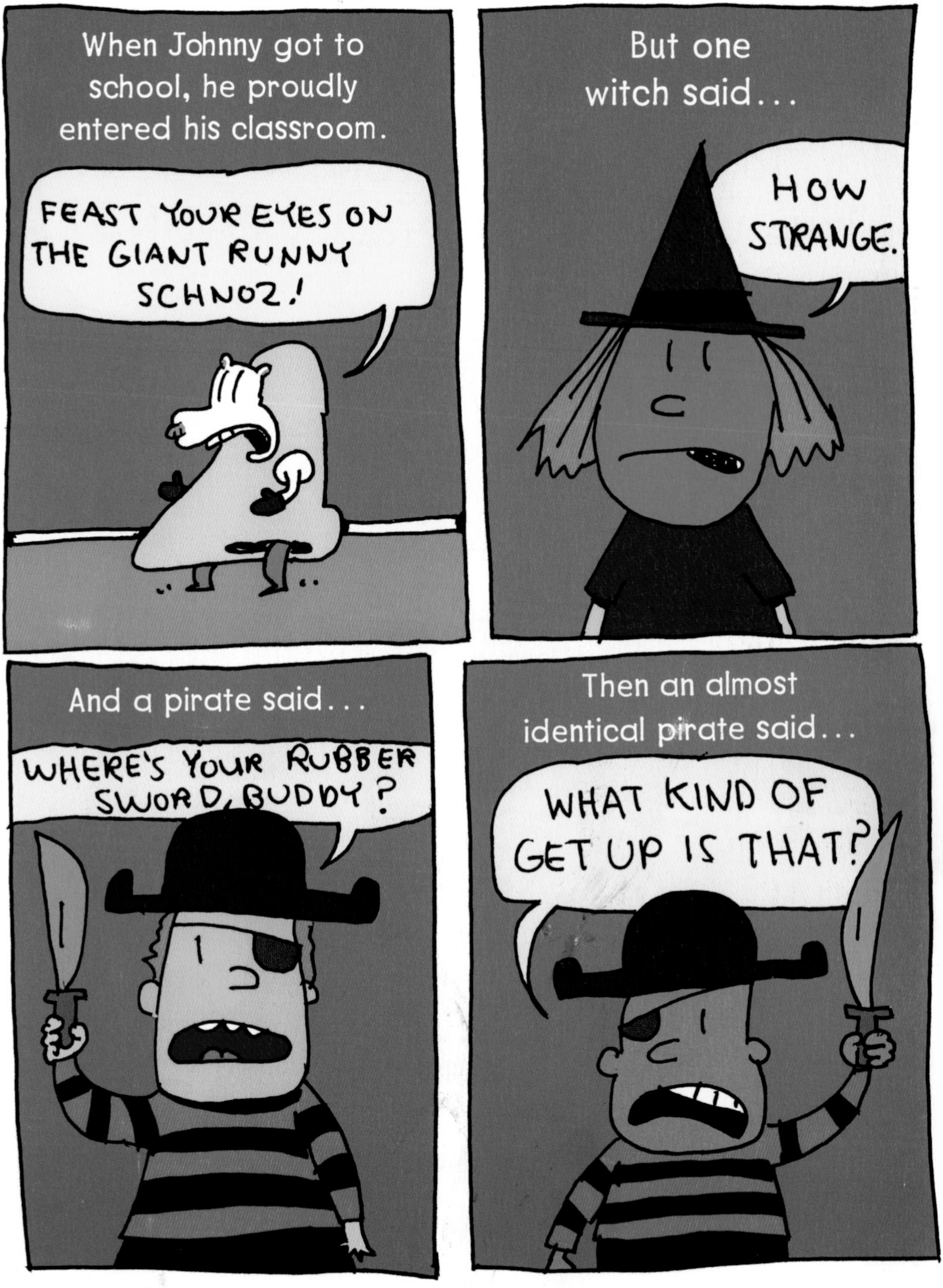
When Johnny got to school, he proudly entered his classroom.
FEAST YOUR EYES ON THE GIANT RUNNY SCHNOZ!
But one witch said...
HOW STRANGE.
And a pirate said...
WHERE'S YOUR RUBBER SWORD, BUDDY?
Then an almost identical pirate said...
WHAT KIND OF GET UP IS THAT?

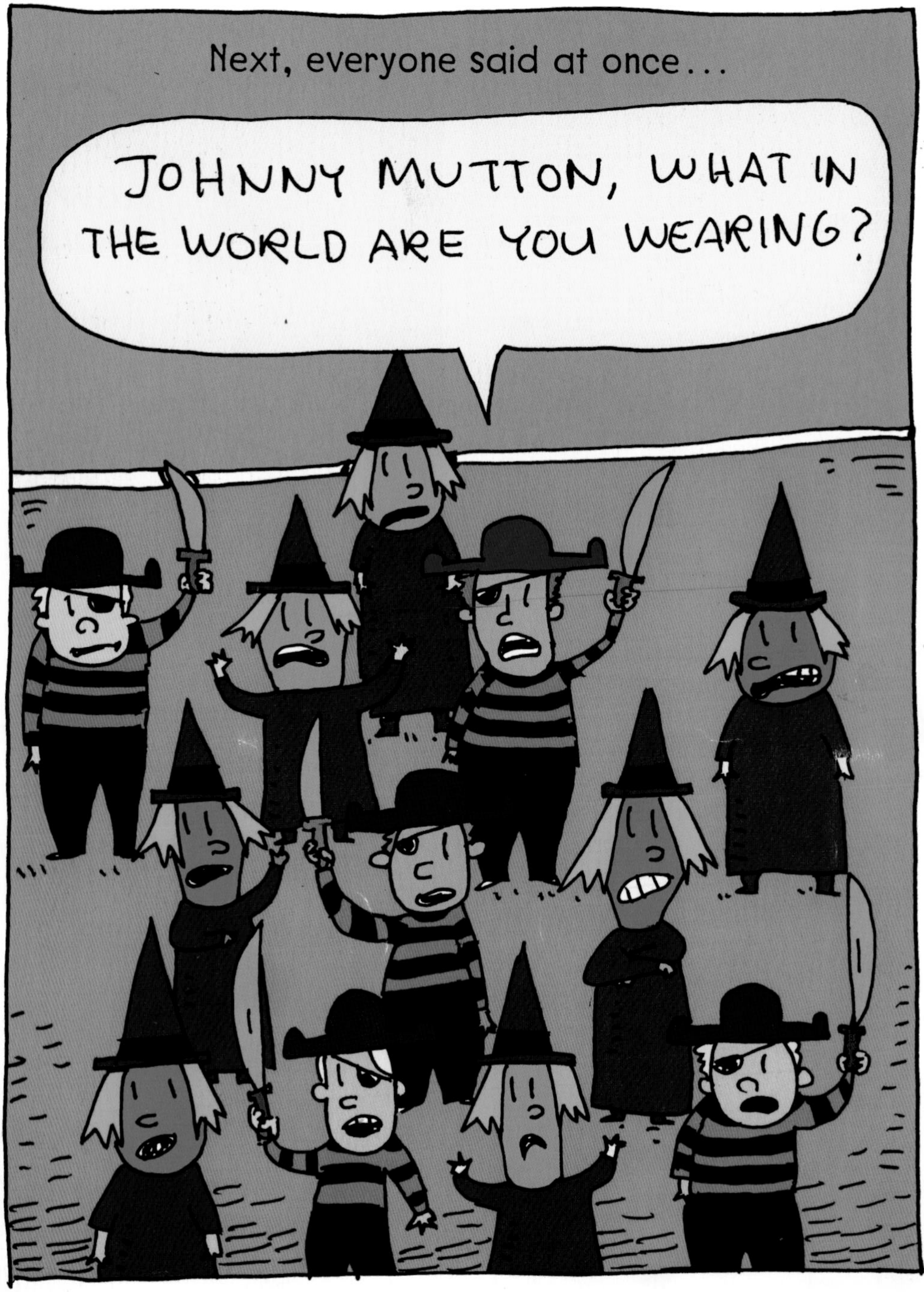
Next, everyone said at once...
JOHNNY MUTTON, WHAT IN THE WORLD ARE YOU WEARING?

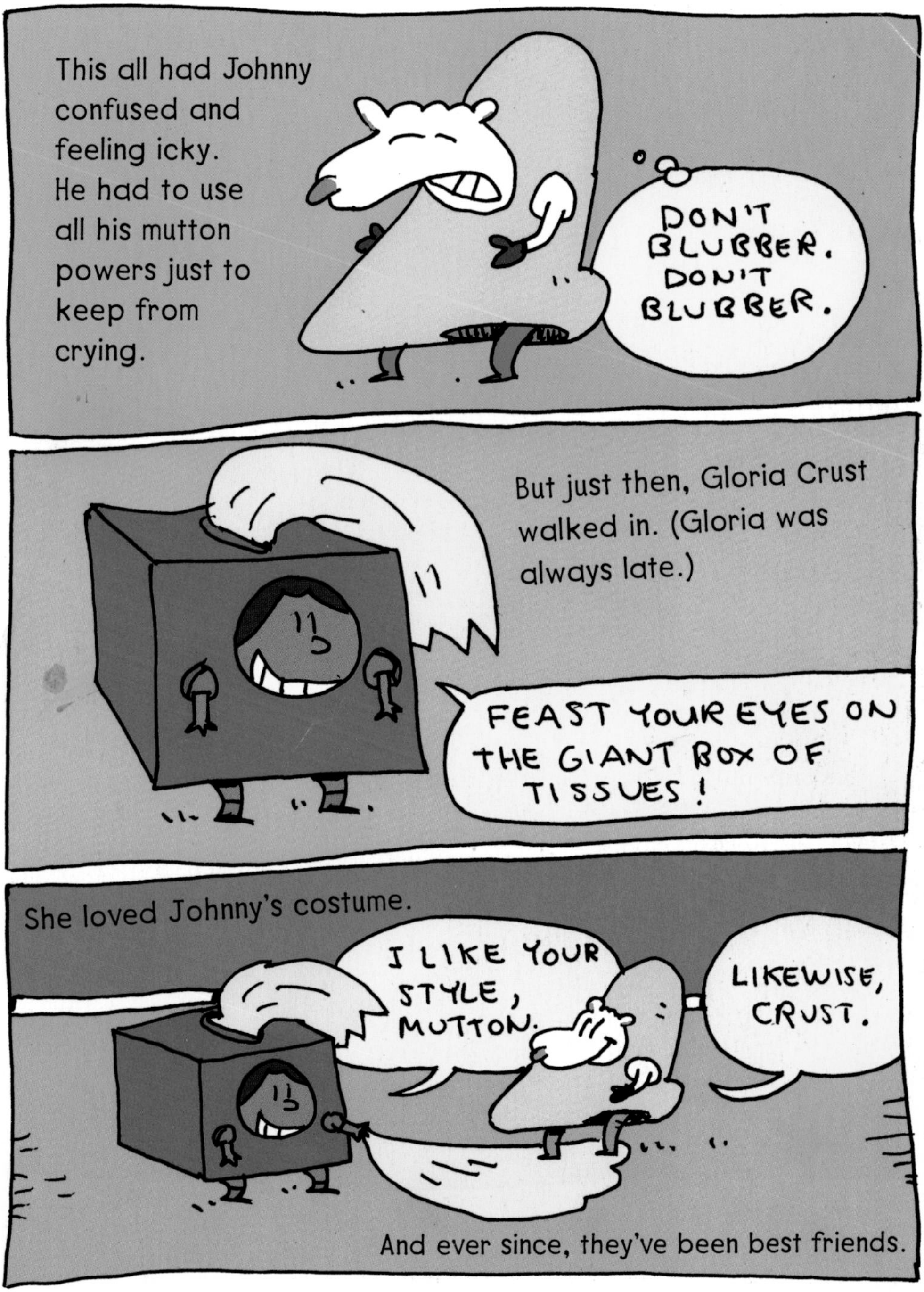
This all had Johnny confused and feeling icky. He had to use all his mutton powers just to keep from crying.
DON'T BLUBBER. DON'T BLUBBER.
But just then, Gloria Crust walked in. (Gloria was always late.)
FEAST YOUR EYES ON THE GIANT BOX OF TISSUES!
She loved Johnny's costume.
I LIKE YOUR STYLE, MUTTON.
LIKEWISE, CRUST.
And ever since, they've been best friends.

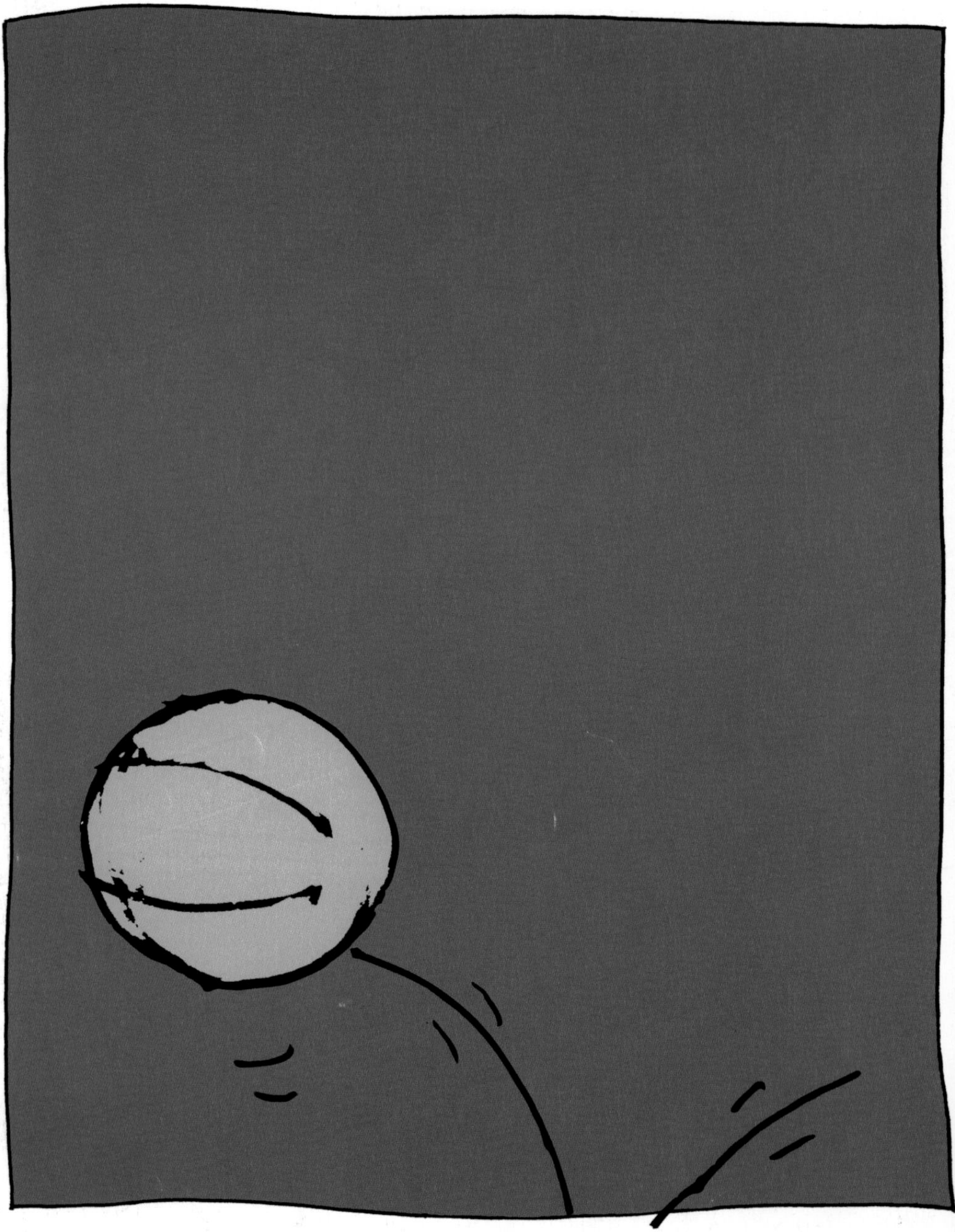

To Dribble or Not to Dribble

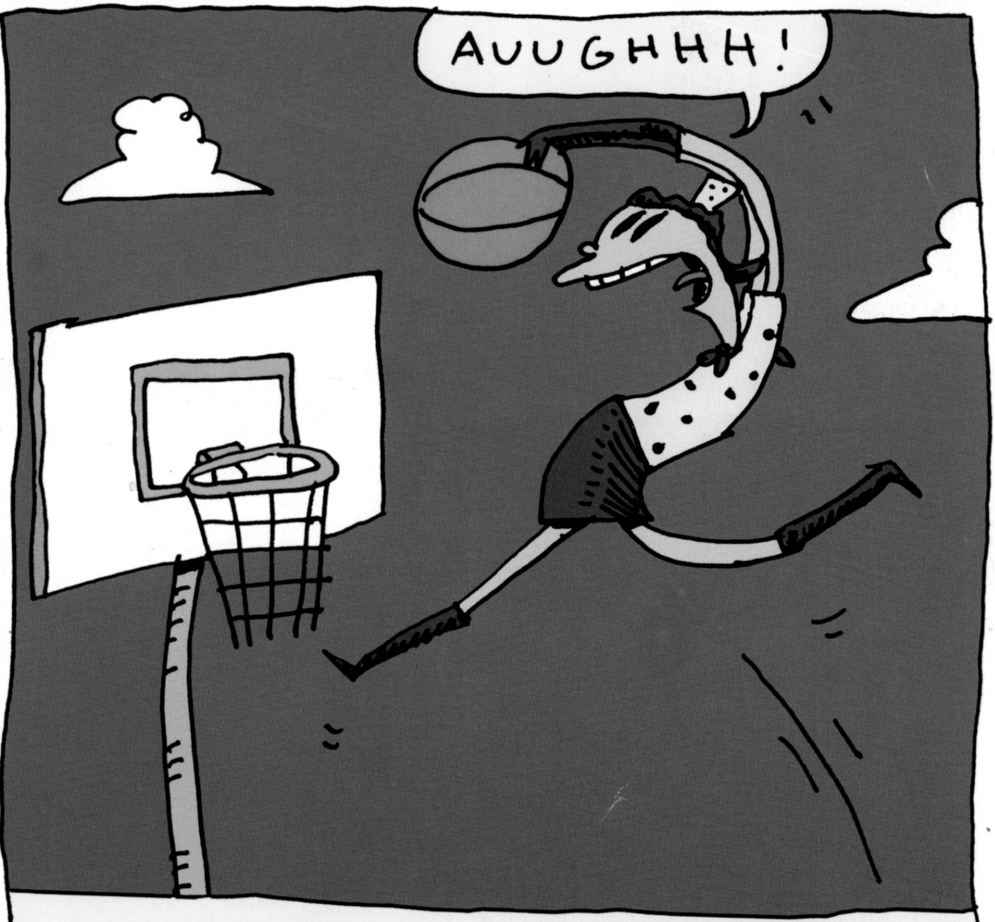
AUUGHHH!

Momma Mutton was a great basketball player.

She wanted Johnny Mutton to be a great basketball player, too. So every day she would throw him a hundred passes.

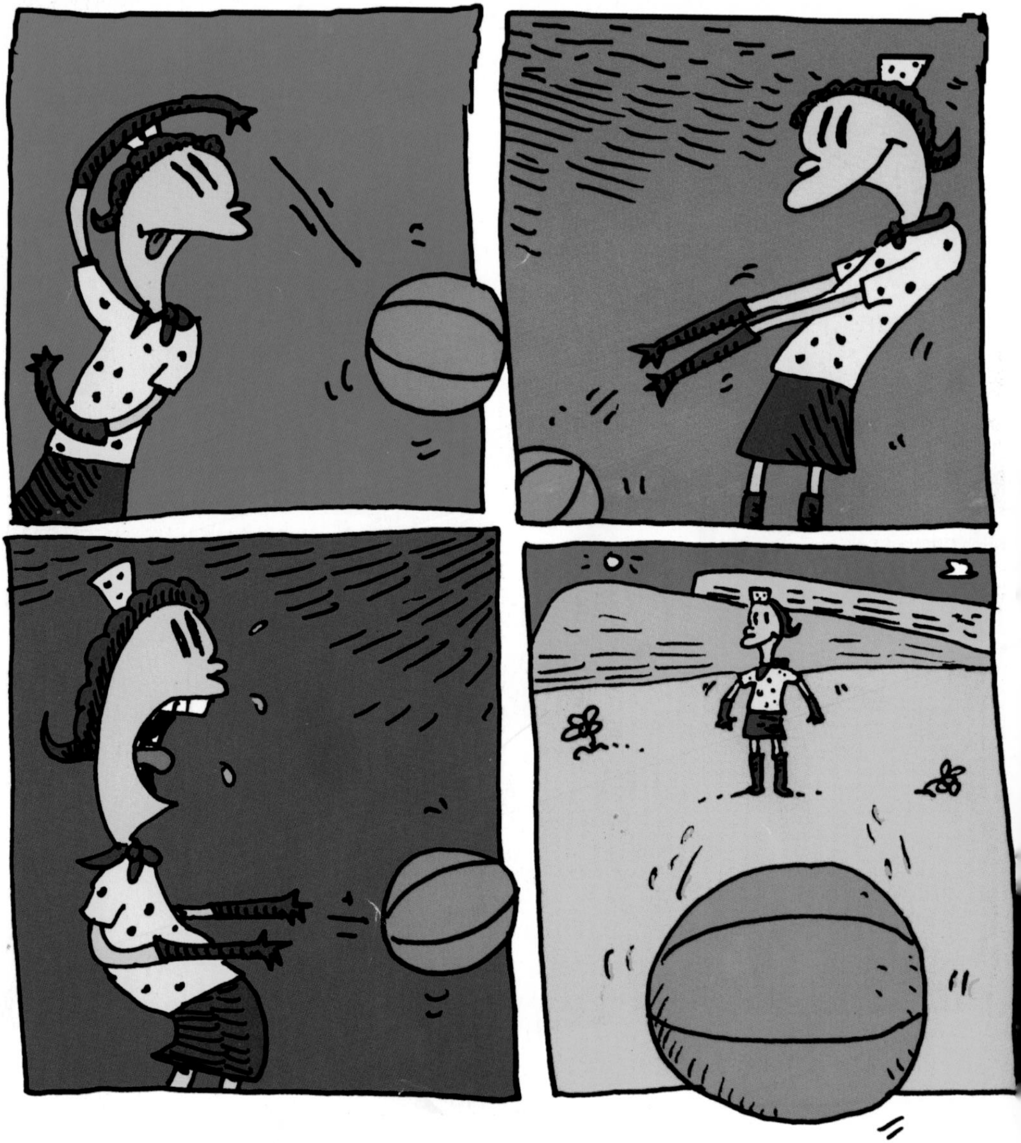

And every day a hundred passes would bounce off his fluffy body.

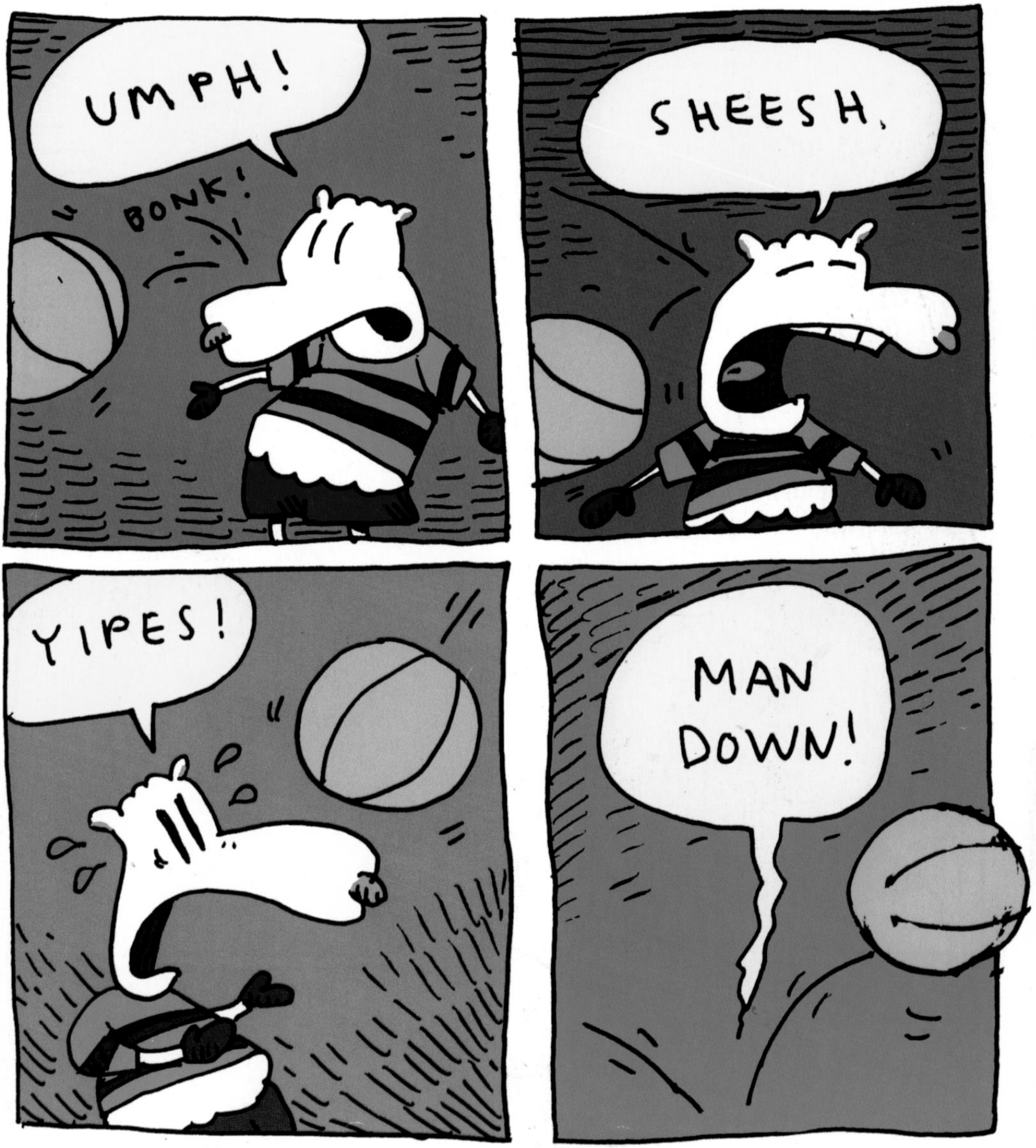
UMPH!
BONK!
SHEESH.
YIPES!
MAN DOWN!

Actually, he did catch one of her passes.
But it was an accident.

One day, the basketball was gone.

NOW WE CAN'T PLAY CATCH TODAY.

WHAT A SHAME.

Just then, Momma noticed a strange "squirrel" up in the tree.

Momma smiled.

HMM.

LA, LA, LA.

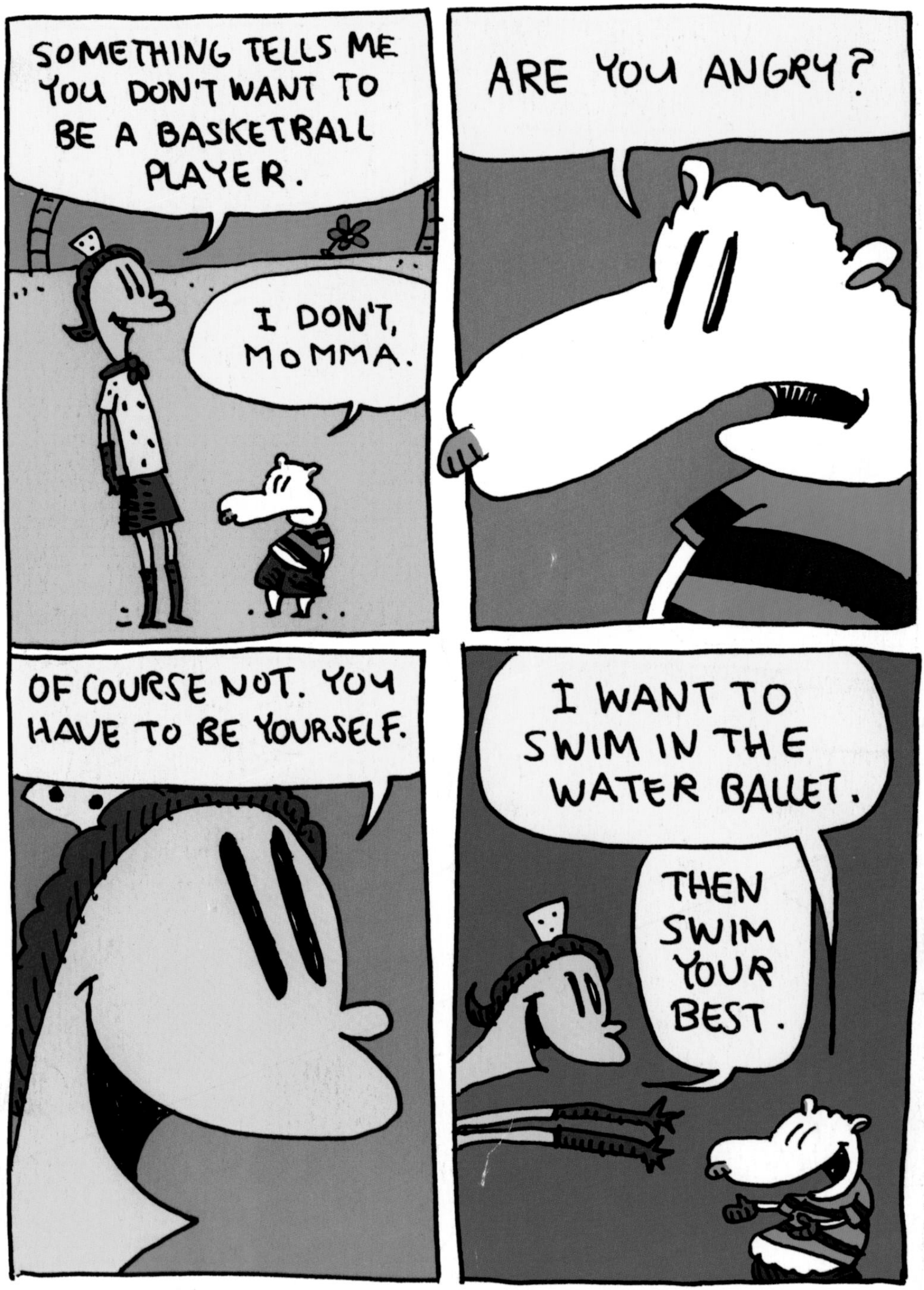
SOMETHING TELLS ME YOU DON'T WANT TO BE A BASKETBALL PLAYER.
I DON'T, MOMMA.
ARE YOU ANGRY?
OF COURSE NOT. YOU HAVE TO BE YOURSELF.
I WANT TO SWIM IN THE WATER BALLET.
THEN SWIM YOUR BEST.

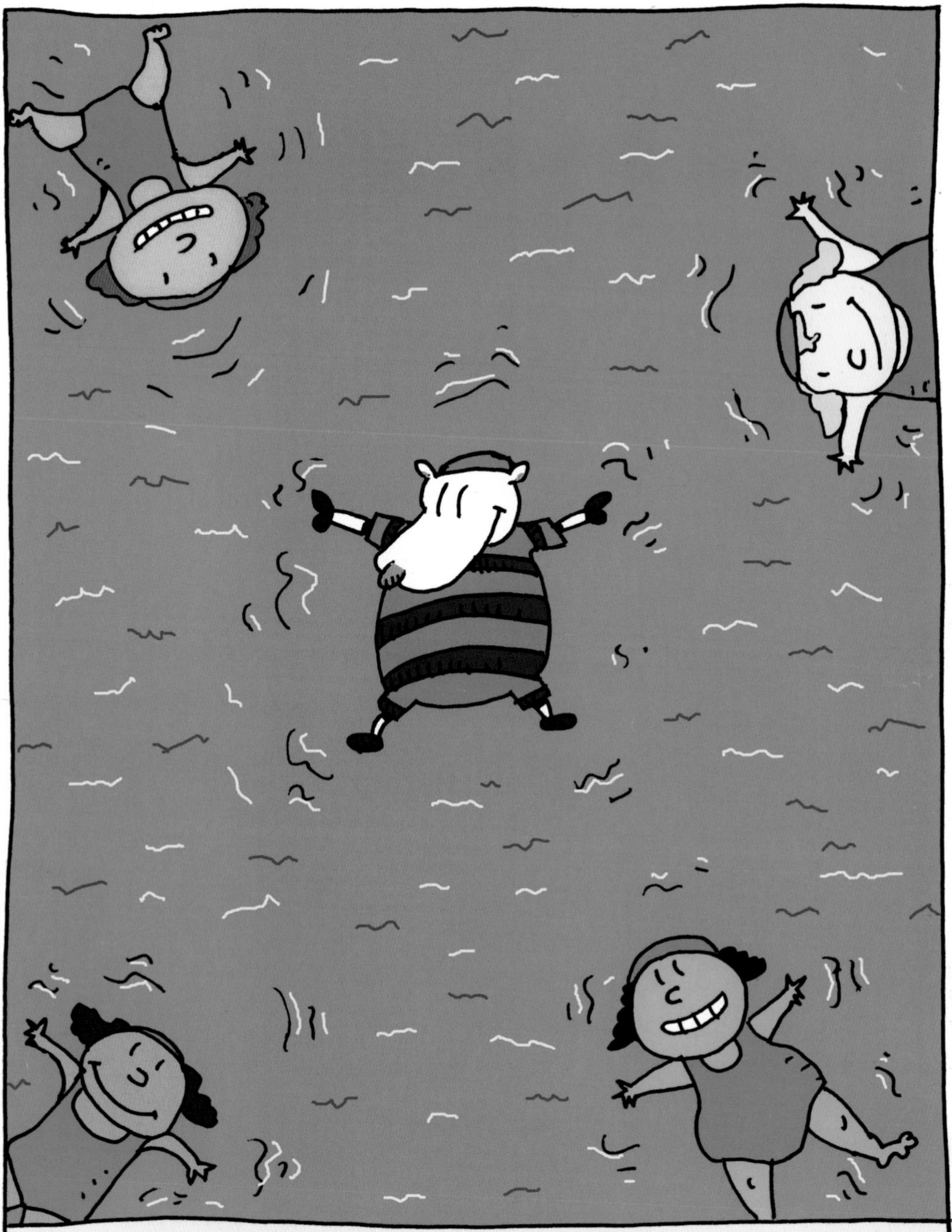

And that's exactly what he did.

Where Are

Johnny Mutton went on to become a national hero by winning twenty gold medals in the Olympics for water ballet.

Mr. Slopdish wound up famous for telling stories about Johnny Mutton on TV talk shows. Eventually he became the Poofy Marshmallow spokesperson— his face on every bag.

They Now?

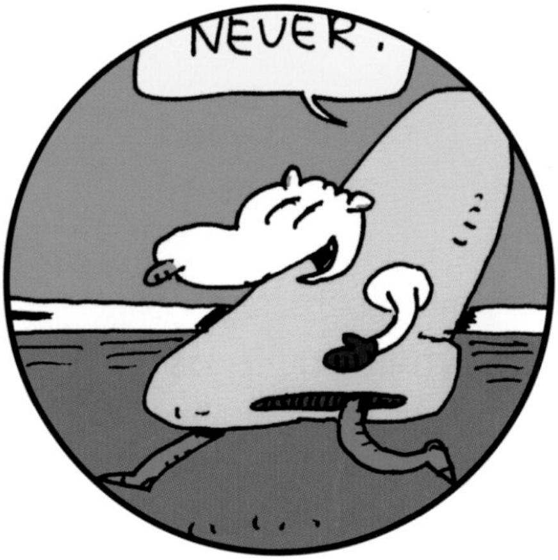
NEVER.

The Halloween after Johnny won those twenty gold medals, all the kids in this book dressed up as Johnny Mutton.

Except for Gloria Crust and Johnny Mutton, that is. Gloria dressed up as a mop. Johnny, as a nasty spill.

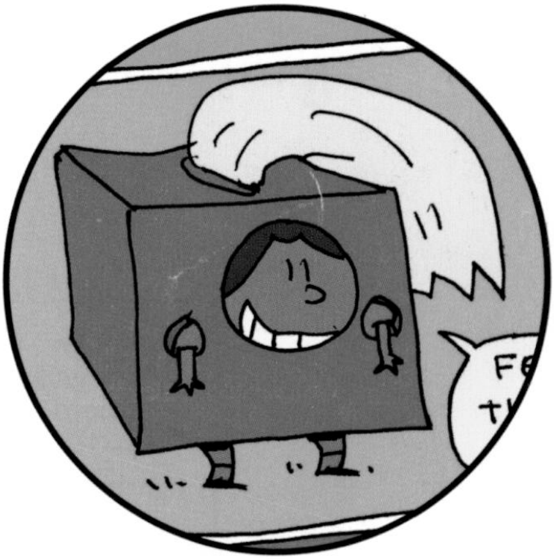

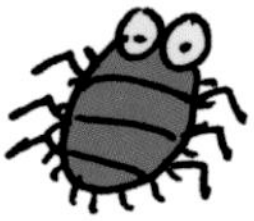

A FUZZY BUG

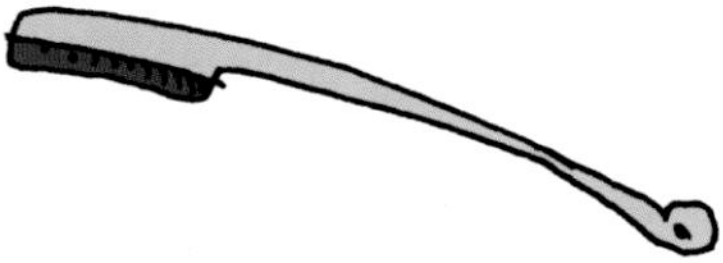

A WINDSHIELD WIPER

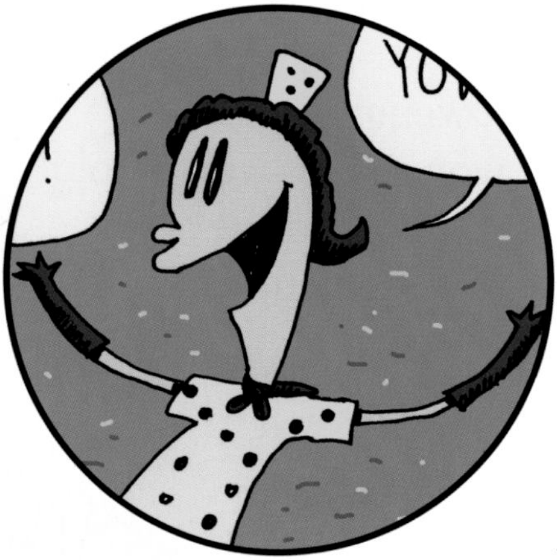

Momma continued to find many interesting items on her front step. But never again would she come across anything quite as wonderful as Johnny Mutton.

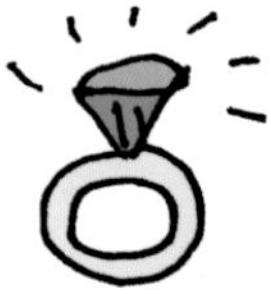

A DIAMOND RING

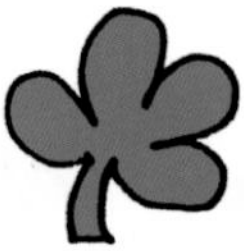

A FOUR-LEAF CLOVER

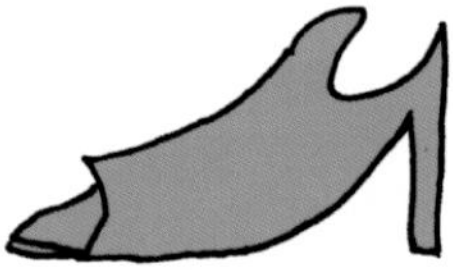

A DOLL'S SHOE

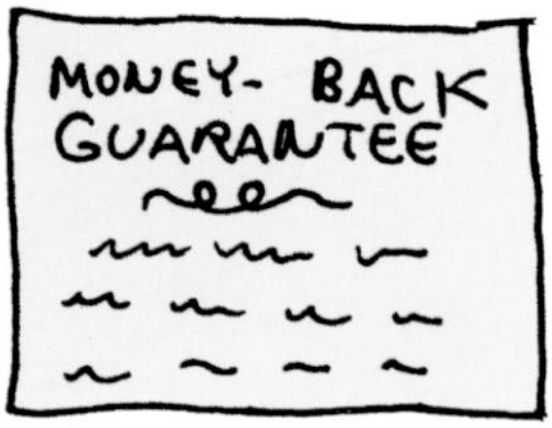
MONEY- BACK
GUARANTEE

A MONEY-BACK GUARANTEE

For Ro Stimo

JOHNNY MUTTON,

HE'S SO HIM!

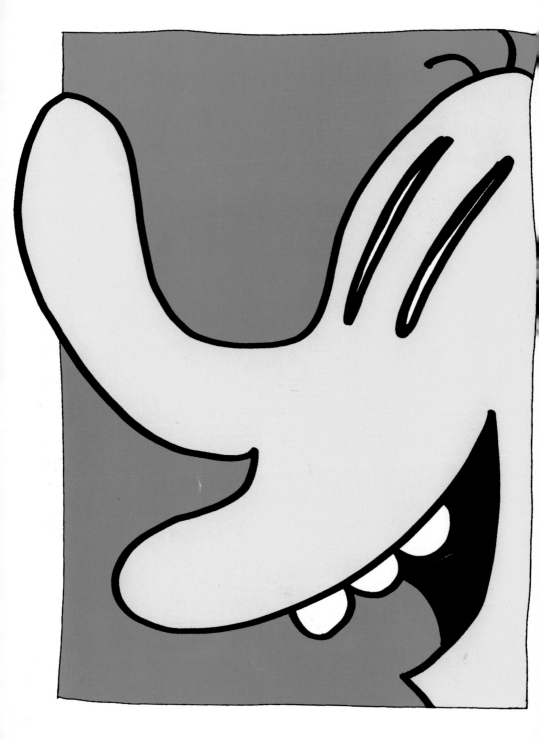

Johnny Mutton Saves the Universe

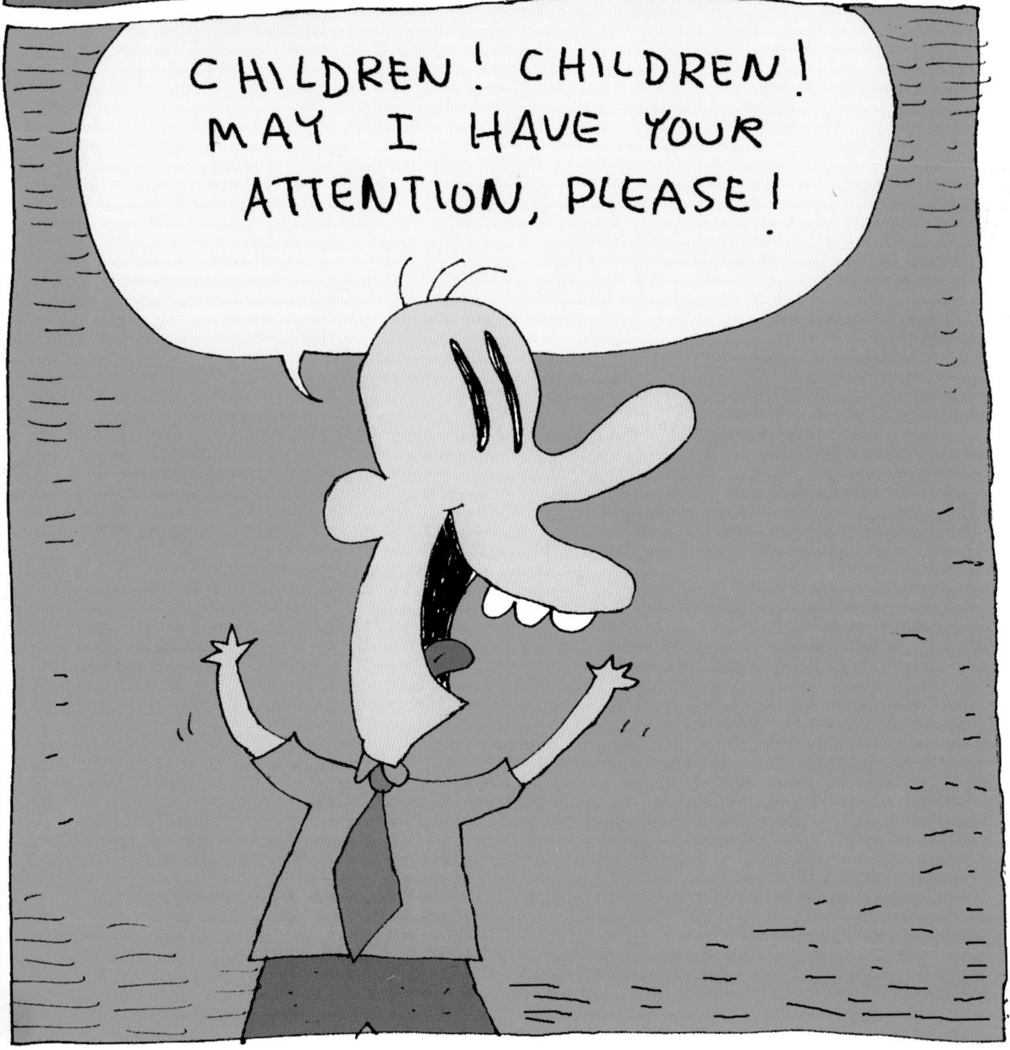
CHILDREN! CHILDREN! MAY I HAVE YOUR ATTENTION, PLEASE!

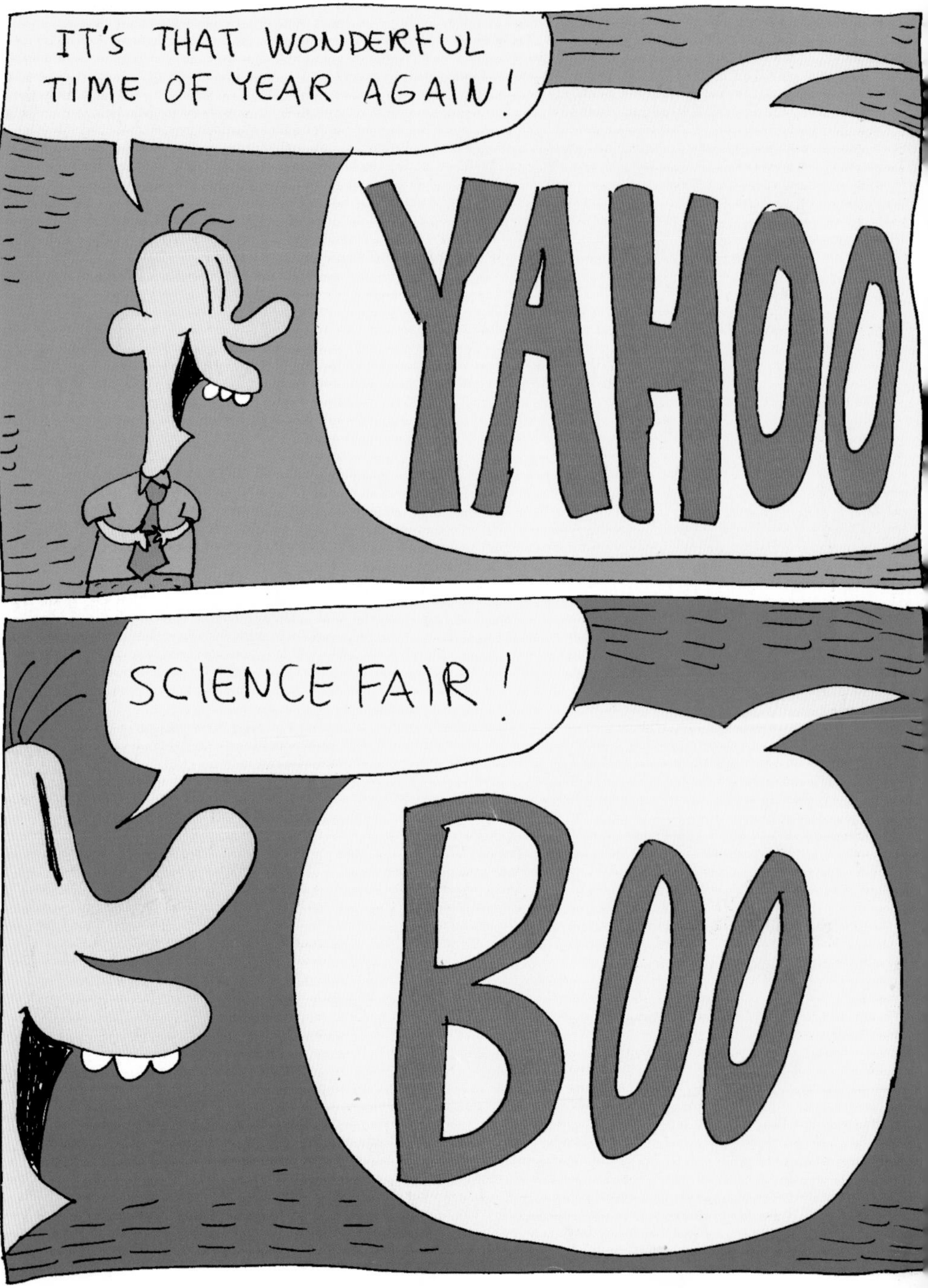
IT'S THAT WONDERFUL TIME OF YEAR AGAIN!
YAHOO
SCIENCE FAIR!
BOO

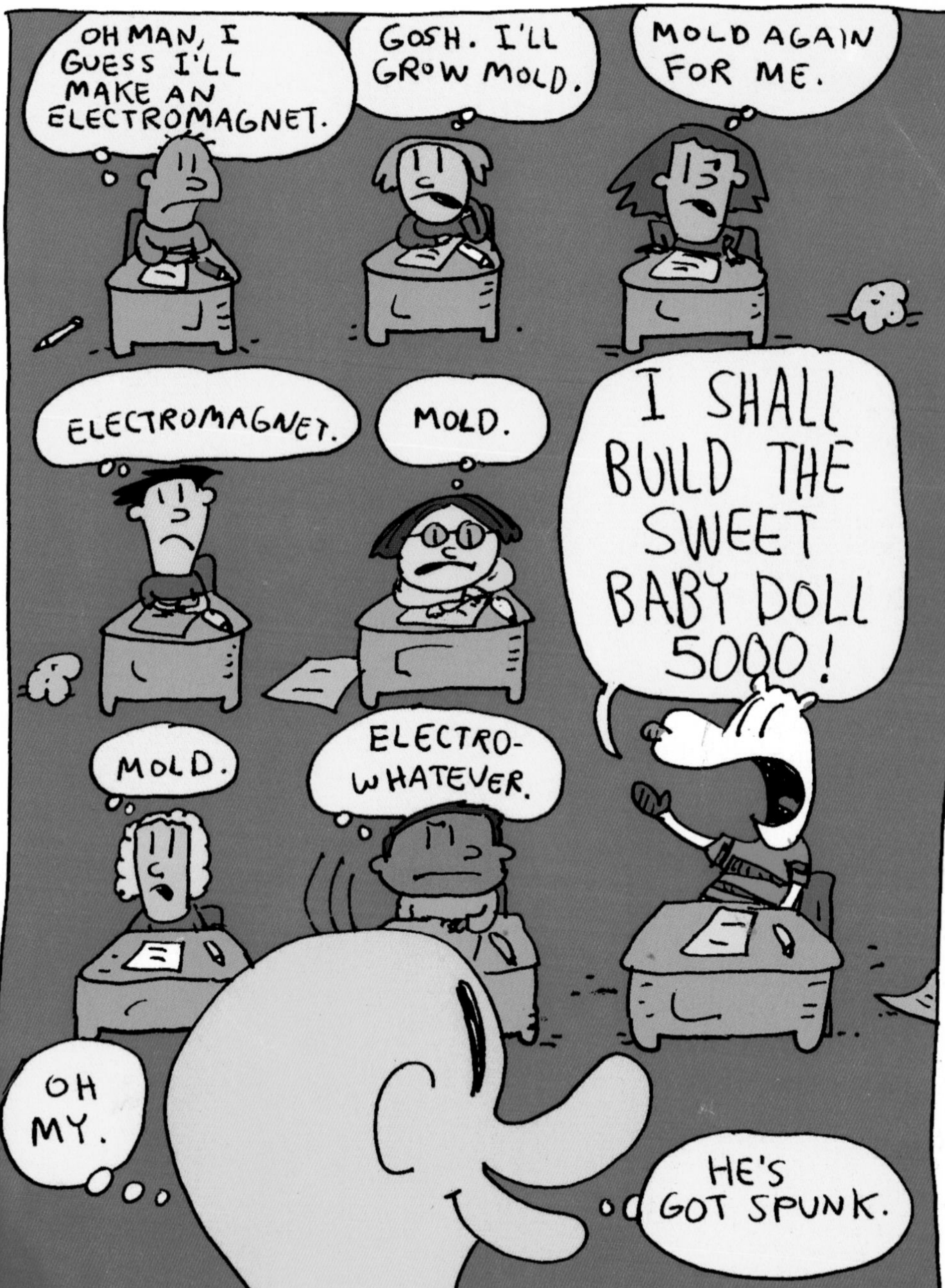
OH MAN, I GUESS I'LL MAKE AN ELECTROMAGNET.
GOSH. I'LL GROW MOLD.
MOLD AGAIN FOR ME.
ELECTROMAGNET.
MOLD.
I SHALL BUILD THE SWEET BABY DOLL 5000!
MOLD.
ELECTRO-WHATEVER.
OH MY.
HE'S GOT SPUNK.

The Sweet Baby Doll 5000 was Johnny's idea of the perfect robot.

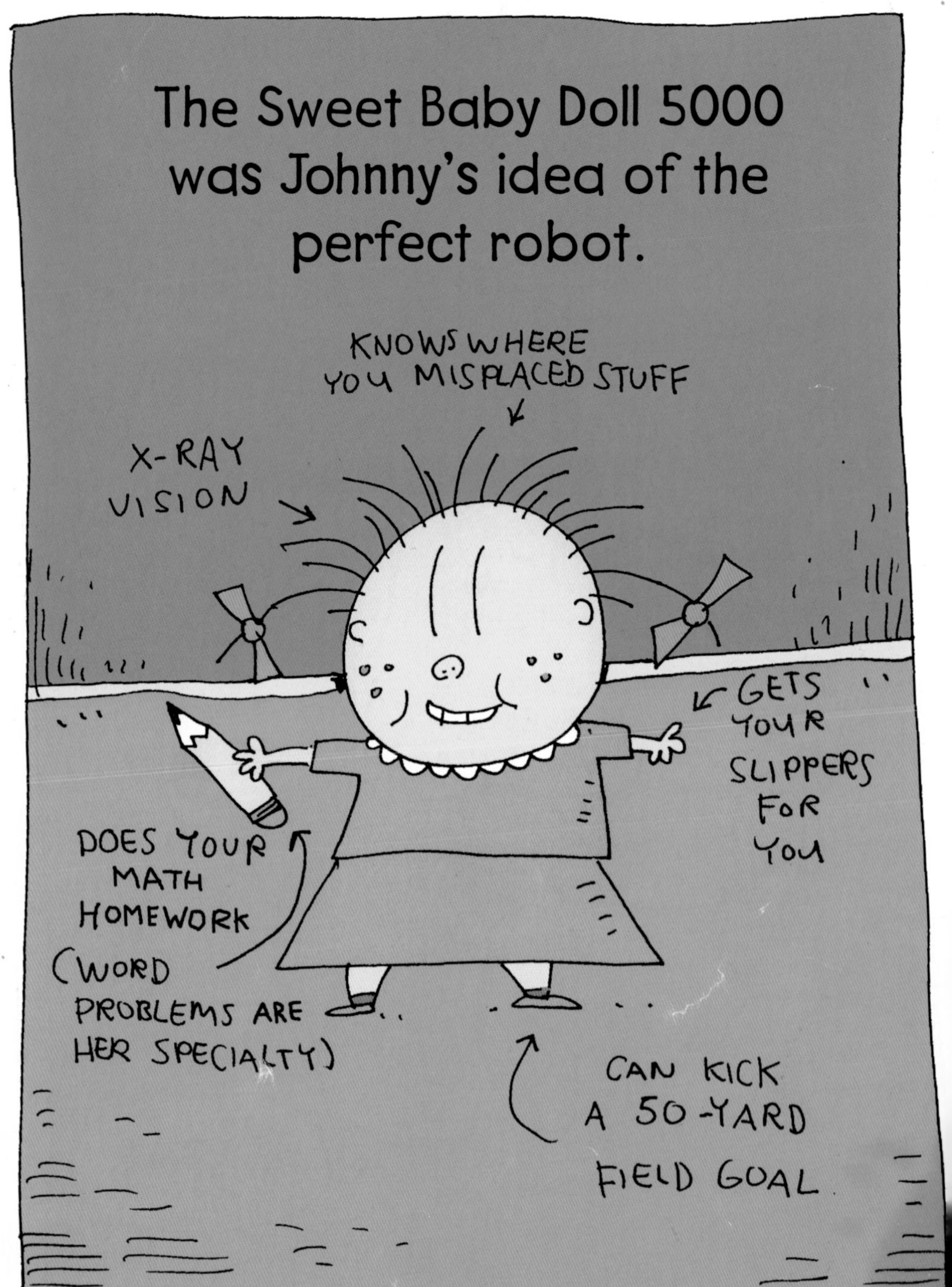
KNOWS WHERE YOU MISPLACED STUFF
X-RAY VISION
GETS YOUR SLIPPERS FOR YOU
DOES YOUR MATH HOMEWORK
(WORD PROBLEMS ARE HER SPECIALTY)
CAN KICK A 50-YARD FIELD GOAL

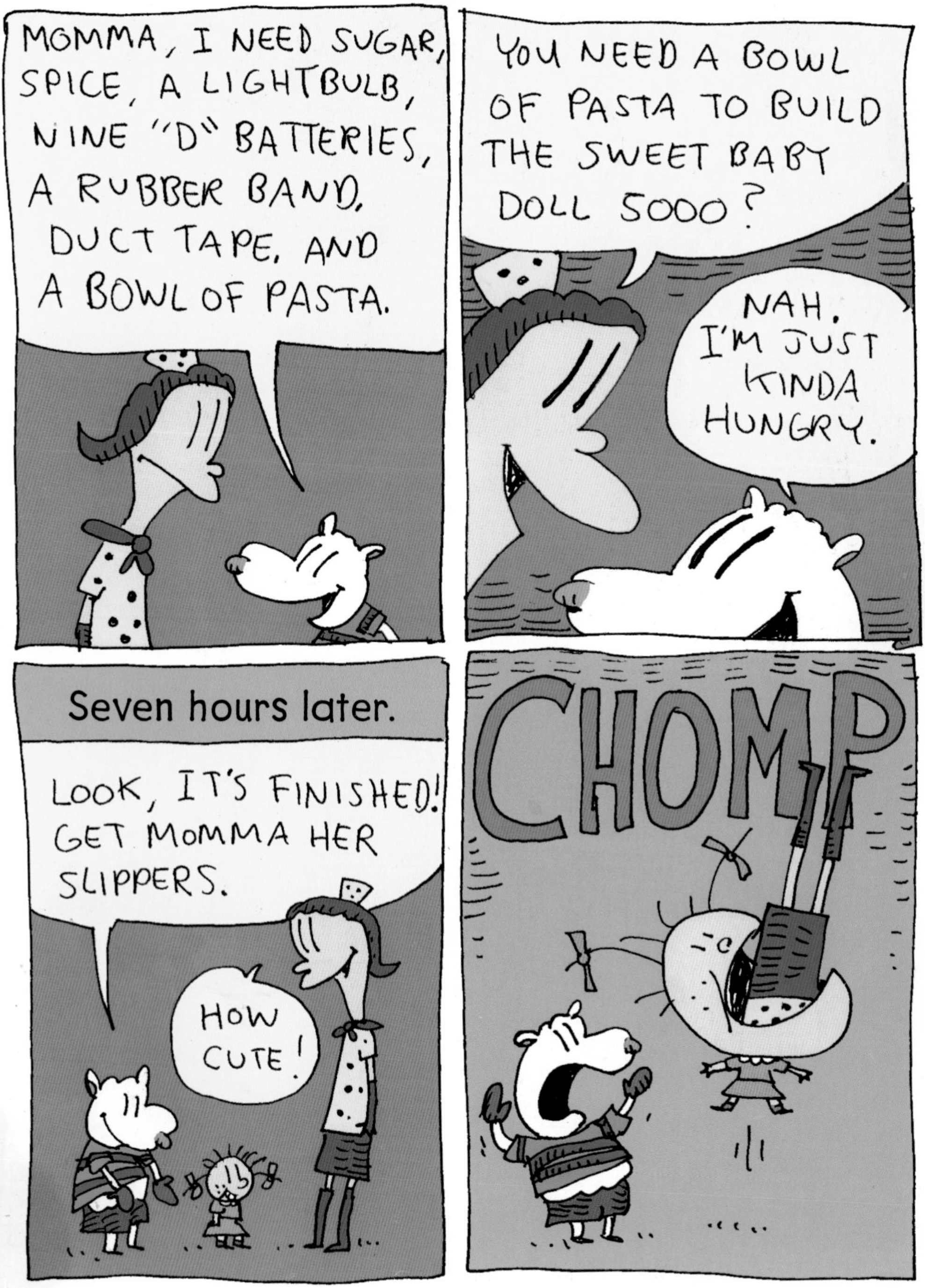
MOMMA, I NEED SUGAR, SPICE, A LIGHTBULB, NINE "D" BATTERIES, A RUBBER BAND, DUCT TAPE, AND A BOWL OF PASTA.
YOU NEED A BOWL OF PASTA TO BUILD THE SWEET BABY DOLL 5000?
NAH. I'M JUST KINDA HUNGRY.
Seven hours later.
LOOK, IT'S FINISHED! GET MOMMA HER SLIPPERS.
HOW CUTE!
CHOMP

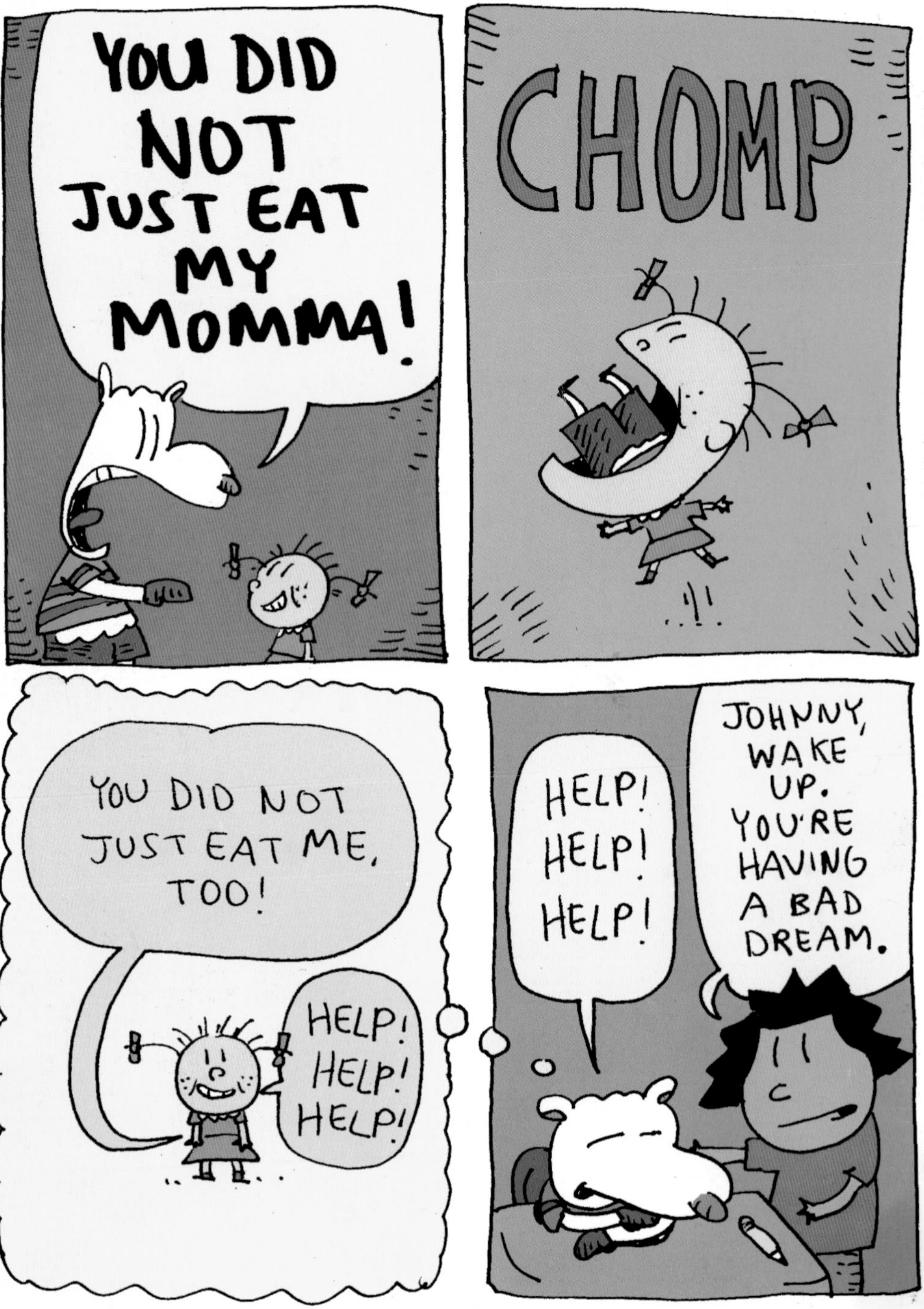
YOU DID NOT JUST EAT MY MOMMA!
CHOMP
YOU DID NOT JUST EAT ME, TOO!
HELP! HELP! HELP!
HELP! HELP! HELP!
JOHNNY, WAKE UP. YOU'RE HAVING A BAD DREAM.

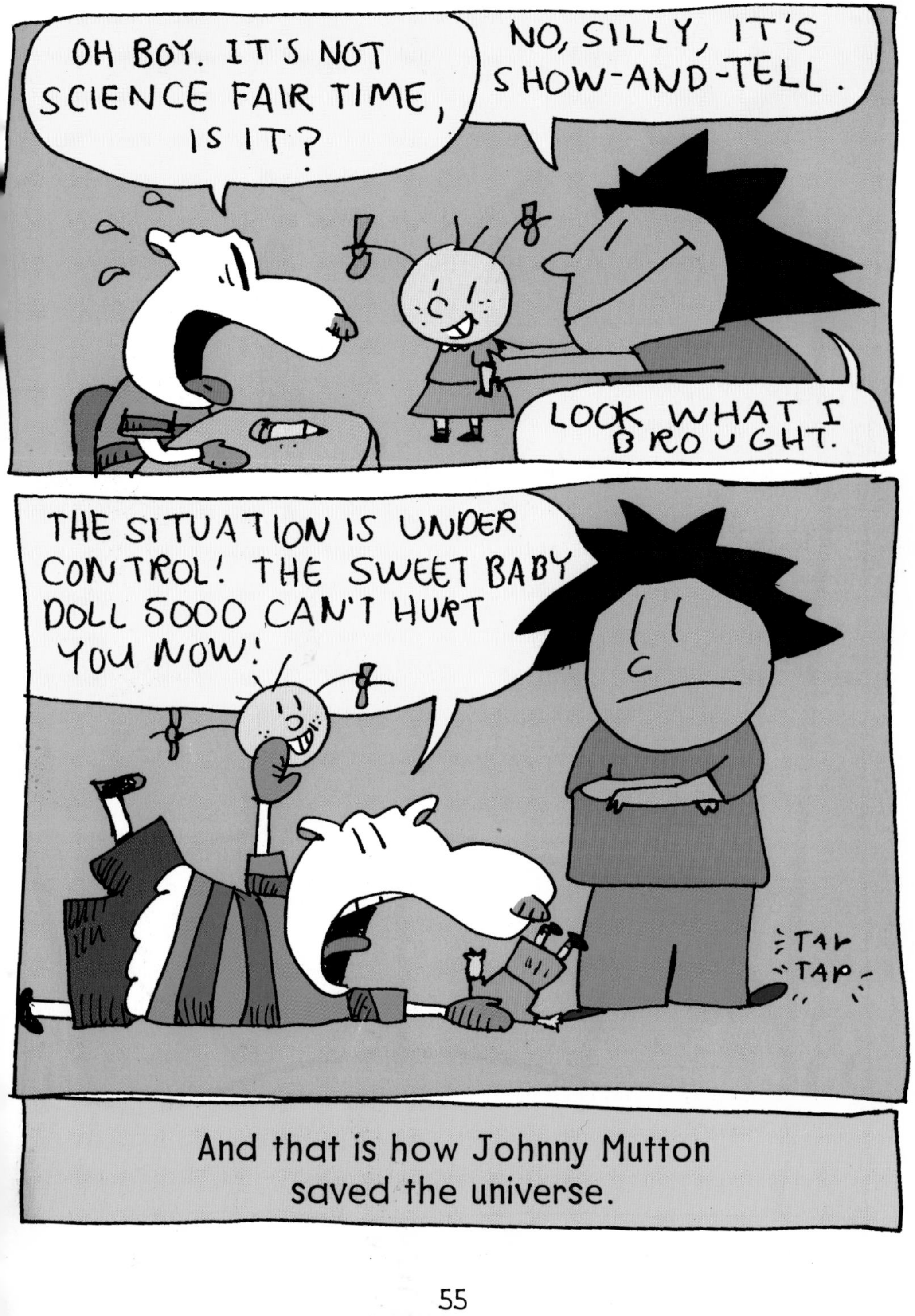
OH BOY. IT'S NOT SCIENCE FAIR TIME, IS IT?
NO, SILLY, IT'S SHOW-AND-TELL.
LOOK WHAT I BROUGHT.
THE SITUATION IS UNDER CONTROL! THE SWEET BABY DOLL 5000 CAN'T HURT YOU NOW!
TAP TAP

And that is how Johnny Mutton saved the universe.

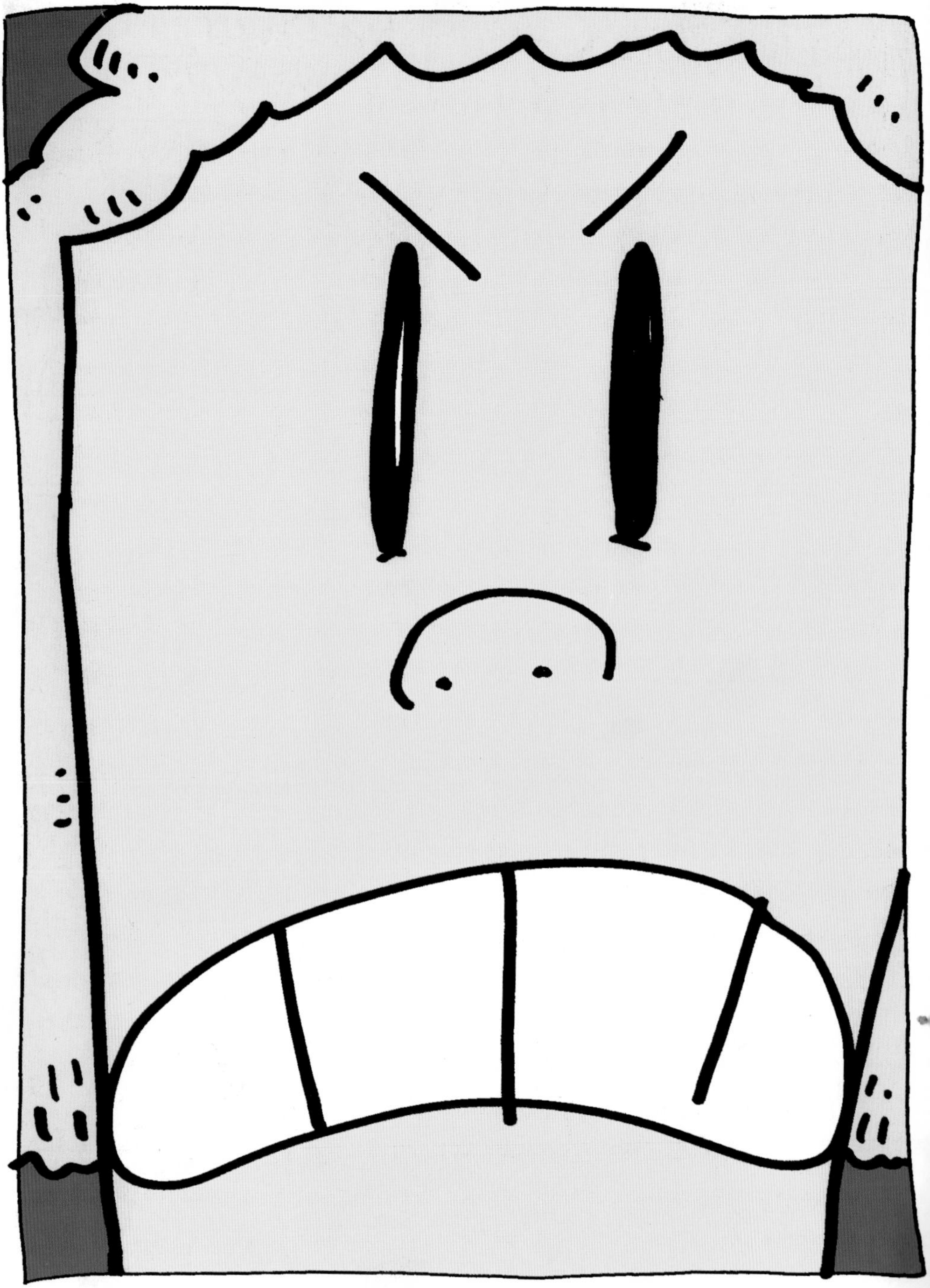

The Cook-Off

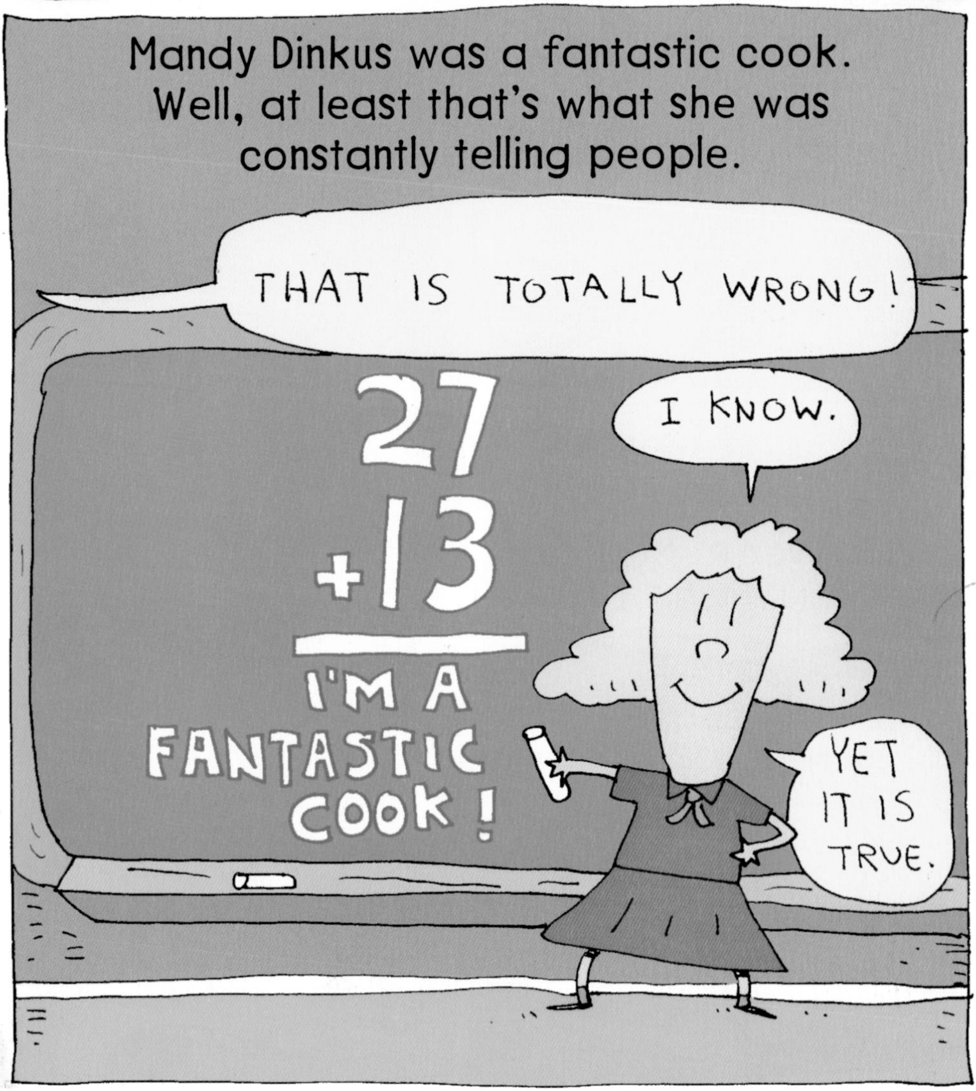
Mandy Dinkus was a fantastic cook. Well, at least that's what she was constantly telling people.
THAT IS TOTALLY WRONG!
27
+13
I'M A FANTASTIC COOK!
I KNOW.
YET IT IS TRUE.

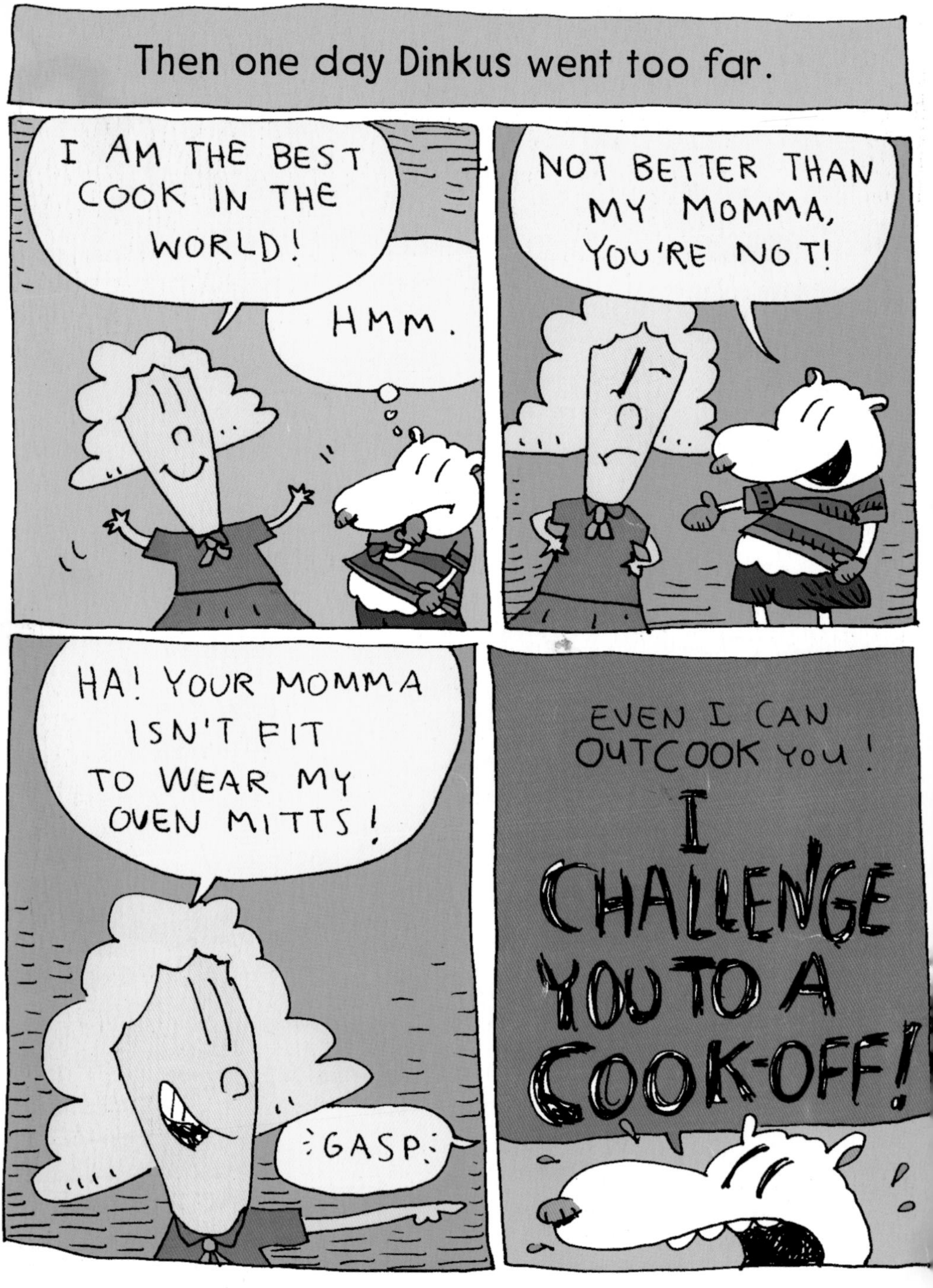
Then one day Dinkus went too far.
I AM THE BEST COOK IN THE WORLD!
HMM.
NOT BETTER THAN MY MOMMA, YOU'RE NOT!
HA! YOUR MOMMA ISN'T FIT TO WEAR MY OVEN MITTS!
GASP
EVEN I CAN OUTCOOK YOU!
I CHALLENGE YOU TO A COOK-OFF!

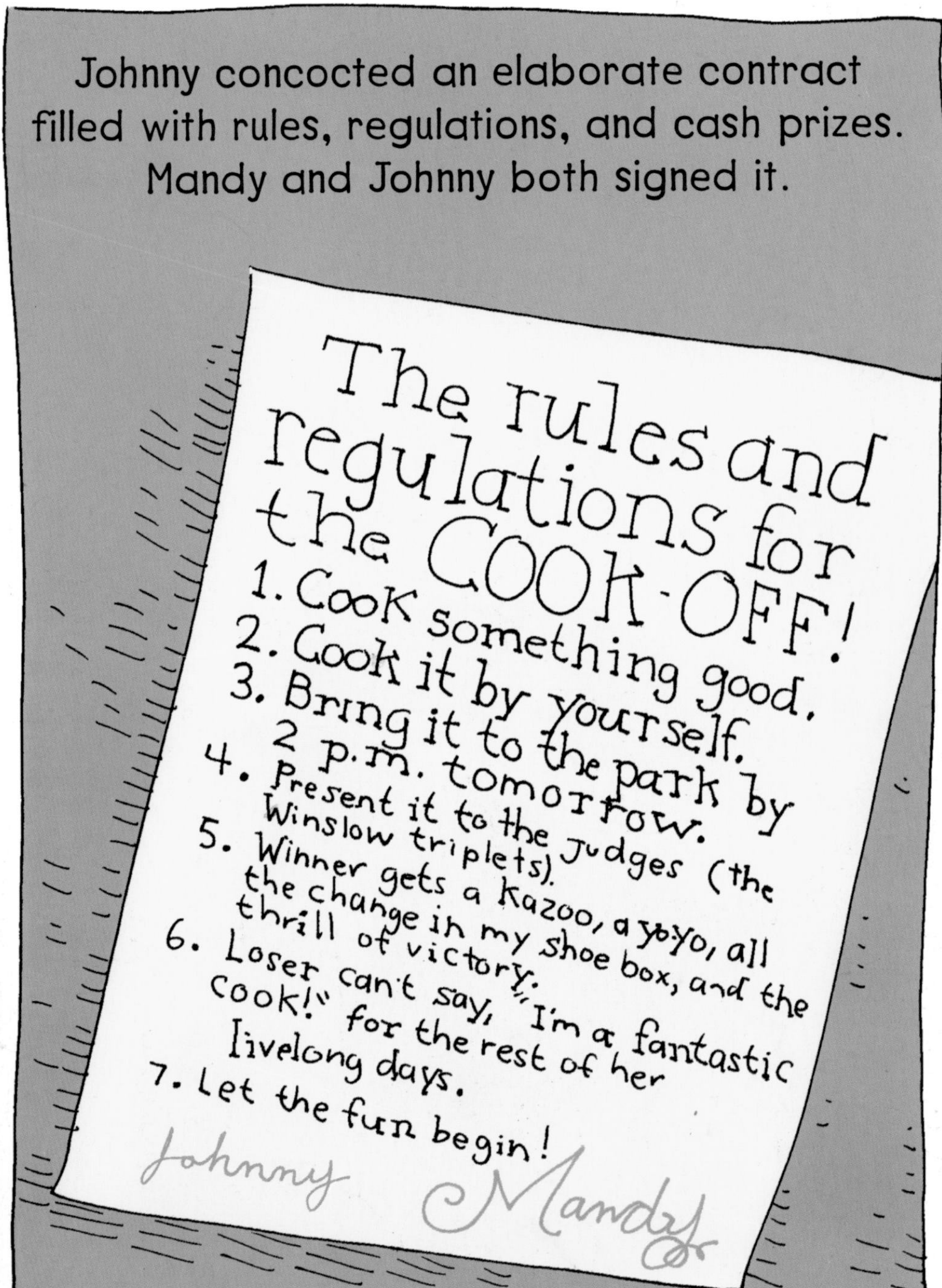
Johnny concocted an elaborate contract filled with rules, regulations, and cash prizes. Mandy and Johnny both signed it.
The rules and regulations for the COOK-OFF!
1. Cook something good.
2. Cook it by yourself.
3. Bring it to the park by 2 p.m. tomorrow.
4. Present it to the Judges (the Winslow triplets).
5. Winner gets a kazoo, a yo-yo, all the change in my shoe box, and the thrill of victory.
6. Loser can't say, "I'm a fantastic cook!" for the rest of her livelong days.
7. Let the fun begin!
Johnny
Mandy

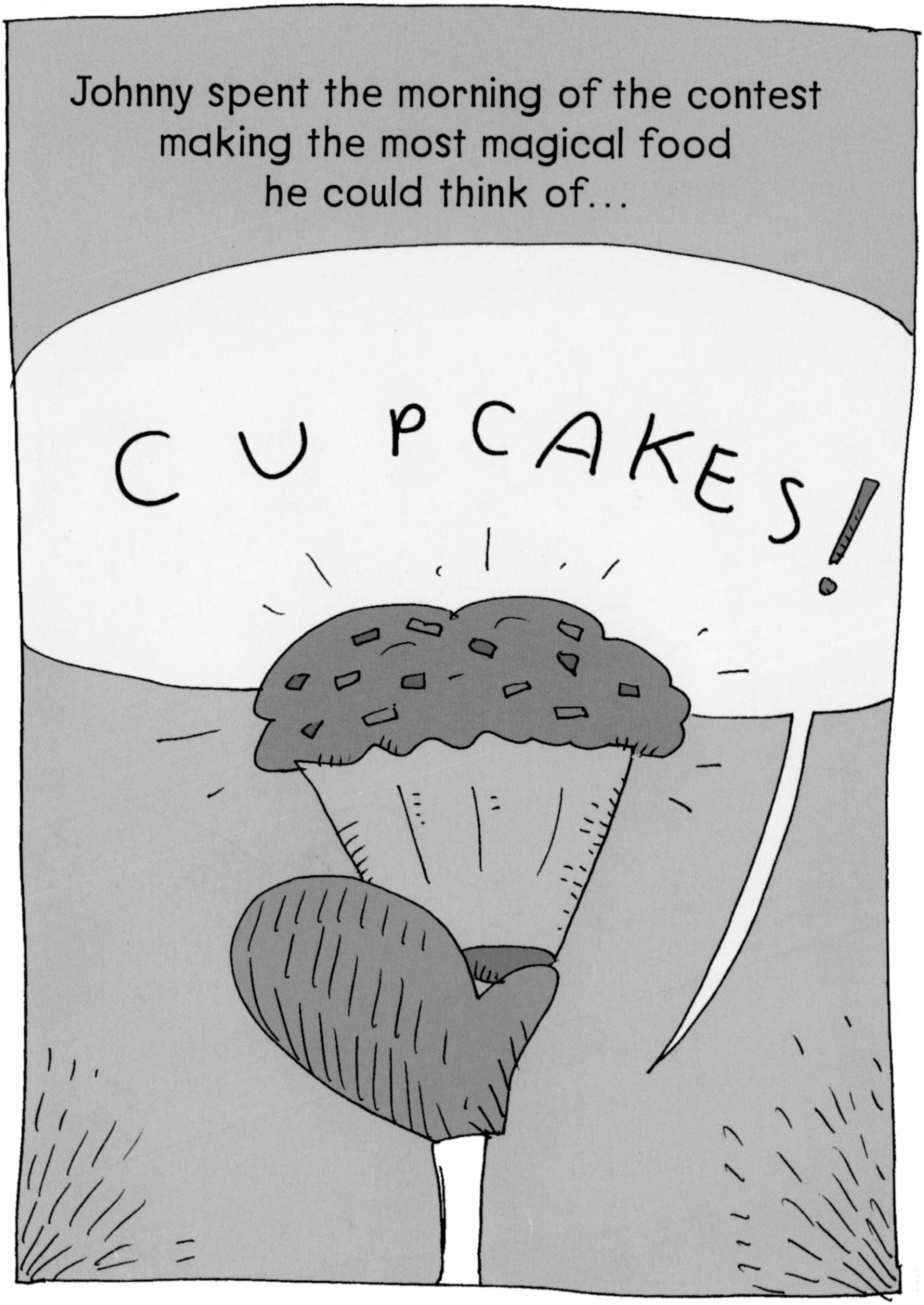
Johnny spent the morning of the contest making the most magical food he could think of...
CUPCAKES!

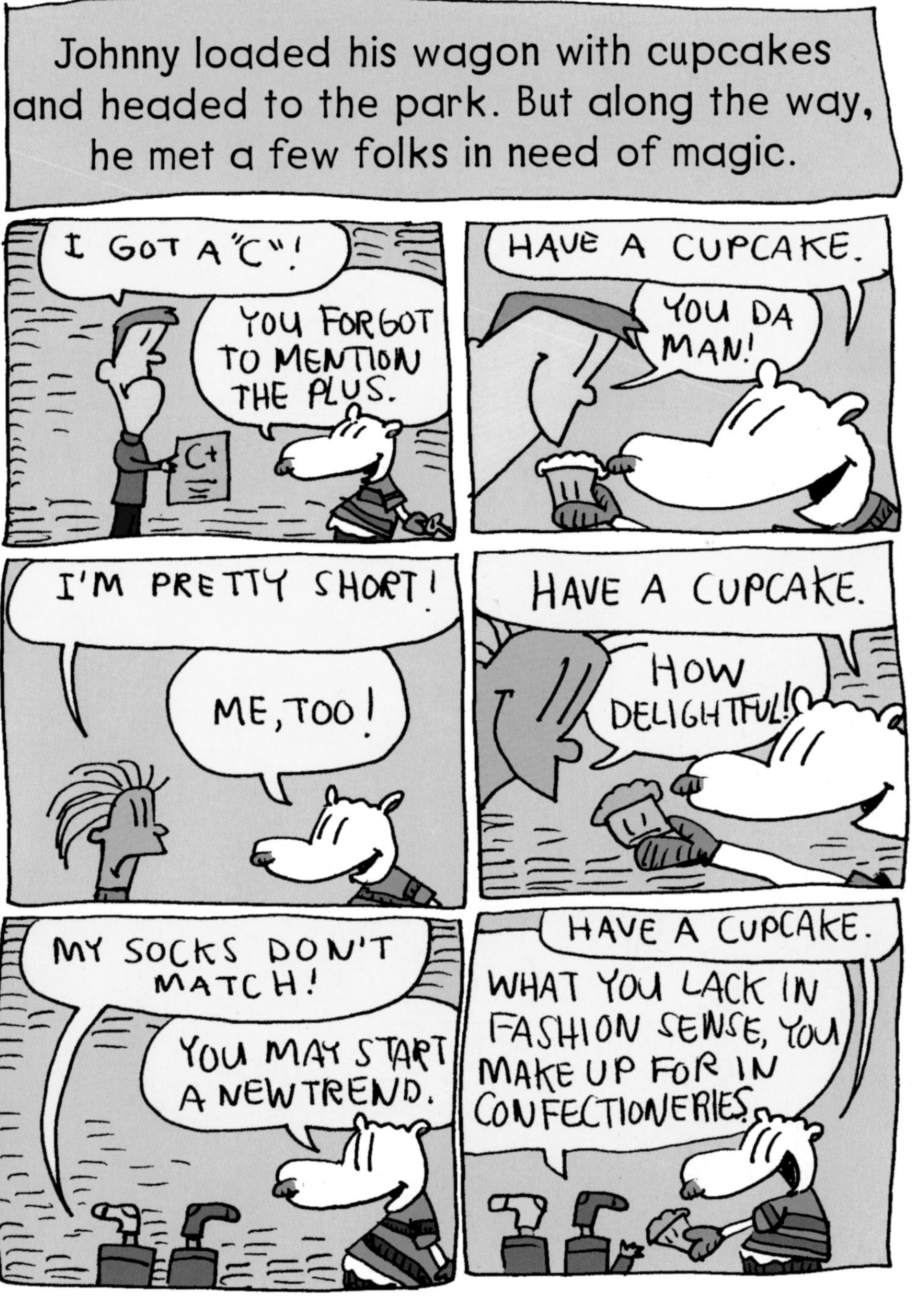
Johnny loaded his wagon with cupcakes and headed to the park. But along the way, he met a few folks in need of magic.
I GOT A "C"!
YOU FORGOT TO MENTION THE PLUS.
C+
HAVE A CUPCAKE.
YOU DA MAN!
I'M PRETTY SHORT!
ME, TOO!
HAVE A CUPCAKE.
HOW DELIGHTFUL!
MY SOCKS DON'T MATCH!
YOU MAY START A NEW TREND.
HAVE A CUPCAKE.
WHAT YOU LACK IN FASHION SENSE, YOU MAKE UP FOR IN CONFECTIONERIES.

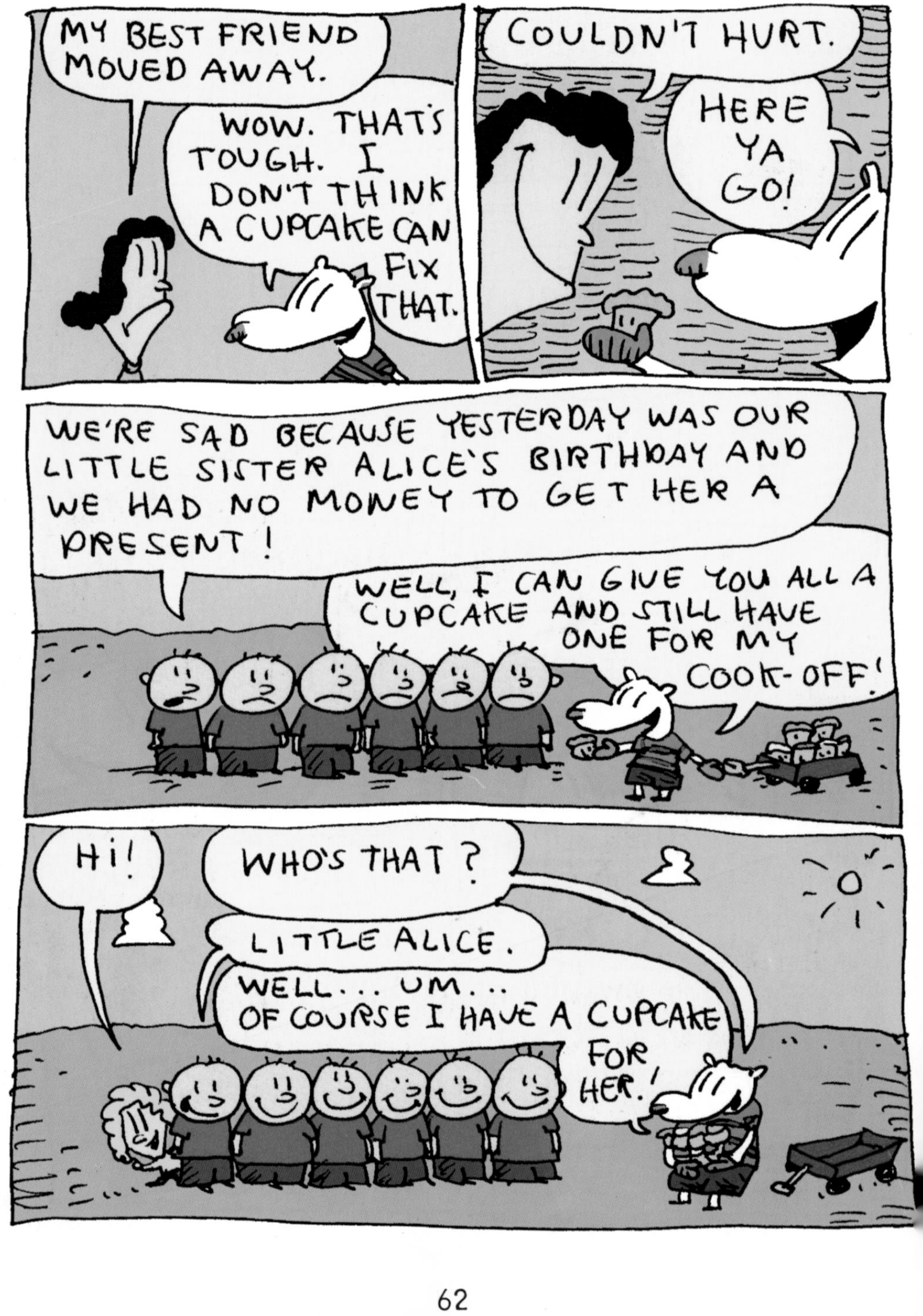
MY BEST FRIEND MOVED AWAY.
WOW. THAT'S TOUGH. I DON'T THINK A CUPCAKE CAN FIX THAT.
COULDN'T HURT.
HERE YA GO!
WE'RE SAD BECAUSE YESTERDAY WAS OUR LITTLE SISTER ALICE'S BIRTHDAY AND WE HAD NO MONEY TO GET HER A PRESENT!
WELL, I CAN GIVE YOU ALL A CUPCAKE AND STILL HAVE ONE FOR MY COOK-OFF!
Hi!
WHO'S THAT?
LITTLE ALICE.
WELL... UM... OF COURSE I HAVE A CUPCAKE FOR HER!

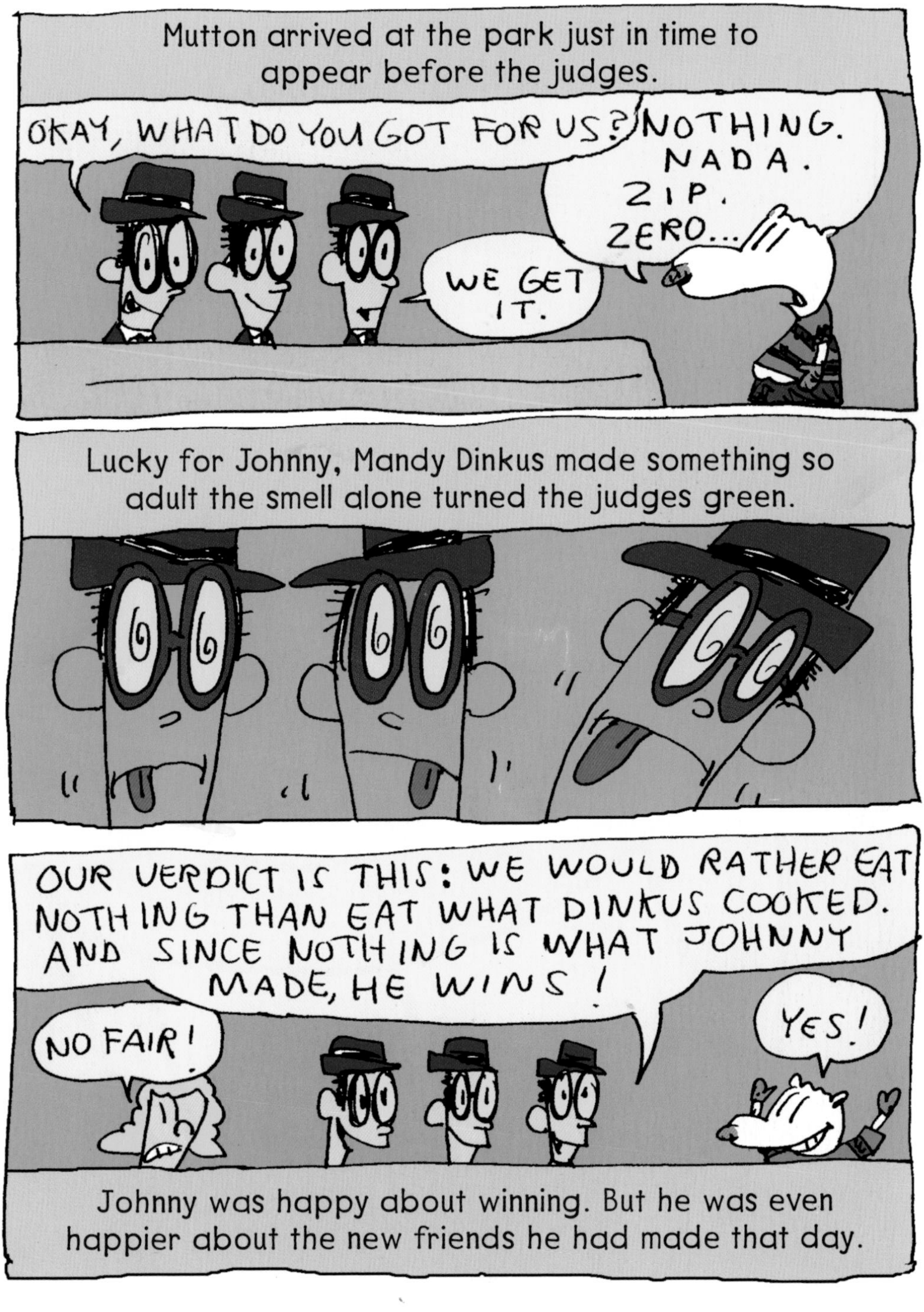
Mutton arrived at the park just in time to appear before the judges.
OKAY, WHAT DO YOU GOT FOR US?
NOTHING. NADA. ZIP. ZERO...
WE GET IT.
Lucky for Johnny, Mandy Dinkus made something so adult the smell alone turned the judges green.
OUR VERDICT IS THIS: WE WOULD RATHER EAT NOTHING THAN EAT WHAT DINKUS COOKED. AND SINCE NOTHING IS WHAT JOHNNY MADE, HE WINS!
NO FAIR!
YES!
Johnny was happy about winning. But he was even happier about the new friends he had made that day.

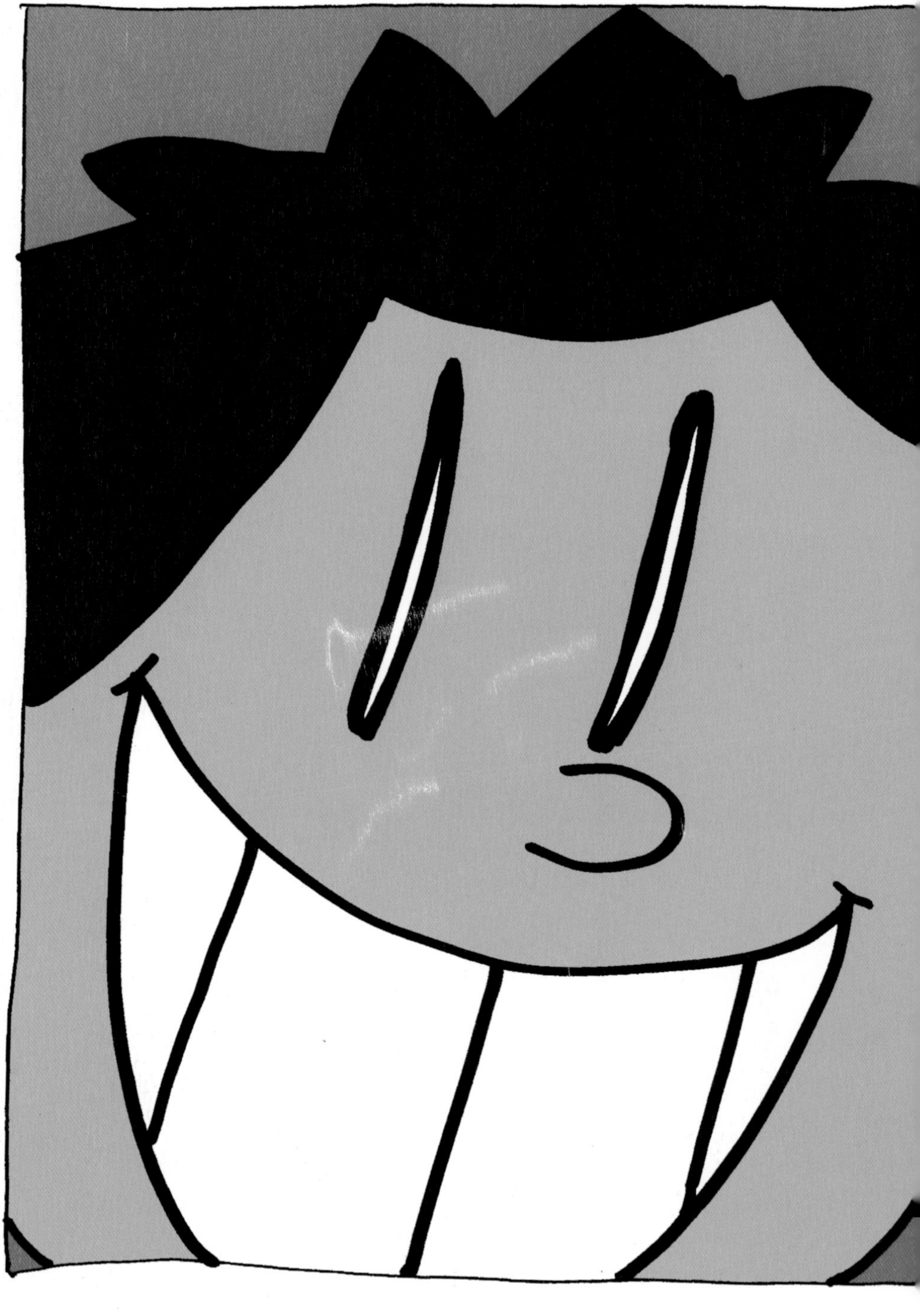

Party Animal

It was one week before her birthday, and Gloria Crust was doing her best to get Johnny to plan a party for her.

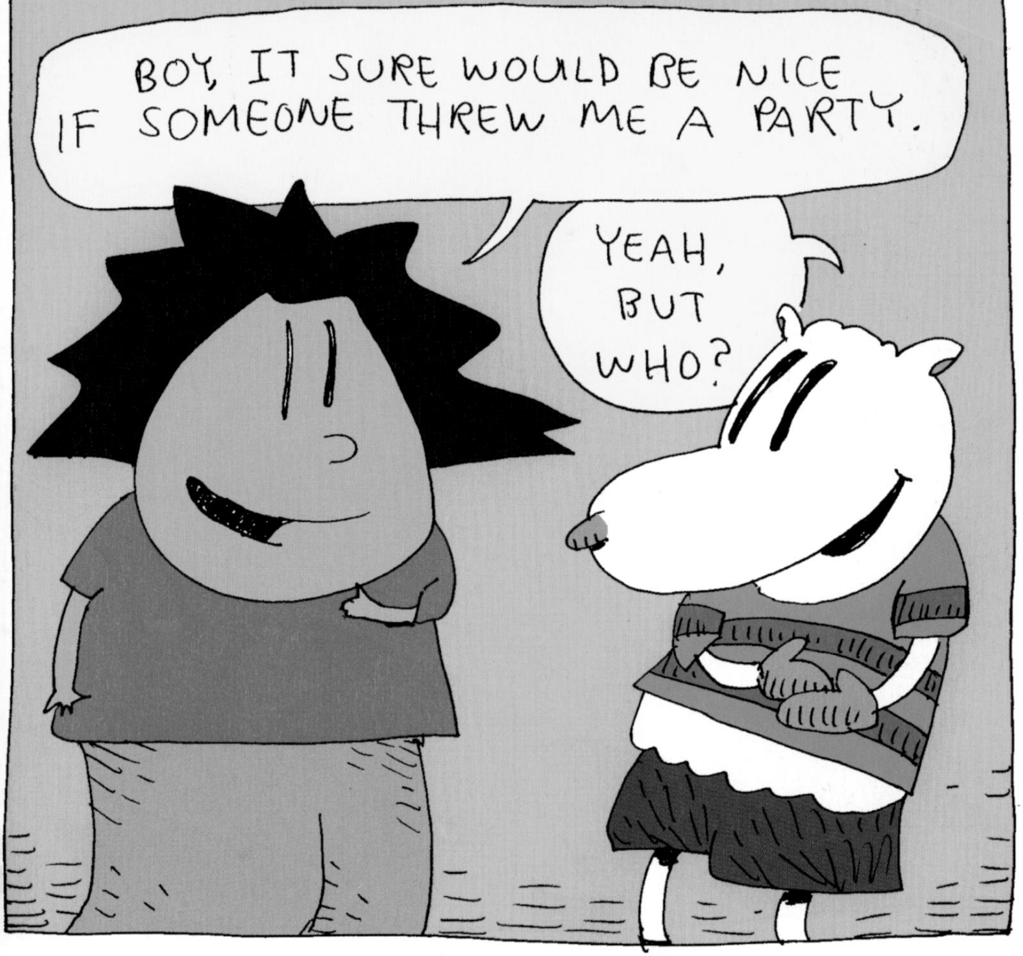
BOY, IT SURE WOULD BE NICE IF SOMEONE THREW ME A PARTY.
YEAH, BUT WHO?

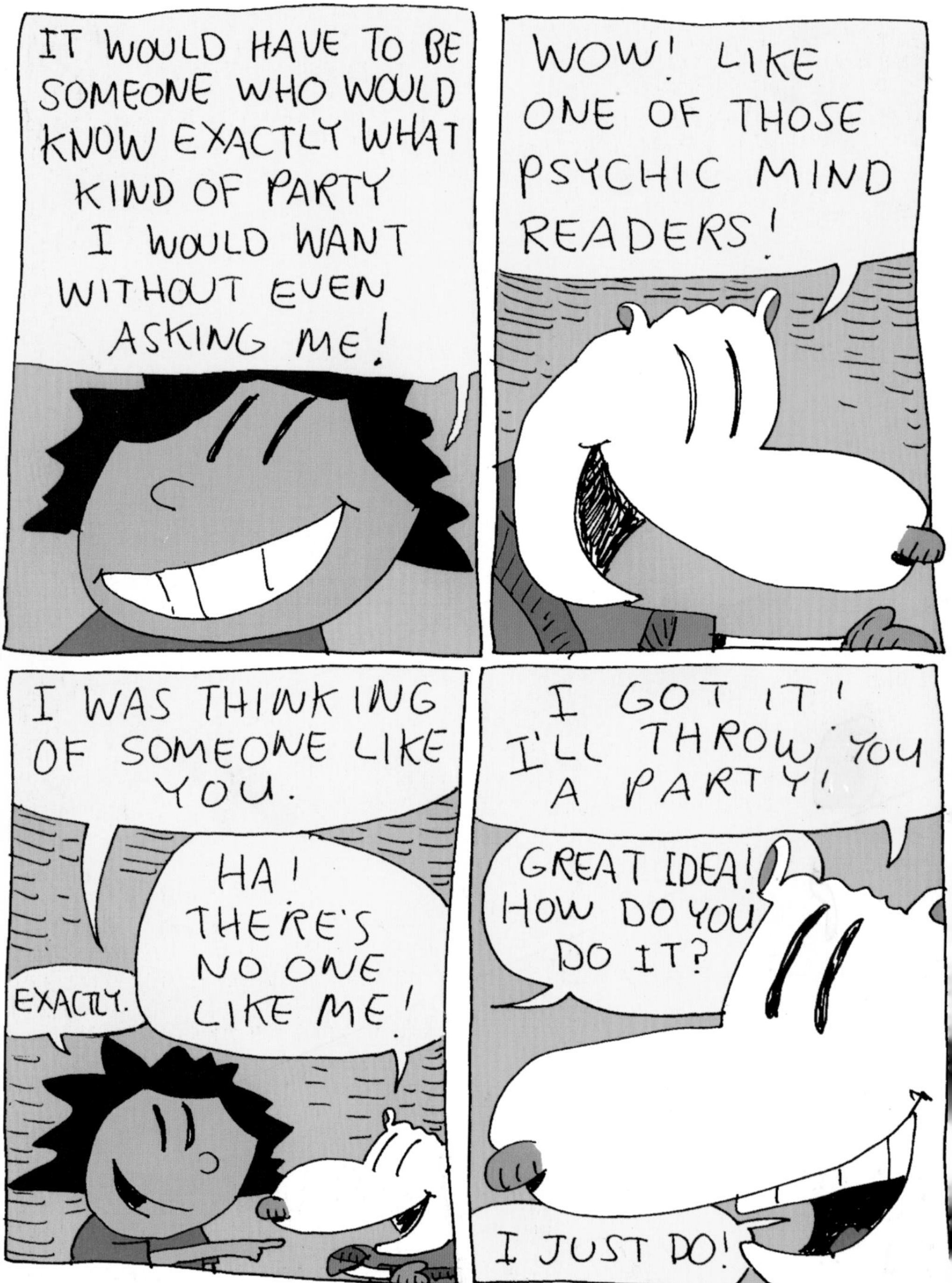
IT WOULD HAVE TO BE SOMEONE WHO WOULD KNOW EXACTLY WHAT KIND OF PARTY I WOULD WANT WITHOUT EVEN ASKING ME!
WOW! LIKE ONE OF THOSE PSYCHIC MIND READERS!
I WAS THINKING OF SOMEONE LIKE YOU.
HA! THERE'S NO ONE LIKE ME!
EXACTLY.
I GOT IT! I'LL THROW YOU A PARTY!
GREAT IDEA! HOW DO YOU DO IT?
I JUST DO!

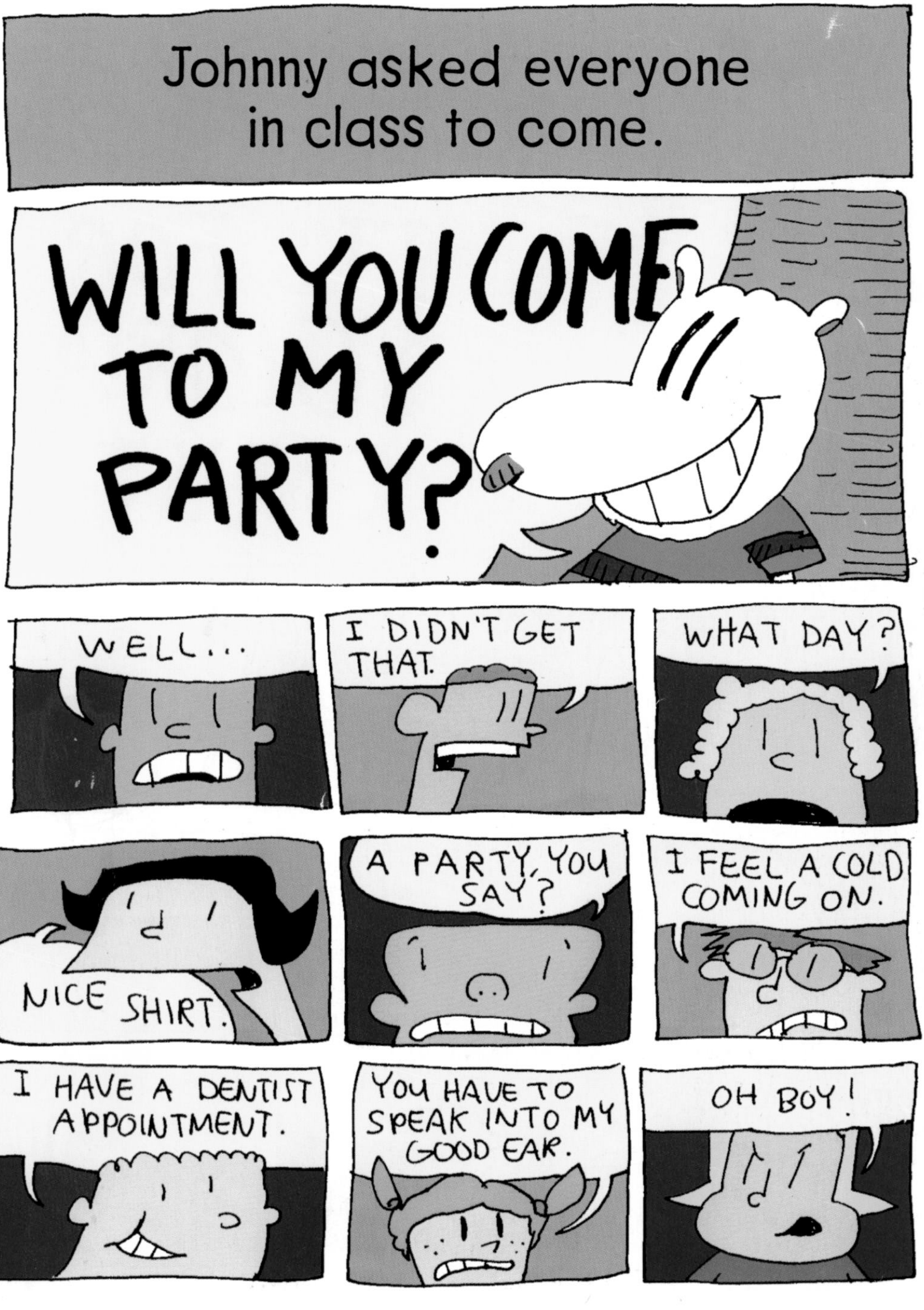
Johnny asked everyone in class to come.
WILL YOU COME TO MY PARTY?
WELL...
I DIDN'T GET THAT.
WHAT DAY?
NICE SHIRT.
A PARTY, YOU SAY?
I FEEL A COLD COMING ON.
I HAVE A DENTIST APPOINTMENT.
YOU HAVE TO SPEAK INTO MY GOOD EAR.
OH BOY!

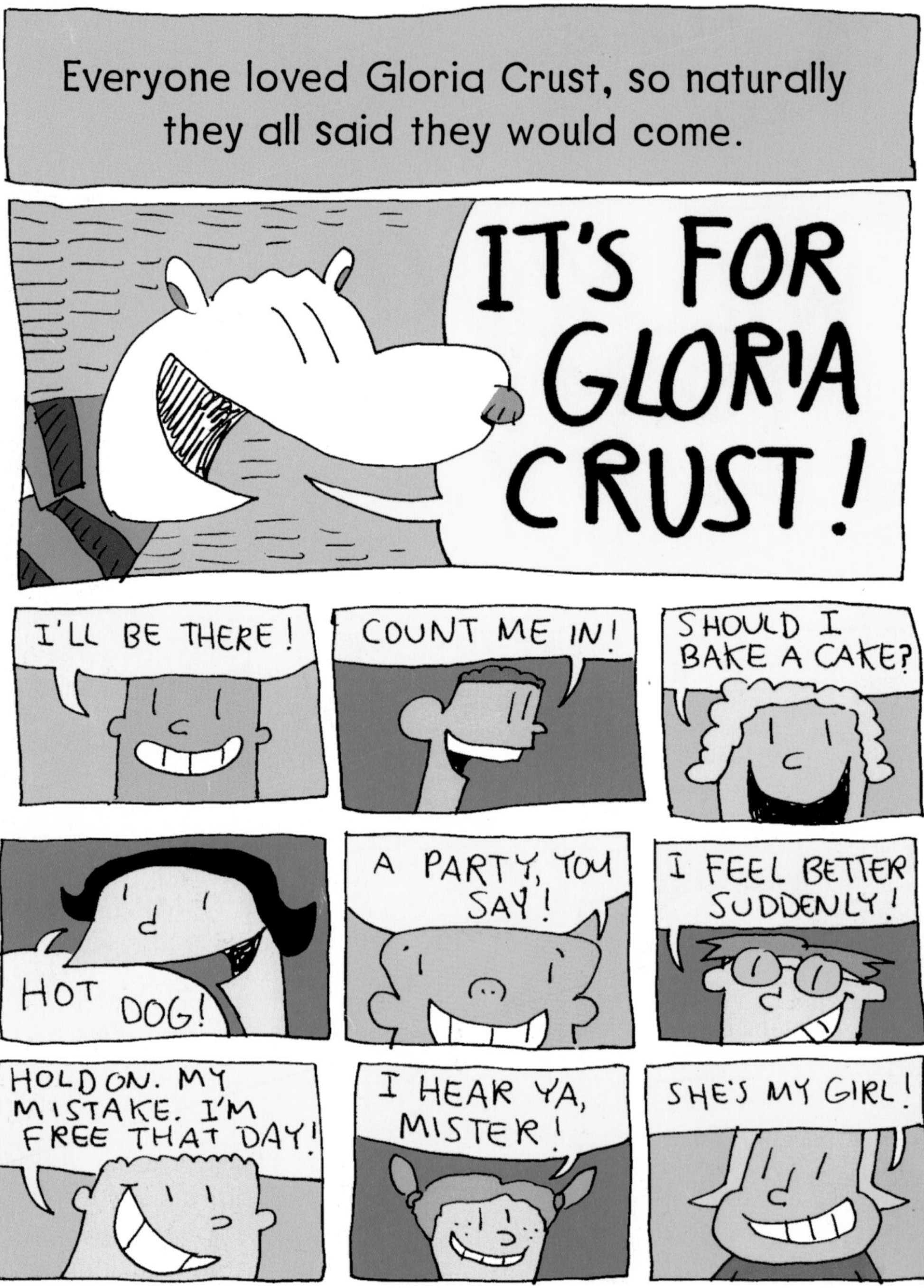
Everyone loved Gloria Crust, so naturally they all said they would come.
IT'S FOR GLORIA CRUST!
I'LL BE THERE!
COUNT ME IN!
SHOULD I BAKE A CAKE?
HOT DOG!
A PARTY, YOU SAY!
I FEEL BETTER SUDDENLY!
HOLD ON. MY MISTAKE. I'M FREE THAT DAY!
I HEAR YA, MISTER!
SHE'S MY GIRL!

Mutton was overflowing with ideas
for the party all week long.
The other kids were not impressed.

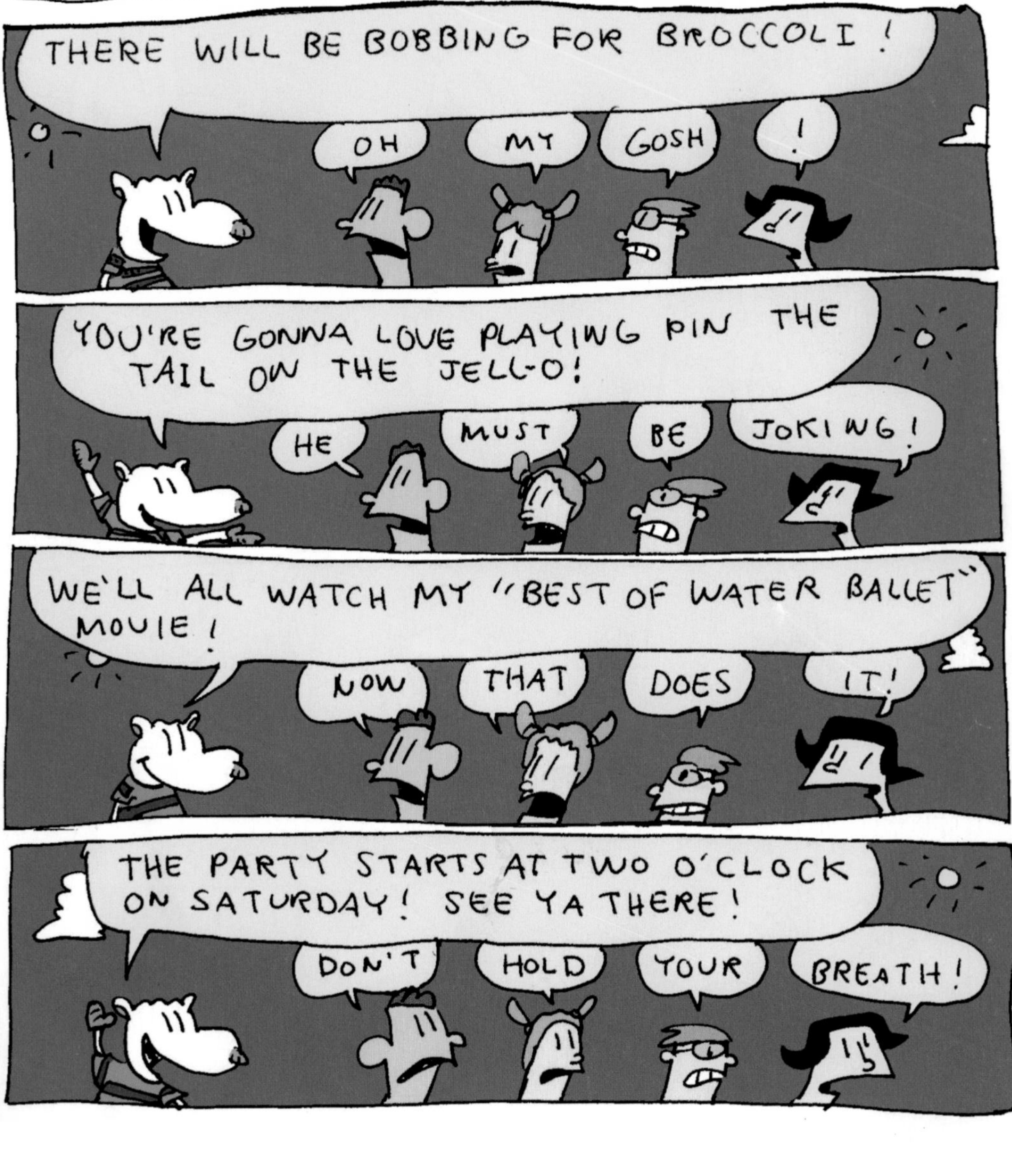
THERE WILL BE BOBBING FOR BROCCOLI!
OH
MY
GOSH
!
YOU'RE GONNA LOVE PLAYING PIN THE TAIL ON THE JELL-O!
HE
MUST
BE
JOKING!
WE'LL ALL WATCH MY "BEST OF WATER BALLET" MOVIE!
NOW
THAT
DOES
IT!
THE PARTY STARTS AT TWO O'CLOCK ON SATURDAY! SEE YA THERE!
DON'T
HOLD
YOUR
BREATH!

Mutton was so excited, he got up at five in the morning on Saturday and began waiting for his guests to arrive.

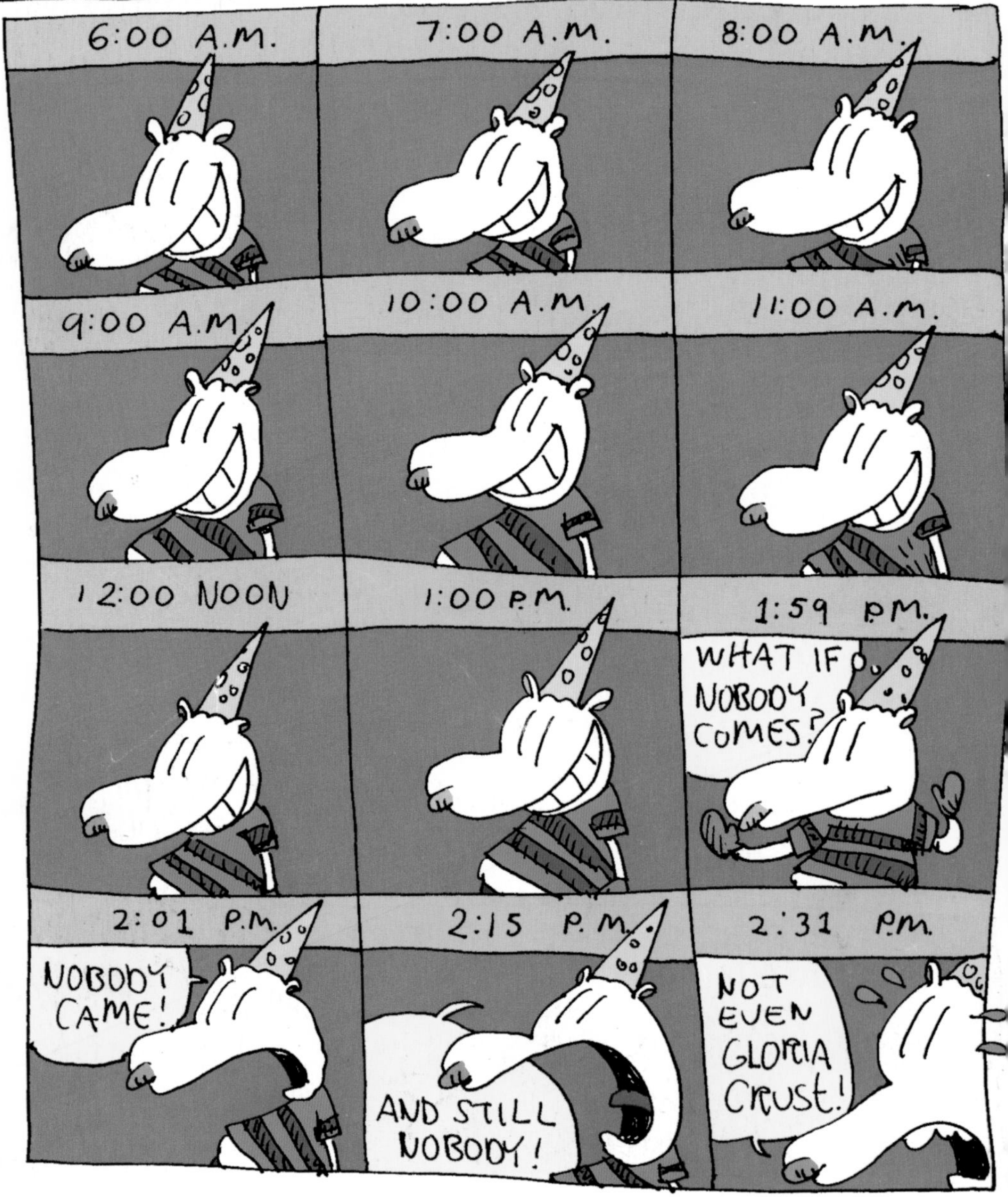
6:00 A.M.
7:00 A.M.
8:00 A.M.
9:00 A.M.
10:00 A.M.
11:00 A.M.
12:00 NOON
1:00 P.M.
1:59 P.M.
WHAT IF NOBODY COMES?
2:01 P.M.
NOBODY CAME!
2:15 P.M.
AND STILL NOBODY!
2:31 P.M.
NOT EVEN GLORIA CRUST!

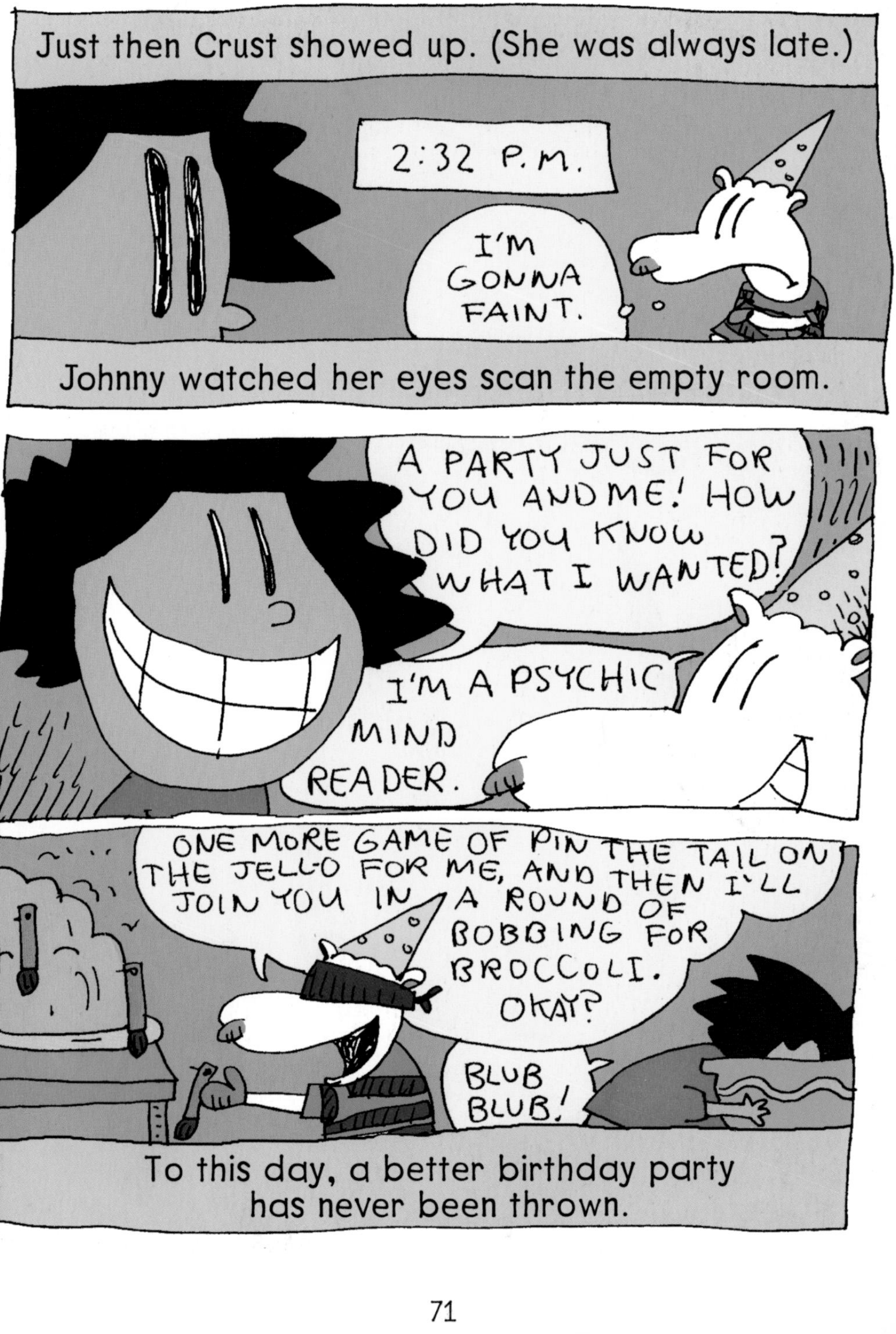
Just then Crust showed up. (She was always late.)
2:32 P.M.
I'M GONNA FAINT.
Johnny watched her eyes scan the empty room.
A PARTY JUST FOR YOU AND ME! HOW DID YOU KNOW WHAT I WANTED?
I'M A PSYCHIC MIND READER.
ONE MORE GAME OF PIN THE TAIL ON THE JELL-O FOR ME, AND THEN I'LL JOIN YOU IN A ROUND OF BOBBING FOR BROCCOLI. OKAY?
BLUB BLUB!
To this day, a better birthday party has never been thrown.

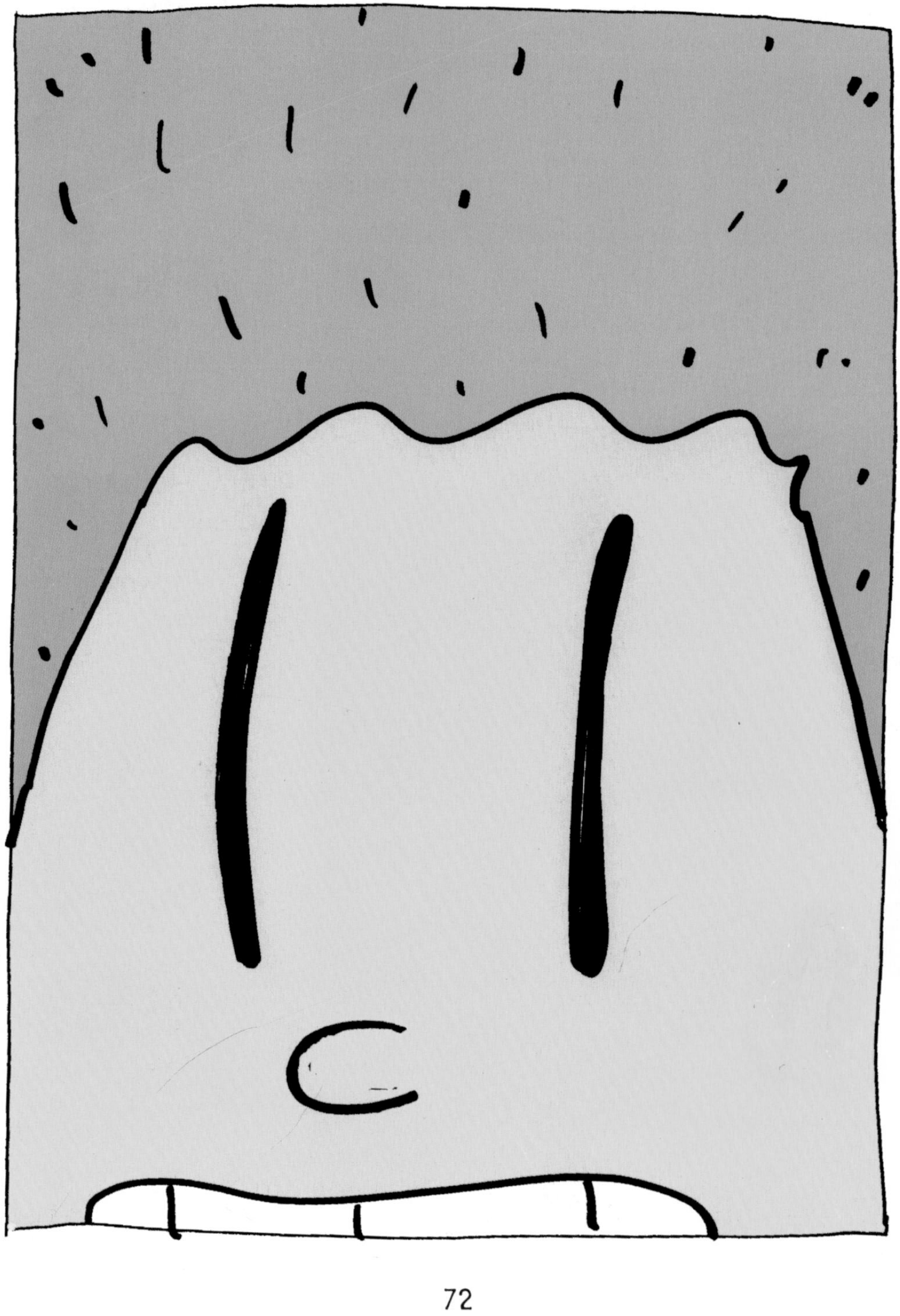

Driving Mrs. Torpolli Crazy

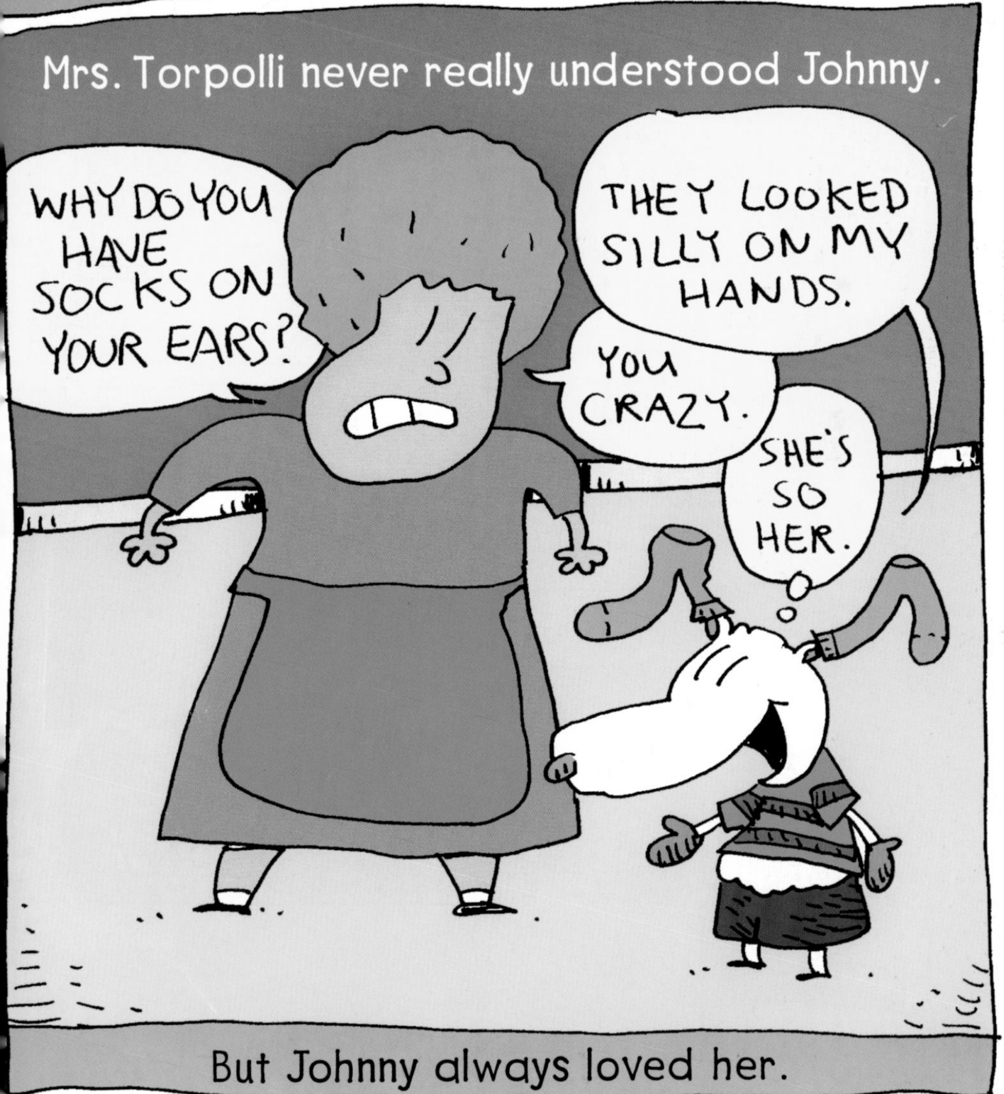
Mrs. Torpolli never really understood Johnny.
WHY DO YOU HAVE SOCKS ON YOUR EARS?
THEY LOOKED SILLY ON MY HANDS.
YOU CRAZY.
SHE'S SO HER.
But Johnny always loved her.

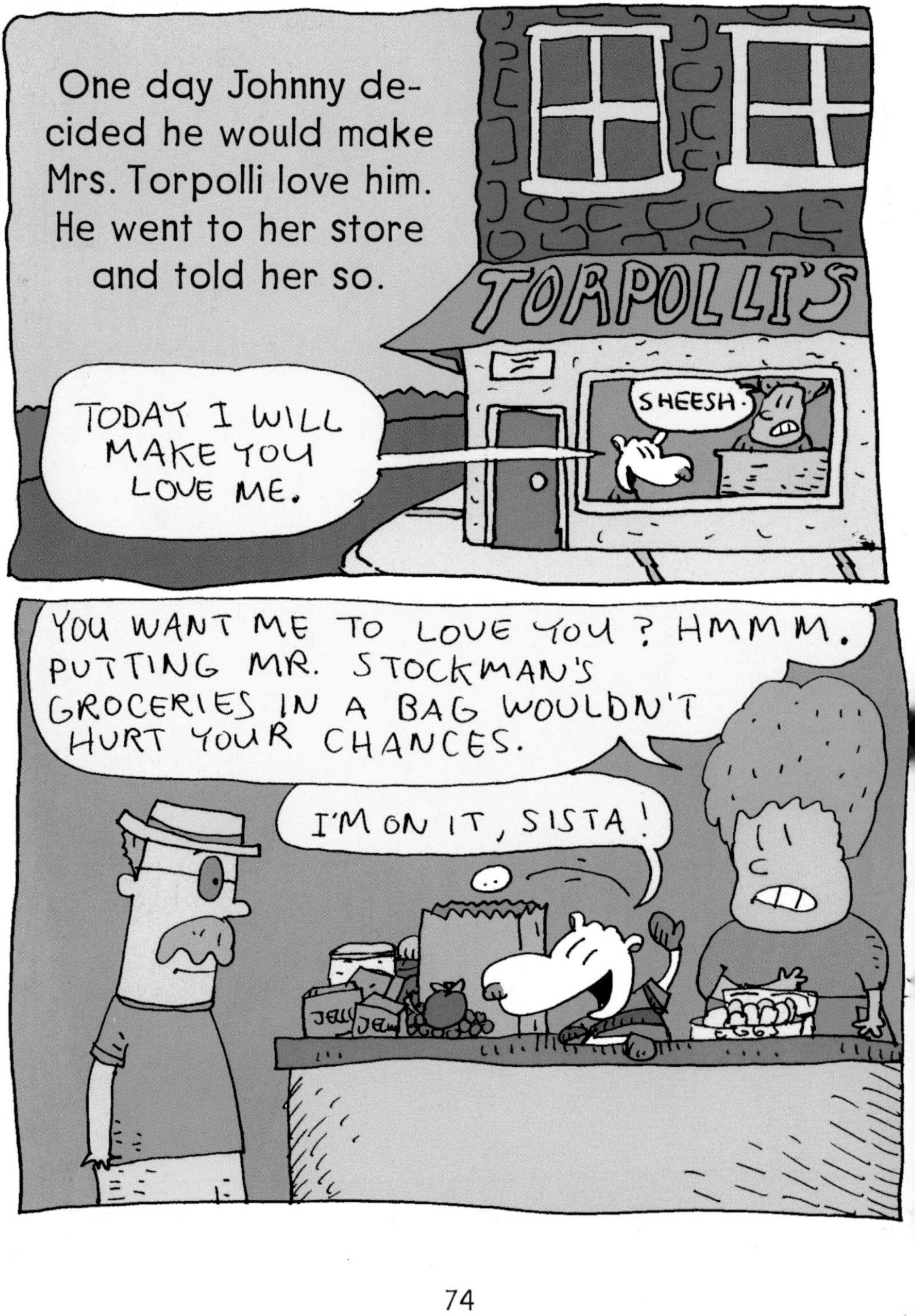
One day Johnny de-
cided he would make
Mrs. Torpolli love him.
He went to her store
and told her so.
TORPOLLI'S
TODAY I WILL MAKE YOU LOVE ME.
SHEESH.
YOU WANT ME TO LOVE YOU? HMMM. PUTTING MR. STOCKMAN'S GROCERIES IN A BAG WOULDN'T HURT YOUR CHANCES.
I'M ON IT, SISTA!

Mutton bagged all that day.
He was awful at it.

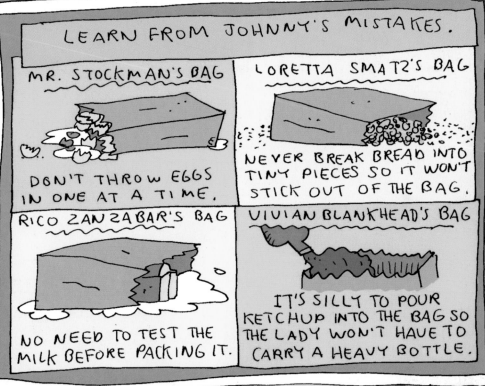

LEARN FROM JOHNNY'S MISTAKES.

MR. STOCKMAN'S BAG

DON'T THROW EGGS IN ONE AT A TIME.

LORETTA SMATZ'S BAG

NEVER BREAK BREAD INTO TINY PIECES SO IT WON'T STICK OUT OF THE BAG.

RICO ZANZABAR'S BAG

NO NEED TO TEST THE MILK BEFORE PACKING IT.

VIVIAN BLANKHEAD'S BAG

IT'S SILLY TO POUR KETCHUP INTO THE BAG SO THE LADY WON'T HAVE TO CARRY A HEAVY BOTTLE.

GET OUT AND STAY OUT!

Mrs. Torpolli told Johnny never to enter
her store again. She was very angry.

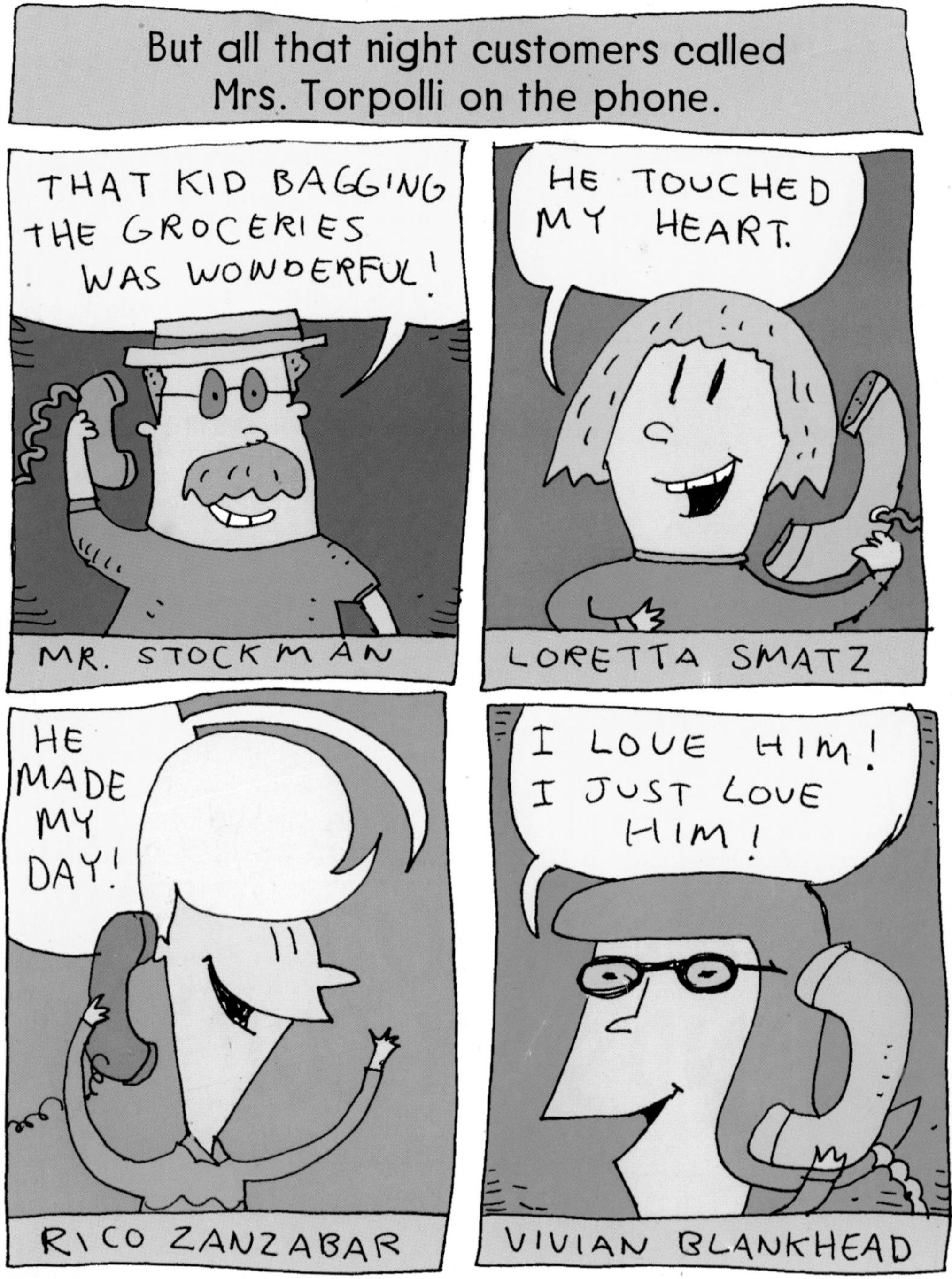
But all that night customers called Mrs. Torpolli on the phone.
THAT KID BAGGING THE GROCERIES WAS WONDERFUL!
MR. STOCKMAN
HE TOUCHED MY HEART.
LORETTA SMATZ
HE MADE MY DAY!
RICO ZANZABAR
I LOVE HIM! I JUST LOVE HIM!
VIVIAN BLANKHEAD

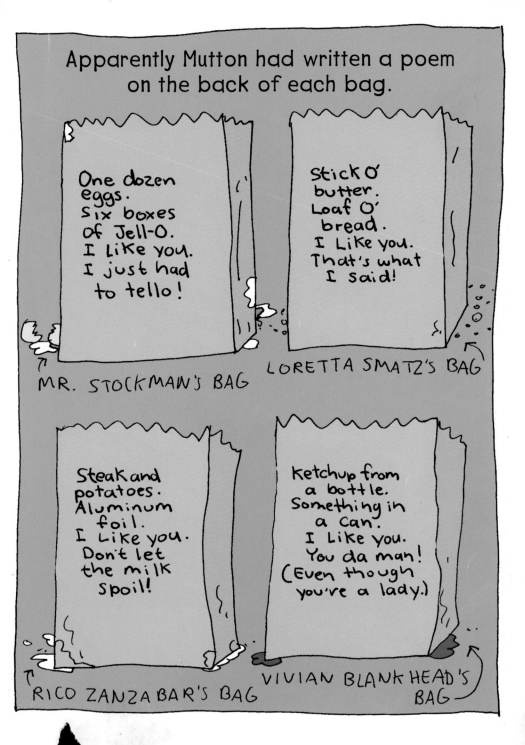

Apparently Mutton had written a poem on the back of each bag.

One dozen eggs.
Six boxes of Jell-O.
I like you.
I just had to tello!

MR. STOCKMAN'S BAG

Stick O' butter.
Loaf O' bread.
I like you.
That's what I said!

LORETTA SMATZ'S BAG

Steak and potatoes.
Aluminum foil.
I like you.
Don't let the milk spoil!

RICO ZANZABAR'S BAG

Ketchup from a bottle.
Something in a can.
I like you.
You da man!
(Even though you're a lady.)

VIVIAN BLANKHEAD'S BAG

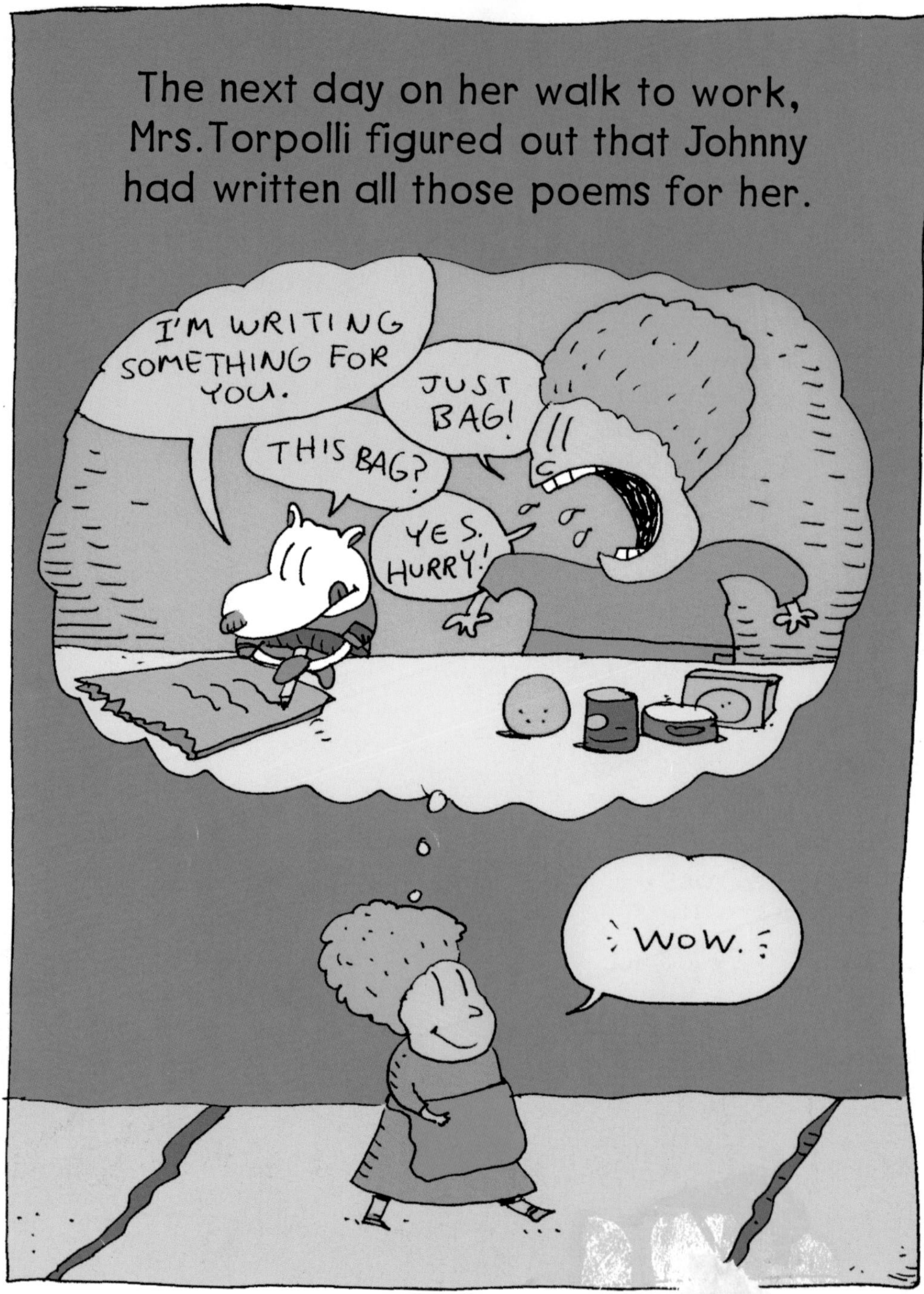
The next day on her walk to work, Mrs. Torpolli figured out that Johnny had written all those poems for her.
I'M WRITING SOMETHING FOR YOU.
THIS BAG?
JUST BAG!
YES. HURRY!
WOW.

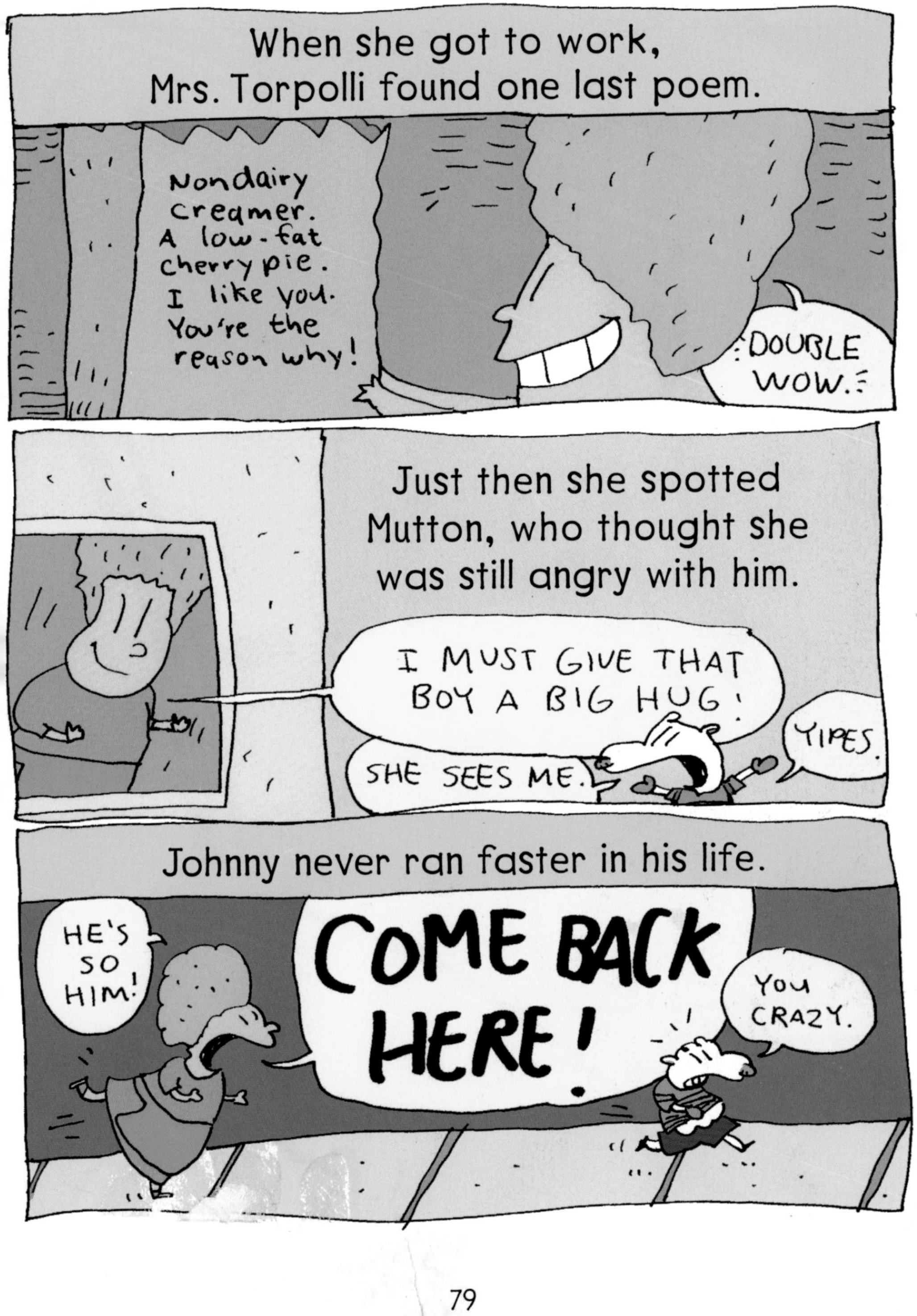
When she got to work,
Mrs. Torpolli found one last poem.
Nondairy creamer. A low-fat cherry pie. I like you. You're the reason why!
DOUBLE WOW.
Just then she spotted Mutton, who thought she was still angry with him.
I MUST GIVE THAT BOY A BIG HUG!
SHE SEES ME.
YIPES.
Johnny never ran faster in his life.
HE'S SO HIM!
COME BACK HERE!
YOU CRAZY.

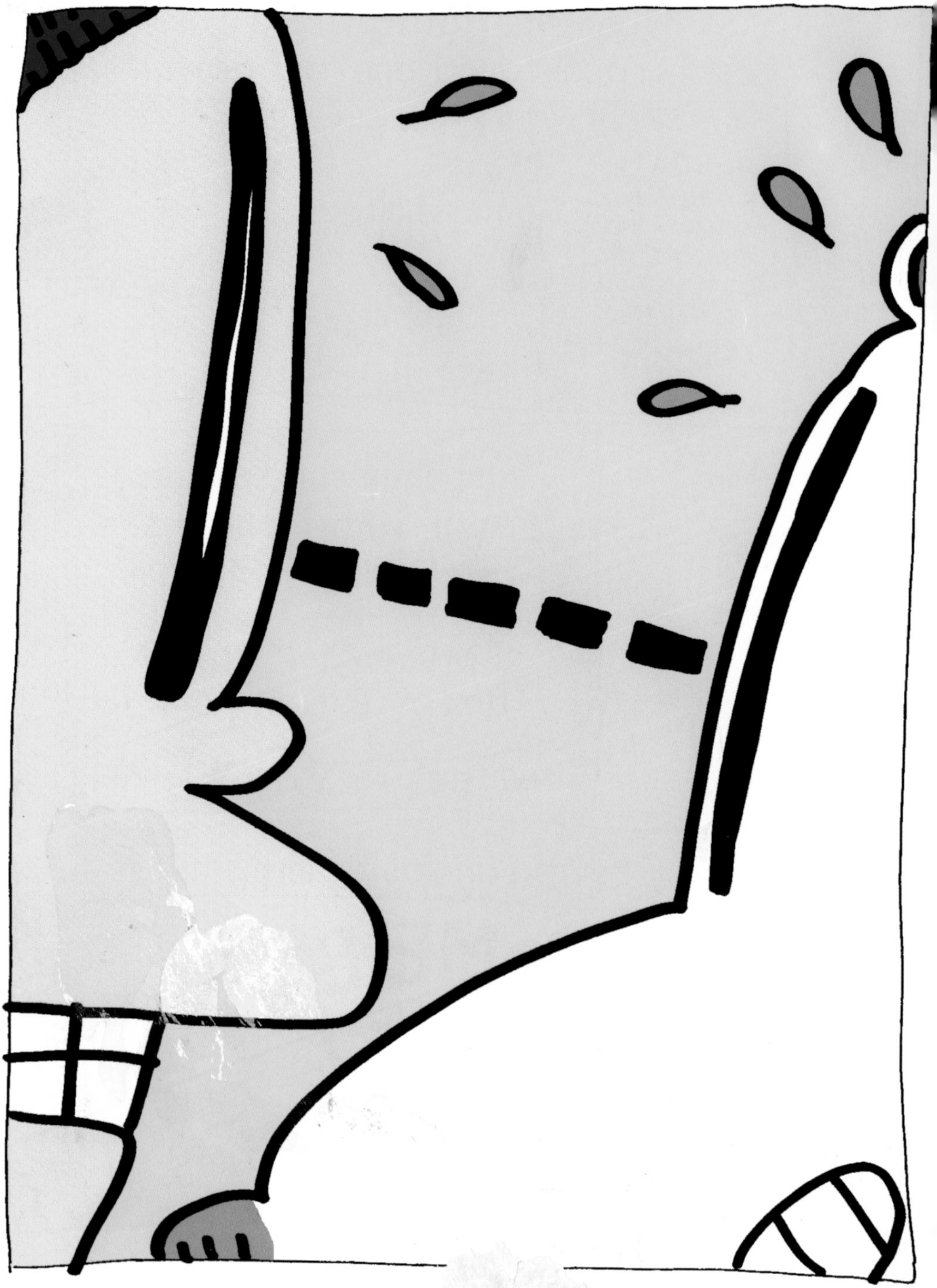

The Staring Contest

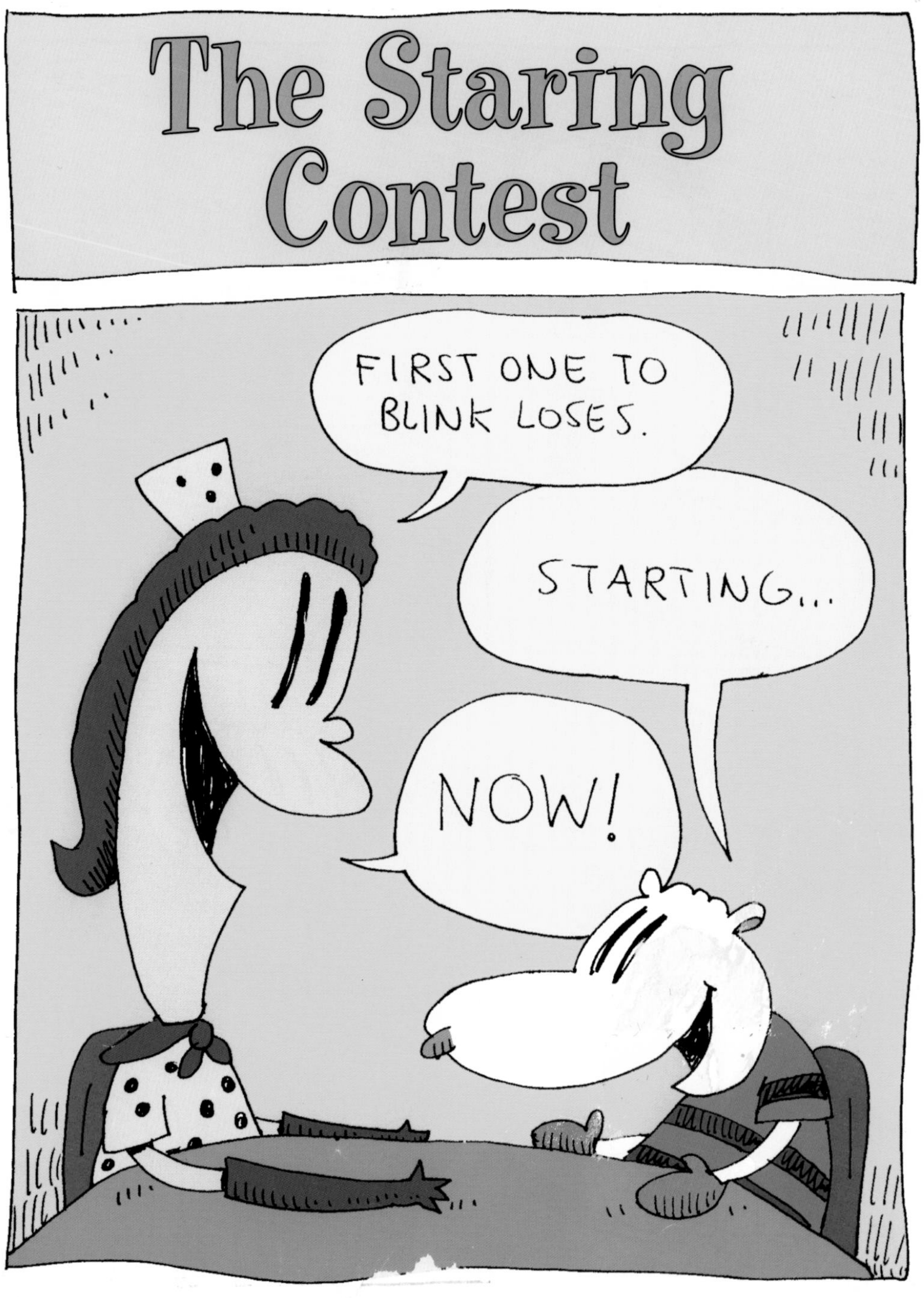
FIRST ONE TO BLINK LOSES.
STARTING...
NOW!

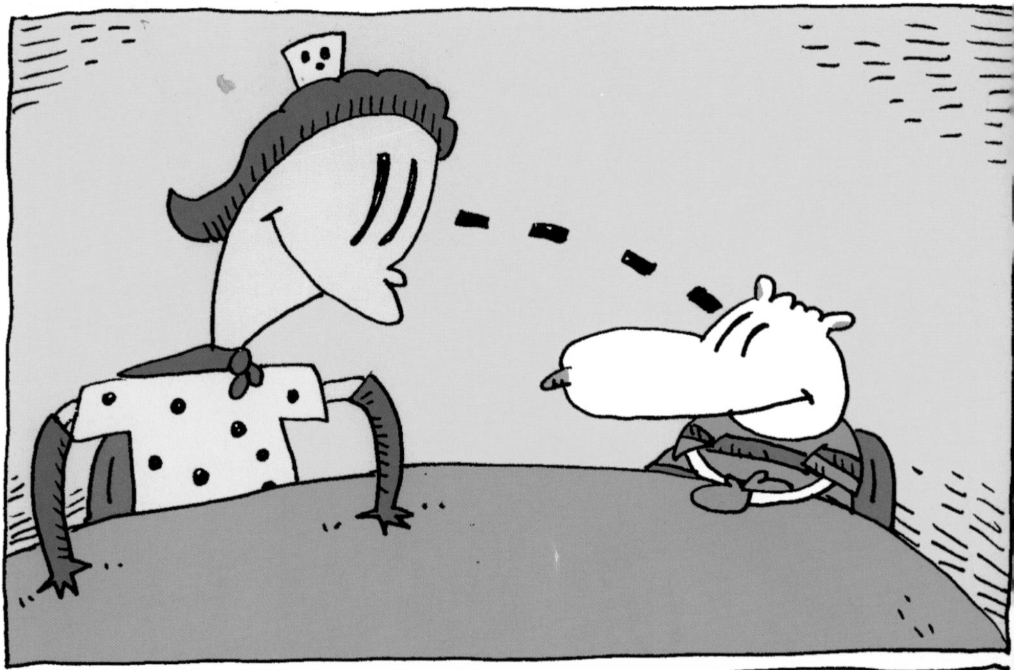

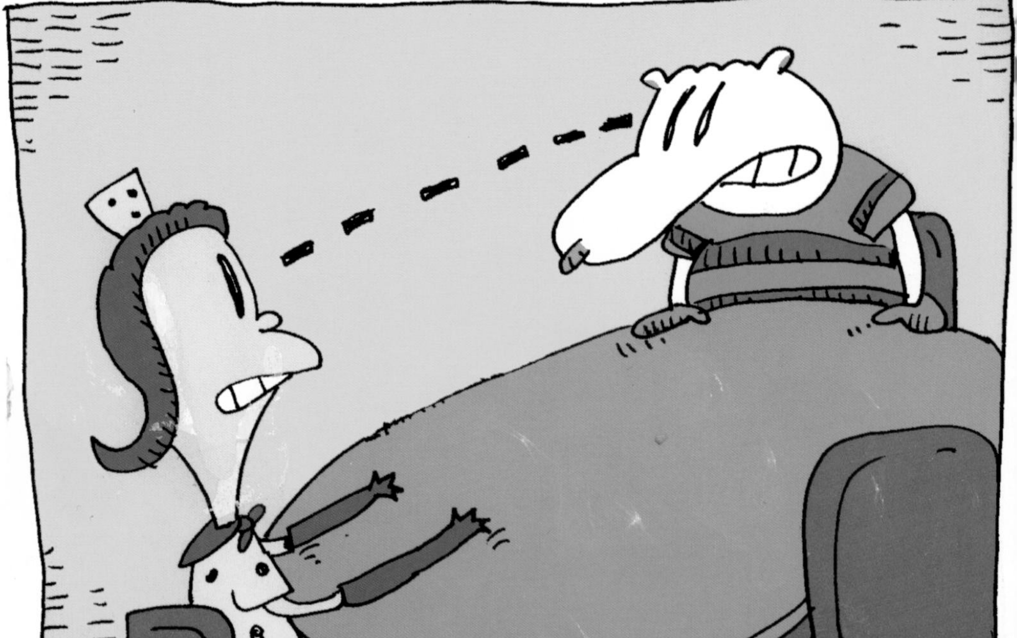

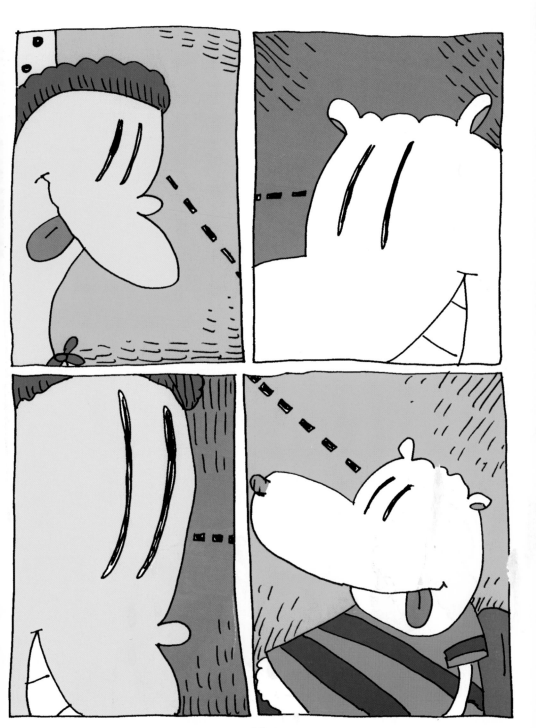

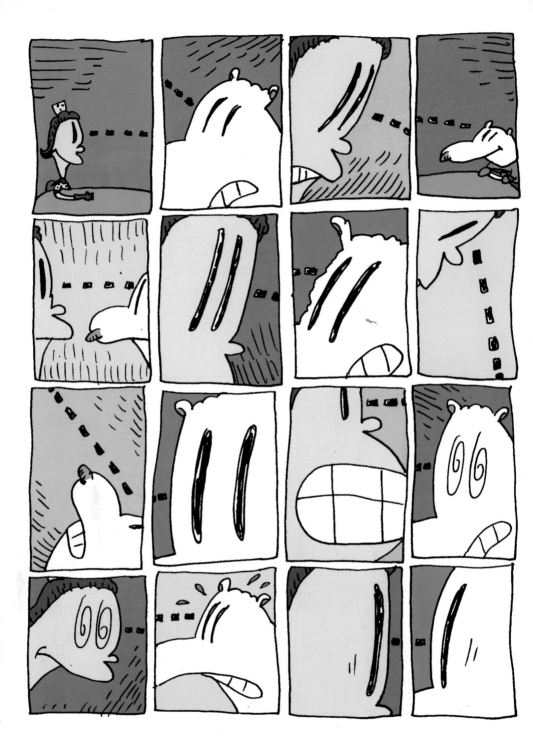

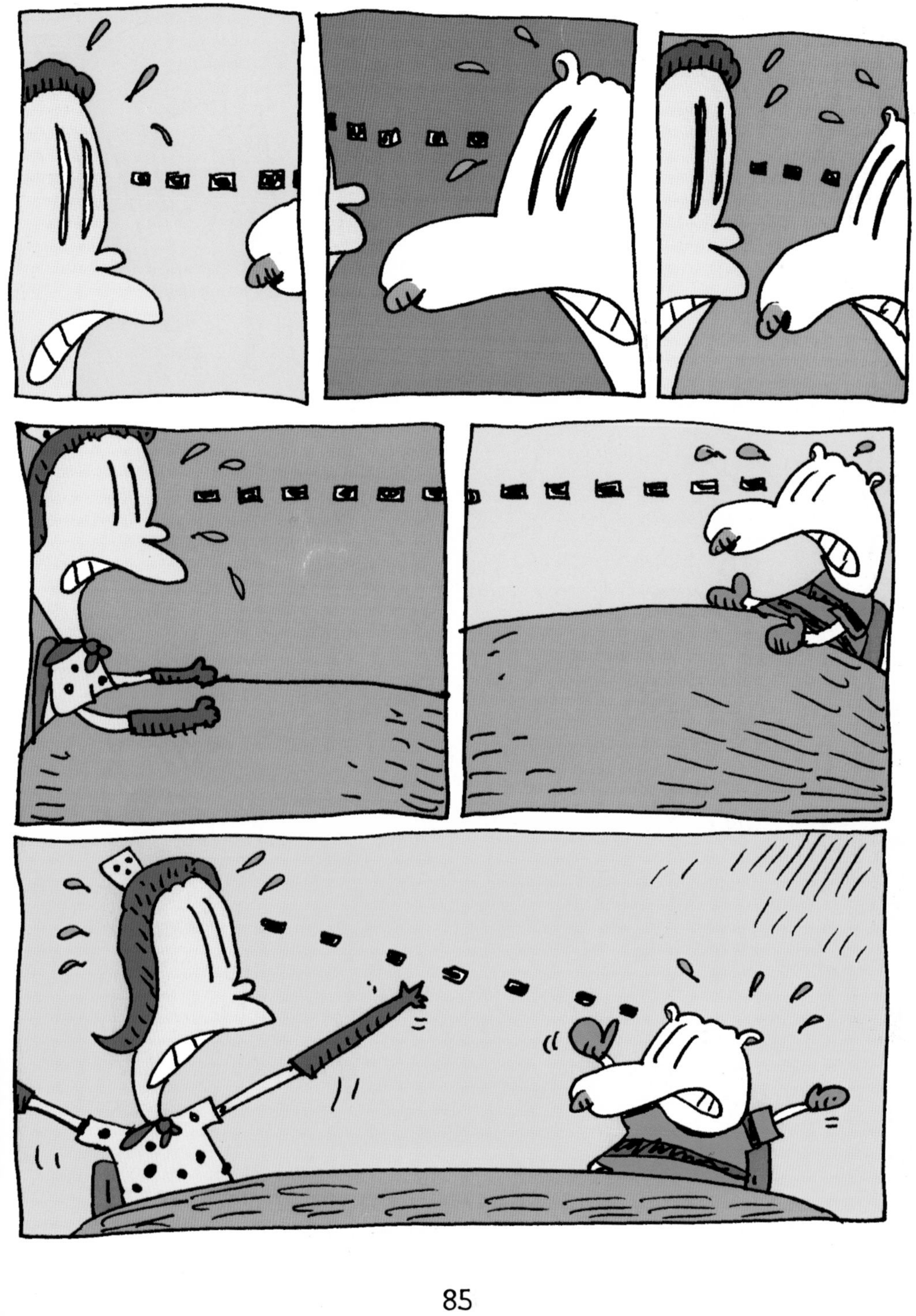

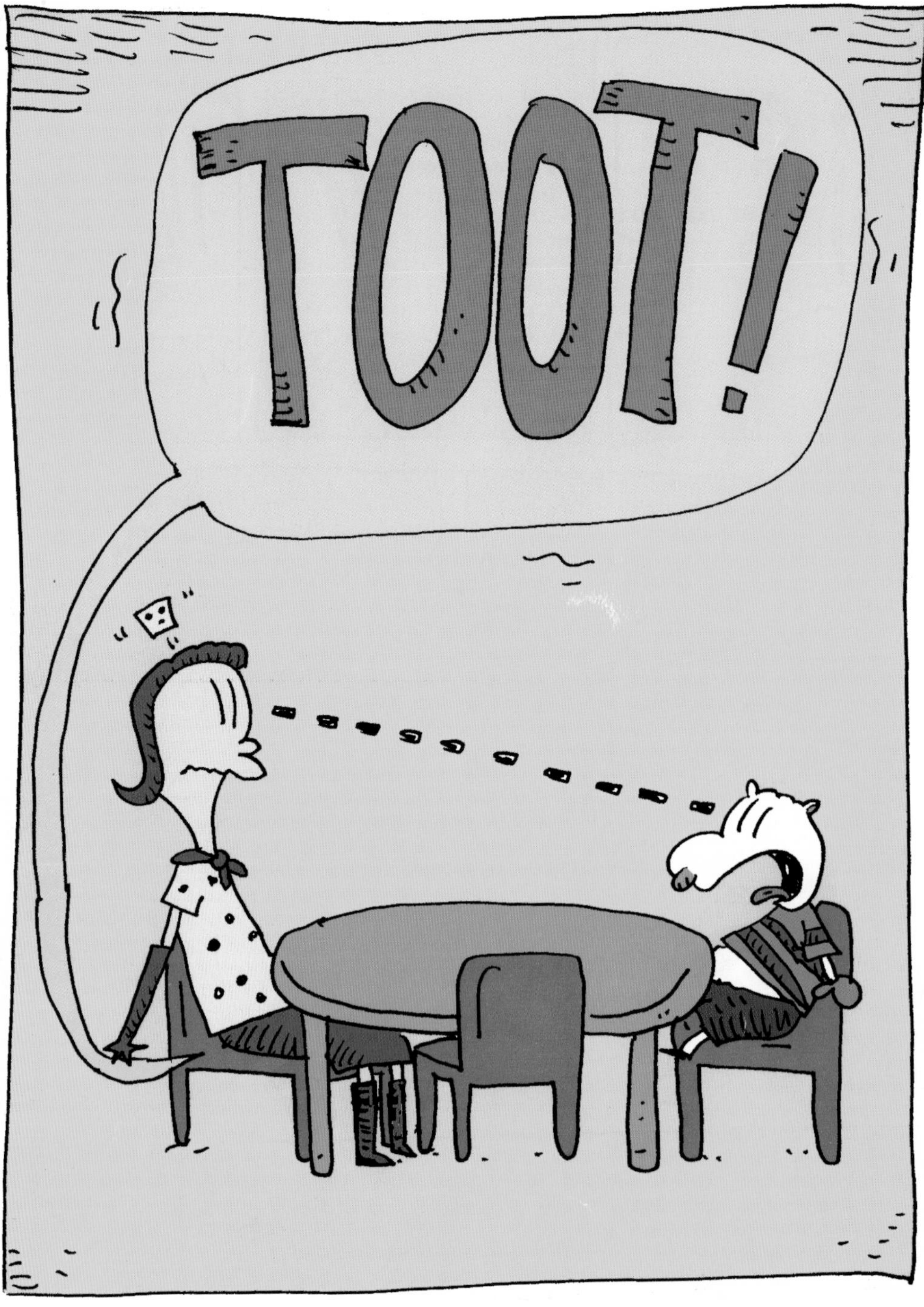
TOOT!

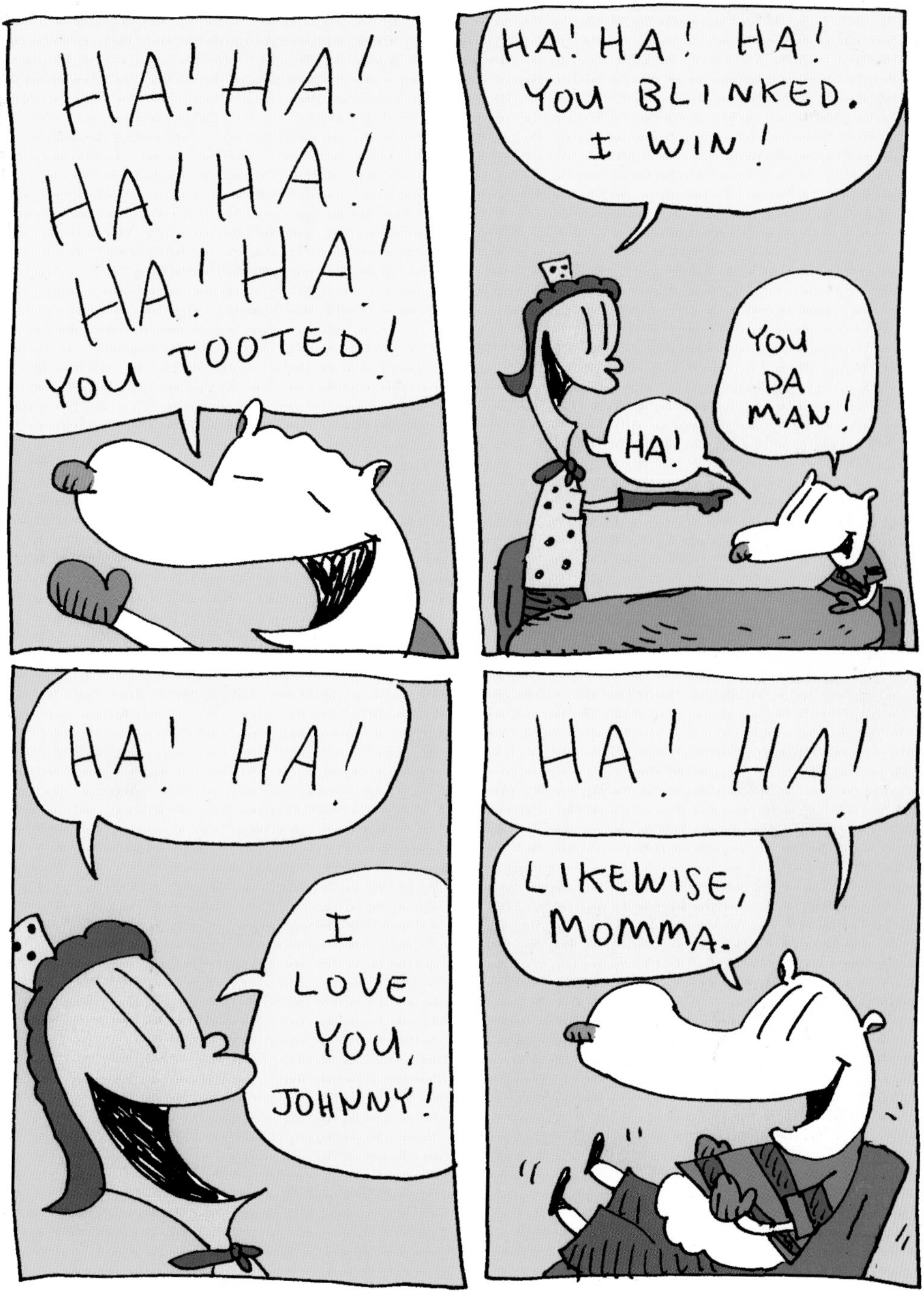
HA! HA! HA! HA! HA! HA! YOU TOOTED!
HA! HA! HA! YOU BLINKED. I WIN!
YOU DA MAN!
HA!
HA! HA!
I LOVE YOU, JOHNNY!
HA! HA!
LIKEWISE, MOMMA.

Where Are

Johnny went on to become President of the World and brought about world peace by instituting "Give-an-Enemy-a-Cupcake Day."

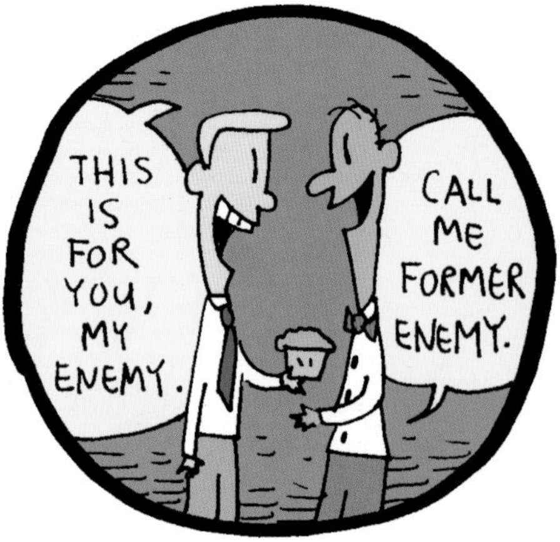
THIS IS FOR YOU, MY ENEMY.
CALL ME FORMER ENEMY.

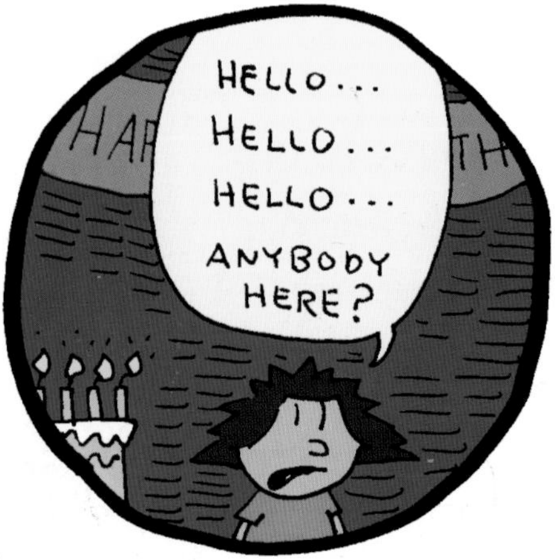
HELLO... HELLO... HELLO... ANYBODY HERE?

On Gloria's next birthday, Johnny decided to outdo himself and throw her a party that even ***he*** wasn't invited to.

They Now?

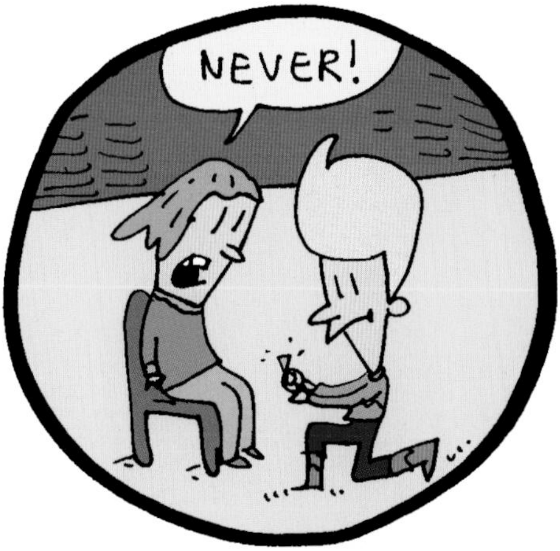
NEVER!

Rico Zanzabar, completely inspired by Johnny's poems, asked Loretta Smatz to marry him.

Rico Zanzabar's broken heart soon mended, and he asked Vivian Blankhead for ***her*** hand in marriage...with much better results.

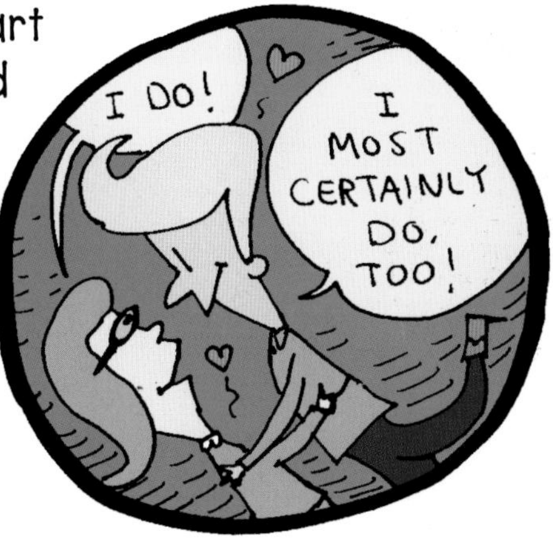
I DO!
I MOST CERTAINLY DO, TOO!

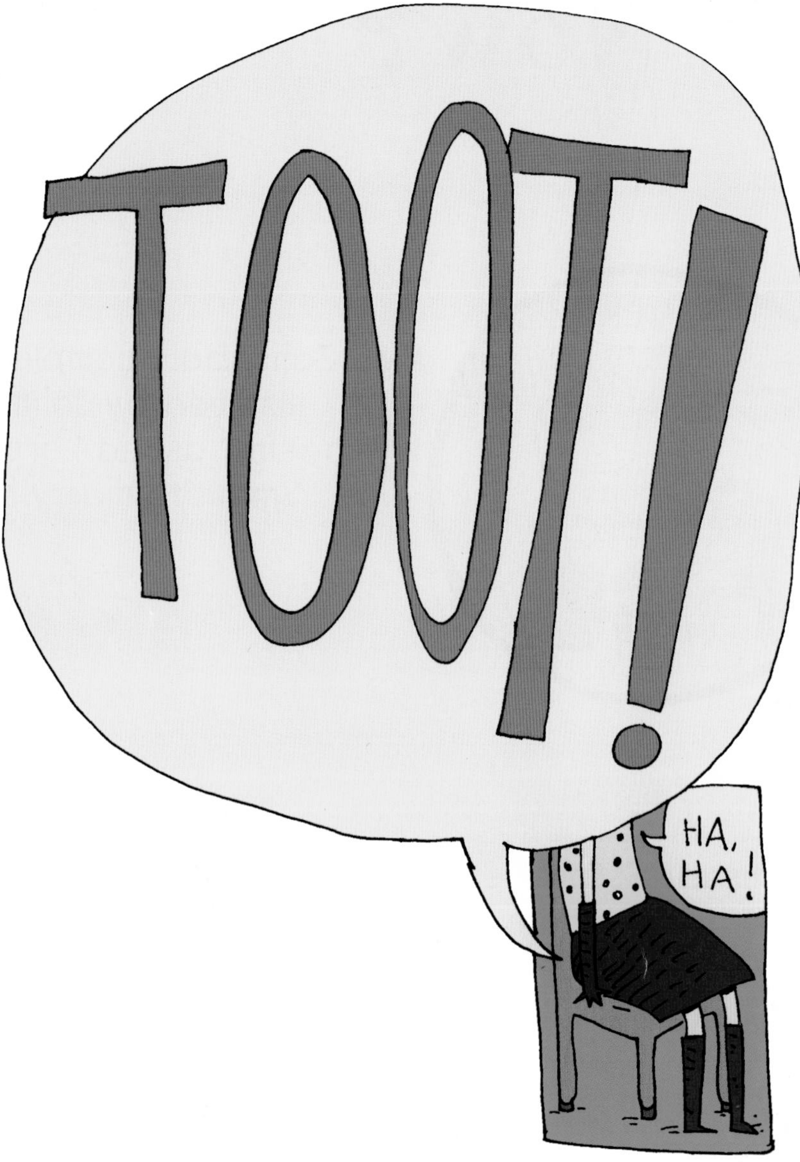
TOOT!
HA, HA!

Momma won the title
"Staring Champion of the Quad-State Area"
by deploying her secret weapon at just
the right moment.

For Karen Grove

MUTTON SOUP

More Adventures of Johnny Mutton

MUTTON SOUP IS 100%. MELTED VANILLA ICE CREAM WITH A CHERRY ON TOP.

In the Dark

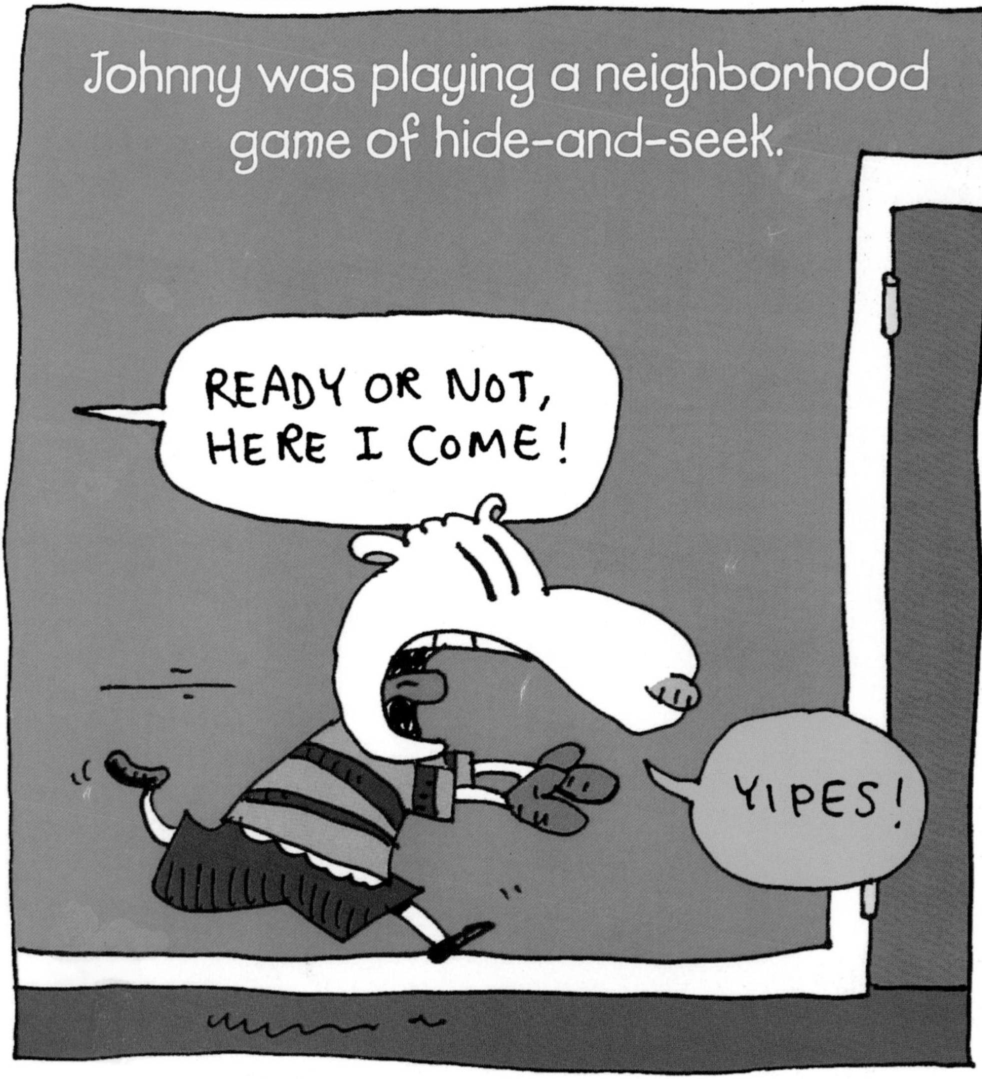
Johnny was playing a neighborhood game of hide-and-seek.
READY OR NOT, HERE I COME!
YIPES!

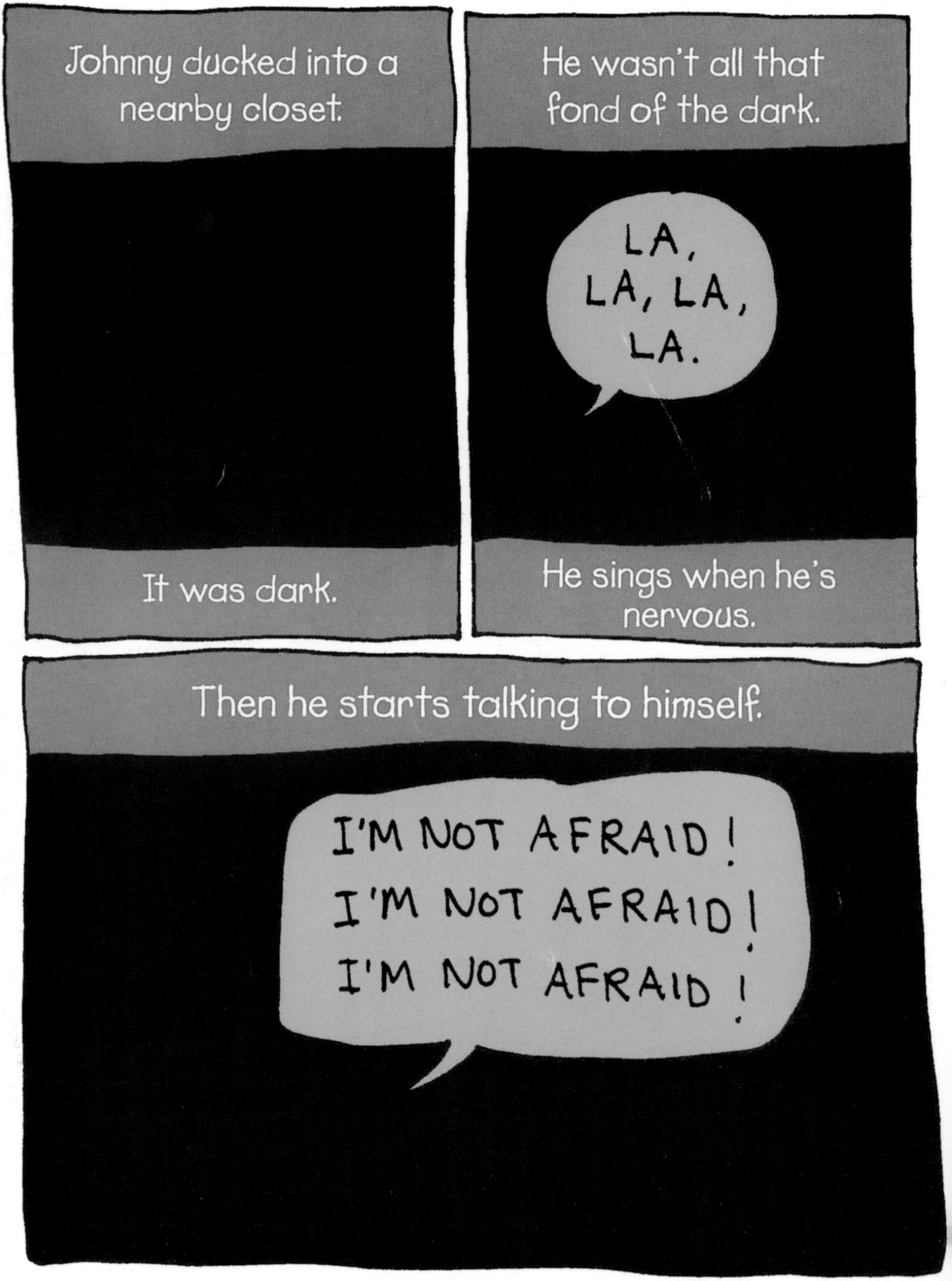
Johnny ducked into a nearby closet.
It was dark.
He wasn't all that fond of the dark.
LA, LA, LA, LA.
He sings when he's nervous.
Then he starts talking to himself.
I'M NOT AFRAID! I'M NOT AFRAID! I'M NOT AFRAID!

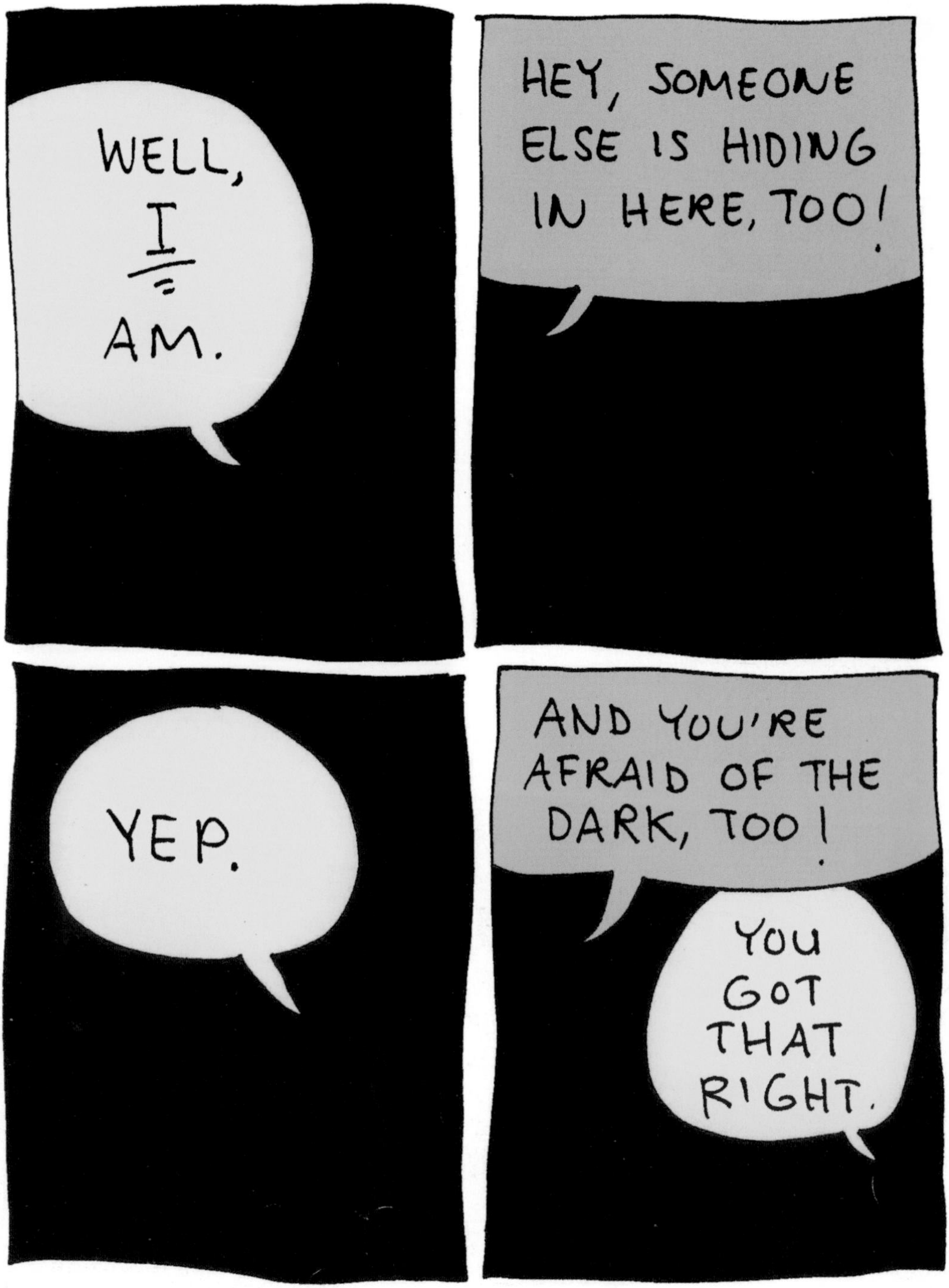
WELL, I AM.
HEY, SOMEONE ELSE IS HIDING IN HERE, TOO!
YEP.
AND YOU'RE AFRAID OF THE DARK, TOO!
YOU GOT THAT RIGHT.

I'M NOT AFRAID OF ANYTHING ELSE.

OH, I AM.

I'M AFRAID OF BEES!

AND DENTURES!

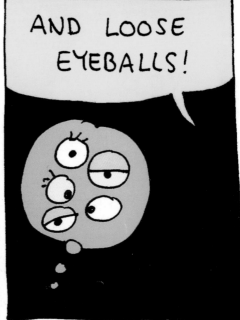

AND LOOSE EYEBALLS!

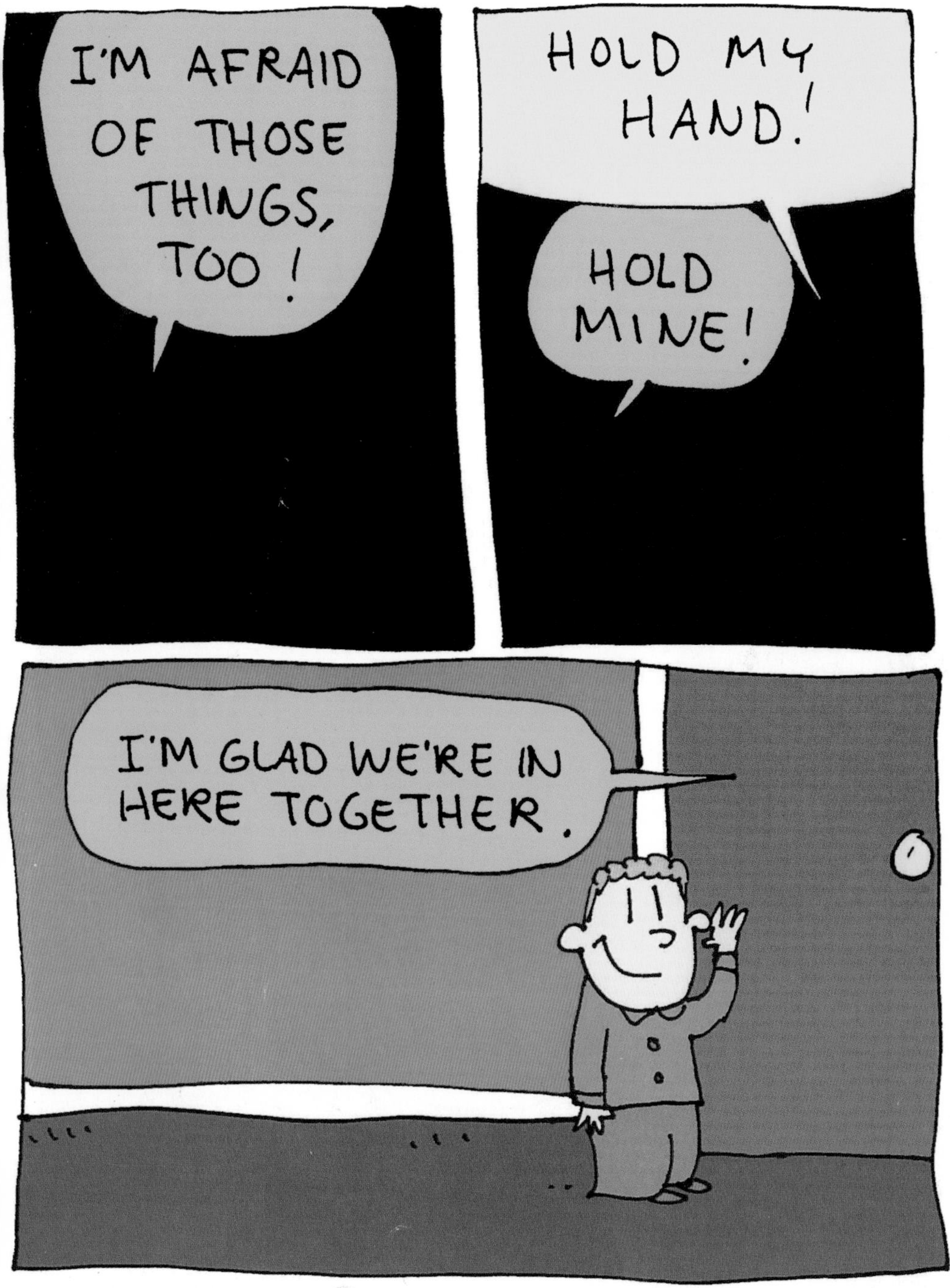
I'M AFRAID OF THOSE THINGS, TOO!
HOLD MY HAND!
HOLD MINE!
I'M GLAD WE'RE IN HERE TOGETHER.

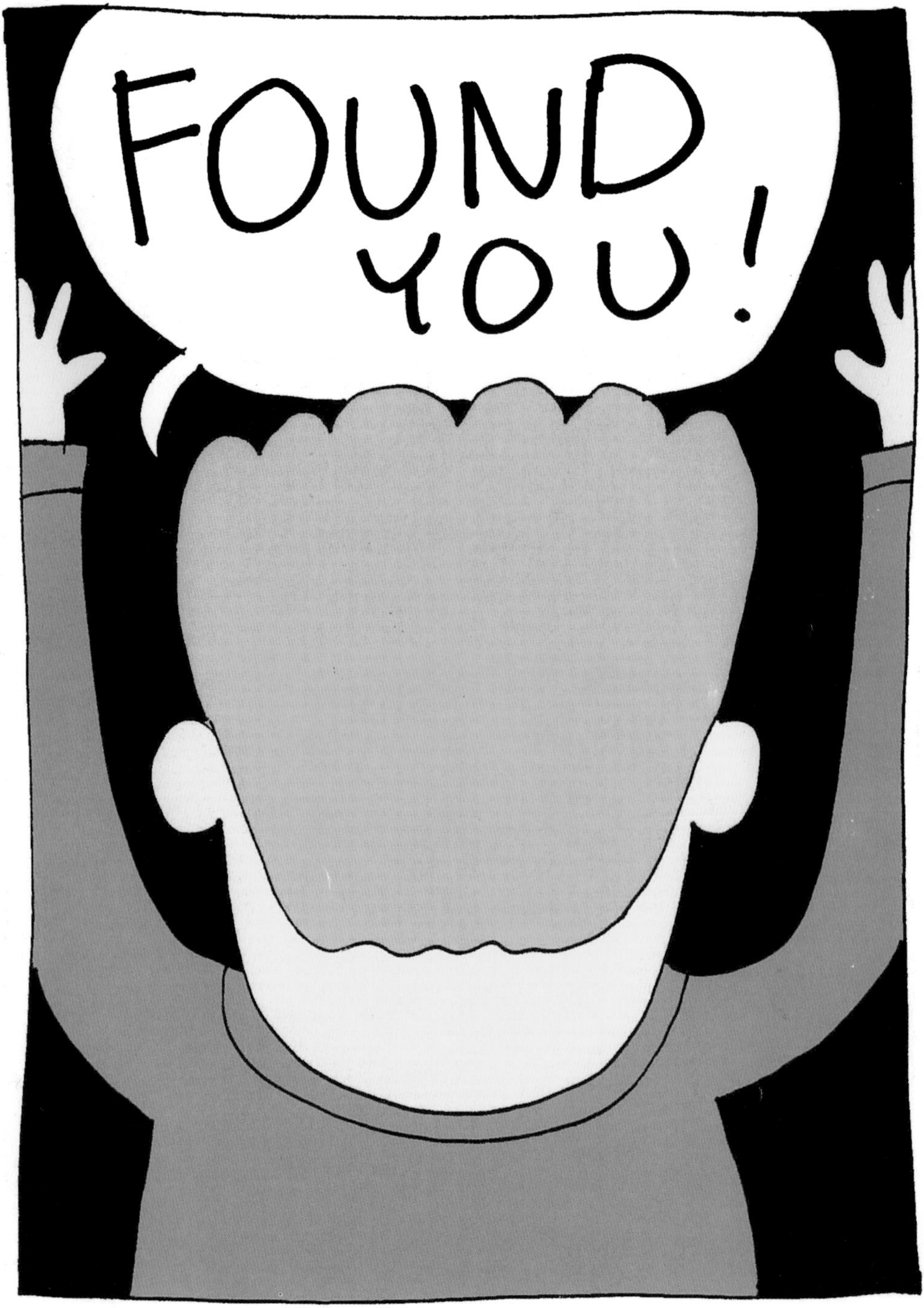
FOUND YOU!

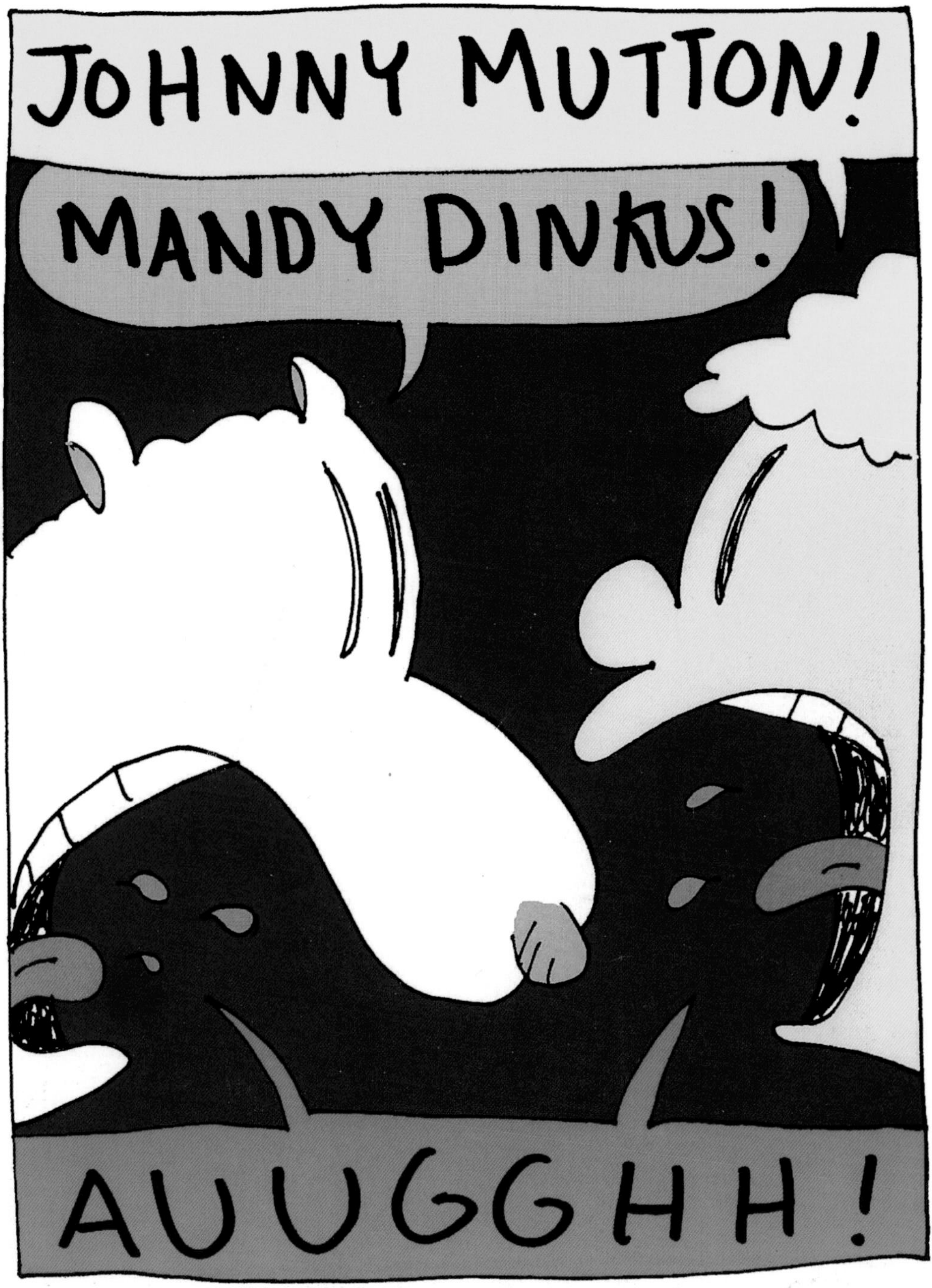
JOHNNY MUTTON!
MANDY DINKUS!
AUUGGHH!

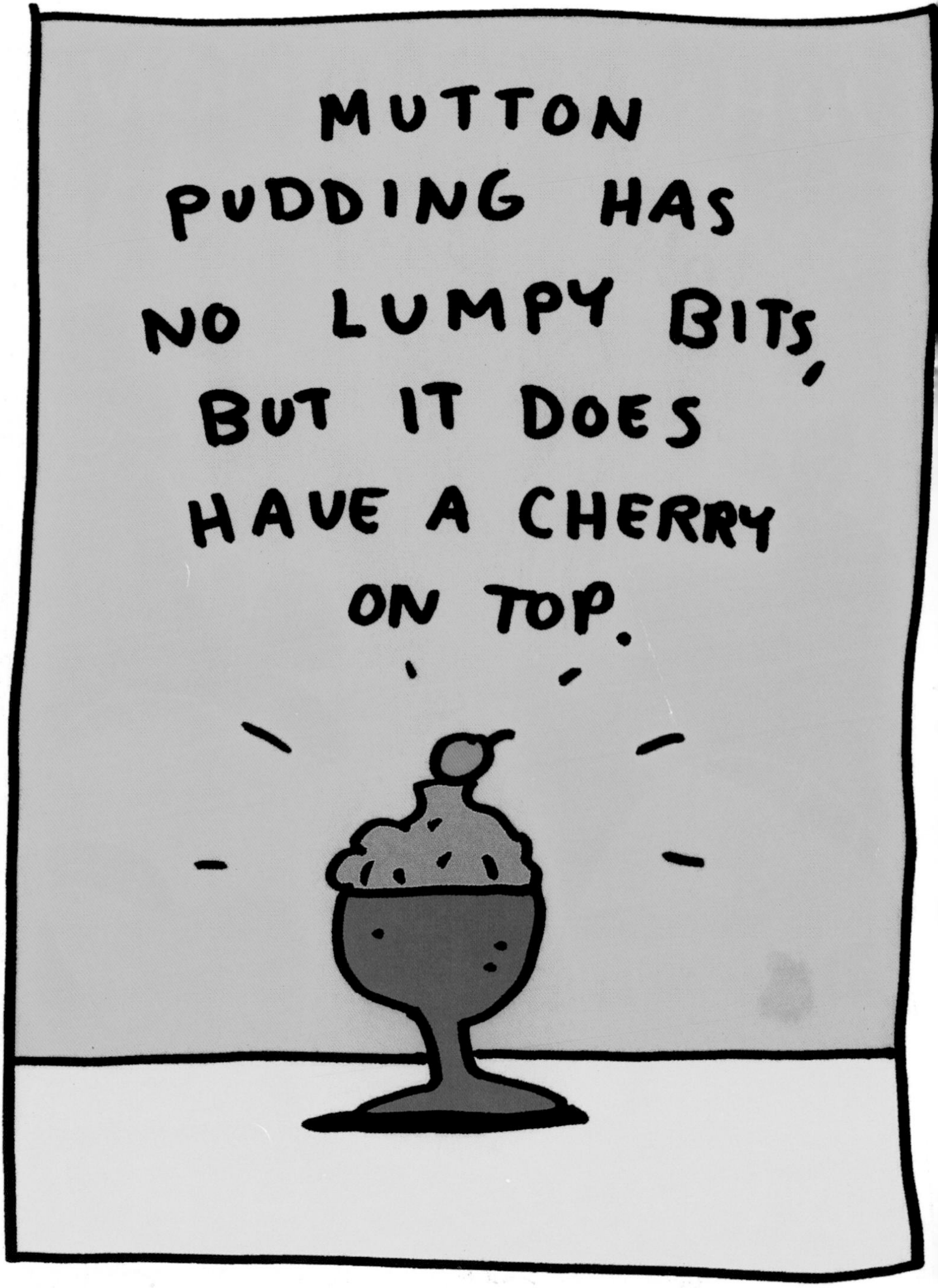
MUTTON PUDDING HAS NO LUMPY BITS, BUT IT DOES HAVE A CHERRY ON TOP.

Bottoms Up

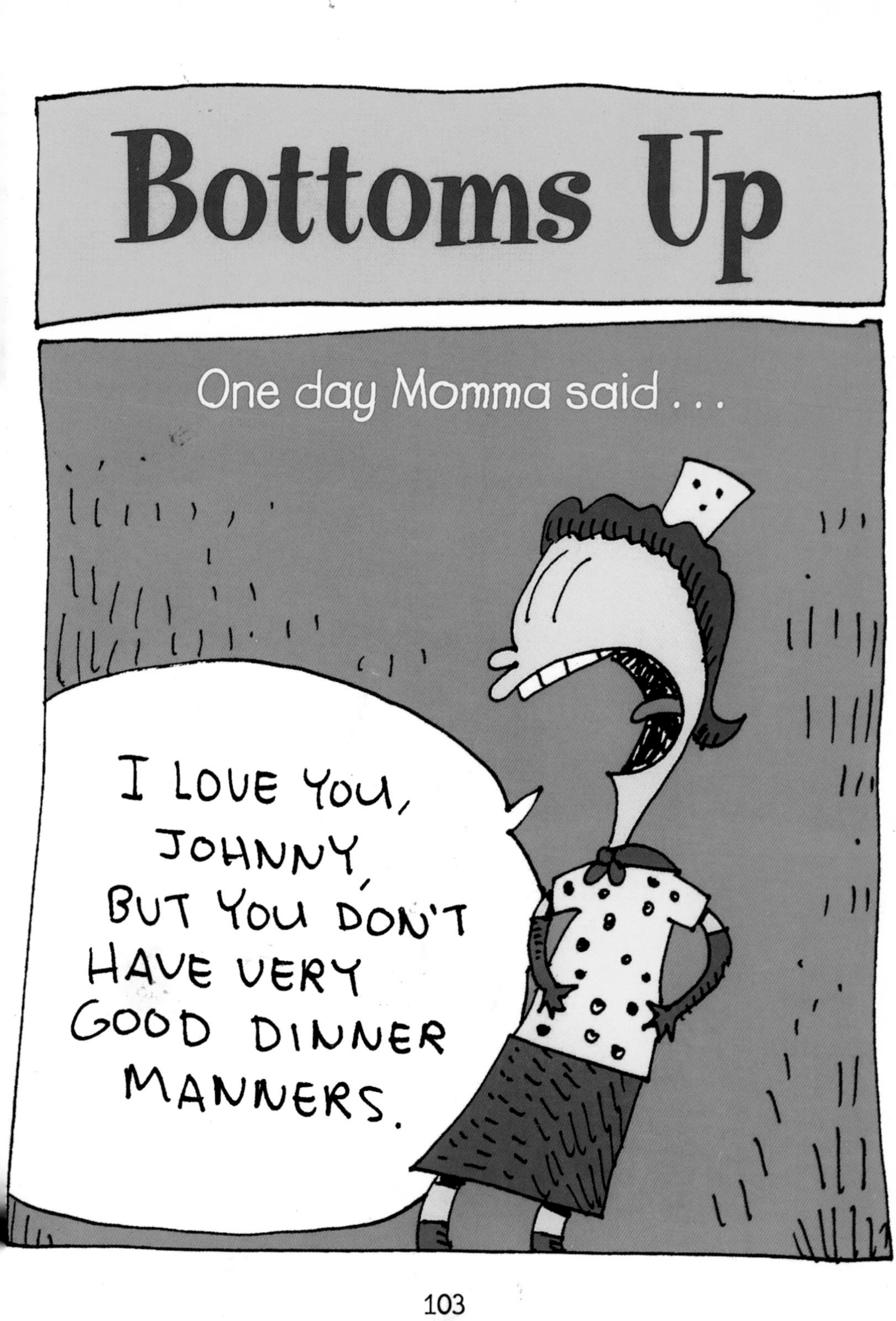
One day Momma said . . .
I LOVE YOU, JOHNNY, BUT YOU DON'T HAVE VERY GOOD DINNER MANNERS.

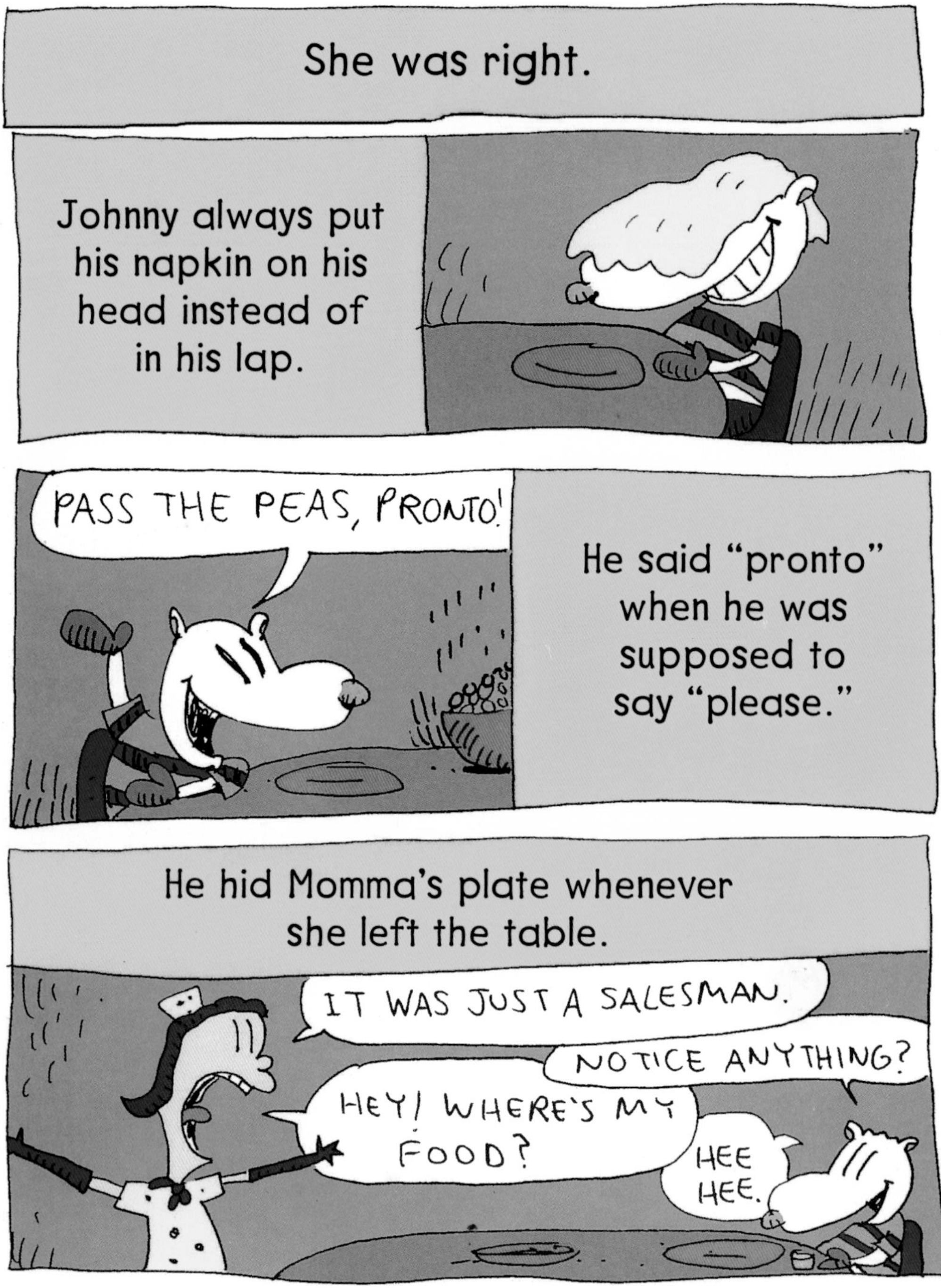
She was right.
Johnny always put his napkin on his head instead of in his lap.
PASS THE PEAS, PRONTO!
He said “pronto” when he was supposed to say “please.”
He hid Momma’s plate whenever she left the table.
IT WAS JUST A SALESMAN.
NOTICE ANYTHING?
HEY! WHERE’S MY FOOD?
HEE HEE.

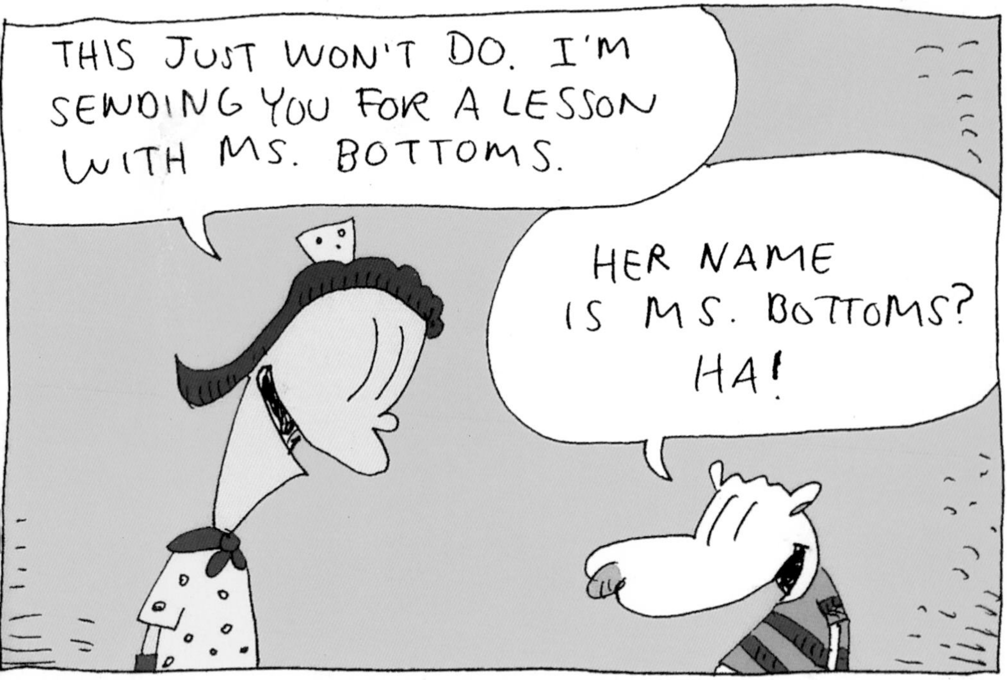
THIS JUST WON'T DO. I'M SENDING YOU FOR A LESSON WITH MS. BOTTOMS.
HER NAME IS MS. BOTTOMS? HA!

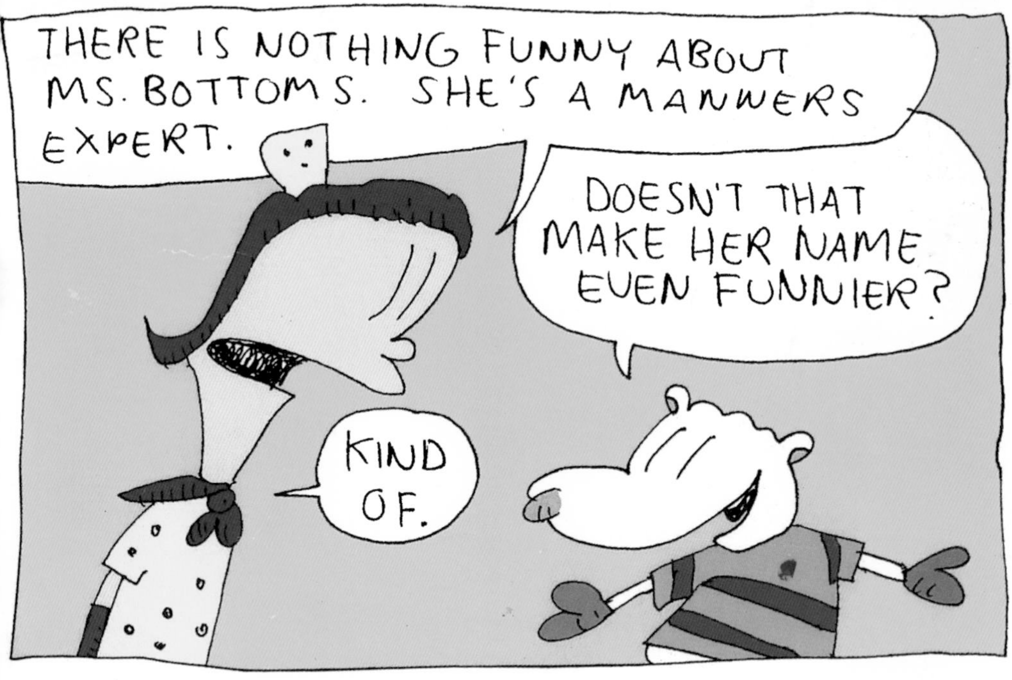
THERE IS NOTHING FUNNY ABOUT MS. BOTTOMS. SHE'S A MANNERS EXPERT.
DOESN'T THAT MAKE HER NAME EVEN FUNNIER?
KIND OF.

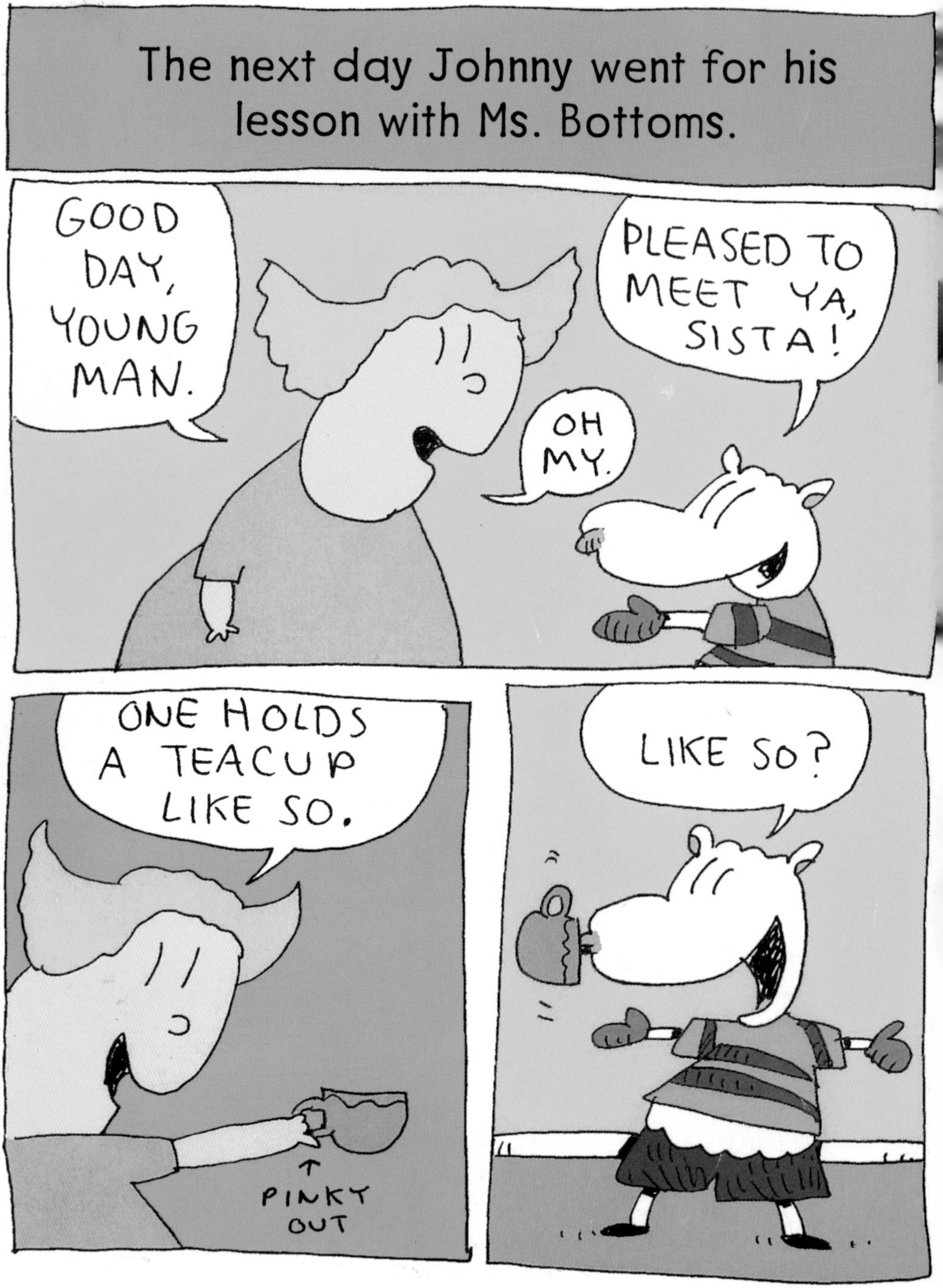
The next day Johnny went for his lesson with Ms. Bottoms.
GOOD DAY, YOUNG MAN.
PLEASED TO MEET YA, SISTA!
OH MY.
ONE HOLDS A TEACUP LIKE SO.
PINKY OUT
LIKE SO?

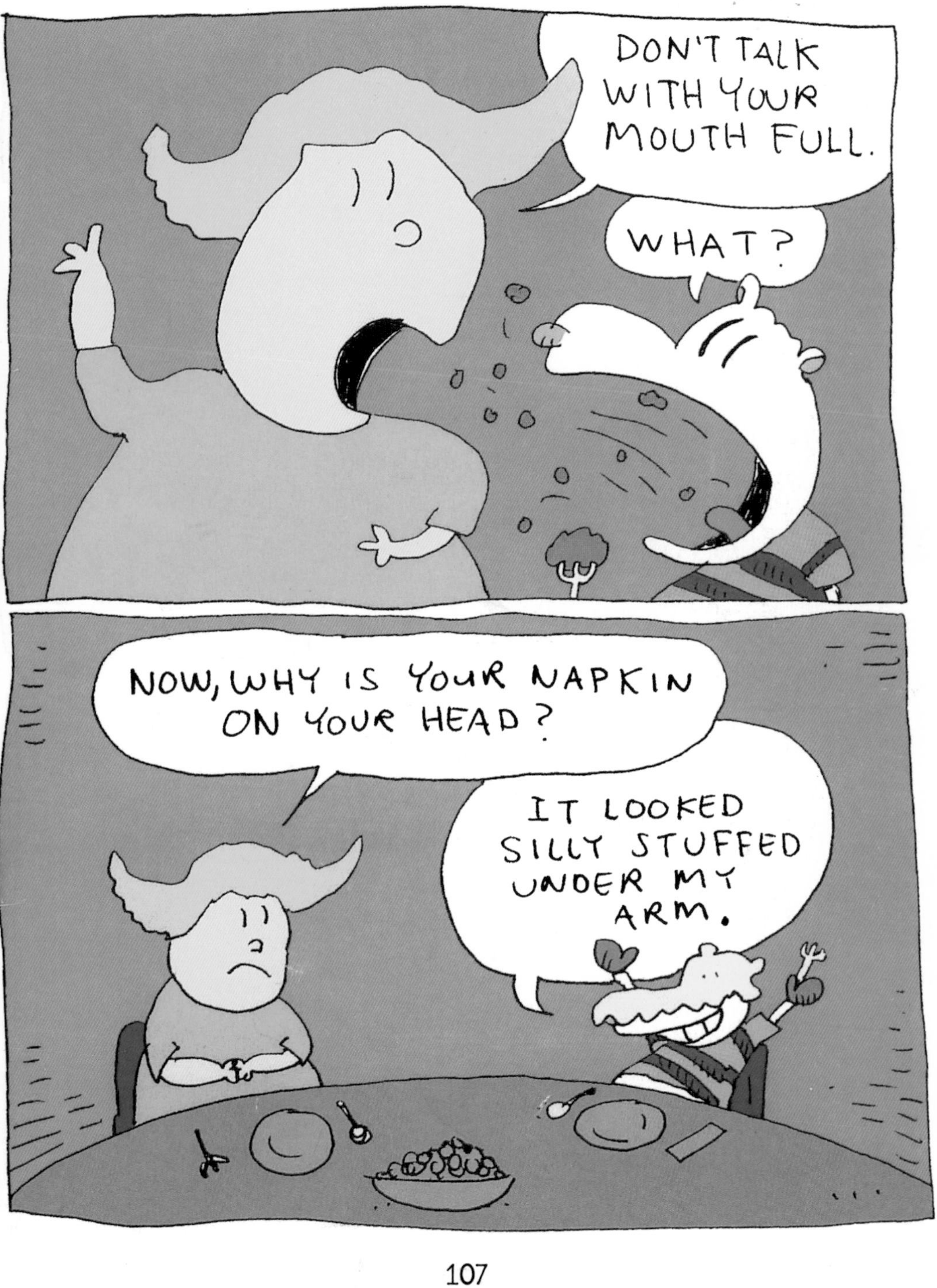
DON'T TALK WITH YOUR MOUTH FULL.
WHAT?
NOW, WHY IS YOUR NAPKIN ON YOUR HEAD?
IT LOOKED SILLY STUFFED UNDER MY ARM.

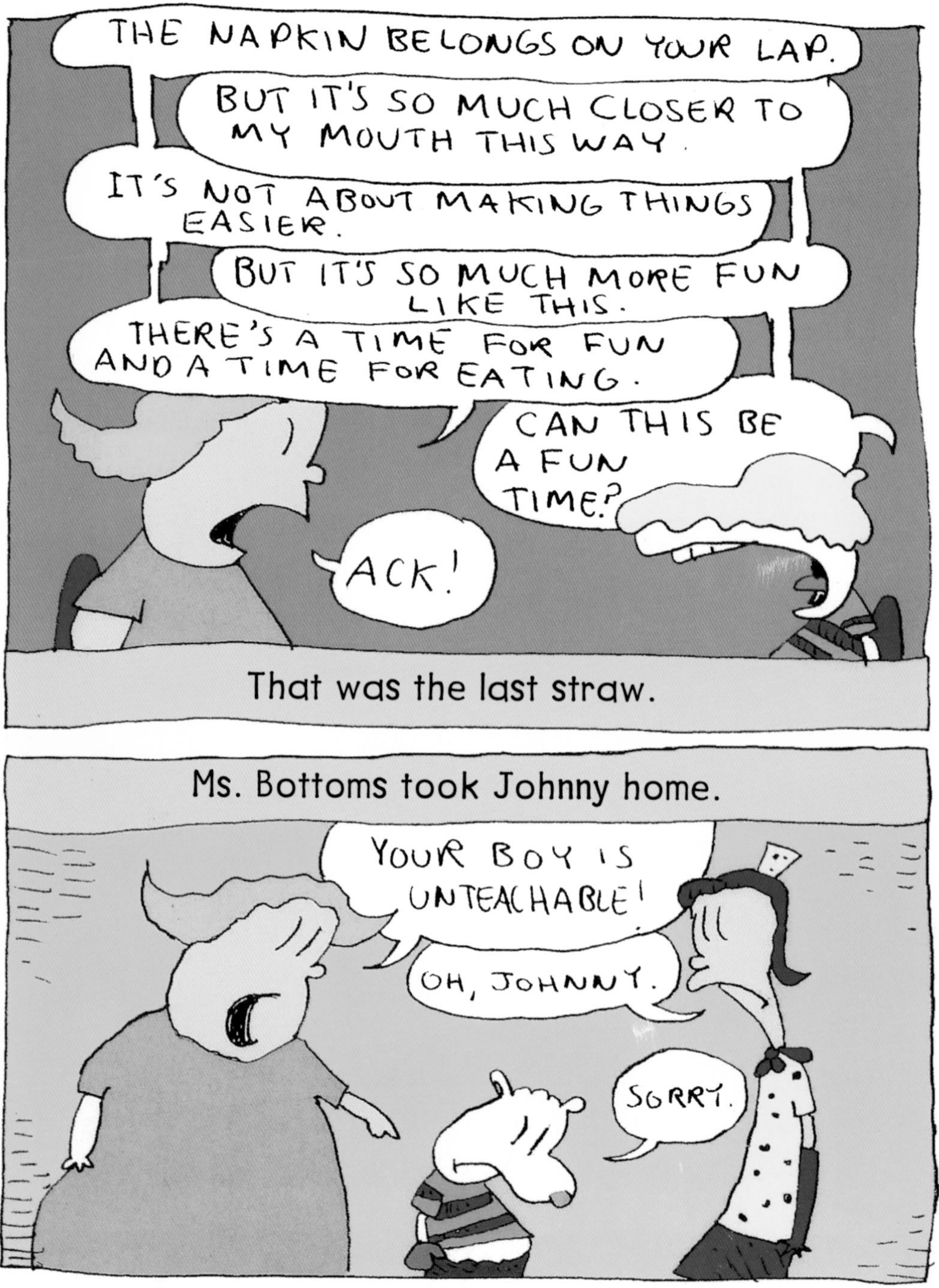
THE NAPKIN BELONGS ON YOUR LAP.
BUT IT'S SO MUCH CLOSER TO MY MOUTH THIS WAY.
IT'S NOT ABOUT MAKING THINGS EASIER.
BUT IT'S SO MUCH MORE FUN LIKE THIS.
THERE'S A TIME FOR FUN AND A TIME FOR EATING.
CAN THIS BE A FUN TIME?
ACK!
That was the last straw.
Ms. Bottoms took Johnny home.
YOUR BOY IS UNTEACHABLE!
OH, JOHNNY.
SORRY.

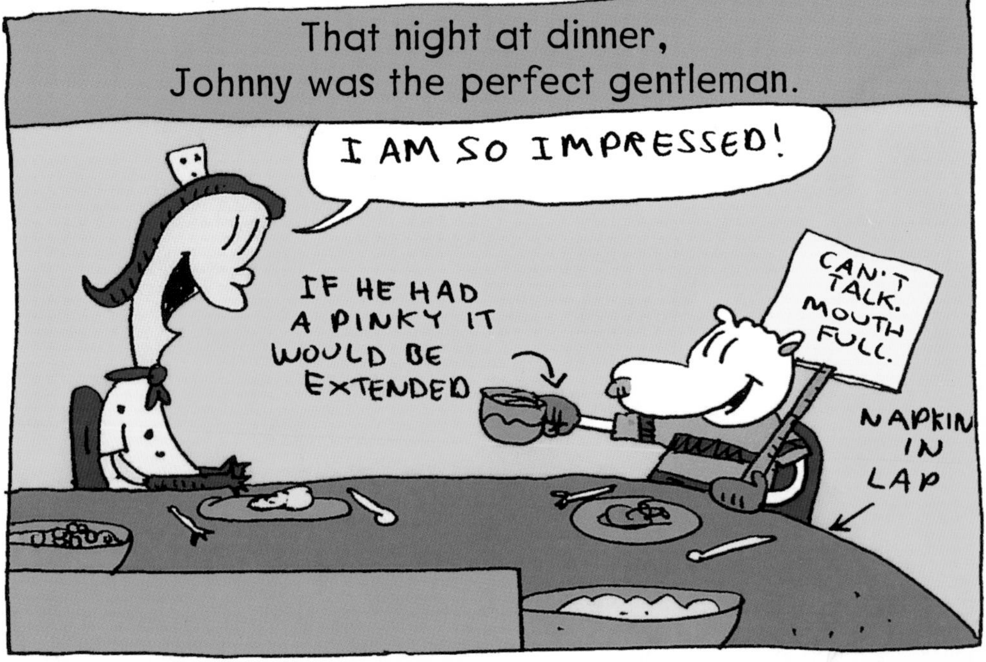
That night at dinner,
Johnny was the perfect gentleman.
I AM SO IMPRESSED!
IF HE HAD A PINKY IT WOULD BE EXTENDED
CAN'T TALK. MOUTH FULL.
NAPKIN IN LAP

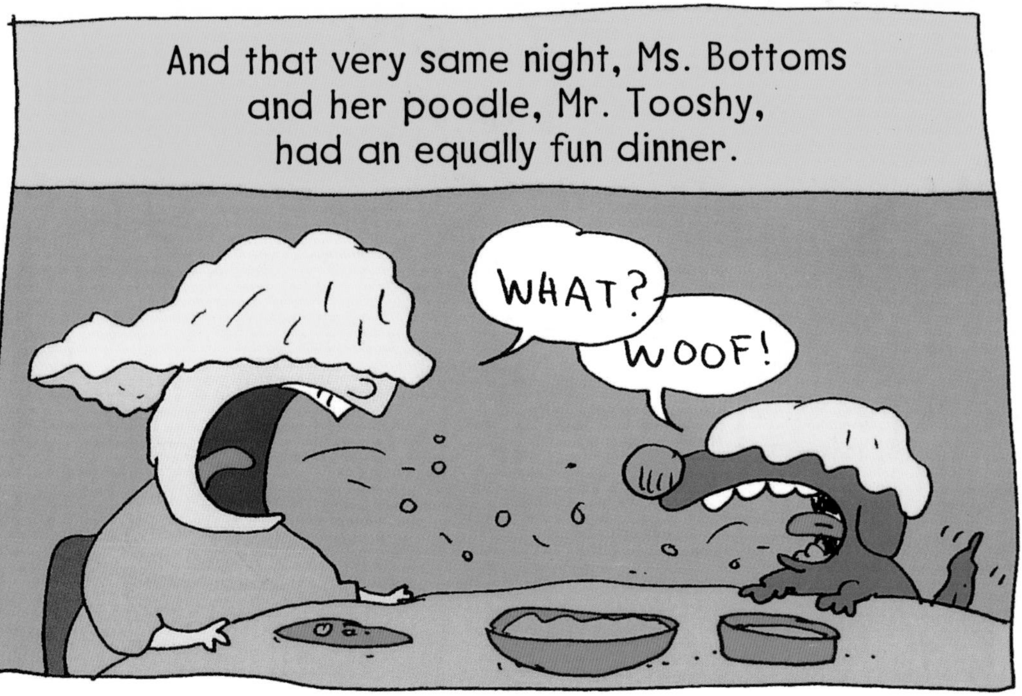
And that very same night, Ms. Bottoms
and her poodle, Mr. Tooshy,
had an equally fun dinner.
WHAT?
WOOF!

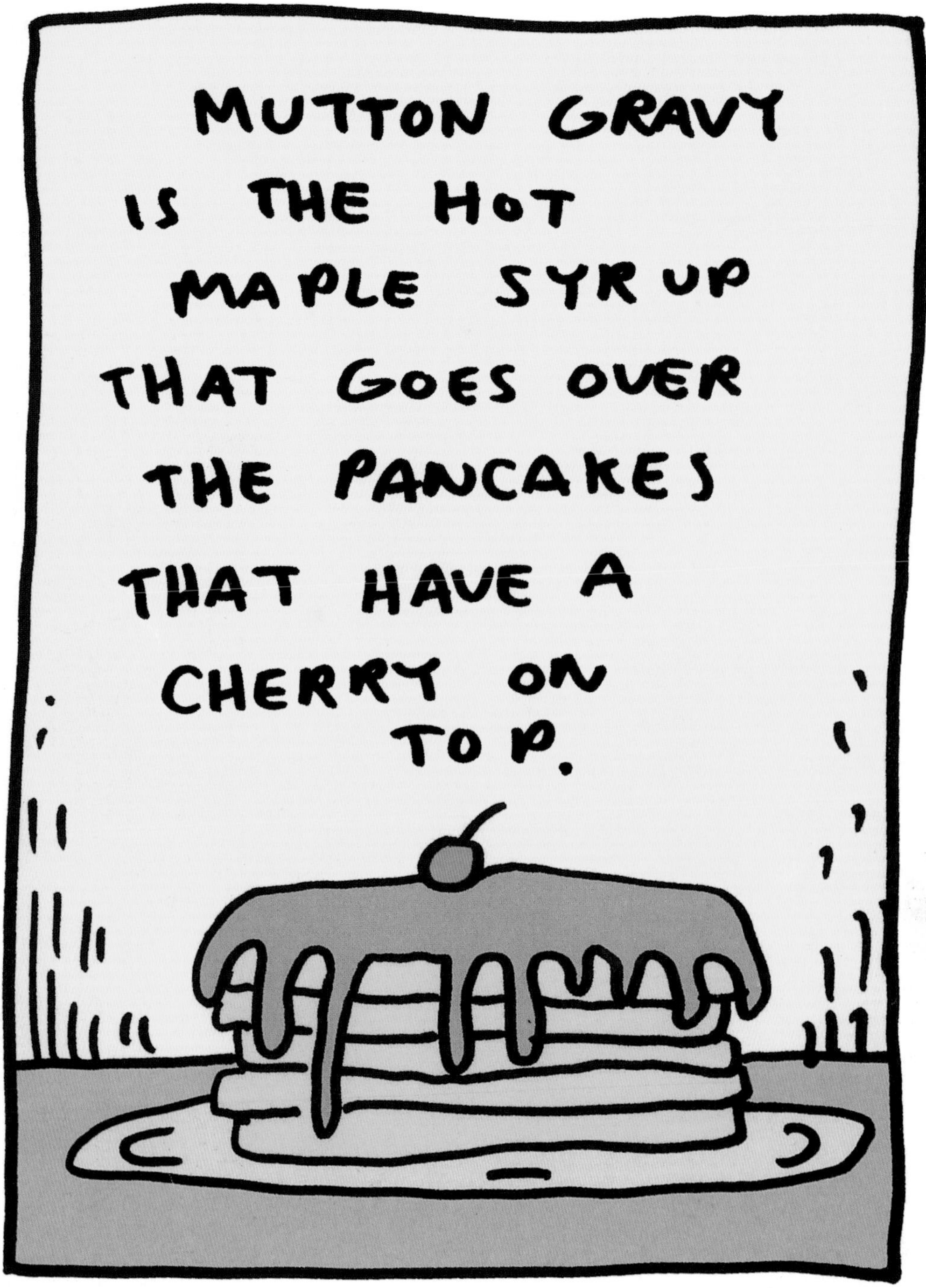
MUTTON GRAVY IS THE HOT MAPLE SYRUP THAT GOES OVER THE PANCAKES THAT HAVE A CHERRY ON TOP.

For the Record

Johnny thought he was one of the most talented guys he knew. And of all his talents, the one he thought he had the most of was his talent for sitting.

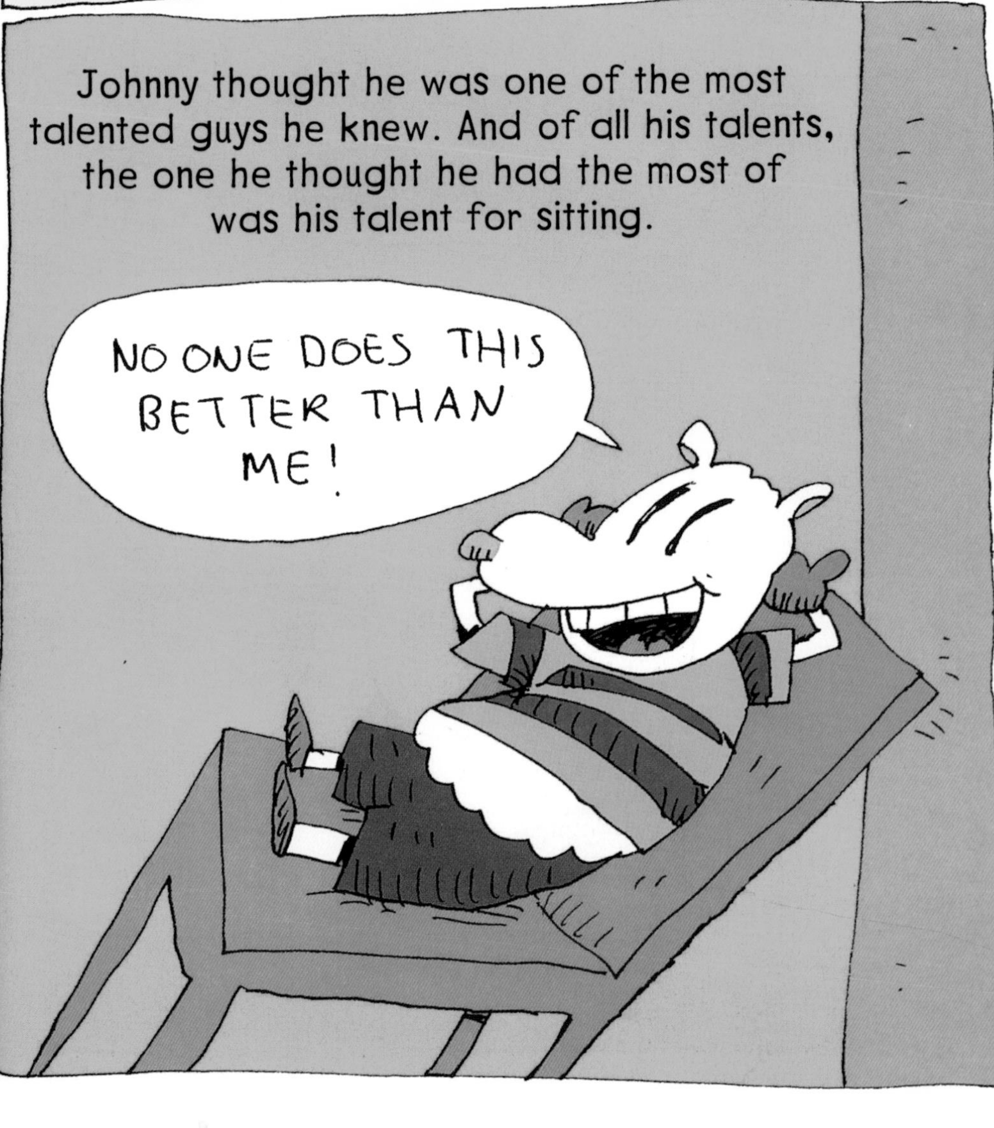
NO ONE DOES THIS BETTER THAN ME!

Most people weren't sophisticated enough to appreciate a great sitter.

LOOK AT THIS!

I DON'T GET IT. YOU'RE JUST SITTING.

OH, BROTHER.

So Johnny decided to set a world record while sitting.

NEXT WEEK I WILL RIDE THE BIGGEST ROLLER COASTER IN THE WORLD 250 TIMES NONSTOP!

THAT'S AMAZING!

AND I'LL BE SITTING!

NATURALLY.

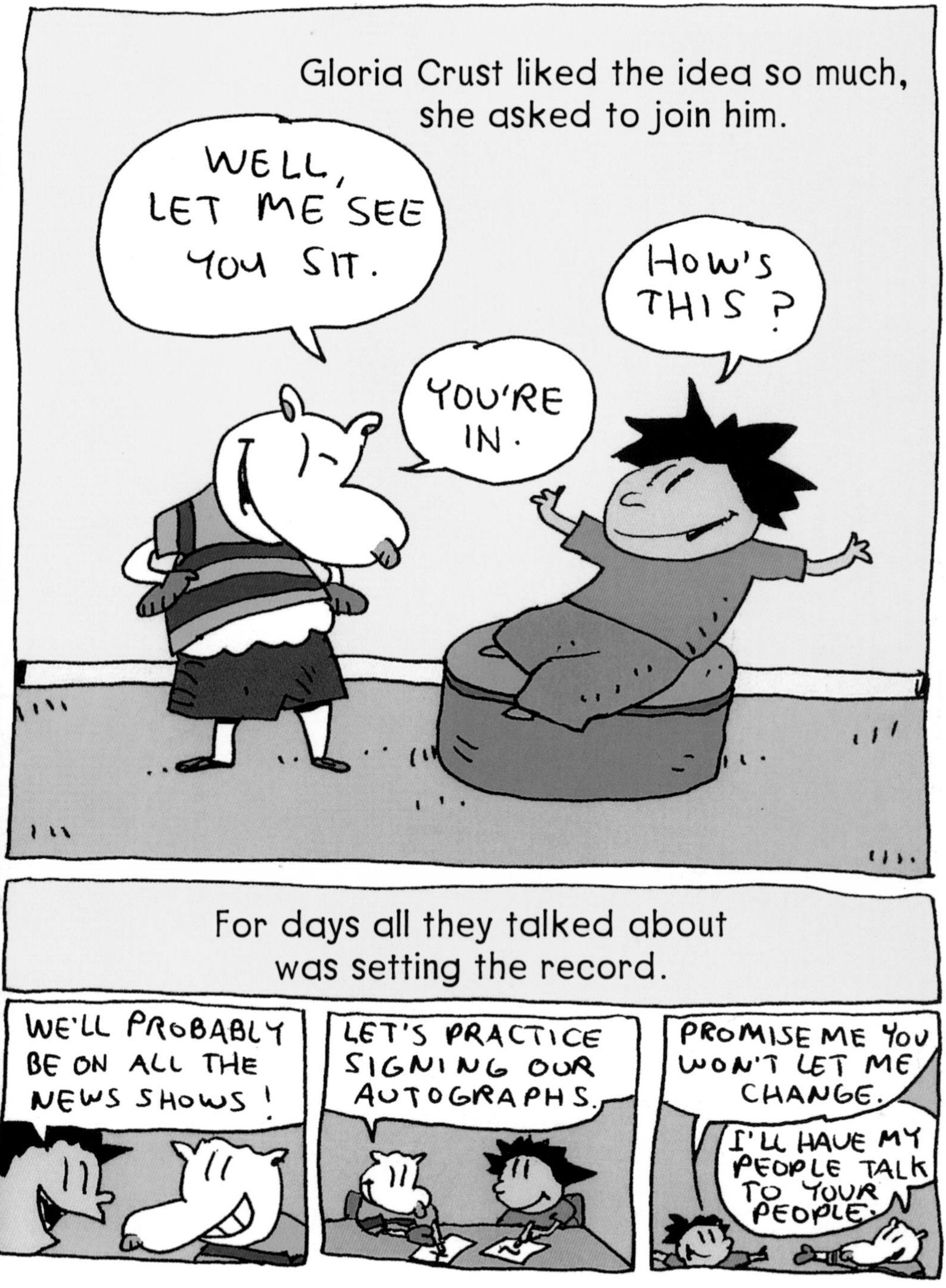
Gloria Crust liked the idea so much, she asked to join him.
WELL, LET ME SEE YOU SIT.
HOW'S THIS?
YOU'RE IN.
For days all they talked about was setting the record.
WE'LL PROBABLY BE ON ALL THE NEWS SHOWS!
LET'S PRACTICE SIGNING OUR AUTOGRAPHS.
PROMISE ME YOU WON'T LET ME CHANGE.
I'LL HAVE MY PEOPLE TALK TO YOUR PEOPLE.

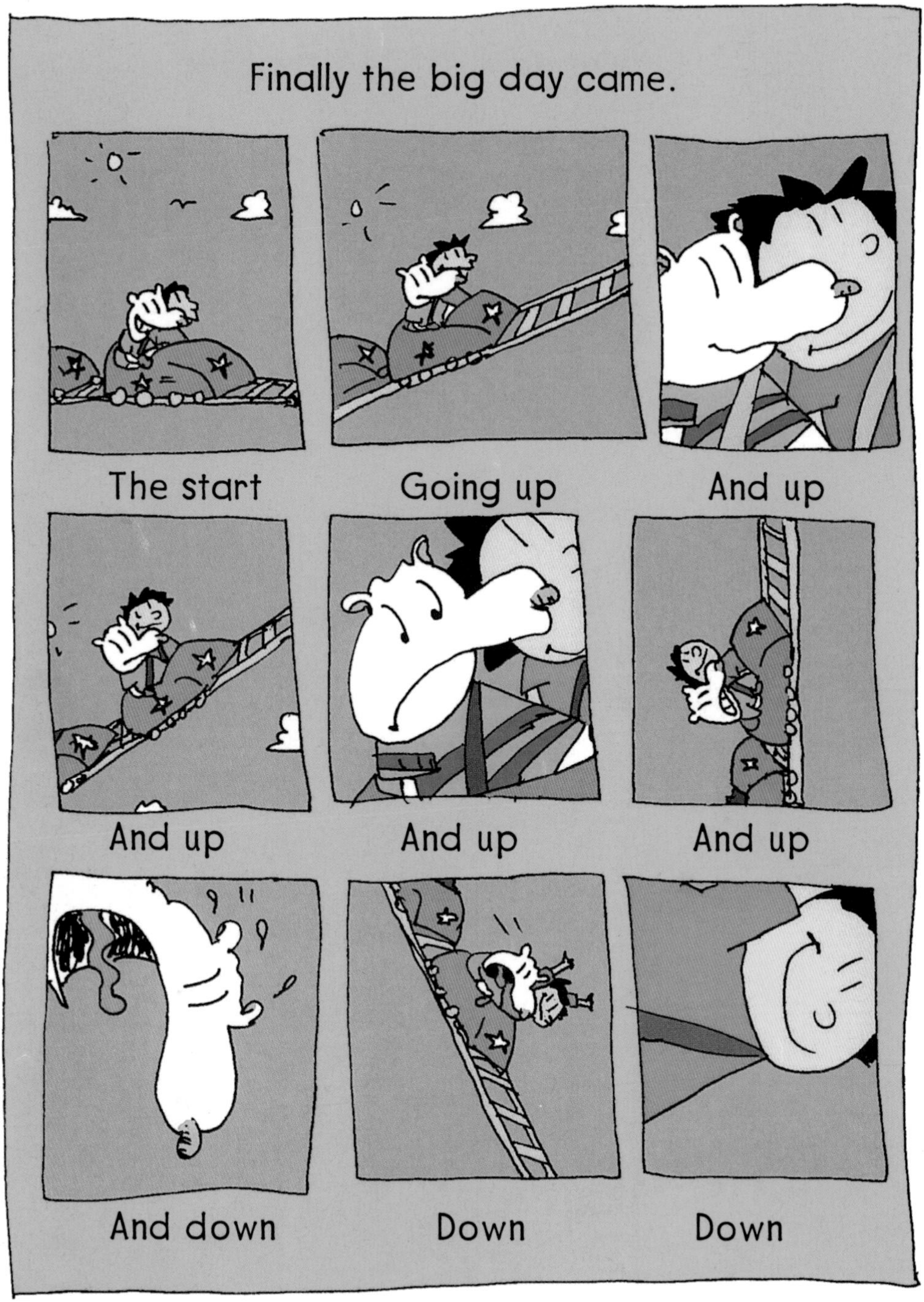
Finally the big day came.
The start
Going up
And up
And up
And up
And up
And down
Down
Down

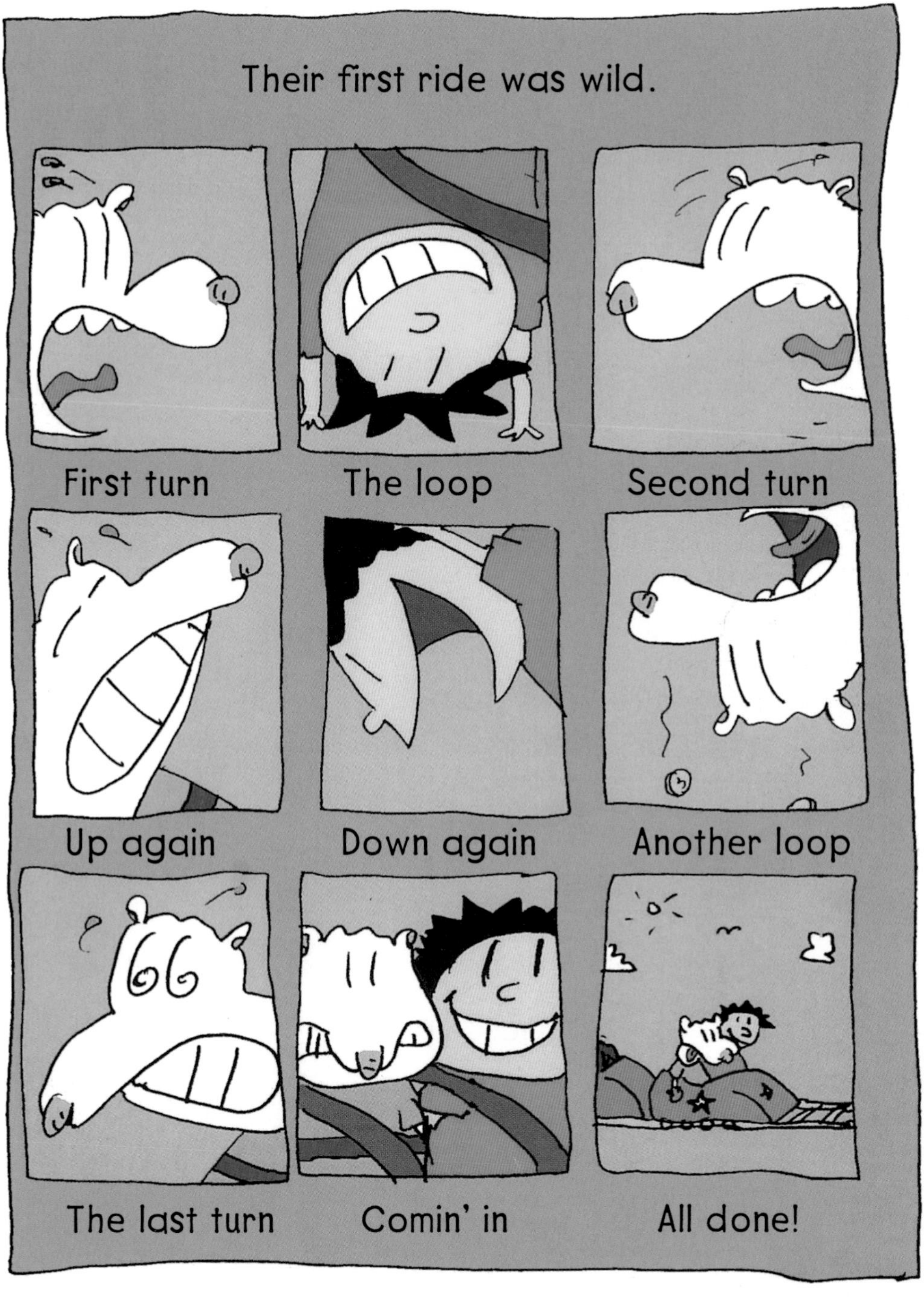
Their first ride was wild.
First turn
The loop
Second turn
Up again
Down again
Another loop
The last turn
Comin' in
All done!

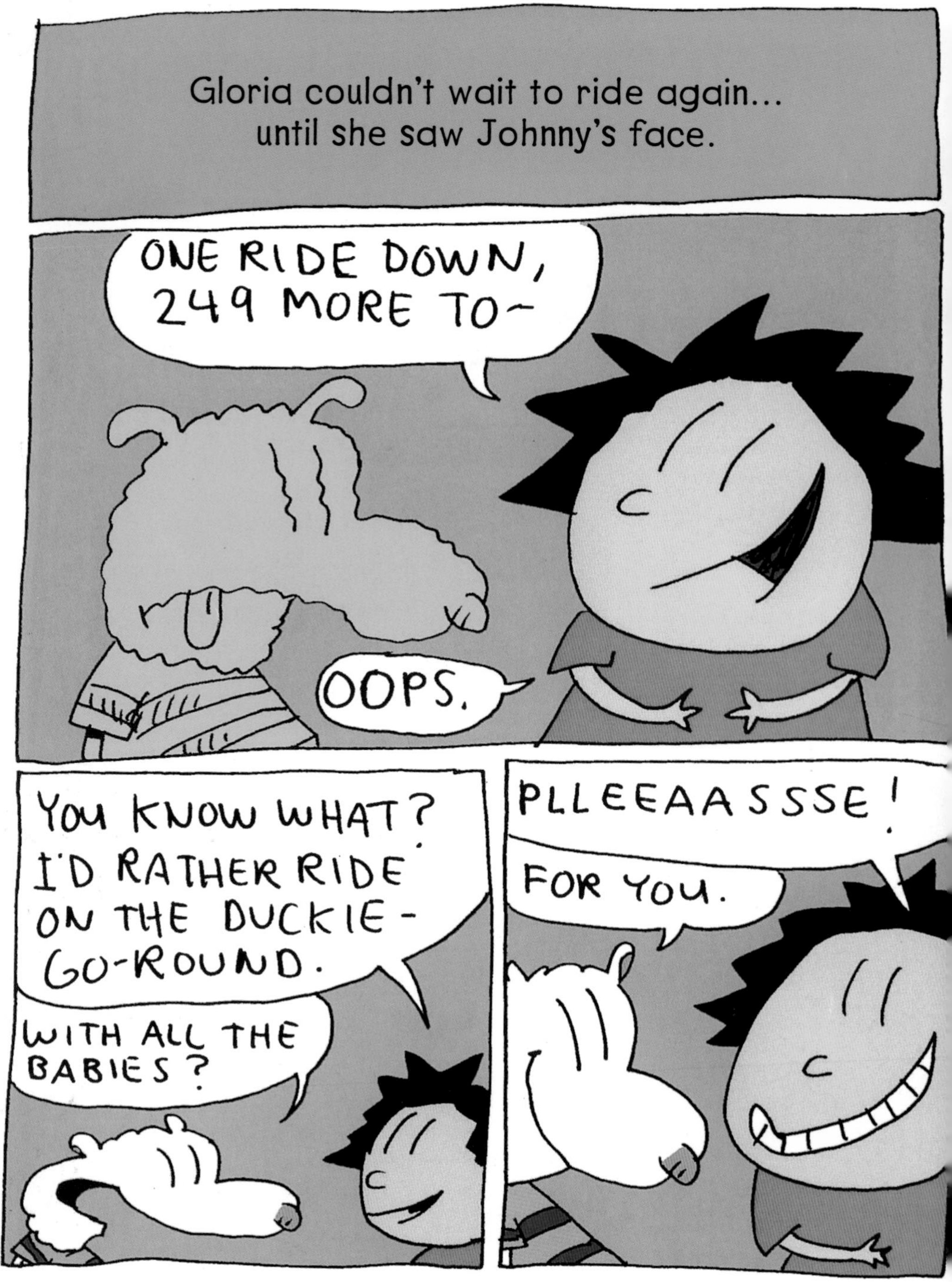
Gloria couldn't wait to ride again...
until she saw Johnny's face.
ONE RIDE DOWN, 249 MORE TO–
OOPS.
YOU KNOW WHAT? I'D RATHER RIDE ON THE DUCKIE-GO-ROUND.
WITH ALL THE BABIES?
PLLEEAASSSE!
FOR YOU.

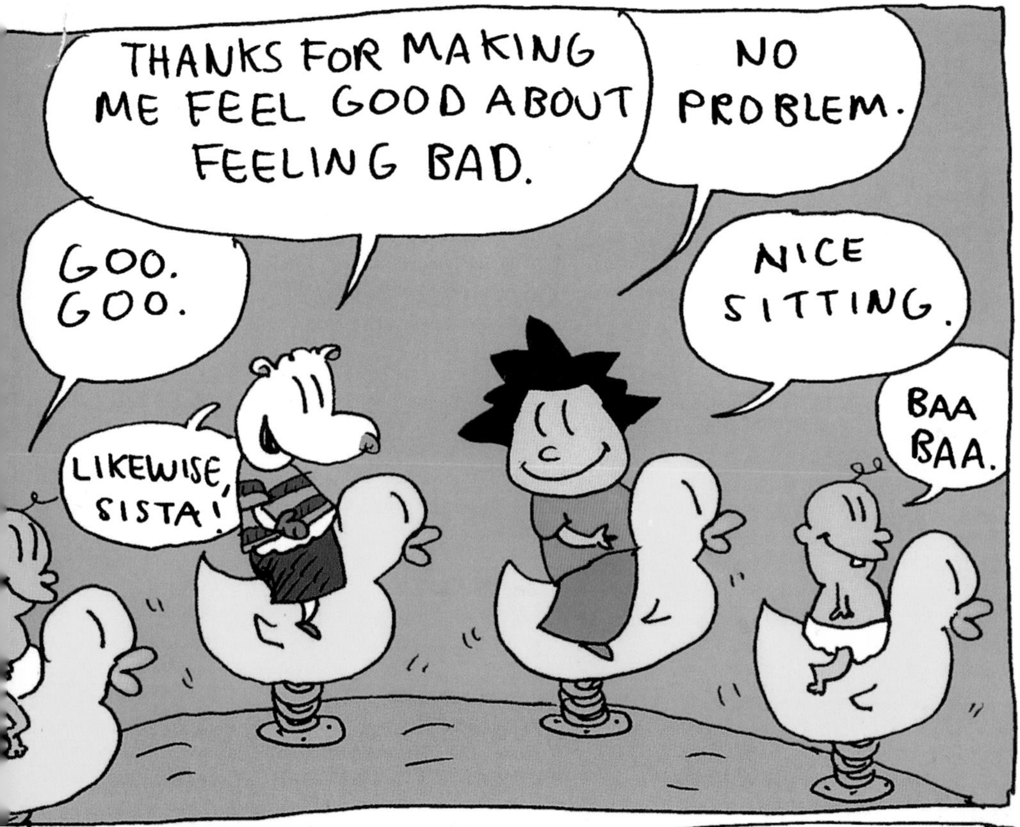
THANKS FOR MAKING ME FEEL GOOD ABOUT FEELING BAD.
NO PROBLEM.
GOO. GOO.
NICE SITTING.
BAA BAA.
LIKEWISE, SISTA!

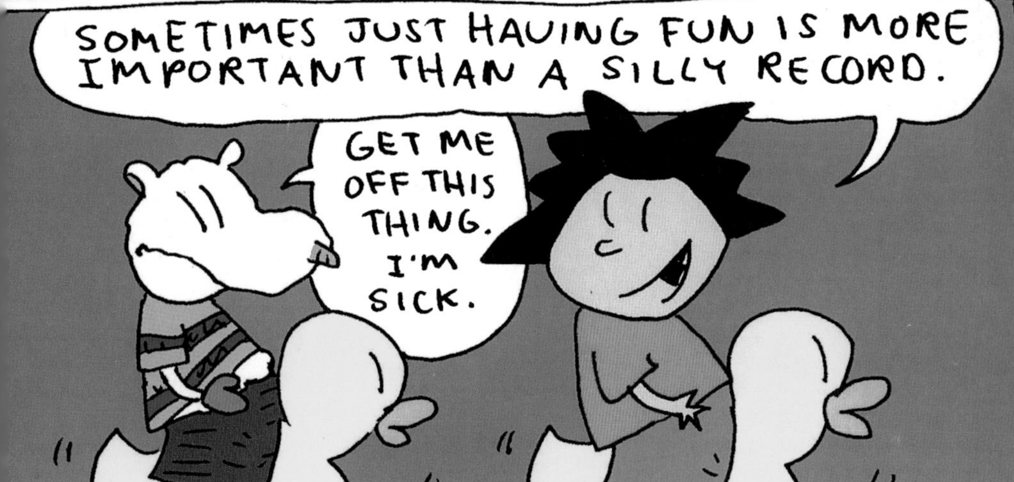
SOMETIMES JUST HAVING FUN IS MORE IMPORTANT THAN A SILLY RECORD.
GET ME OFF THIS THING. I'M SICK.

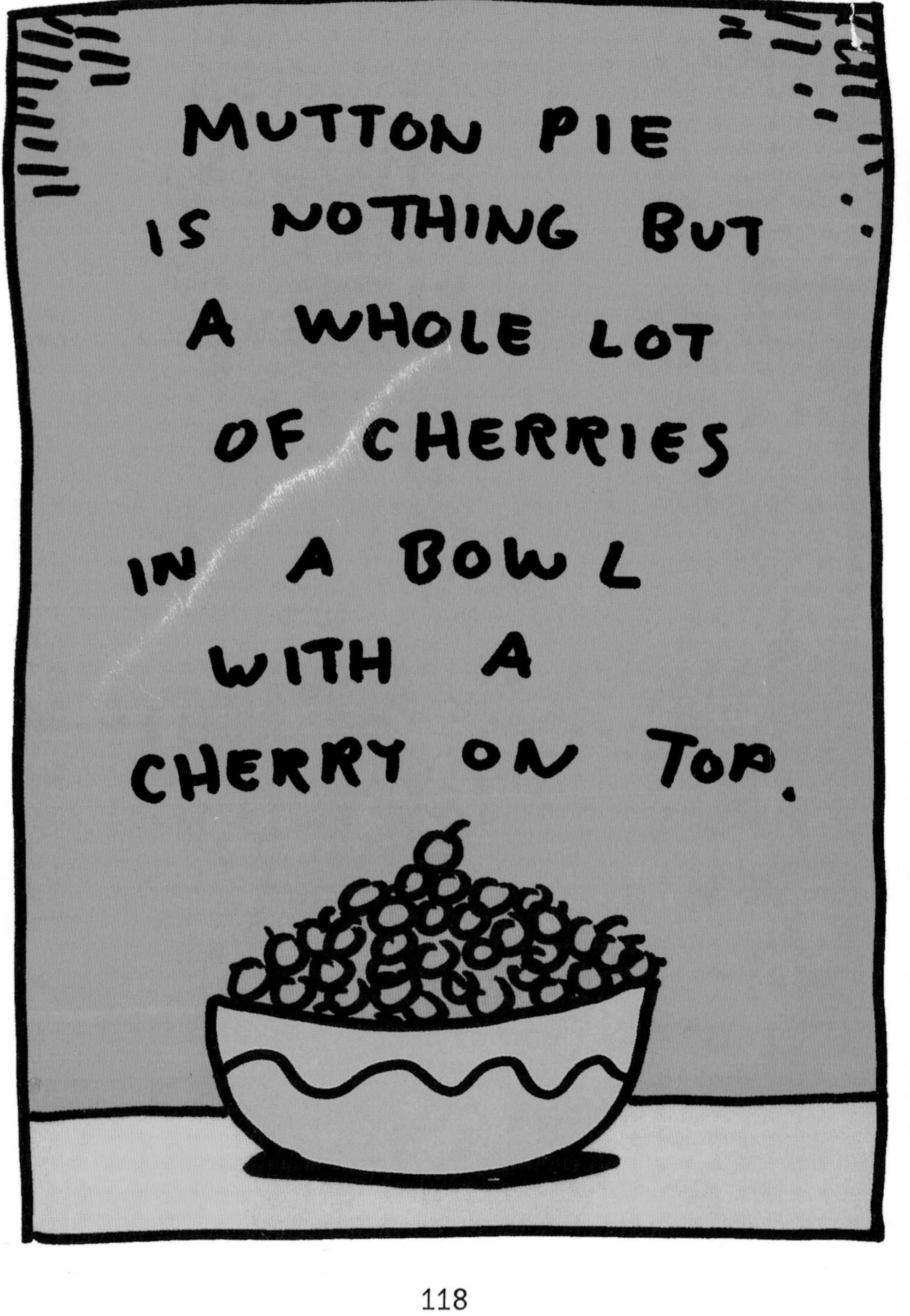
MUTTON PIE IS NOTHING BUT A WHOLE LOT OF CHERRIES IN A BOWL WITH A CHERRY ON TOP.

My Dinner with Dinkus

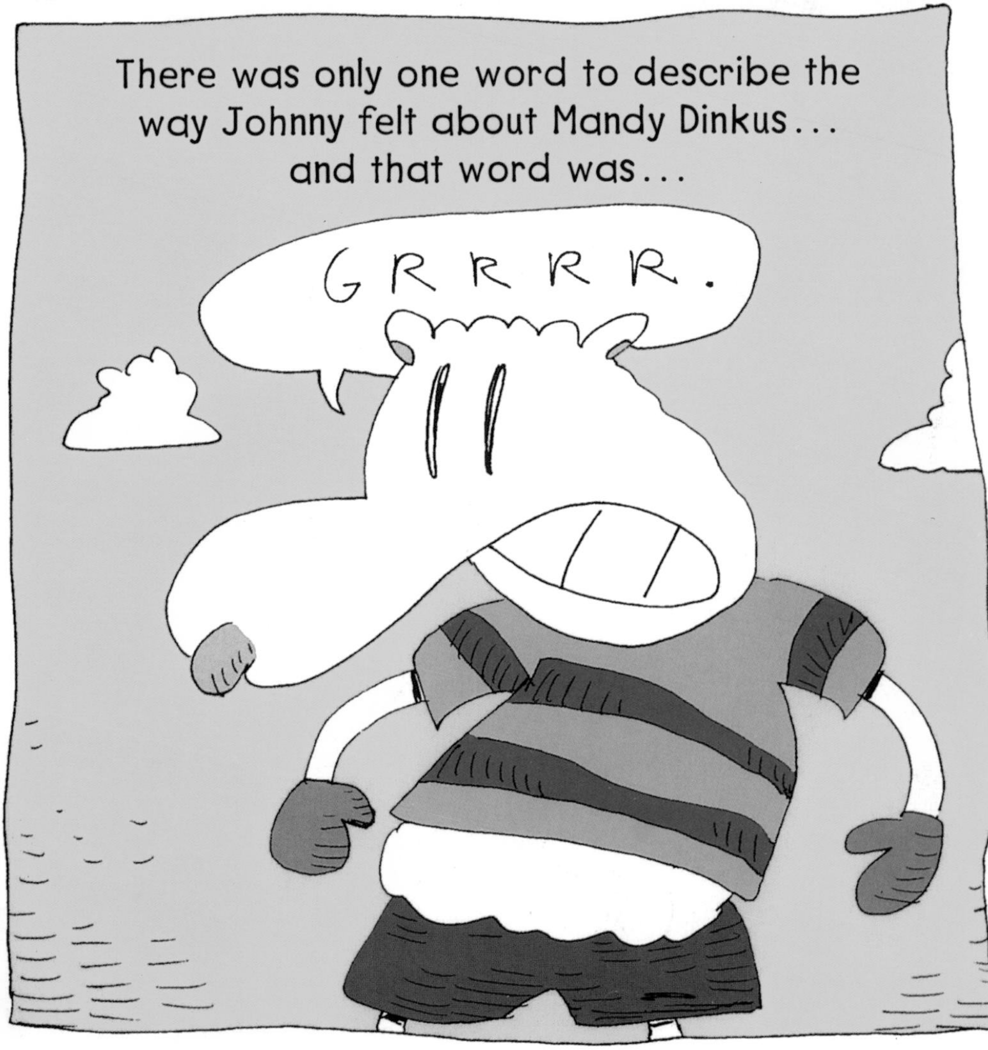
There was only one word to describe the way Johnny felt about Mandy Dinkus...
...and that word was...
GRRRR.

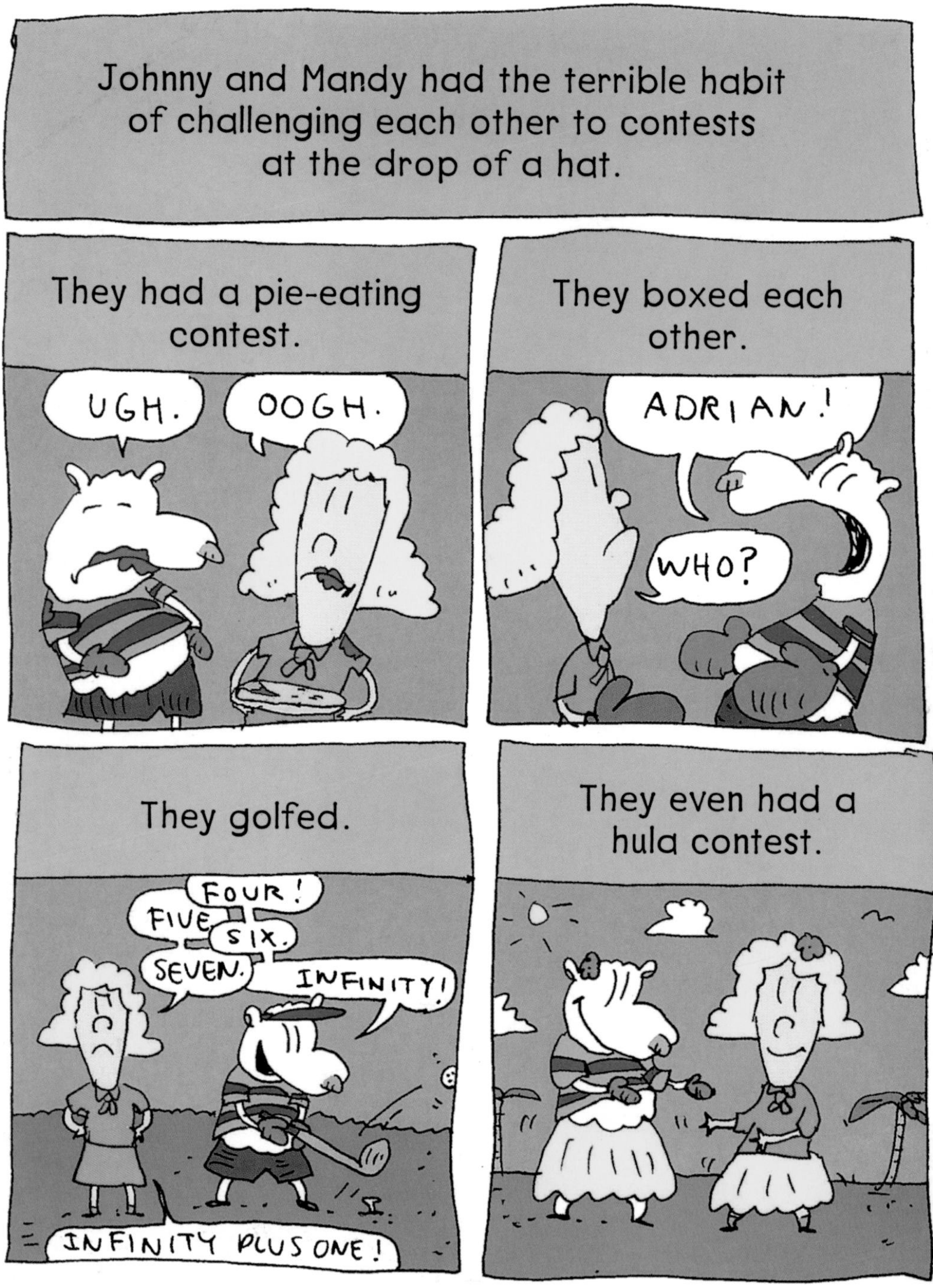
Johnny and Mandy had the terrible habit of challenging each other to contests at the drop of a hat.
They had a pie-eating contest.
UGH.
OOGH.
They boxed each other.
ADRIAN!
WHO?
They golfed.
FOUR!
FIVE.
SIX.
SEVEN.
INFINITY!
INFINITY PLUS ONE!
They even had a hula contest.

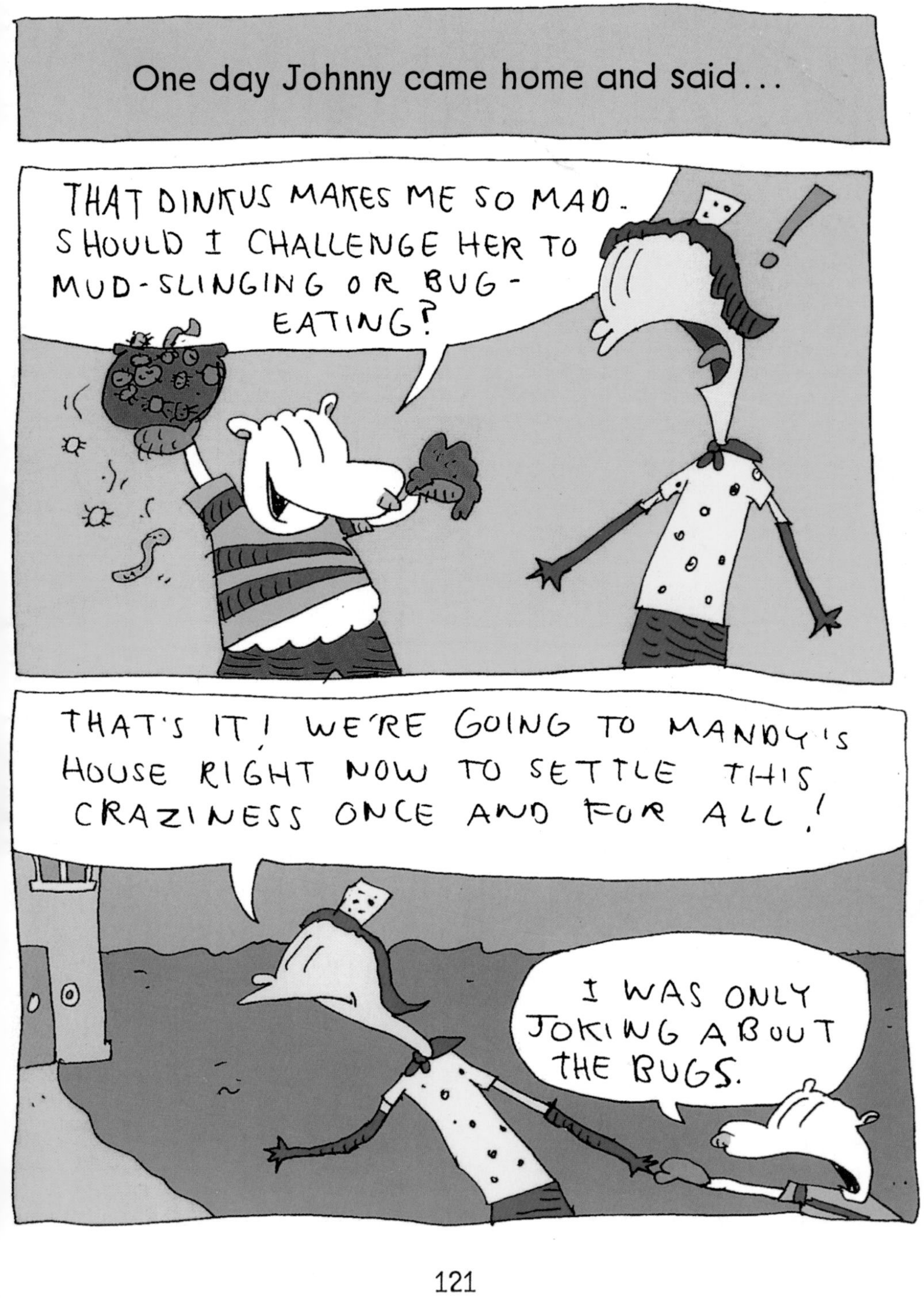
One day Johnny came home and said...
THAT DINKUS MAKES ME SO MAD. SHOULD I CHALLENGE HER TO MUD-SLINGING OR BUG-EATING?
!
THAT'S IT! WE'RE GOING TO MANDY'S HOUSE RIGHT NOW TO SETTLE THIS CRAZINESS ONCE AND FOR ALL!
I WAS ONLY JOKING ABOUT THE BUGS.

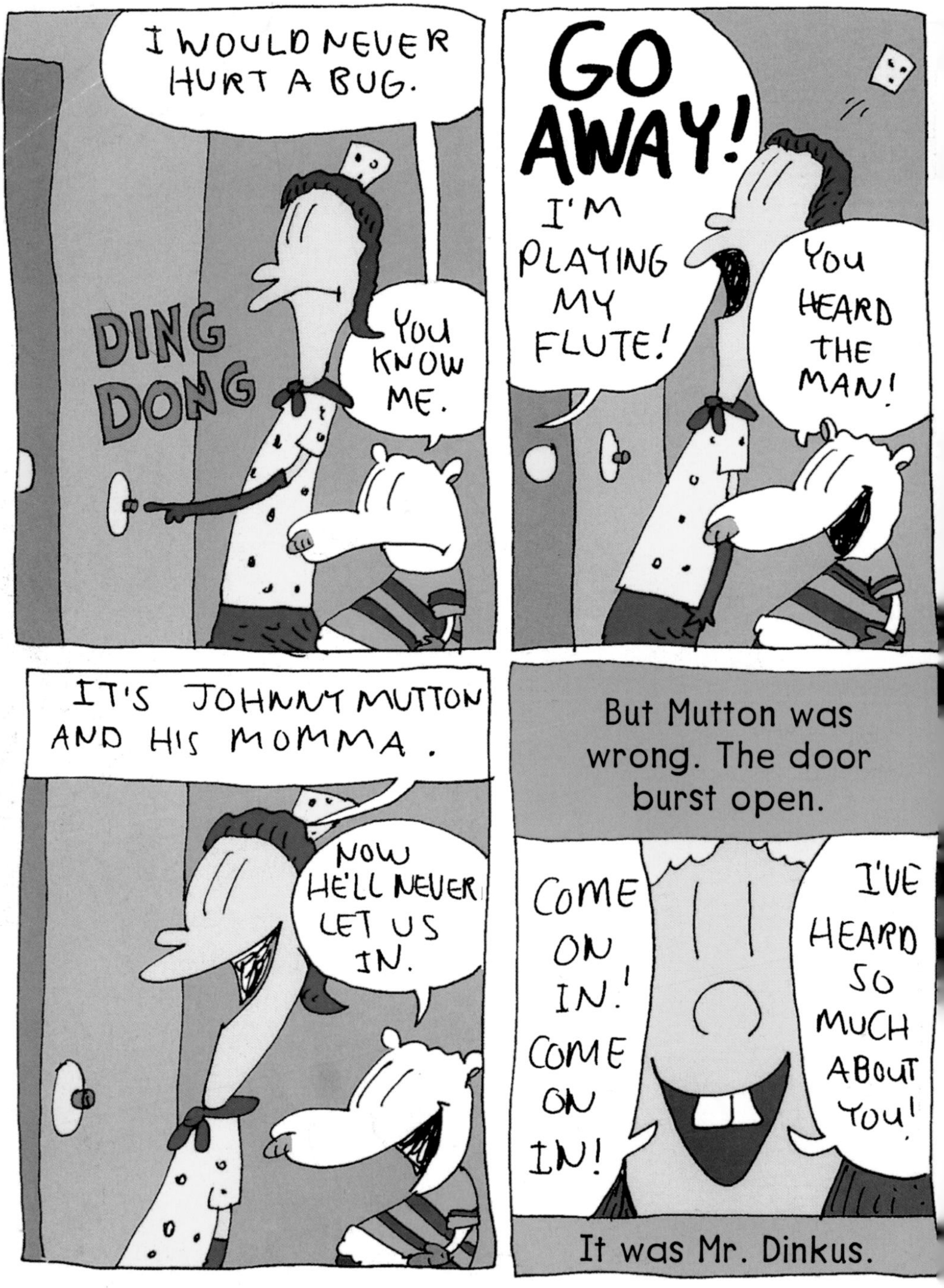
I WOULD NEVER HURT A BUG.
DING DONG
YOU KNOW ME.
GO AWAY!
I'M PLAYING MY FLUTE!
YOU HEARD THE MAN!
IT'S JOHNNY MUTTON AND HIS MOMMA.
NOW HE'LL NEVER LET US IN.
But Mutton was wrong. The door burst open.
COME ON IN! COME ON IN!
I'VE HEARD SO MUCH ABOUT YOU!
It was Mr. Dinkus.

Mr. Dinkus invited Momma and Johnny to have dinner with Mandy and him.

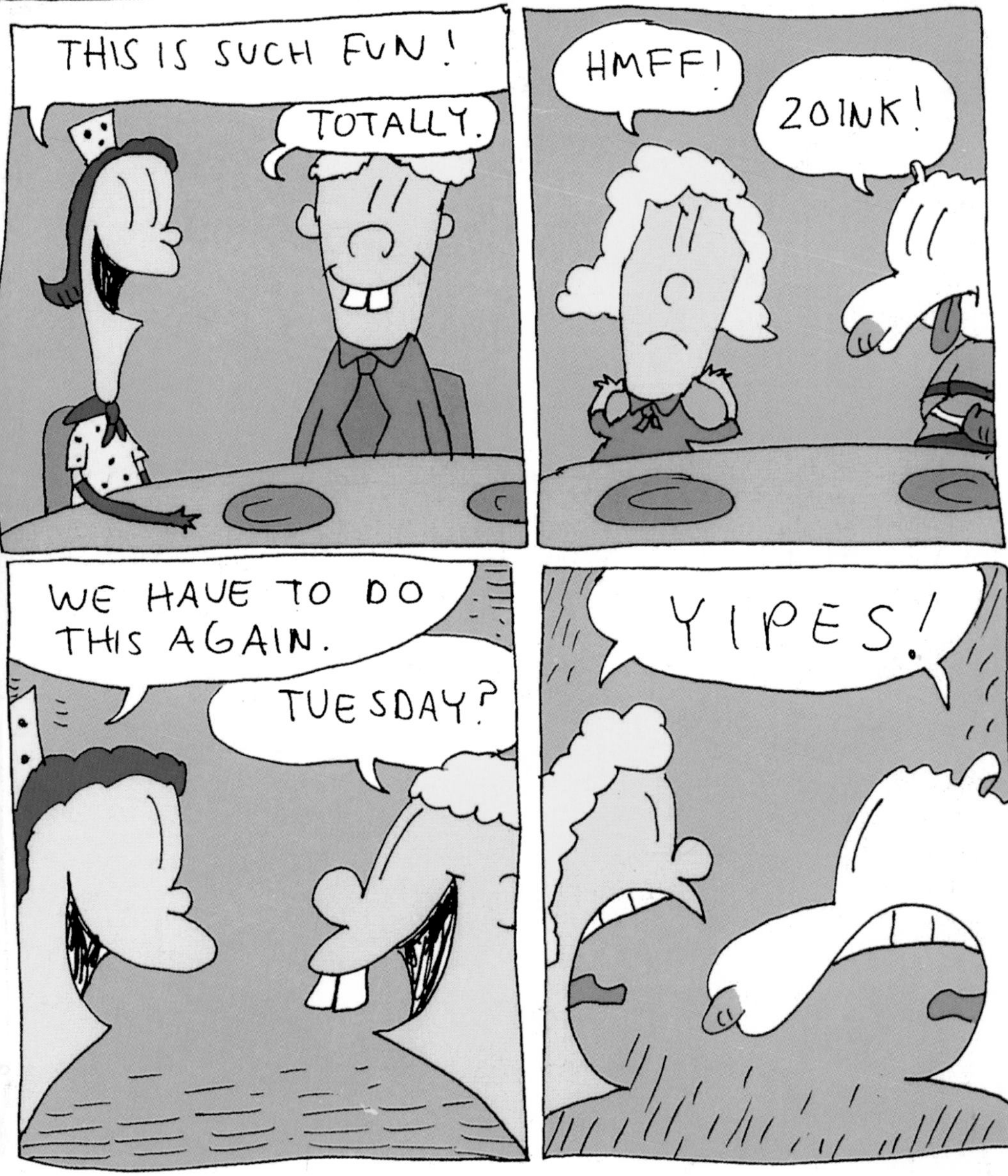
THIS IS SUCH FUN!
TOTALLY.
HMFF!
ZOINK!
WE HAVE TO DO THIS AGAIN.
TUESDAY?
YIPES!

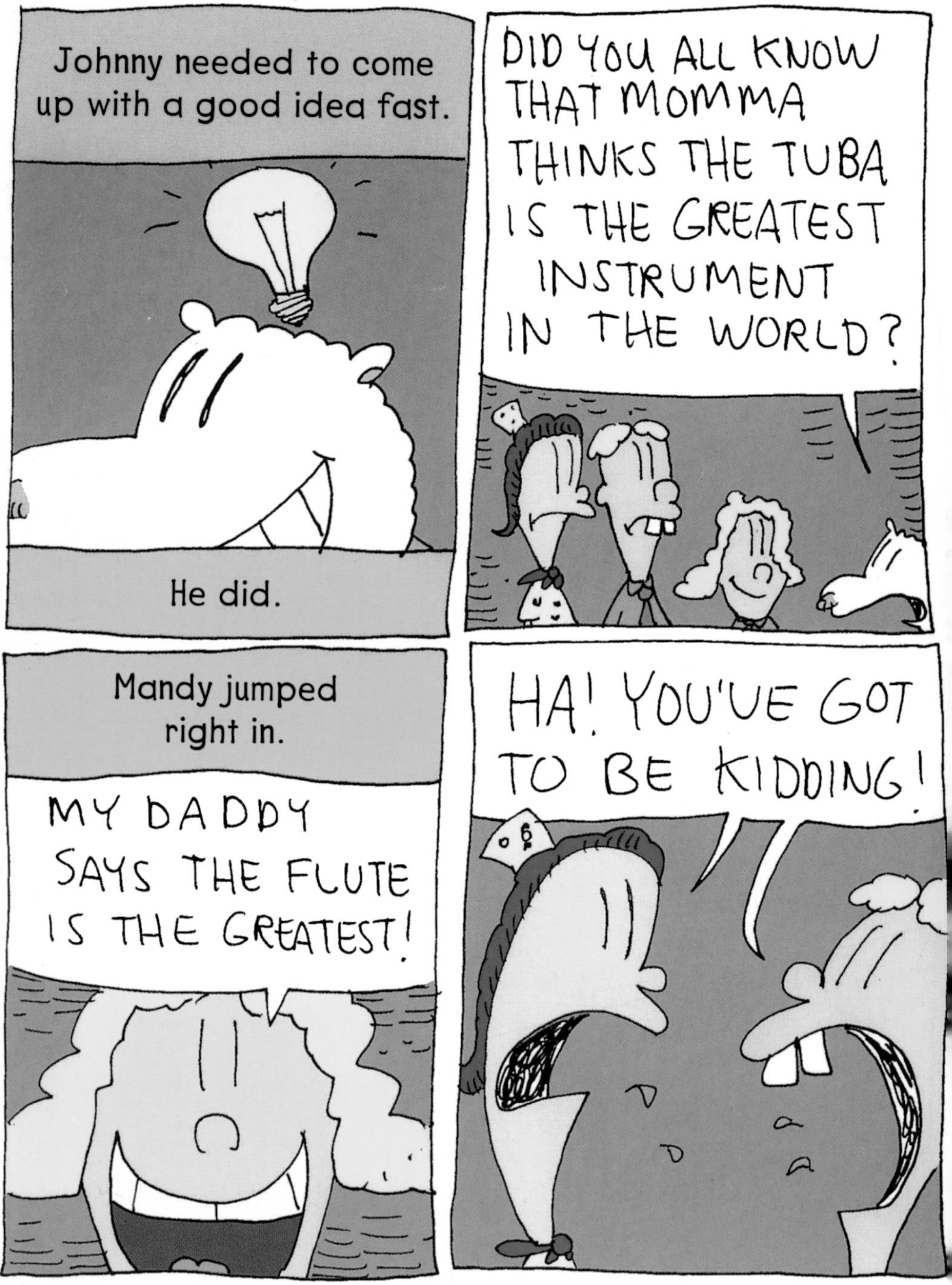
Johnny needed to come up with a good idea fast.
He did.
DID YOU ALL KNOW THAT MOMMA THINKS THE TUBA IS THE GREATEST INSTRUMENT IN THE WORLD?
Mandy jumped right in.
MY DADDY SAYS THE FLUTE IS THE GREATEST!
HA! YOU'VE GOT TO BE KIDDING!

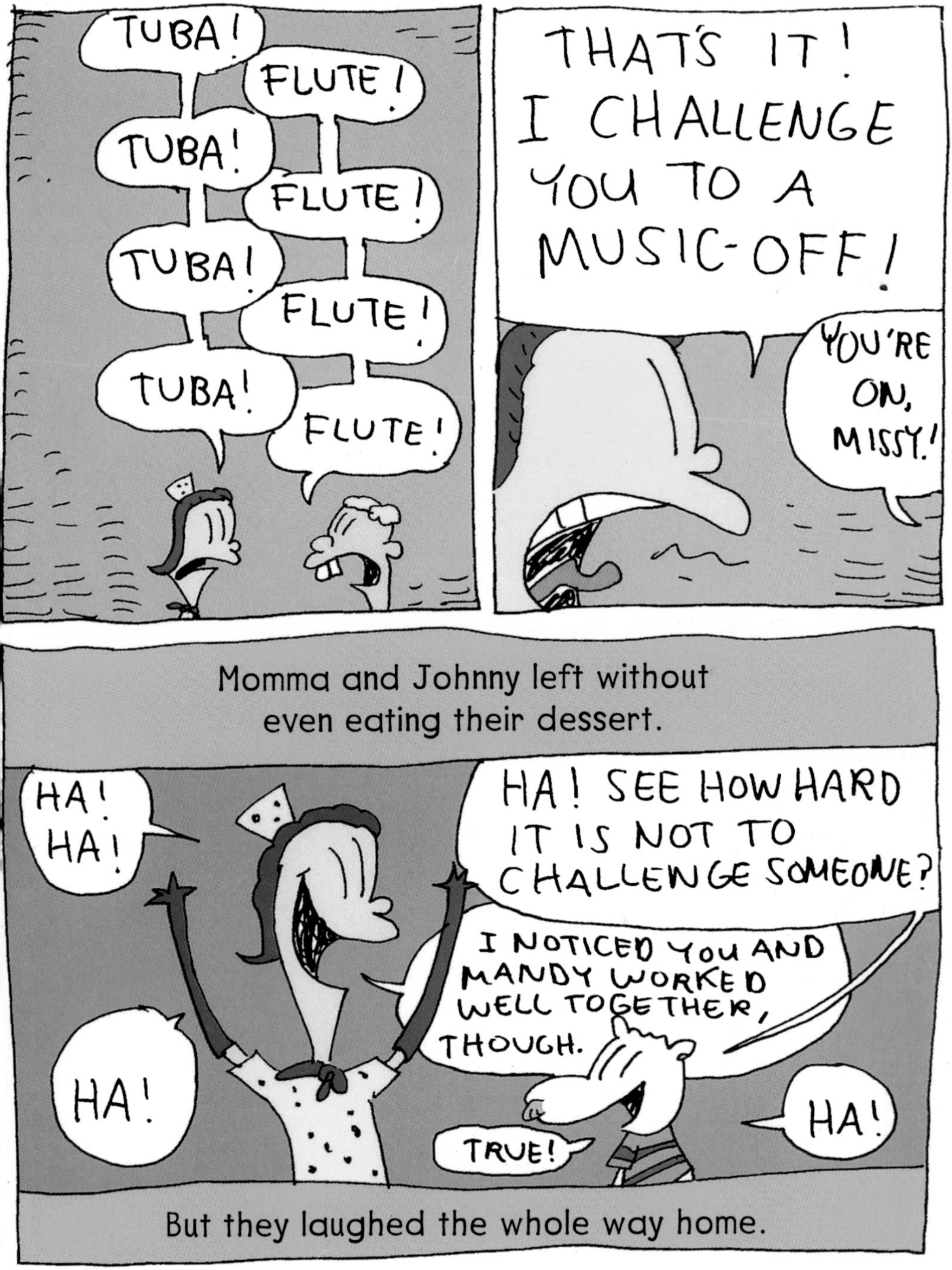
TUBA!
FLUTE!
TUBA!
FLUTE!
TUBA!
FLUTE!
TUBA!
FLUTE!
THAT'S IT! I CHALLENGE YOU TO A MUSIC-OFF!
YOU'RE ON, MISSY!
Momma and Johnny left without even eating their dessert.
HA! HA!
HA! SEE HOW HARD IT IS NOT TO CHALLENGE SOMEONE?
I NOTICED YOU AND MANDY WORKED WELL TOGETHER, THOUGH.
HA!
TRUE!
HA!
But they laughed the whole way home.

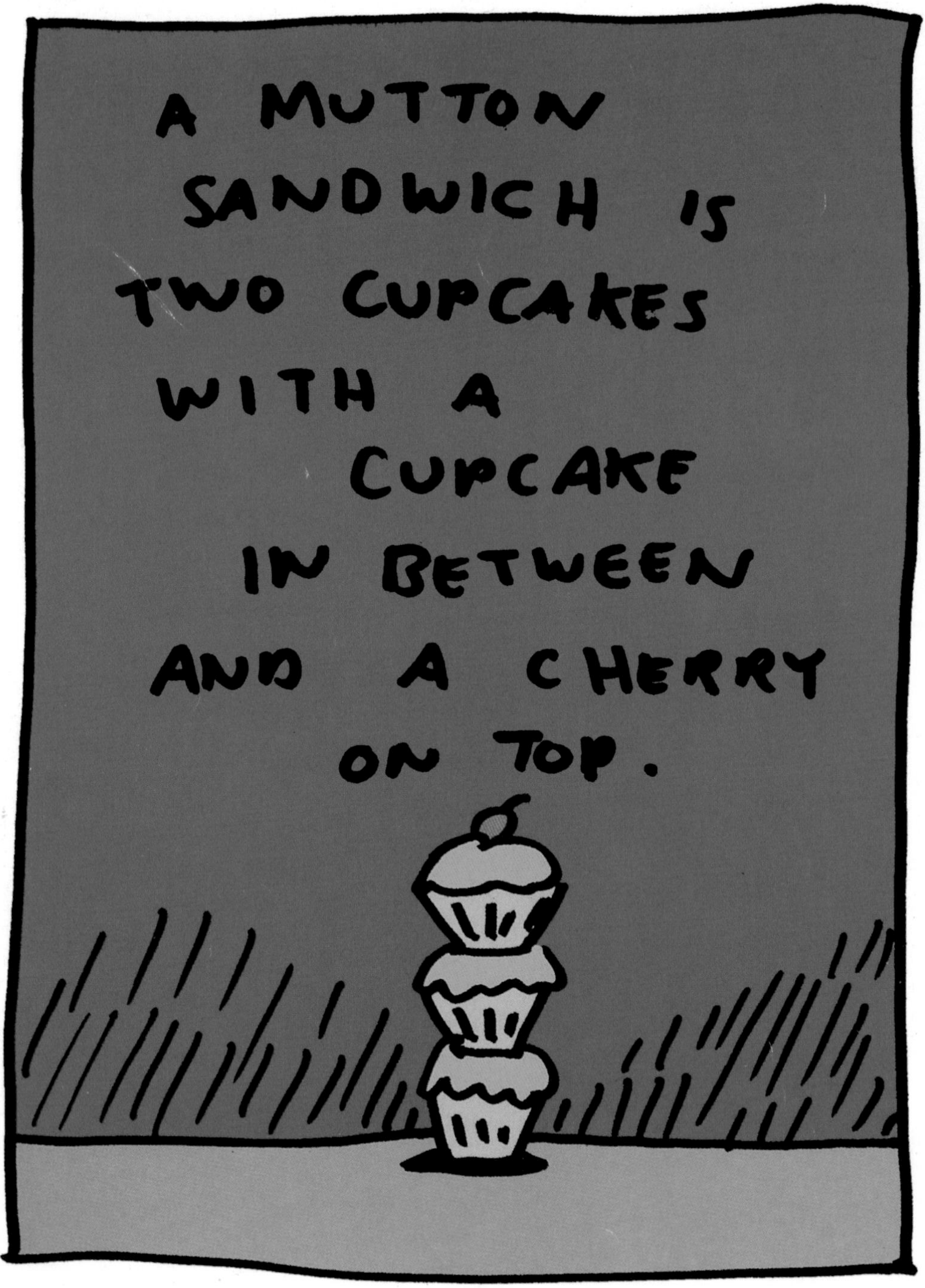
A MUTTON SANDWICH IS TWO CUPCAKES WITH A CUPCAKE IN BETWEEN AND A CHERRY ON TOP.

Old Man Stagglemyer

One day Johnny was walking and listening and walking and listening to the Winslow triplets tell one of their famous long stories.

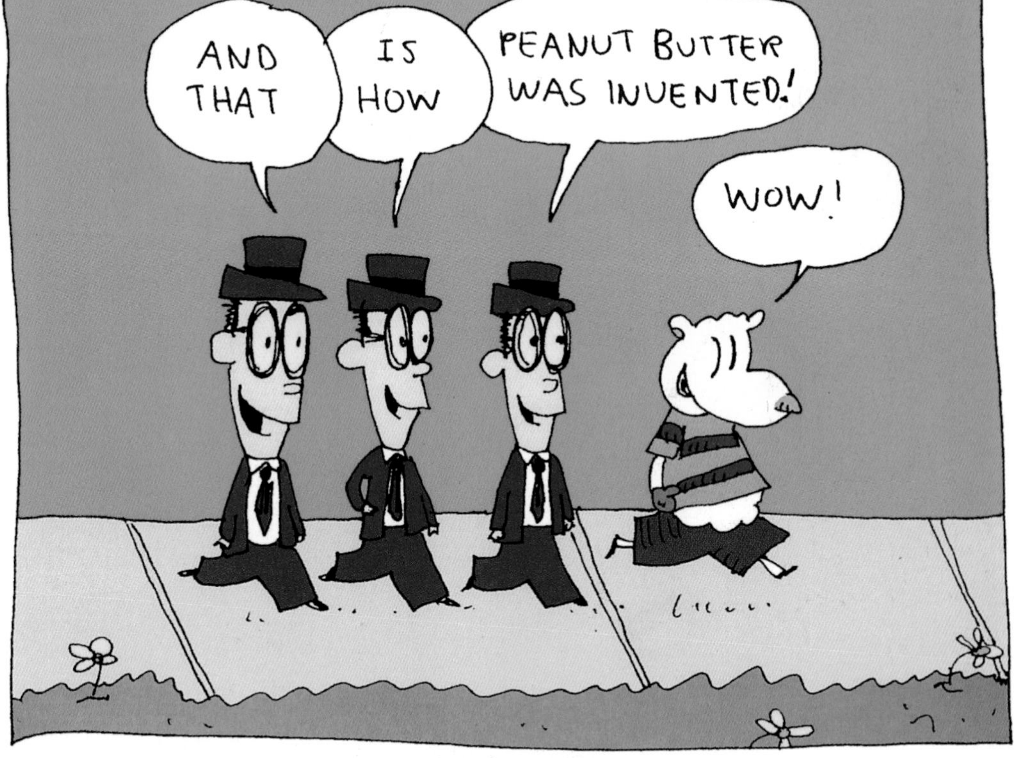
AND THAT
IS HOW
PEANUT BUTTER WAS INVENTED!
WOW!

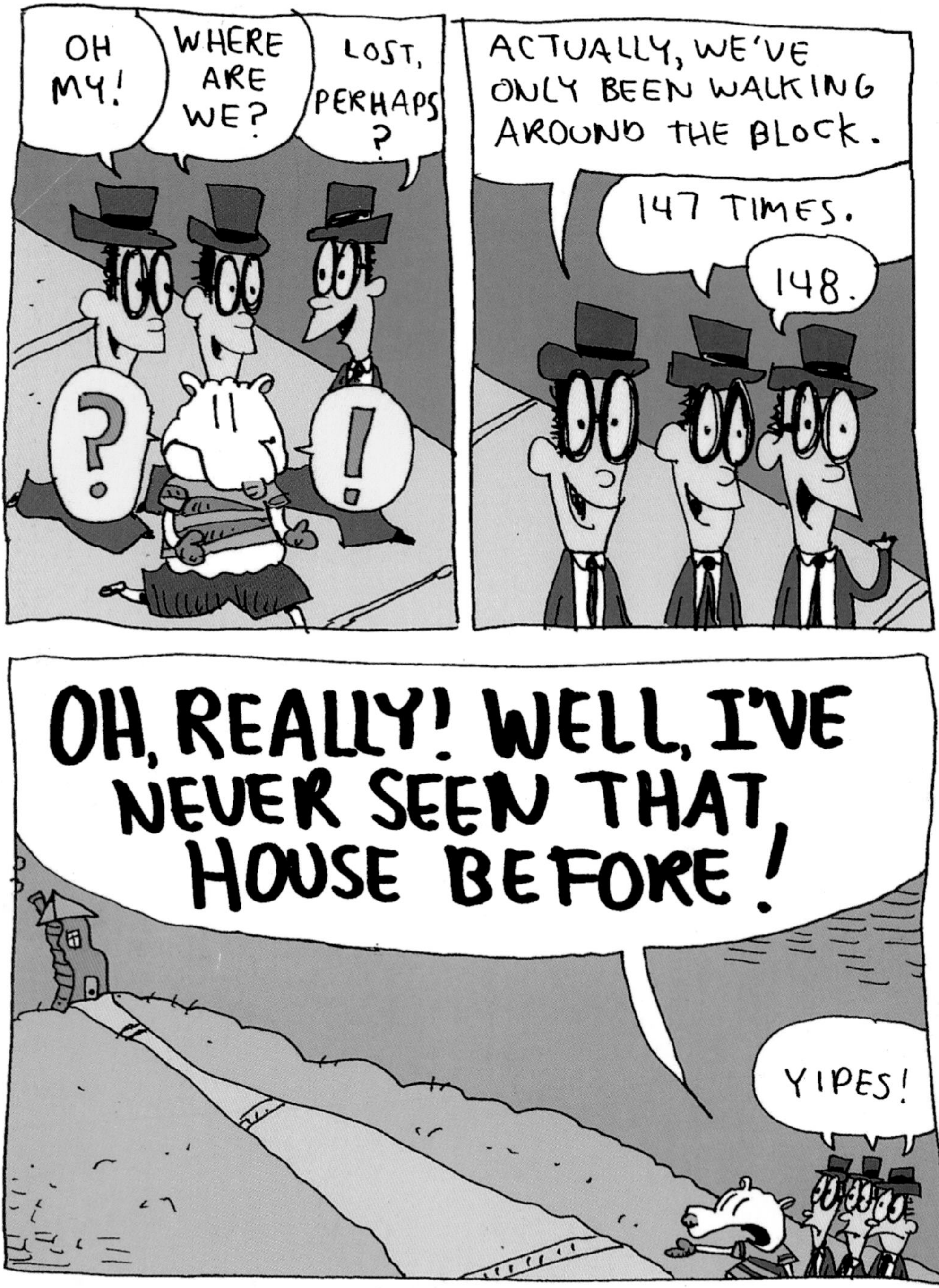
OH MY!
WHERE ARE WE?
LOST, PERHAPS?
ACTUALLY, WE'VE ONLY BEEN WALKING AROUND THE BLOCK.
147 TIMES.
148.
OH, REALLY! WELL, I'VE NEVER SEEN THAT HOUSE BEFORE!
YIPES!

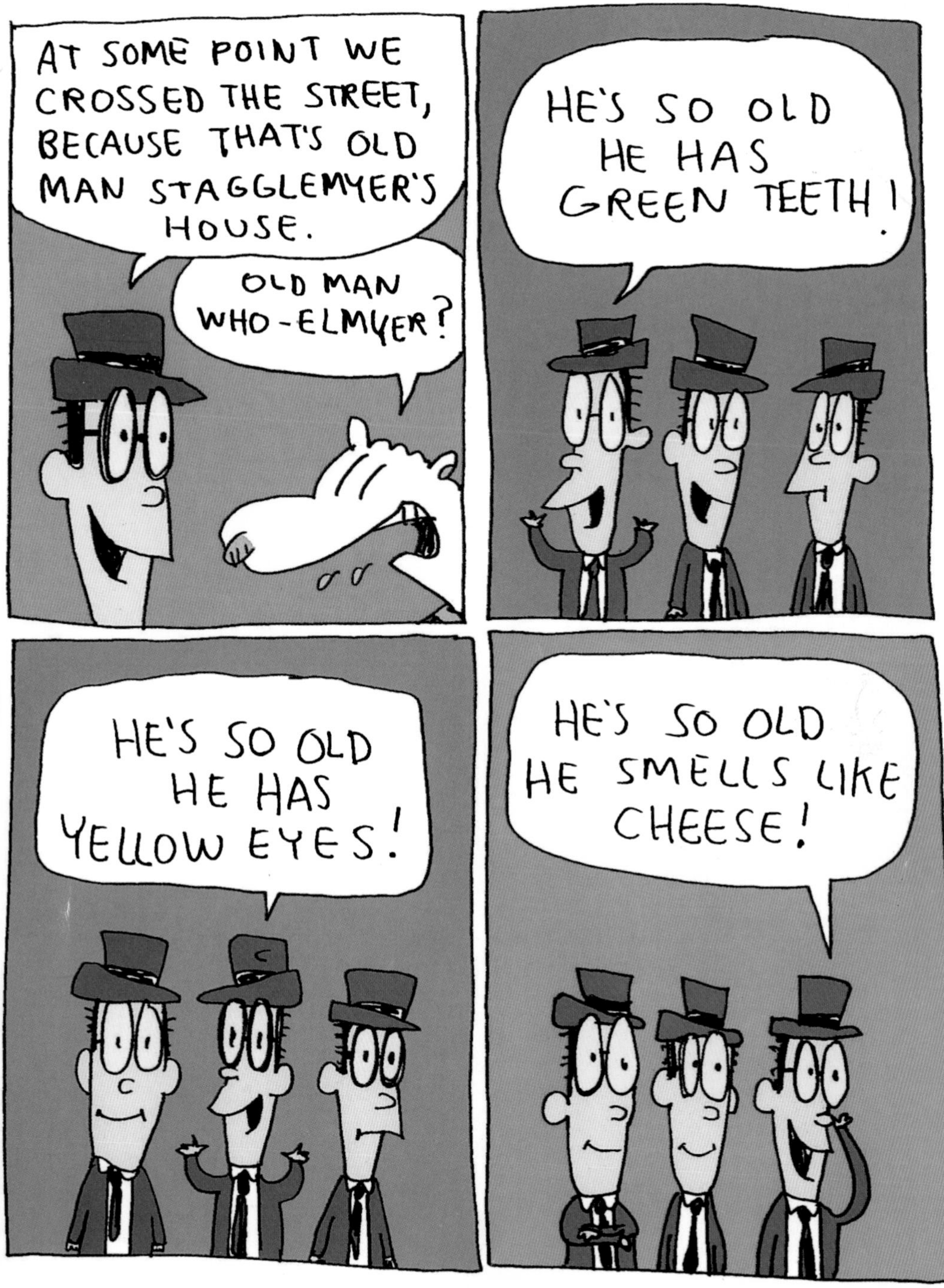
AT SOME POINT WE CROSSED THE STREET, BECAUSE THAT'S OLD MAN STAGGLEMYER'S HOUSE.
OLD MAN WHO-ELMYER?
HE'S SO OLD HE HAS GREEN TEETH!
HE'S SO OLD HE HAS YELLOW EYES!
HE'S SO OLD HE SMELLS LIKE CHEESE!

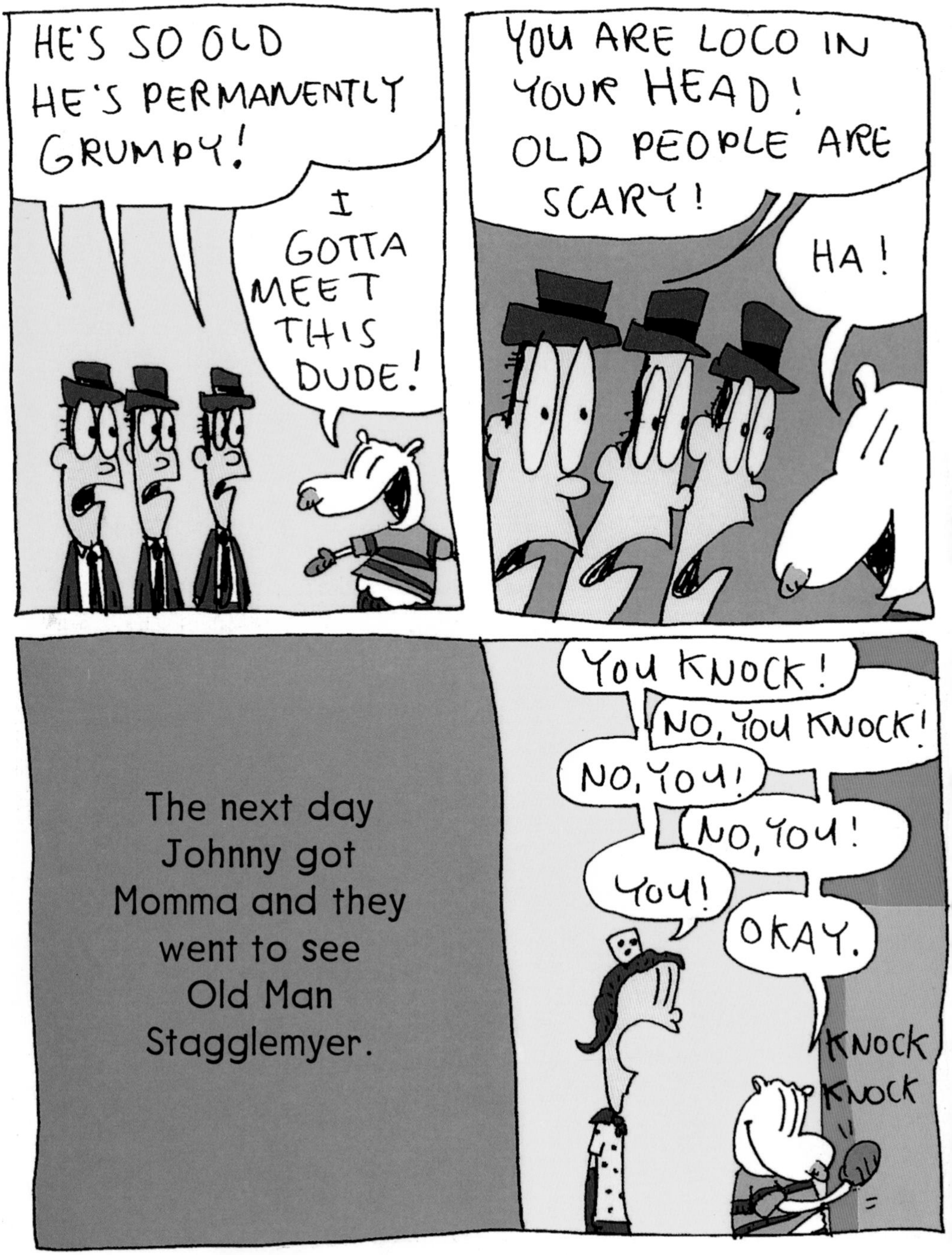
HE'S SO OLD HE'S PERMANENTLY GRUMPY!
I GOTTA MEET THIS DUDE!
YOU ARE LOCO IN YOUR HEAD! OLD PEOPLE ARE SCARY!
HA!
The next day Johnny got Momma and they went to see Old Man Stagglemyer.
YOU KNOCK!
NO, YOU KNOCK!
NO, YOU!
NO, YOU!
YOU!
OKAY.
KNOCK KNOCK

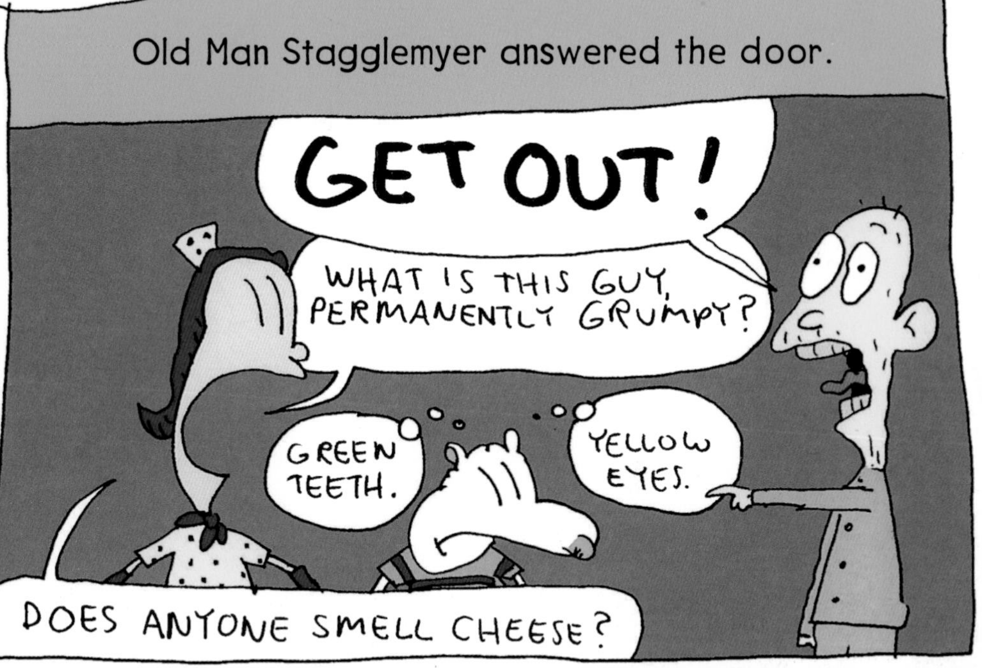
Old Man Stagglemyer answered the door.
GET OUT!
WHAT IS THIS GUY, PERMANENTLY GRUMPY?
GREEN TEETH.
YELLOW EYES.
DOES ANYONE SMELL CHEESE?

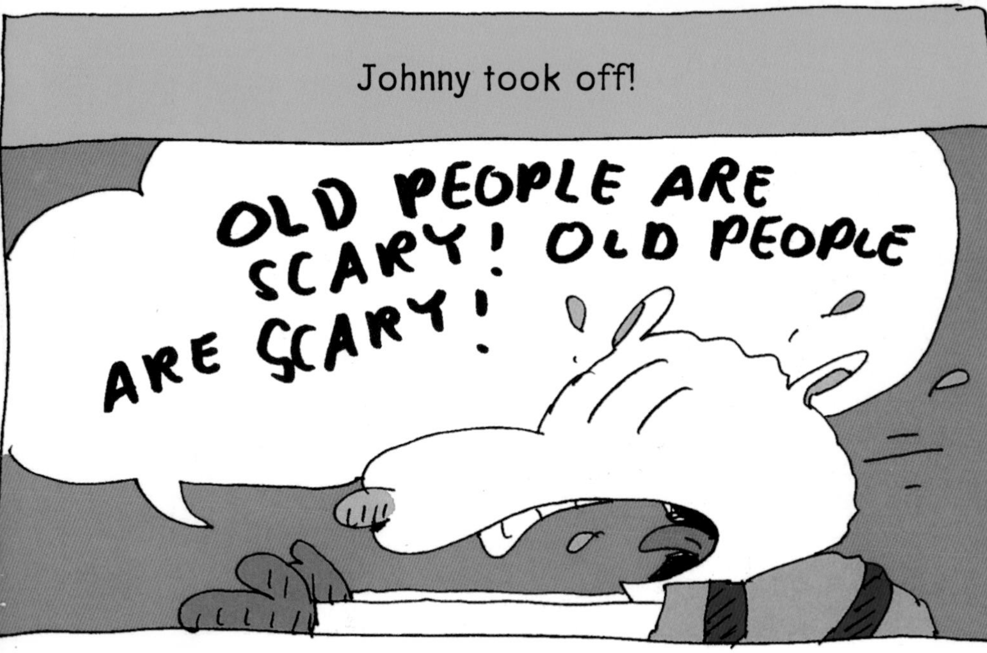
Johnny took off!
OLD PEOPLE ARE SCARY! OLD PEOPLE ARE SCARY!

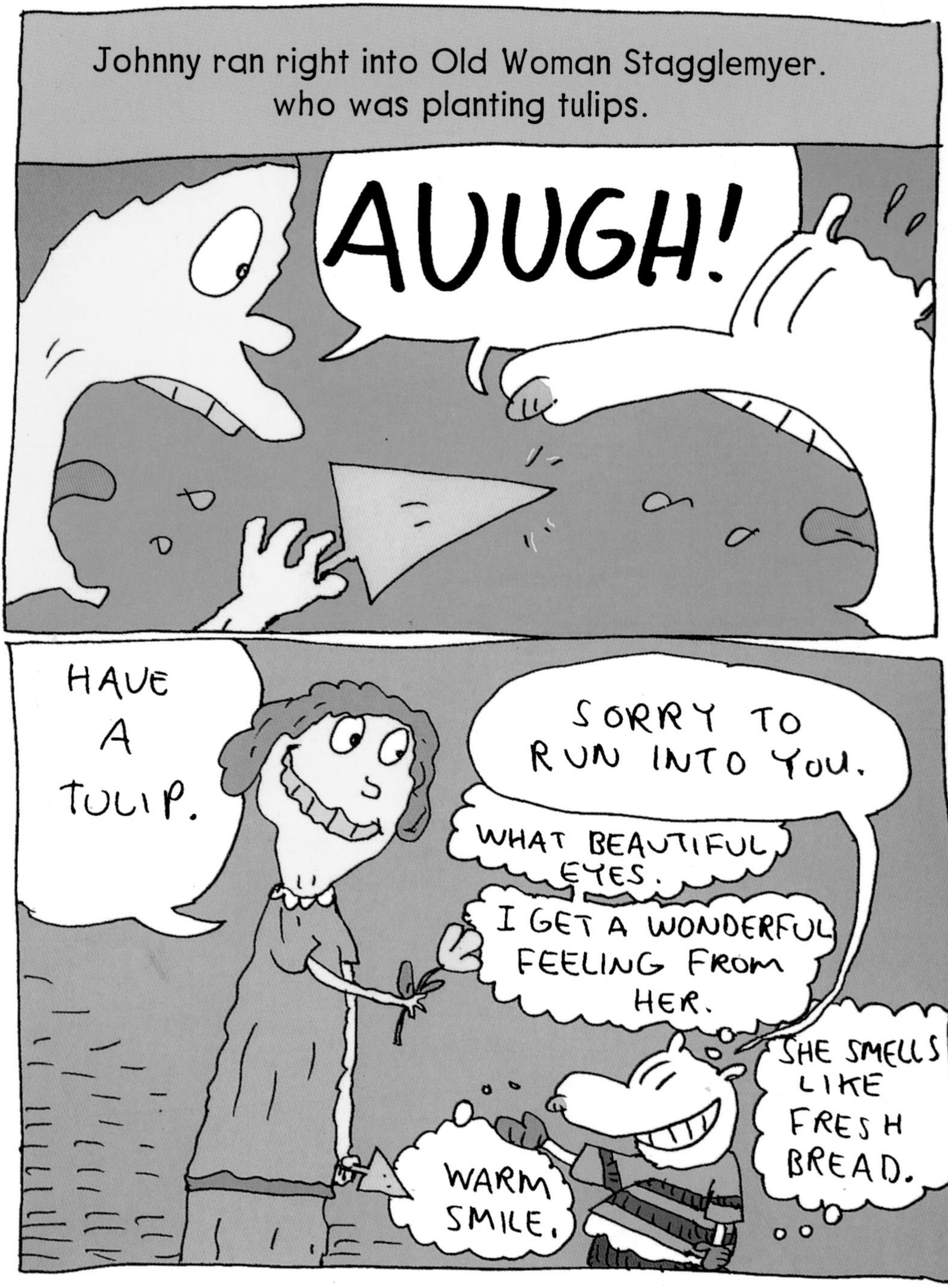
Johnny ran right into Old Woman Stagglemyer. who was planting tulips.
AUUGH!
HAVE A TULIP.
SORRY TO RUN INTO YOU.
WHAT BEAUTIFUL EYES.
I GET A WONDERFUL FEELING FROM HER.
SHE SMELLS LIKE FRESH BREAD.
WARM SMILE.

Old Woman Stagglemyer and Johnny became great friends. In fact, they skateboard together every Friday!

And every so often,
Old Man Stagglemyer joins them.

Where Are

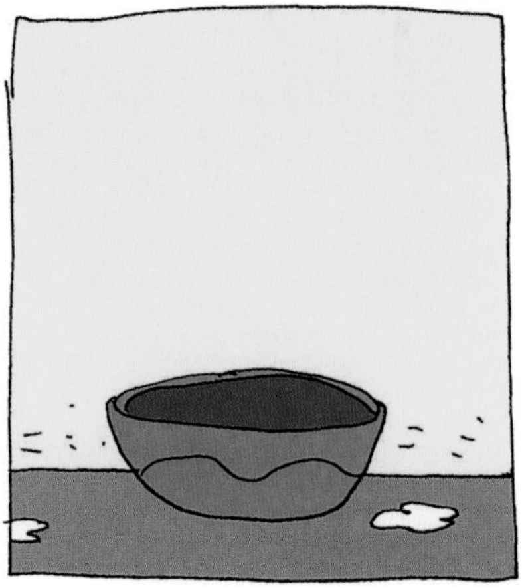

The soup is gone.

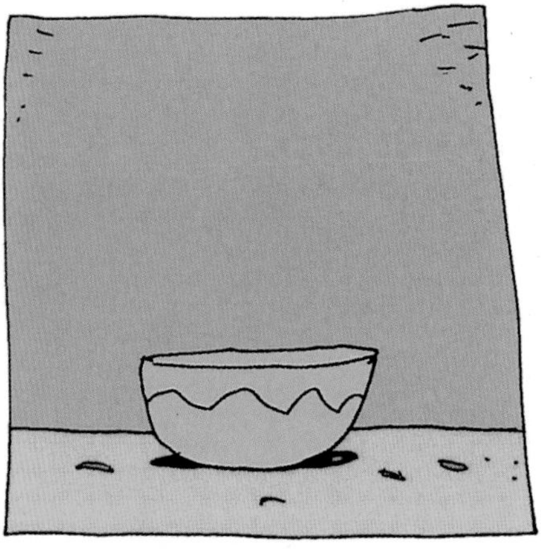

The pie has disappeared.

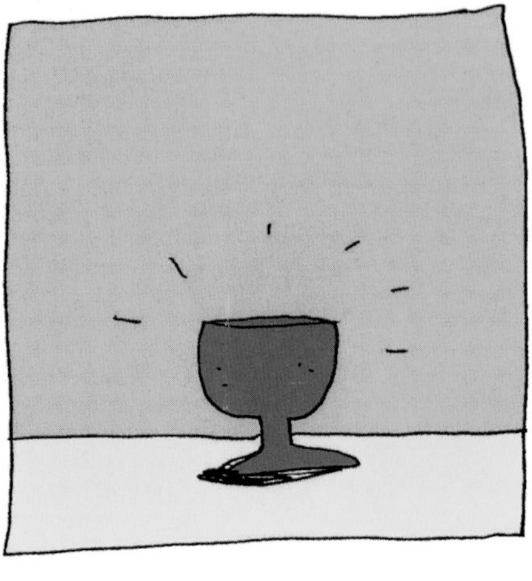

Who knows where the pudding went.

They Now?

The gravy isn't here.

The sandwich has vanished.

Where's Johnny?

He's in bed with a tummy ache.
You gotta love him.

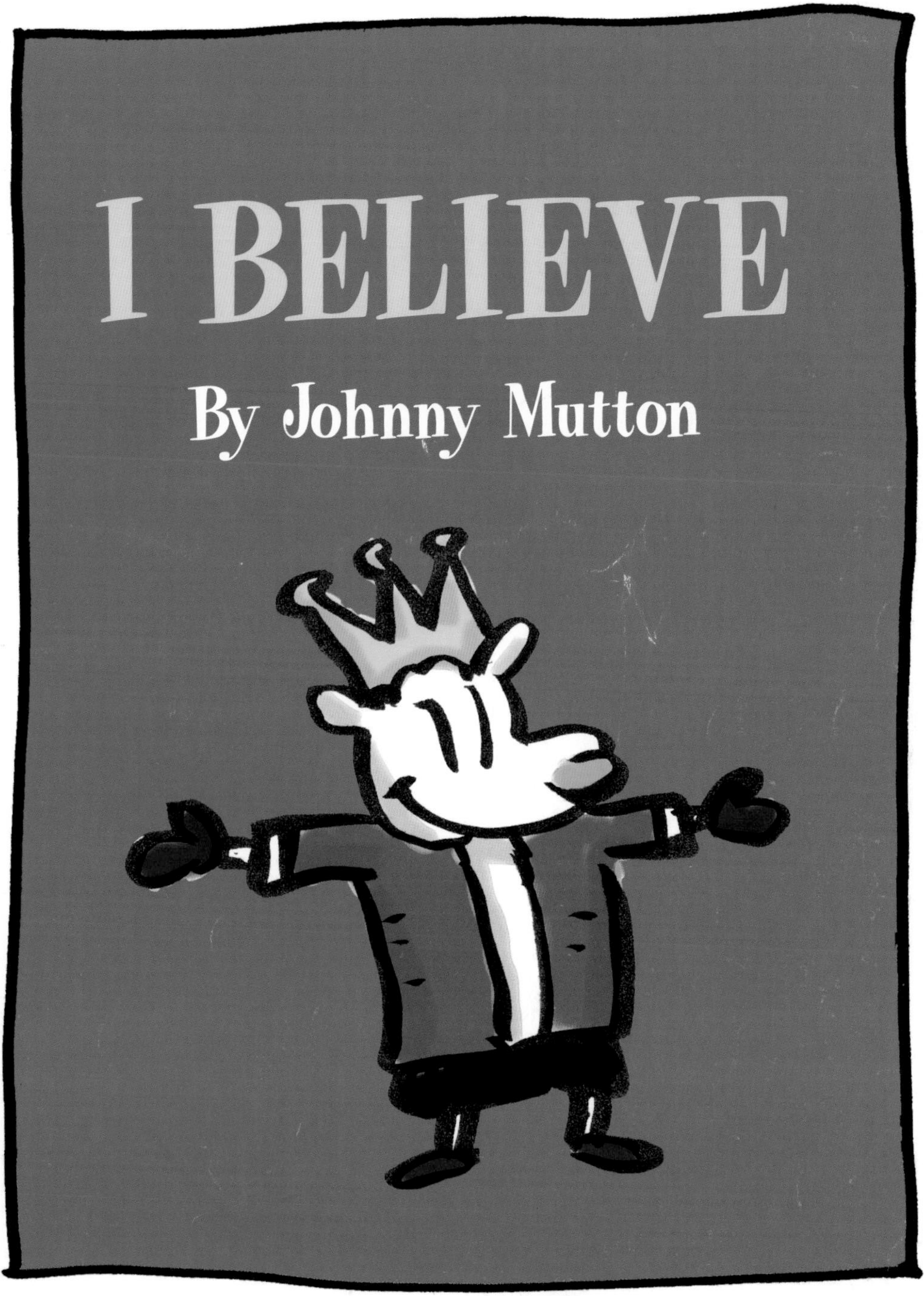
I BELIEVE
By Johnny Mutton

I believe that bees sting out of love.

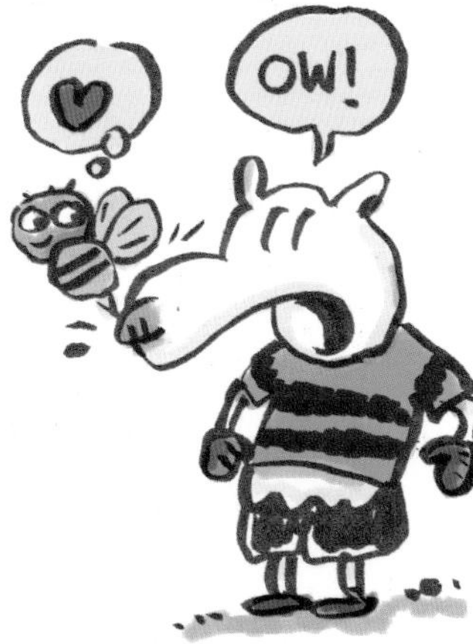
OW!

I believe that slides are often not slide-y enough.

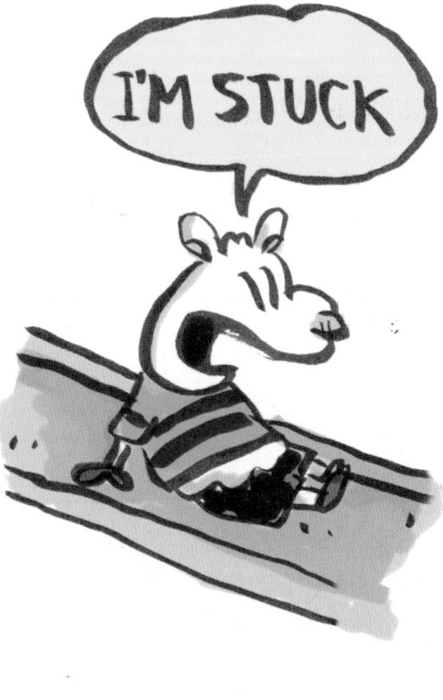
I'M STUCK

I believe that you can catch more flies with honey than you can with broccoli.

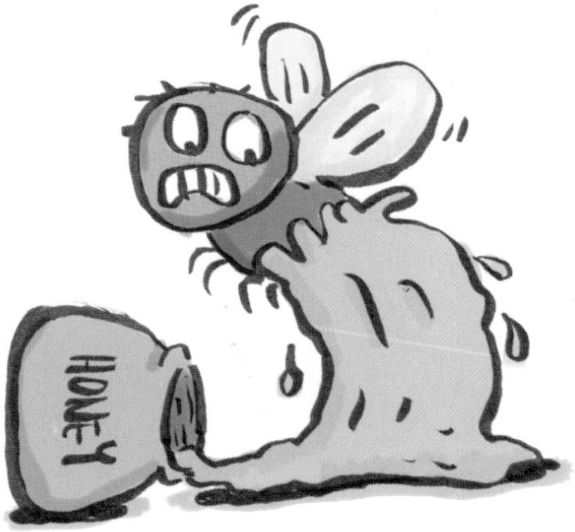
HONEY

I believe zippers are easier than buttons.

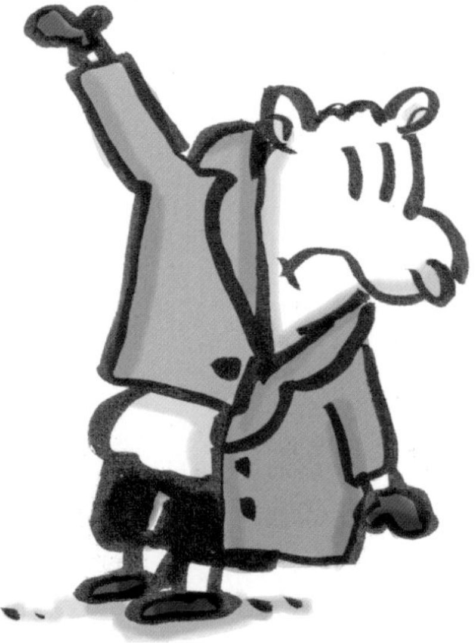

I believe that a staring contest can be won with a toot.

I believe stick and stones will break my bones but words hurt as well. So be careful what you say.

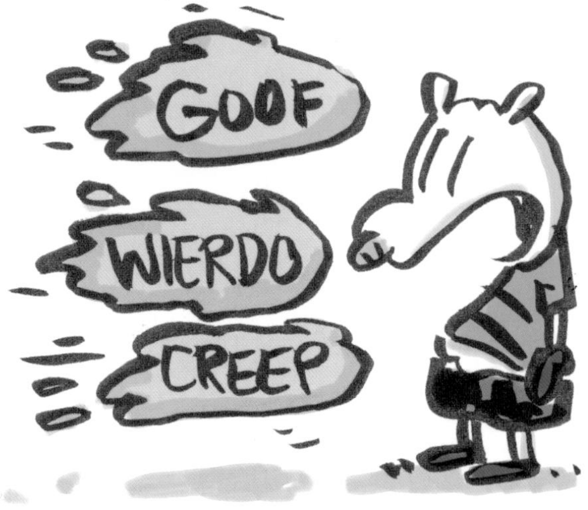
GOOF
WIERDO
CREEP

I believe that there is another way to do whatever it is you're doing.

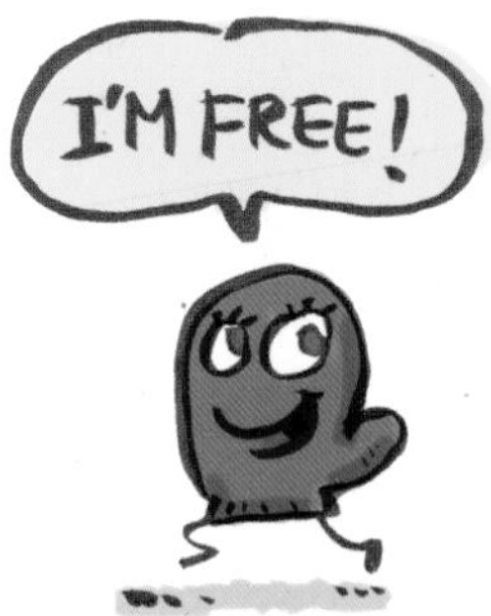
I'M FREE!

I believe mittens like to run away from home.

I believe that Gloria Crust has got what it takes.

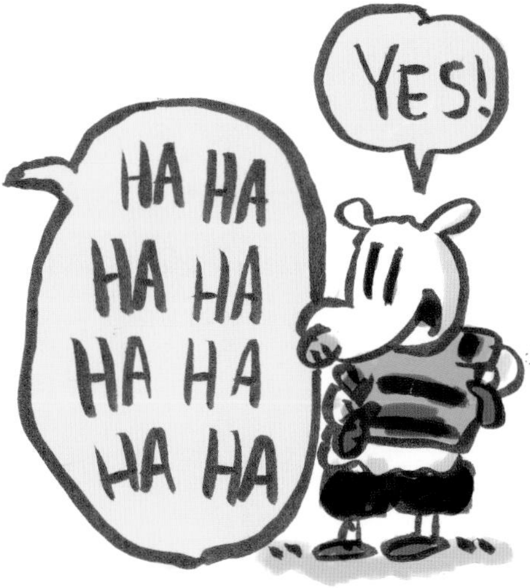
HA HA
HA HA
HA HA
HA HA
YES!

I believe Mrs. Torpolli will one day get a joke I crack.

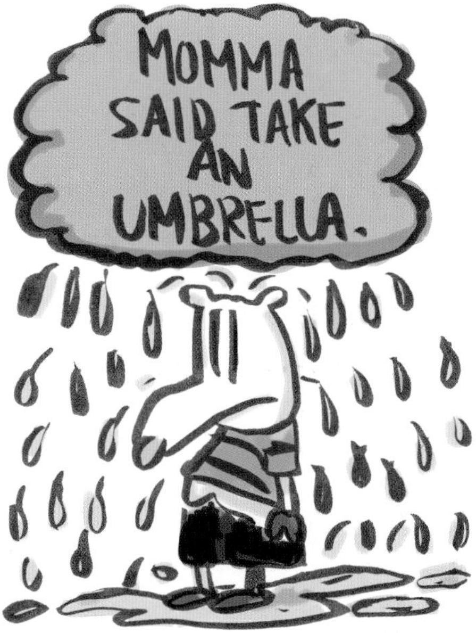
MOMMA SAID TAKE AN UMBRELLA.

I believe you best listen to Momma.

I believe guacamole is delicious.

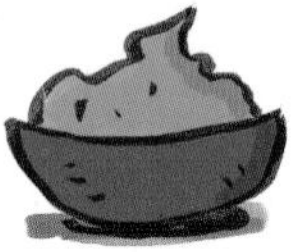

I believe you should stop and smell the roses. But watch out for those bees I mentioned earlier.

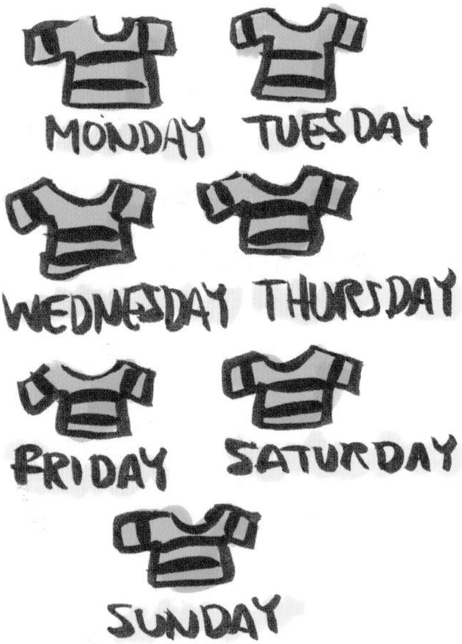
MONDAY
TUESDAY
WEDNESDAY
THURSDAY
FRIDAY
SATURDAY
SUNDAY

I believe I will wear a green striped shirt every day this week.

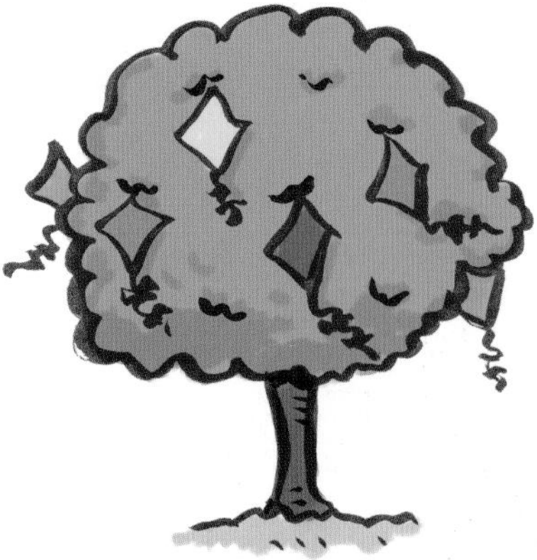

I believe a better name for a tree would be a "kite magnet."

I believe that doing a cartwheel on the spur of the moment is the perfect cure for the blahs.

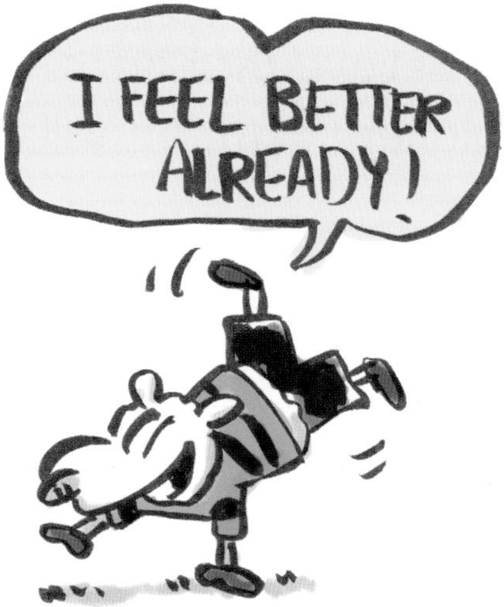
I FEEL BETTER ALREADY!

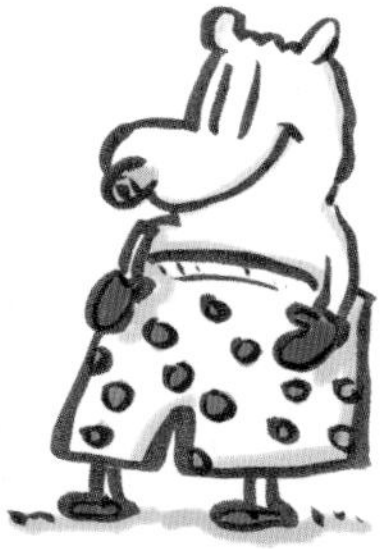

I believe that a big giant pair of polka-dotted underwear is just plain hilarious.

I believe that if you bow after you say something, people will applaud.

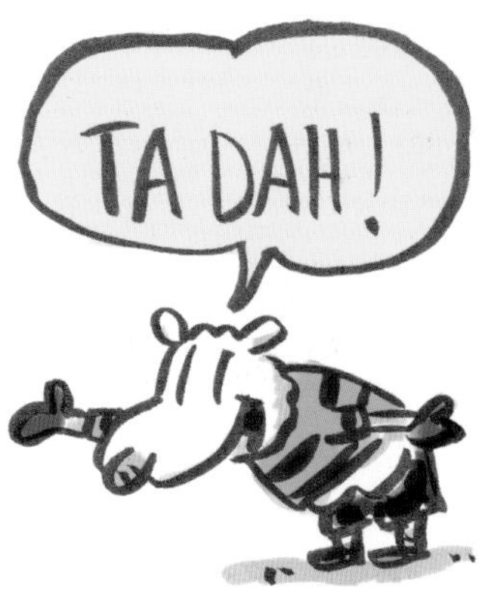
TA DAH!

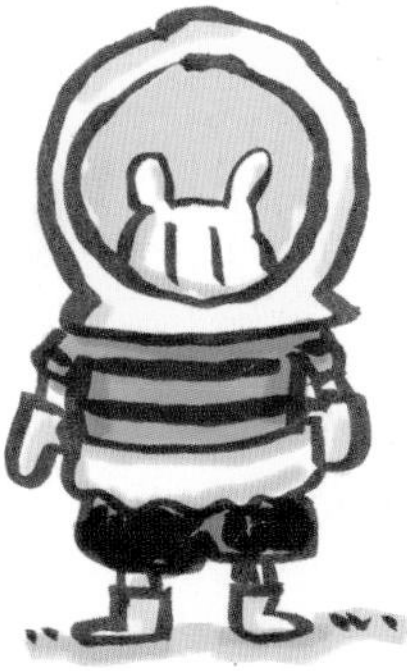

I believe that one day a sheep will land on the moon.

I believe that upon said sheep's arrival back to planet Earth, he will be voted King of the World.

I believe he will be the greatest king ever. His signature achievement will be changing every day of the week to Saturday. Except for Wednesday, which will of course be Spaghetti Day.

I believe this is the end.

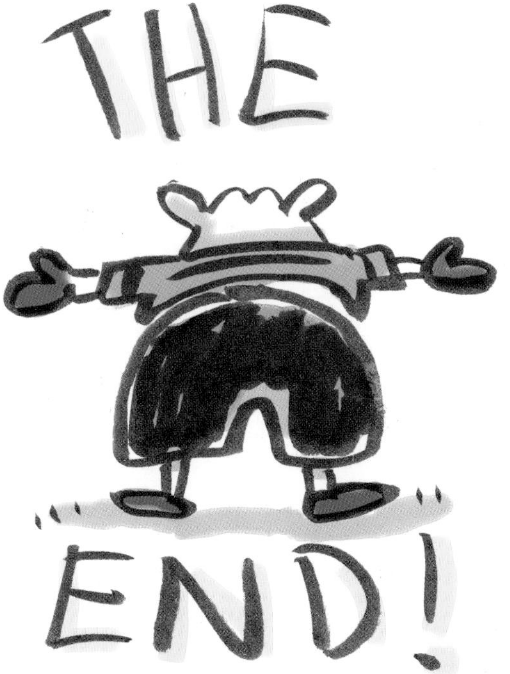
THE
END!

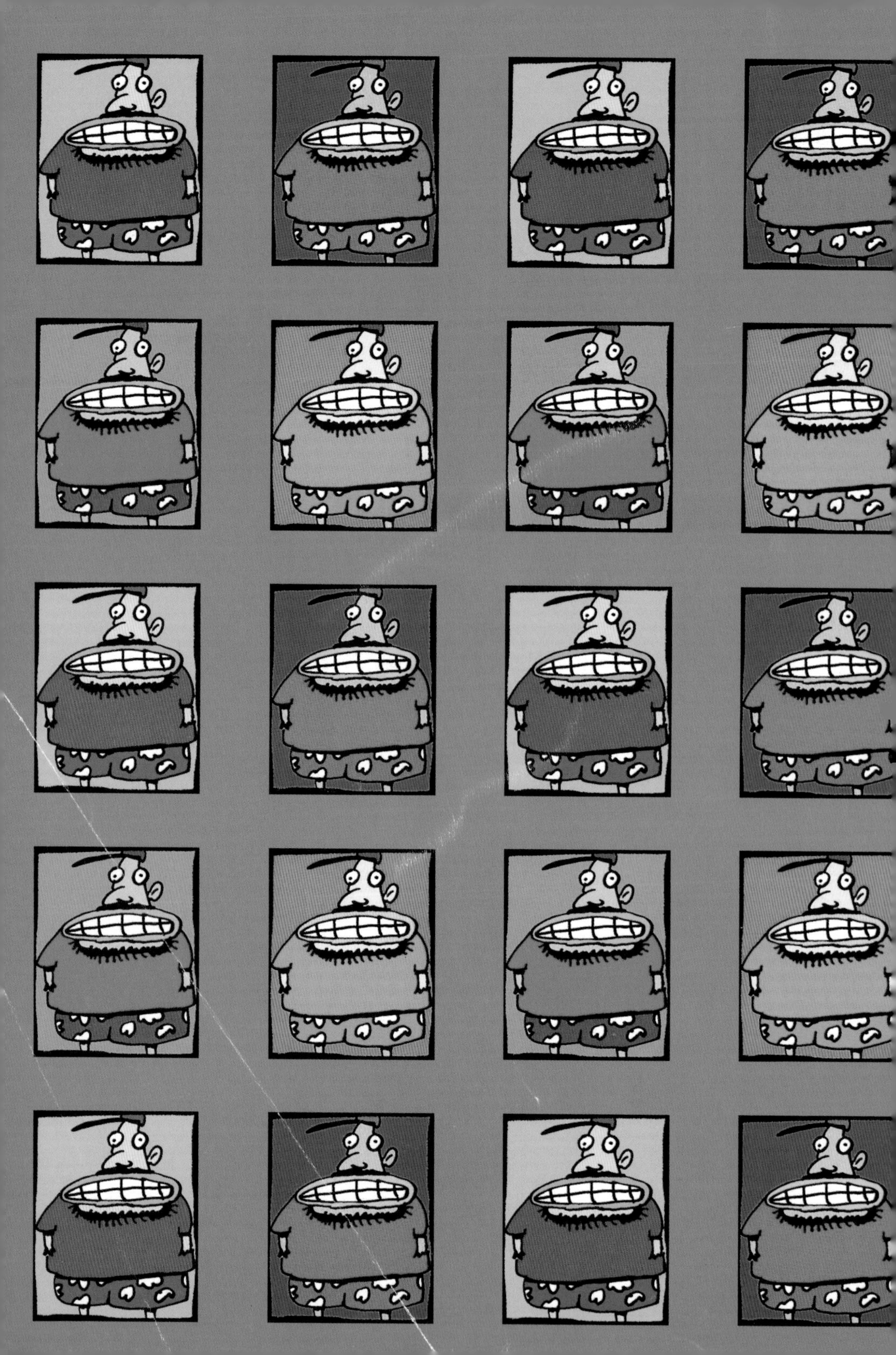

A Conversation with James Proimos

Q. Have you ever won a spelling bee?

A. Nevver. Wich is surprizing.

Q. What do you like on your pizza?

A. The only ingredients I like on my pizza are cheese, basil, garlic, cheese, and tomato sauce. And hands off! It's all mine.

Q. Are you as good at basketball as Momma Mutton?

A. No one is as good as Momma Mutton. It is an insult that you would even ask. I'm leaving this interview now. Well, right after I finish eating this pizza, I mean.

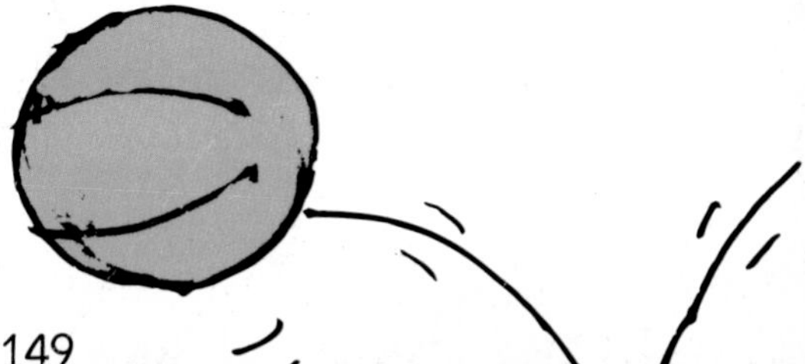

Q. What was your favorite book when you were seven and a half?
A. *Where the Wild Things Are.*

Q. What's your favorite color?
A. I like blue. Unless we are talking about food. I rarely eat anything blue.

Q. What is the meaning of life?
A. Once I get a life I will let you know.

Q. Who taught you to draw?
A. Drawing came natural. I don't even hold a pencil correctly. The important thing for my style of art is that I never lost the ability to draw like a young child does, without thinking about technique or perspective—or anything, really.

Q. If you were stranded on a desert island, what three things would you wish for?
A. I would wish for a good book, a glass of root beer, and a boat to get me off this stinking island!

Q. Did you know a girl like Mandy in school?

A. Mandy is a girl I knew in school. Her name was Mandy.

Q. Did you ever get sent to the principal's office?

A. I was once sent to the principal's office, but it was by mistake. My parents meant to send me to Paris.

Q. Why is Johnny a sheep? Why not an antelope?

A. Johnny is a sheep because I was making a little opposite joke. Sheep are generally portrayed as followers and Johnny does not follow! Johnny is so him!

Q. Is there anything you want to say to us that you haven't gotten to say yet?

A. This pizza was delicious. Now I must be going. Thanks.